Alex,

ELITE

ELITE DOMS OF WASHINGTON

ELIZABETH SAFLEUR

So lovely to meet you!

XO,
Elizabeth Safleur

Elizabeth SaFleur LLC
PO Box 6395
Charlottesville, VA 22906
Elizabeth@ElizabethSaFleur.com
www.ElizabethSaFleur.com

Edited by Nancy P.
Cover Design by Cosmic Letterz

ISBN: 978-1-949076-12-7

For Marilyn and Patricia

Dear Reader,
This book is a work of fiction, not reality. My characters operate in a compressed time frame. A real-world scenario involves getting to know one another more extensively than my characters do before engaging in BDSM activities. Please learn as much as you can before trying any activity you read about in erotic fiction. Talk to people in your local BDSM group. Nearly every community has one. Get to know people slowly, and always be careful. Share your hopes, dreams and fears with anyone before playing with them, have a safeword and share it with your Dom or Domme (they can't read your mind), use protection, and have a safe-call or other backup in place. Remember: Safe, Sane and Consensual. Or, no play. May you find that special person to honor and love you the way you wish. You deserve that. XO ~Elizabeth

1

The Jefferson Suite had a reputation. Everyone said so.

Christiana Snow watched Henrick, the sous-chef, slip a red rose into the silver bud vase on the room service tray she'd been tasked to deliver. "There are some naughty stories about the guests that stay in that suite." He winked. "Let me take you to dinner, and I'll tell you all about it."

She turned her back on Henrick's smirk—and his eyes that never seemed to travel farther north than her neck. Since the day Christiana started working at The Oak she'd fought the desire to bend her knees to force his gaze to her face. It would only give him the wrong idea.

Instead she threw back two ibuprofens with her milk and then set the glass into a nearby bin of dirty dishes. Gossip made her head hurt.

She felt Henrick's eyes travel her body as she pushed the room service cart into the elevator. "For a reporter's daughter, you aren't very curious," he called after her.

Curiosity wasn't the issue. The Oak, which stood mere blocks from the White House, attracted politicians and paparazzi—and dozens of men, sporting earbuds attached to wires disappearing into their dark suits, sent to watch them both. It took real concentration to ignore the stories that the hotel's staff collected like trophies.

At least the tips were good at the boutique hotel and restaurant, and the mundane work gave her time to think—or *think forward*, as her father always said. And that's what she was going to do—think forward and *move* forward. She didn't have time to get wrapped up in other people's lives and certainly not the pseudo reality of the D.C. politicos.

The elevator creaked to a stop. Water sloshed in the silver pitcher as Christiana leaned over the cart to push the slatted metal door aside. A dusty, oil-paint smell greeted her as she started down the hallway, lined with canvases of hunting scenes set in over-sized, gilded frames higher than she was tall and wider than her arms could stretch.

Christiana took in a lungful of the stagnant air as she reached the Jefferson Suite's double doors at the end of the corridor. She knocked and listened for the sound of footsteps. No one came.

Her leg danced with impatience. Mrs. DeCord's order was Christiana's last task of the day, and she wanted to finish it as fast as possible to rush off to meet Avery, her best friend. Christiana had agreed to be her "date" at some society fundraiser that afternoon.

Christiana studied the rich mahogany crown molding, lining the long hallway. Gold brocade wallpaper led her eyes to images of smiling women, draped in gossamer swaths of pastel blue and green fabric. They stared down from their ceiling mural home, their eyes cold and full of secrets.

Christiana knocked on the door once more. After no response, she pulled her master key card from her apron pocket and slipped it to the lock slot. The door cracked open but stopped against something on the other side. Through the gap in the door, she saw a man's shoe lying on its side.

She called into the room, "Hello? Room service. Ma'am?" No one answered though muffled voices resonated deeper within.

Well, she couldn't wait. She pushed harder on the door, and the shoe slid aside.

The cart's wheels whispered over the marble entryway floor. She announced herself one more time. No reply. She picked up the man's dress shoe, an expensive leather smell wafting to her nose. She set it down beside a tufted chair in the hall.

A male voice echoed from the bathroom off the suite's master bedroom. "No, Yvette."

"Please take me. I won't say a thing." Mrs. DeCord's voice reverberated off the tile.

"You know our agreement."

Mrs. DeCord whined, "I don't understand why I wasn't invited. I'll show up anyway."

"You won't do any such thing, Yvette." He spoke her name like a caress. "Take off your panties."

Christiana's insides seized at the man's abrupt change in tone. Maybe she had heard wrong. After a long silence, she urged the cart forward, but the wheels bogged down on the plush carpet in the living area.

The voice spoke. "Bend over, put your hands on the counter. Good. Look in the mirror. Eyes on me, Yvette."

Smack! A sharp slap pierced the air, and Christiana jerked backward as if stung. Mrs. DeCord moaned. Was she hurt?

Christiana couldn't break her gaze, eyes glued on the bedroom doors. They weren't closed completely. They were slightly ajar, a sliver of the interior showing through a small crack.

"Open your legs." The man's voice, sandpaper and velvet, rooted Christiana in place even though her heart fluttered wildly. "Very nice, baby."

Christiana took a deep breath to steady herself, inhaling musk mixed with the fragrance of lilacs. Something else hung heavy in the air.

Mrs. DeCord's whimpers grew louder.

Should she call, so they knew she wasn't trying to hide her presence? If they saw her, would they realize she had overheard? Should she leave? If she abandoned the lunch, they'd know she'd heard and run away, probably to gossip.

"Mmm, you like that, don't you, sweetheart?"

Christiana licked her lips at the man's chocolate-caramel tone. She tried to place the voice—maybe he was a radio announcer. No, he sounded too sexy and way too dangerous.

Slap! Slap! Christiana's leg bumped into the cart and silverware clanked. Water splashed on the linen, and she stilled, but no new sound came from the bedroom.

She couldn't abandon the lunch in the middle of the living room. She'd just have to be quick. Christiana maneuvered the cart to the small bay window overlooking Pennsylvania Avenue. She set up the silver and lifted the dome on Mrs. DeCord's salad.

"Touch yourself," the deep, rich voice said. Christiana's heart punched at her ribs, and she lifted one hand to her breast to still it. Her eyes darted to the doors.

She gulped and tried to shake off the sound of the man's sexy intonation. Christiana tiptoed over to the French doors of the master bedroom and risked a peek into the room. The bed's comforter wilted over one side of the bed, and sheets bunched in a tight wad at the foot, bulging through the brass rails of the footboard. Pillows lay scattered on the floor. Braided black ropes hung limply from the frame of the headboard. She envisioned a restrained body, spread-eagle and helpless on the bed. *Oh, god.*

A chill broke out across her body. Instinct told her to click the doors shut. She winced at the snick of the door jam. *Did they hear her?*

More whispers escaped from behind the closed doors. She couldn't make out the words, but the sensual rhythm of his voice rose and fell in a soothing, hypnotic cadence. Christiana's ears strained for the man's instructions, for what he wanted Mrs. DeCord to do next. Footsteps brushed across the carpet in the bedroom. The man spoke in rumbling purrs, approaching the bed.

She bit her bottom lip when a thought arose about that strange, human scent. *Sex.* A pang hit between her thighs as an image slipped into place of the faceless man—with that voice—putting his mouth on Mrs. DeCord's neck.

A long wail and an ecstatic groan drifted from inside the bedroom.

Christiana stepped back. She needed to leave—*now.* If caught eavesdropping, even accidentally, she'd be dismissed. She clutched the silver dome to her chest like a shield and slunk to the marble foyer. The man's smoky voice oozed into the main room as the suite's front door clacked behind her, a barrier to . . . what?

She jogged down the long hallway to the elevator, punched the call button, and tried to steady her breathing as the elevator creaked upward. The man's voice still reverberated in her chest. Relief coursed through her body, glad she hadn't run into either of them inside, especially him. One look and he would have guessed she'd heard, had sucked in the air, heavy with sex, and understood.

Her imagination settled on Mrs. DeCord pressed into the mattress under a dark, mysterious man. His lips floated over her breast. Christiana shook her head in a vain attempt to stop the image from evolving into the man slipping his hands between the woman's legs.

Christiana hit the button twice more. *Come on.* She gave up on the antiquated elevator and headed to the stairs. More questions surfaced with each step downward.

Did Henrik's wink mean he knew? Who was Mrs. DeCord hooking up with in the Jefferson Suite? The mystery man had done something carnal to her, something she'd wanted done, though Christiana couldn't imagine what. *Something with ropes and slaps and Lord knows what else.* Maybe she should've listened when the other waitresses, huddled in the employee break room, tittered about who slipped through the hotel lobby trying not to be noticed.

Then again, maybe not. She began to understand why her manager, Brian, had directed staff to drop off the orders and avoid looking around. He had warned, "In the political climate of Washington, D.C., some things are best not to see."

Christiana dislodged her overactive daydreaming and ran to the staff room to gather her things before clocking out. She jumped when her phone rang.

"Hey, get here already! I'm guarding your dress in the main ladies room. You know where," Avery said. "I never wore it, and you seem to like blue."

Avery's closet enjoyed a regular turnover, as the budding socialite wouldn't be caught dead photographed in anything twice. Christiana was the grateful recipient of Avery's generosity. Her hand-me-downs were really more like hand-me-ups for Christiana.

She grabbed her purse from her locker. "I'm leaving right now. How come this event is so early?"

"Mom said it'd be like happy hour. It's really so they can all start drinking earlier. Serve anyone interesting today?"

"No one special." She glanced in the small mirror inside

the door and smoothed down a few wispy bangs to cover up the two-inch scar on her forehead, now pink from exertion.

"Oh, come on. It's an election year. Everyone wants to be seen."

Christiana laughed. "You sound like my dad." The silence on the other end signaled Avery wasn't pleased with the comparison. Another faux pas—something Avery said Christiana was very good at making, like wearing the same dress to a charity event more than once.

"Um, do you know Mrs. DeCord?" Christiana asked.

"Sure. Former Miss Dallas, married to a high-powered lawyer. Well, at least for now. Women like that go through men like wardrobe changes. Why? What'd she do? Spill it."

"Oh, nothing. She comes in from time to time." Damn, she shouldn't have asked. Avery's natural investigative nature came alive when a fellow socialite's name arose.

"Who was she with today? Not her husband?" Avery's voice lit up with excitement.

"I don't know what her husband looks like. It was probably him."

Avery snorted. "Yeah, right. No one goes to The Oak with who they're *supposed* to be with."

"I'll take your word for it. Look, I'll be there as soon as I can, okay?"

Christiana stuffed her phone into her purse and sprinted to the garage.

Cars choked Constitution Avenue even on a Saturday. Tourist season had begun in Washington. Families clad in matching t-shirts and people carrying maps and cameras would soon replace D.C.'s full-time residents, who would escape the city for Rehoboth Beach on most muggy summer weekends.

She shifted in her seat and adjusted the air conditioning vents to blow directly over her clammy chest. Christiana glanced to the National Mall alongside Constitution Avenue. Stopping at a red light every thirty-five feet never used to bother her. It gave her time to take in the sights. But lately the Washington Monument's constant pointing to the sky created an unsettling feeling. It only reminded her nothing really changes in D.C.

Christiana pulled up to the entrance of the Rosemont Country Club only ten minutes late. Sunlight bounced off the brass plaque on the white brick pillars, the only announcement to the outside world that the elite of Washington gathered at the other end of the dogwood-lined driveway. Members of Congress discussed budget negotiations while golfing and bored wives complained about Neiman Marcus inventory while sunning themselves on the terrace.

Avery's family had held membership here since the club opened in the 1920s. Her great-grandfather was one of the founding members. The Churchill women had spent countless hours flipping from their backs to their fronts by the swimming pool and attending mixers and events in the cool evenings. Avery reveled in the ambience. Butterflies usually took over Christiana's stomach at the thought of crossing the threshold of the country club though she attempted to raise a little gratitude for Avery's generosity in letting her tag along. *Or drag me along.*

Christiana handed her keys to the valet, whose traditional red coat was replaced by a ridiculous number in black and pink. Oh, right, today's event was a fundraiser for breast cancer research. Great, she'd be in blue while everyone else draped themselves in various shades of fuchsia and rose. She hoped no one would notice. She knew everyone would. Even when helping a great cause, Washington feasted on mistakes, and failure to heed dress codes was a major gaffe. It took a lot of time and money—none of which she had—to conform to all the rules of Avery's world.

She shook her head and tried to focus on not tripping up the stairs in her high-heeled sandals. But memories of work today and what she'd overheard at the Jefferson Suite kept replaying in her mind. *Stop it. Chris. Think forward.* She slipped through the massive oak door.

2

Jonathan Brond thrummed on the steering wheel impatiently at another stoplight on M Street. He hadn't expected his little pet to be so demanding this morning, and now he was late, very late. Hell, he'd missed the opening speeches on the latest developments in medical research on breast cancer. Never mind, he had done his own breast study that morning.

His cell phone interrupted his recollection.

He smiled as he answered. "Sarah, I'm begging you."

Soft laughter filled his ear. "You haven't done that in years."

"You get him off my back, and you can have anything."

"What makes you think I have any pull with Brond Senior? I'm just the step-daughter."

"He likes you better than me. Tell him you met a nice accountant from Baltimore, and he has a sister. We'll double date. Orioles game."

She laughed. "Let me guess. Such unmasked desperation must mean your father arranged a not-so-blind blind date with Marla Clampton."

"He never lets up." A beep alerted him to another call. A

quick glance showed it to be the one person he didn't want to talk to. *Shit.* "Speak of the devil. Call him. Tell him something. Come up with any story at all. Just that I am *not* taking Marla to the July Fourth fundraiser."

"You owe me."

"Anything." He switched to the second caller, steeling himself for an inevitable lecture. "Yes, Father, I'm on my way."

"Why aren't you there yet?"

Jonathan sighed heavily into the phone. "Obviously, your spies have checked in on time."

"Don't change the subject. You need to get on the Senate majority leader's bandwagon. His bill will pass before the election. You could use some positive attention before October."

"Father, it's Saturday."

"That means nothing for a freshman trying to get re-elected. What's this I hear about you jetting home yesterday for a fundraiser? Don't take on too many charity cases, Son. Too much hand-holding will bleed you dry. Looks desperate."

"I fail to see how attending an event to raise money for a child's medical bills is *hand-holding.* And they were desperate."

"Yes, yes, of course. It's good publicity and all that."

"Not everything's about publicity, Father. In my position it's important to—"

"Like hell. You're running for office, not a papal honor. Look at your mother and me. We don't give—"

"Stepmother," Jonathan corrected shortly, having barely eked through a yellow light past a taxicab stopping short for a woman with her hand outstretched in a hail. Jesus, where did all the traffic come from on a Saturday afternoon? Most

Washingtonians fled like lemmings to the cooler beach on Memorial Day weekend.

His father cleared his throat, the signal Jonathan was about to get a speech. "Claire always said your heart's too soft for office and too hard for family."

"I'm surprised she recognizes a heart."

"Don't start, Jonathan. She's done nothing but—"

"Support me. I know, I know."

Jonathan's stepmother, Sarah's mother, had smiled through event after event at his father's side to show support for Jonathan's re-election campaign. It wasn't her fault she married the one person who had traded in his own heart for influence long ago. It wasn't her fault Brond Senior forgot the purpose of public office—to serve the public. "Lobbyist" fit him perfectly today.

"So, how are you going to handle the Collins show?" his father asked.

"I'll play the game."

"Good. Because, Son, you need to land in the middle on this thing."

"I understand the middle very well, Father." Christ, did he understand. His two years in office seemed one single, endless meeting, where the only place to land was the middle. More experienced politicians called it "consensus building"—the height of success in Washington. Fuck, he hated compromise. Everyone walked away with a little something but disappointed because they didn't get enough.

"Well, when Shane told me—"

"Why are you talking to my staff?" Jonathan rubbed his forehead. The early summer heat must be taxing his patience.

"It's the only way I find out anything. Jonathan, you've got to select an issue on which you can build consensus, not turn the whole First Amendment on its ear."

Jesus. The old man's relentlessness had kicked up a notch today. At least he wasn't bringing up his son's love life—a recent favorite topic.

"Father, aren't you missing a golf game or something?" Jonathan spun his palm on the steering wheel as he turned into the Washington Rosemont Country Club. "Listen, I'm here. Gotta go."

Jonathan repeatedly tried to dredge up some sympathy; his father had been hit hard by his own failed re-election six years ago. But his parental manipulation dried up any empathy he might muster. Jonathan had his own agenda—a ten year master plan, actually, where each election would draw him closer to his real life, not his father's version of living. He couldn't—wouldn't— get lost in his father's ambitions.

Jonathan handed his keys to the valet and gave a quick wave to the photographers, who had set up camp at the entrance of the club. His first lesson in office had been to play nice with the paparazzi, especially during crises. Just last week, a fellow congressman had been caught in *flagrante delicto,* cheating on his wife with his assistant. The cliché alone made headlines.

"Congressman," they called. "Give us your thoughts on this whole Blanchard affair."

"Nothing to say, boys." Jonathan brushed past a camera shoved in his face. Being nice didn't include feeding the bloodsuckers.

Jonathan stepped into the cool air of the club's domed entranceway and followed the roar down the plush-carpeted hall. He hated arriving late, even to an event he'd never wanted to attend in the first place. Tardiness showed an utter lack of command of one's environment. *Undisciplined.*

He rounded a corner. "Jesus." A young woman had landed

in his arms. Long blond hair and an opera-length pearl necklace swung out as she stumbled backwards out of his hold.

"Pardon me, I didn't mean to run over you." He trailed his fingers down her soft skin, as he steadied her—and studied her.

She shivered in response. "Sorry. My fault, sir."

The lovely woman's face drew Jonathan's eyes. Although she wasn't blatant about it, she appraised him, too.

Pretty. Blue eyes. Pale skin. Dress understated. He ran an inventory on her assets, an automatic reaction whenever presented with something beautiful. Jonathan paid attention to women in general. He loved everything about them. He didn't plan to get heavily involved, much less married, for some time. His political career wouldn't allow for such attachment. Yet, when they offered themselves, they gave a gift, and he took it—at least while it lasted.

"It appears the event's in full swing," he said.

"Oh, yes." She glanced up and met his eyes briefly, then ducked her head, fidgeting with her necklace, running the pearls through her fingers—first up, then down. She released the necklace as soon as she realized he'd noticed and smoothed down the front of her plain blue silk dress.

On any other woman, the dress choice would scream, "Don't notice me!" On the lovely young lady standing before him, it presented an elegance that couldn't be overlooked.

"May I escort you inside, Miss . . . ."

"Snow. Um, Chris."

"Jonathan Brond." He held out his hand. She took it with reticence, as if she had never shaken hands before. He didn't release her slender fingers when she tried to pull away.

"Have we met before?" he asked. She seemed familiar.

"I don't think so, sir."

His cock twitched at her soft, sultry "sir."

"Well, having a good time?" He stared at her naked pink

lips. *No lipstick. Very nice.* He never understood why women covered up such assets with smears of paint and grease. He preferred no barrier to the tender slips of flesh.

"Yes. Are you?" she asked.

He laughed. "I could be. Come dance with me."

"I don't think—"

"Don't think. Dance."

"Oh, I couldn't." She pulled her hand loose.

Perhaps a boyfriend waited around the corner, though her eyes held an intelligence that would outclass most of the single men trotted out for the debutantes who gathered at such places. No wedding ring, either.

A woman, sporting a pouf of platinum blond hair that looked like a swirl of cotton candy appeared by his side. *Damn, Mrs. Darden.* She slid her hand up his back and around his shoulders.

"Congressman, darling," she purred. "It is sooo good to see you."

The taut skin over her face drew back as her mouth stretched into a thin-lipped smile. It was a look shared by all the Washington professional wives. If he had to guess, Dr. Levine, one of the finest plastic surgeons in Washington, was responsible for her permanent "deer in the headlights" look.

"Mrs. Darden. Wonderful to see you, too." He gave her "Euro" kisses on her heavily made-up cheeks.

He allowed Christiana Snow to scoot by them, her anxious blue eyes cast to the ground. Yes, he recalled exactly who she was now. Her face rose up from a memory. She was pulling her father from a reception a few months ago. His legislative assistant, Shane, caught him staring and offered up her name.

Mrs. Darden latched onto his arm. "Really, Jonathan, isn't it awful, this Blanchard thing?"

"Yes, terrible." He let himself be led across the ballroom threshold.

❦

Christiana slipped into the ladies' room. Running into the charismatic *Congressman* Jonathan Brond ratcheted up her nervousness. Running into him? She'd practically mowed the man down! He probably wondered why she didn't recognize him. Mrs. Darden's unctuous cooing signaled his high place on the congressional food chain.

Already the event was like every other big society affair she'd attended—over her head. Christiana tried to get into the spirit, feed off the excitement of being surrounded by powerful people with important jobs and positions. But they rarely held the entertainment promised. She'd find Avery and make her excuses. Perhaps a headache or last-minute change to her work schedule.

"Jesus, Chris, come on." Avery's reflection appeared in the mirror.

Christiana jumped. "Hey, I—"

"You'll never guess who's here. Congressman *Brond*," Avery whispered. She stiffened when a few of the primping women threw backward glances at their reflections in the mirror.

I know. I nearly ran him down.

Avery pulled her out the door and steered her toward the music. Her friend wore the requisite pink that most women modeled that day, and her glossy chestnut curls bounced in a messy bun, a style that easily could have taken an hour.

"This event is looking up. We might even get you a date," Avery said at the ballroom entrance. "Now stop touching your scar."

Christiana pulled her bangs down to cover her forehead.

She didn't mind her scar. It's just someone always asked about it, and she wasn't about to share *that* story with anyone.

"Oh, Avery, I might—"

"No. You are going to talk to people, make some new *hot* friends, and not abandon me."

Avery had read her mind. Okay, Christiana could do one hour.

Swaths of rose-colored parachute fabric, interspersed with swags of white fairy lights, draped the walls. Inside, a mob of women in magenta, cherry, and white gowns gave air kisses to one another between tables draped in fuchsia linens with coordinating pink and white striped chairs. Bejeweled fingers and wrists sparked the air like paparazzi flashbulbs as women waved at one another across a crowded parquet dance floor. Only the fidgeting tuxedoed men, lining up before the bars in each corner of the room, broke the sea of pink.

The room looked like someone had slaughtered a flock of flamingoes.

Maybe she'd stay thirty minutes.

Avery drew her closer. "It's hunting time. Remember, if anyone asks, we're part of the committee. Don't you dare mention waitressing." Avery spun on her heel and headed toward her mother, the fundraiser's organizer, off in a corner laughing at something two women said. They bestowed the requisite air kisses on each other's cheeks.

Marcella "Coco" Churchill stood regally still as ever, in contrast to Avery's fidgeting. Though Christiana had admired her beautiful friend's poise when they were in high school, Avery had acted like a bird caught in a screened-in porch since returning from Stanford University a few weeks ago.

Could Avery be silently wishing they'd skip this event

too? They'd both already met versions of anyone they might meet here—the politicians hoping for connections, impassioned do-gooders convinced their organization could right some wrong, and socialites soliciting fat checks from the concerned and hopeful.

Christiana tried not to bump into anyone as she weaved through the tables, scanning the room for people she'd seen on political television shows or events she had attended with her father.

"The real success of a D.C. fundraiser is who actually shows up," her father had told her at the first such event. "Be sure to note where people are seated. You'll tell pecking order by table placement." Her father should know. He wrote for *The Amendment*, a paper dedicated to watching the comings and goings of Capitol Hill. He was an expert on power—who had it and who wished they did.

Christiana found her table tucked into a corner. As soon as she sat down, a waiter filled Christiana's wine glass. After a tentative sip, she wrinkled her nose. The Chardonnay probably cost seventy-five dollars a bottle. It still smelled like dirty feet.

"Hey, Chris." Christiana jumped as her friend crouched by her chair. "See the gorgeous blond guy at that middle table? Next to the facelift? That's *him*."

Not even the dim lighting prevented her from recognizing Congressman Brond. How could anyone *not* see him? If Mrs. Darden hadn't used his title, Christiana would have pegged him for a model. His symmetrical cheekbones would've been stunning on any man—or any woman for that matter. But his intense green eyes, framed by dark lashes, tipped him into a whole new category of good-looking.

"God, I hope he remembers me. We met two years ago, but he kind of disappeared from the club scene. He's one of the youngest members of Congress. And *single*," Avery breathed.

Christiana recalled how his hands trailed down her arms. He probably thought Christiana was the most ignorant woman he'd met and certainly the rudest, not acknowledging his position and refusing his polite offer to escort her inside. *Good going, Chris.* She could have been more gracious, even if Congressman Brond was an insurmountable, completely out-of-her-reach fantasy. Powerful men like him ended up with the Avery Churchills of the world.

Avery stood. "I'm going to ask him to dance."

"Oh?"

"You should start talking to all the hot guys here too. Don't waste your chance." She pulled Christiana's wine glass from her and took a big swallow. "But don't drink too much, Chris. You can't handle it."

Avery swept back toward the head table, her pink satin dress swishing from side to side. Christiana blinked back irritation at Avery's tone, shook it off. Something had been bothering Avery for the last two weeks since she'd returned from school. But she'd turned away every question Christiana had asked about her year at the glamorous California college. Maybe she found her freshman year as disappointing as Christiana did. It sure wasn't what she expected—high school on steroids.

Within minutes, servers danced around one another, putting plates of filet mignon and asparagus, swimming in hollandaise, in front of the seated guests. The clamor of voices and clanking silverware rose over the music. The real jousting had begun.

"Conversation is the best swordplay in Washington, Chrissy," her father told her just that morning. Christiana hoped no one expected her to parry.

She sneaked a look at Congressman Brond. He dipped his

head, dodging the wild gestures of the man to his left who accentuated his speech with arm waves and punches to the air. The congressman's bland expression showed he wasn't enthralled by the exchange.

"Are you a friend of the Churchills? I saw you talking with Coco's *gorgeous* daughter." The silver-haired woman next to her washed her meat down with a swig of what smelled like scotch.

"Avery's my best friend." Christiana studied her hands.

"Well, tell me, dear, why are you here alone? A beautiful girl like you?"

Christiana's face heated.

"You should take a page out of your friend's book." The woman nodded to Avery, now standing next to Congressman Brond's table, offering him a glass of champagne. Of course, he smiled up at her.

Christiana took another sip of the smelly wine but then set her glass down. Getting tipsy might feel good for an hour, but it wouldn't change her life. Besides she had to drive herself home . . . alone.

3

If Avery Churchill pushed her breasts any closer to Jonathan's face, he'd be tempted to give her a good, hard spanking.

"Well, I guess I should return to my committee's table." Avery lowered her eyelashes. "Let me know about that dance."

"Miss Churchill." He rose but couldn't return her handshake with any enthusiasm. Her practiced, child-like moves raised his ire and added to the tedium of the affair. But she presented a good escape route. He'd kept an eye on Christiana Snow since she entered the ballroom; she'd vanished from her corner table.

Jonathan entered the deserted hallway. The sweet-looking blond likely headed to the ladies' room. It's where all women ended up at some point in the evening.

Christiana barreled into his chest as he rounded the corner.

"Well, Miss Snow, I seem to keep running into you—literally." He smiled as he caught her arms.

"Oh, Congressman, I don't know what's gotten into me."

Fuck, he'd like to get into her. "You can repay me with that dance."

"Oh, really, I couldn't . . . ."

"You don't like to dance?" He dropped her arms.

"Oh, no, it's not that. I wouldn't want to take advantage."

"You're that good, huh?"

"Oh, no, sir. It's, well, you'll want to be seen with someone more—"

"More what?"

"Helpful to the fundraising effort." She bit her bottom lip. "I really should go. My table must be wondering where I am."

He watched her hair swing in time with her hips as she marched away from him toward the ballroom. Christiana Snow wasn't anything like he'd imagined.

Jonathan had seen the beautiful girl twice before with her father, famed reporter Peter Snow, who hadn't been too steady on his feet either time. The first was only a glimpse of her helping the intoxicated man into a taxicab outside a Georgetown restaurant but the second wasn't much longer— when she pulled her father out through a reception exit. After Shane revealed the man was her father, he'd tucked her name away but hadn't thought to follow up then.

Now, up close and in person, Christiana's shy but genuine demeanor piqued his interest. A yearning lay behind those sapphire eyes. Someone so young rarely showed such depth.

How old was she? He would find out.

Jonathan took in the traces of her vanilla perfume left in the stale air of the hallway. *Lovely.* Such a woman would be the antidote to his bland and oh-so-politically correct work activities planned that summer.

His logic kicked him in the pants. What was he thinking? He shouldn't go there.

His imagination went there anyway.

The other women at the reception had had every

molecule of originality polished out of them at their finishing schools, debutante balls, and girls' colleges, ensuring a future husband a blank slate to write upon. Thoughts of Christiana, a wildflower in a sea of hothouse orchids, giving her trust to someone—to *him*—fed his erection and his interest. He imagined she'd be tentative at first, allowing only a little bit of intimacy at a time. Christiana would require proof of his intentions. She'd need to be coaxed, calmed and lured forward. Her hesitancy would prove too frustrating for most men. It would only power Jonathan's resolve. Because, when she did let go, the results would be titanic.

Christiana was something he hadn't encountered in years. Maybe never. Christiana Snow was real.

Christiana's moment of swagger dissolved three steps later, and she slowed, entering the main reception room. She realized the low to which the night's potential had plummeted. *Well, hell.* Christiana's feet ached as she stood inside the doorway and stared at the dance floor. She should go home.

Her focus snapped to a point just behind her back. She sensed *him.*

Christiana turned to face Congressman Brond. No more than a foot separated them. His eyes showed his self-assurance hadn't wavered in the two minutes they were apart. Neither had her sense of being out of her element diminished. She didn't know where to look—his radiant green eyes smiling down at her, his hair catching the light, or his broad shoulders.

He took her elbow before she had a chance to choose.

"Shall we?" He pulled her toward the whirling mass of color on the dance floor.

When her foot hit the parquet, the up-tempo music changed. People melted into one another, stilling to a slower beat. He snaked an arm around her waist and pulled her into him with an unyielding strength. She'd been unmistakably seized.

They started off slowly, his eyes never leaving her face.

The band played a bluesy number. It wasn't an easy rhythm, but he had no trouble finding it. He turned sharply, and her pearl necklace swung out.

"You can dance," he said.

She swallowed. "My father taught me."

"Ah, yes. The gregarious Peter Snow."

"You know my Dad?"

"Only by reputation." His face held practiced neutrality. *Not good.*

The congressman twirled her through the swaying crowd. On tiptoes, she tried to stay loose for his lead. Her father could have taken lessons from this man. The congressman had woven them through the crowded floor to an almost deserted corner in seconds. His grace sent her heartbeat into a strange cadence.

"So, you are friends with the Churchills," he said.

"Yes. Avery is my best friend."

"I see." He sounded pleased.

Of course. He wanted more information about Avery. But he mustn't know Avery very well. Holding Christiana this close would only bring out her legendary temper. Of course, if she could extricate herself, Avery could move in.

"I'm sure Avery would love to dance with you," Christiana said.

"I'd rather talk about you. Tell me about yourself."

"What do you want to know?"

"How about a little bit of everything? At least for now."

Christiana couldn't help but smile. "What would be after everything, then?"

"Oh, that's good." He twirled her in a tight circle. "So, you're a model," he said, definitively.

"No, I'm in school." She was a little thrilled he would think such a thing after the long day she'd had.

"Well, you're quite lovely, Christiana."

She flushed more at the stunning richness of his voice than the compliment. "Thank you."

"No, thank you." He swung her in a big arc, and her skirt swirled out. His warm breath ran through her hair.

Christiana inhaled deeply, taking in his scent. It reminded her of an exclusive men's store, with hints of linen, wool and a trace of leather.

"How do you find the event?" His voice broke her trance.

"Oh, good, I guess. It's an important event." *There. That's something Avery would say.*

"The cause, yes. But the party seems a little over-the-top, don't you think?" He winked.

Her shoulders dropped a little under his warmth. He honestly seemed interested. *Well, he is a politician.* Yet despite his obvious charm, he seemed so normal—but not ordinary.

She exhaled heavily. "To be honest, I never understood why they spend so much money just to raise money. Why not just funnel it all to the charity?"

He laughed. "You should run for office."

Christiana dipped her eyes to his lapel. She hoped the scar on her forehead wasn't at his eye level. She tried to concentrate on the music, but the vibrations between her legs threatened to pull her off rhythm. As if reading her mind, he pulled her closer. Her nipples hardened as the bodice of her dress grazed his suit jacket. She should say something, make polite conversation. She could have used the distraction herself.

"Christiana."

She peeked up at him under her lashes.

His face held a resolve, like a man used to wielding power. "Are you here alone?"

"Sort of."

He smiled. "Have someone on standby?"

"No, sir. Nothing like that."

"A date, then?"

She shook her head.

"Then I'm glad you agreed to dance with me, Christiana."

Had she agreed? It didn't matter. Christiana followed his steps . . . and his scent. Her arm lay heavy against his chest as his height allowed only her hand to reach his shoulder. Underneath his tuxedo, his muscles felt tight and hard. His strong thighs brushed hers. *God, what he must look like under that suit.*

He twirled her in a double spin that made her gasp. He smiled down at her, bemused. The music had changed to a Frank Sinatra song. He didn't let her go. *Don't let me go. Not yet.*

A steady craving warred with her nerves—and her good sense. One more dance, she told herself. *Then you'll leave.*

His hand moved farther down her back, and a strange desire spiked, winning the battle. She wanted him to drop his hand lower, cup the curve of her bottom and draw her closer. Without thinking, she leaned into his body.

He loosened his hold as if he'd heard her inappropriate thoughts and meant to rectify the situation. "What are you doing this summer?" he asked.

"Sir?" His direct tone penetrated her haze. She searched for a suitable answer. What first flashed in her mind couldn't be what he meant. *Waiting tables, wasting time at the pool, helping my father with . . . everything.*

He frowned. "Tell me what you're thinking."

"Oh, nothing, really."

"When we're together, I expect you to always tell me what you're thinking."

Before she could process his words, someone spoke into a microphone, announcing something Christiana was too flustered to catch, and couples separated. The congressman let her go.

"Meet me outside in ten minutes. In front," he said.

Avery's voice scissored between them. "Why, Congressman, you are quite the dancer. Perhaps you'll show me some of your moves?"

"Yes." Christiana cleared her throat and crashed to earth. "Avery's a wonderful dancer."

Avery's eyes flashed with resentment, but they paled in comparison to the storm in the congressman's. Christiana left the two of them standing together before the tempest broke. She had to go elsewhere to reclaim her mind. She had to get away from his penetrating eyes, his seductive voice and his scent. Besides, her replacement had arrived.

She made it out the front door and onto the lawn near the parking lot. The late-spring air hung heavy, ripe with the scent of freshly mown grass. She tilted her head up to the starless sky and wished for a breeze to stir the stifling air and maybe cool the stickiness between her legs.

She should go home. Her feet refused to move.

"What were you two talking about?"

Christiana startled at Avery's voice. "He asked me how I knew your family. I said you and I were friends and that he would enjoy dancing with you."

"I don't need you to do that. What were you really doing?" Avery snapped.

"He wanted to dance. That's all."

"Yeah, I hear he likes spreading himself around. Ya' know, so no one gets the wrong idea."

A jolt of irritation ran through Christiana at her friend's tone. "What do you mean?"

One of the plastic surgery brigade, who Christiana recognized from Coco Churchill's bridge club, looked out through a half-open door. "Ah, Avery! There you are. Your mother's looking for you."

Avery huffed. "Duty never ends. Later, you have to tell me everything."

Christiana, watching Avery hurry across the lawn and disappear through the door, stayed perched on the edge of one of the Adirondack chairs, ignoring the rough surface pulling threads from Avery's blue dress. She scanned the darkened sky. The moon peeked from behind gathering storm clouds, and the air bore down on her chest.

Jonathan hurried down the hallway. He managed to avoid dancing with the ersatz Avery Churchill but got stopped by the Dardens for another bout of mundane small talk. He only hoped Christiana Snow hadn't left. He wasn't disappointed when he slipped out the wide front door.

He waited a moment, drinking in the sight of Christiana's pert ass perched on an Adirondack chair on the front lawn. After telling his cock to stand down, he jogged down the wide steps onto the grass.

"You didn't tell me how you're spending your summer," he said to her back.

Her face turned, whispers of blond hair falling off her shoulder. She didn't rise right away, but her elegant profile showed she smiled.

He drew closer. "Surely, a beautiful young lady such as yourself has a full dance card by now."

She cleared her throat and stood to face him. "No, I don't."

Her hair shone in the soft glow from the gaslights surrounding the lawn.

"Um, how do you know my full name? Everyone calls me Chris, but when we were dancing, you called me Christiana."

"You seem like someone a person should know."

"A waitress from The Oak Room?" She blushed. "At least 'til I go back to school later. To Virginia, uh, UVA."

"Good restaurant. Good school." He walked toward her, and she stepped backward nearly sending herself over the side of the chair in response. He reached out and grasped her arm, steadying her for the third time tonight. She stilled, hardening his most manly parts at her reaction to his touch.

"UVA is my alma mater," he said. "Law school, anyway. Charlottesville is a beautiful town."

"Yes, well, I don't get out much. Studying and all that."

He released her arm. "That's a shame. There's much to experience there. I could show you."

She looked up at him quizzically and then sank back down on the edge of the chair. Perhaps she wasn't interested —as if that would stop him from persisting to learn more about the girl. It would take more than her natural shyness to make him stand down his pursuit.

"Grad student?" he asked.

"Oh, no, I'm a sophomore this fall."

"Oh. You're twenty?"

"Um, nineteen."

Damn. Full stop. Exactly when did young girls start looking like they were twenty-five? Obviously much younger than he recalled. Christiana Snow could easily have passed for one of those public relations girls working down in the Watergate offices or an art studio assistant in some one room gallery in Dupont Circle.

She clutched at her fingers and cast her eyes down, obviously uncomfortable at how long he'd been staring. He just couldn't believe her youth. Everything about Christiana Snow spoke of having lived far longer than nineteen short years.

He sighed. "I'd have taken you for someone older. Your maturity exceeds your age." He took her hand and kissed it. Jonathan was no stranger to disappointment, but when she trembled as the stubble of his upper lip brushed over her wrist, he nearly cursed the Gods for presenting such a temptation before him.

"You really are exquisite, Christiana."

She blinked as if she hadn't heard him.

And then he did the only thing he could do. He walked away.

4

Rain peppered Christiana's bedroom window, and flashes from lightning bolts darted through the curtains. She couldn't sleep with the thunder hammering outside and inside her head.

Christiana sat up, and a wave of clammy dizziness washed over her whole body. *Wine is so not worth this.* She pulled herself out of bed, steadying herself on the nightstand. Her tongue stuck to the roof of her mouth, tasting a strange, acrid fuzz.

She stumbled into the kitchen and downed a large glass of water along with three Advils. "I don't know how Avery drinks wine. Two sips and I'm toast."

Yawning, she shuffled to the living room. Dust motes floated in the stale air, highlighted by the gloomy morning light that shone through the bay windows. Newspapers, mail, and half-written essays with red pen marks cascaded from piles around her father's faded, brown recliner. Or, as he liked to call it, his throne.

Christiana leveled a pile of magazines on the coffee table and fluffed a few of the gold pillows on the green couch. She folded the red plaid blanket, thankful her father hadn't slept on the sofa. Comfort seeped through her limbs as she set about straightening things so familiar.

Since her mother had died, Christiana had kept up her mother's ritual of cleaning the house on Sunday mornings. Housework brought a sense of solace that she had missed those mornings away at school. By the state of the living room, the house missed it too.

An image of green eyes and a warm hand on her waist swam up from the back of her mind, interrupting her focus. The remnants of last night's dreams—rose-colored silk, a dark chocolate voice, and the feel of wool against her skin—wouldn't retreat.

Christiana tamped down her imaginings. It was absurd, these daydreams. Why would a congressman pay any attention to a girl who didn't fit with the society crowd? *Pity, probably.* If she had her wits about her, she would have recognized the clues—the misgivings that ran across his face when he said goodbye.

Water trickled through the pipes and Christiana switched on the radio in the kitchen. Rihanna's singing didn't quite drown out the groans coming from her father's shower, a clear sign he drank too much last night.

Maybe Avery downed too much champagne at the reception and wouldn't remember Congressman Brond's hand on Christiana's back.

Fat chance, Chris. Add that to your growing list of delusions.

Speaking of lists, Christiana needed one for all the things she intended to do this week. *Get oil changed in Dad's car, turn in her semester admission fee, get insurance, update Quicken . . . get a life.* Her tasks ran through her head like a chant as she washed the dishes. *Call the dishwasher repairman.*

Her father lumbered into the kitchen, hair still wet. He sported the family uniform of sweatpants and t-shirt.

"Talking to ourselves a little early, doncha think?" She hadn't realized she'd been chanting her list out loud.

As he reached for the coffeepot, Christiana snapped him with a dish towel.

"Good. You're up," she said. "Lots to do today, Dad. In fact, about this insurance . . . ." She waved a form at him. It had lain on the kitchen counter the entire two weeks she'd been home from school.

"I'll get to it. So, what was the charity event like?"

"Very pink. Lots of champagne. They had beef Wellington."

"I would expect nothing less of the Honorable Churchill. So, anyone interesting there?"

"Business men. A few congressmen. Oh, and this horrible woman with too much plastic surgery." *The one who couldn't keep her hands off Congressman Brond.* Christiana shook her head, and some coffee sloshed over her mug onto the counter.

"Careful there, Chrissy." Her father picked up a sponge and wiped away the spill. "Which congressmen? Any pundits?"

He must be desperate for specifics. Her father wouldn't touch a sponge unless he was trying to ingratiate himself.

"Umm, I think I saw Tyrone, Carroll. I don't know who else." She swallowed the name she wanted to say. "Hey, did you file that tax extension?"

"What were they talking about?"

She sighed. Her father's focus was singular. "I don't know. Lots of back slapping, drinking, dancing, watching Avery . . . ."

Her heart twinged when he glanced up at the mention of Avery.

Christiana's father delighted over her friendship with the most popular girl in school and her resulting connection to one of Washington's most powerful families. Yet, too often his fatherly eyes cast the question neither had ever asked. Why did Avery befriend Christiana in the first place? Avery spent the last three years schooling Christiana on the ways of a socialite—and failing repeatedly. Still, it had been nice to have a friend who tried.

Her father stared at her. "What about their wives?"

"I don't know what their wives look like."

"Well, anyone you recognized?"

"Not really, Dad. Look, I'm getting a headache—"

"You're not changing the subject on me."

"Dad, I'm not—fine, I'm changing the subject to this insurance form. I really need you to fill it out."

"I'm gonna do it."

"When?"

"After *Meet the Press*." He took it. "See?"

She gave him a weak smile.

"Did you see a man with—"

"Dad!"

"Alright, alright. I'm going to watch TV now." He left Christiana in peace to make another pot of coffee.

Her father would've killed to attend the club fundraiser last night. He loved events, any kind where he could angle for an interview or test his theories on someone. But given his penchant for social networking—and scotch—Avery wouldn't have extended an invitation to him even if Christiana had begged. Christiana thought how alike her father and Avery were about social gatherings. No occasion went unconsidered. Few events went unattended.

"Keep your eyes and ears open," her father always said. "You might learn something, Chrissy." But, really, how many different ways can a girl smile at the nothings she heard?

How many Sunday brunches, ballroom dinners, mansion soirees had she attended with her father? Some guy always seemed to angle her into a corner of the kitchen where he breathed liquor fumes down the neckline of her dress. Or worse, focused on her forehead and reminded her of things better forgotten. Christiana would duck away as soon as the booze forced him to clutch the edge of the counter with both hands. Her father would be talking loudly in the living room, barely holding on to a tumbler of scotch. When they were the only ones left, she'd help him to the car.

Several male voices thundered from the TV in the living room. Christiana sighed and moved to join her father. If she didn't, he would yell from his throne about how a reporter or consultant had just said the stupidest thing he'd ever heard.

Christiana curled her feet underneath her on the sofa and picked up her laptop. She launched Quicken to start updating the household accounts. They'd been woefully abandoned. The data entry work would distract her from the noise of the Sunday political television show.

A lot of words for a whole mess of nothing.

She was deep into reconciling her father's checking account when a familiar, rich baritone pulled her gaze to the TV. *Oh! Him.*

On the screen, Congressman Jonathan Brond's eyes shone more sea-green than emerald. She held her breath when he spoke. Her inner parts tingled as she remembered how he said her name.

The congressman leaned forward. "Privacy is on everyone's mind right now, David. Public confidence in online security seems to be lessening as usage of the Internet and social media, in particular, is growing."

The political pundits around the table watched him as if mesmerized, drawn in like Christiana. The congressman's conviction was palpable. Even the host, David Gregory, stared, engrossed by his words.

"There is mounting evidence that security holes exist," he

continued. "We need to construct a protective framework, including legislative action, without violating the First Amendment. If we don't protect the American people from false information, fake news stories, and predators, who will? For one, allowing cyber bullying is criminal."

"Look at him. He can control a room," her father said. "But, then the Bronds always could."

The Bronds. She rolled the name over her tongue, silently.

"Listen to this, Chrissy. This social media thing has got some issues, and he seems to be the only one taking action."

Most politicians' voices dripped with air kisses and firm handshakes, affable and approachable, telling you what you wanted to hear. But Jonathon Brond had an edge. The man didn't hide the power in his voice.

Congressman Brond scratched his chin. Her belly clenched at the thought of his hands and how strongly they'd held her on the dance floor.

"You and your friends may fill your days and nights on YouTube and Facebook," her father said. "But, mark my words, all this exposing yourself so freely online is going to get ugly soon. That poor girl who killed herself from online bullying. Shameless." Her father spat his last word.

Christiana wished her father would stop lecturing her on social media; he knew she hated Facebook and Instagram and all those vanity selfies.

No, she wanted to hear what her father knew about the Bronds. "So, the Bronds have a prominent history in D.C.?"

"Political family. Very wealthy. Legacy politicians like the Kennedys and the Rockefellers. The Bronds started out in the Midwest somewhere and then hit the national stage sometime in the forties. Then they decided to get away from their roots. Moved the whole kit and caboodle to Rhode Island. Well, that wasn't too popular," he said.

"Why wasn't it popular?" Christiana couldn't imagine anyone disliking Jonathan Brond.

"Some big scandal. A divorce, I think. Not a very smooth move by his father, Senator Brond. Then, of course, that whole mental health debacle the good Senator started. The family's not very graceful."

Not graceful? She recalled Congressman Brond's smooth movements as he twirled her on a dance floor. "I danced with him last night," she said to the TV.

"You danced with Congressman Brond at the fundraiser?" Her father pointed an accusing finger at the television. "You *danced* with him."

"Jeez, Dad. Yes. One dance. That was it." She snapped the laptop shut and stood to retreat into the kitchen.

Her father lurched from his recliner and followed. "Well, what did you talk about?"

"Nothing. Typical politician. All charm and small talk." The ache between her eyes returned.

"Tell me everything."

Christiana turned to face him. "Are you kidding me?"

"You said he was charming," He held up his hands in mock surrender.

"Charitable. Taking pity on a girl who he thought was alone."

Her father's eyebrows raised. "A famous politician who's known for womanizing."

"I wouldn't know."

"Did he talk about the Internet bill? It's your generation who—"

Christiana's phone rang, down the hall. She pushed herself from the counter's edge and jogged to her room to answer, glad for an excuse to leave the awkward discussion.

"Chris." Only Avery could scold someone by saying their name.

"Hi, Avery."

"Where did you go last night?"

"Everyone seemed to be leaving, so I thought I'd call it an early night." Christiana flopped on her bed.

"Well, what did you and the hot congressman talk about on the dance floor?"

The tight band around Christiana's head turned into a vise. Little stars of light pricked her vision. *Great. A migraine.*

"Not much," Christiana said. "I told you everything. But you danced with him later, right?" Christiana's chest filled with both pride and guilt. She knew he hadn't. She had the handsome man's attention first although the thought was difficult to enjoy with the invisible screws boring into her head.

"No, he said he had to go. Early meeting or something. Then, I got caught by the dreaded twins."

"The twins?"

"Yeah, those two college guys. Dad made me talk to them. Something about clerking for him. He wanted me to convince them Washington was the most fun place to be, *ever*." Avery's earring clinked against the phone. "So, did you meet anyone?"

"Um, not really."

Avery sighed into the phone. "What about that guy at your table? He was cute."

"Who?"

"Jeez, Chris. I've never met anyone less interested in guys in my life."

"Like I've ever raised my hopes around guys?" Of course, one man in particular hadn't left her thoughts since she'd met him.

"Whose fault is that? Jesus, you'll never get anyone's attention if you don't go for it. But, I've got great news. I managed to get out of going to church. What do you want to do today? Shopping's the only option. Stupid rain."

Christiana didn't know what would be worse, being cross-examined by her father at home about a man she'd never attract or being steamrollered in a shopping mall by Avery's chatter about all the men *she* could attract.

"I have to spend time with Dad." At least at home she could hide in her room.

"Not another one of those parties, Chris! You won't meet anyone suitable there."

"No, it's just I'm leaving in a few months, and Dad's been alone all year. I've got some catching up to do. Dad hasn't touched Quicken since I left. And, I—

"You shouldn't be doing all that. I'm rescuing you. You and I are going to the pool on Tuesday. It'll be sunny. No arguments."

"I don't—"

"Don't tell me you're working. God, Chris. I don't know how you stand it, serving food to all those tourists."

"Those tourists leave great tips." Christiana rubbed the back of her neck, vainly attempting to coax the blood flow to continue.

"Okay, girl. Tuesday. Be at my house at nine-thirty. We have to get good placement," Avery said.

Christiana's phone silenced. She pushed deeper into her pillow and stared at the little rosettes on her bedroom walls. *Little-girl wallpaper.*

Christiana closed her eyes and shut out the pink. The hum of distant voices from the television drifted down the hallway. The reverberation of his deep, rich voice strummed over her body. She inhaled and remembered the scent of leather, wool and the mysterious ingredient unique to a man named Jonathan Brond.

Her hands trailed over her belly, and she slipped nervous

fingers under the waistband of her sweats, dipping into the silky hair beneath. She cupped her breast with the other hand and rubbed her thumb over her nipple. She imagined pressing her breasts against his hard chest. The steel band around her forehead relaxed. Updating her dad's accounting could wait.

The congressman's rich vocals vibrated through the paper-thin walls, a deep string instrument, teasing, yet serious. The sound wrapped around her fingers and urged her to continue. She dipped a finger through her fleshy folds into dampness.

Echoes on the other side of the pink-rose barrier grew more pressing. Someone said something another didn't like. She focused on his muffled voice, and let it drive the rhythm of her hand.

Her middle finger rubbed up and down over her hardened clit. Licks of warmth built to a fire as recollections of strong arms holding her on a remembered dance floor blocked out the sounds in the living room. Christiana lifted her other arm over her head. She curled her hand around an iron scroll in her headboard, recalling black braided ropes hanging over the edge of a bed in the Jefferson Suite.

Christiana spread her legs and slipped a finger inside herself as her thumb rubbed her sensitive pearl. The congressman's deep voice entered the room—and shut out all others. She plunged her finger in and out, her longing coating it with her juices.

Her hips lifted to meet her penetrating finger. She danced on the edge of tipping over. She wanted to hold back a little, to follow the murmurs floating through the room.

His charged words cut through the debate. "I intend to dig in deep, blow things wide open."

Air shot out of her lungs as her body arched off the bed in a tidal wave of sensation. She rode the last of her orgasm and released the voices on the other side of the wall. She slipped her fingers free from her wet, swollen tissues and tuned into her own breathing.

Maybe he did it intentionally. Was he talking to her in some secret code in that rich, stunning voice?

You really are exquisite, Christiana.

Clarity struck her like a lightning bolt. She knew where she'd heard that velvet purr. Congressman Brond was the man from the Jefferson Suite.

5

Jonathan kept his regard on Shane and ignored the demanding vibration of his phone blinking his father's name repeatedly. Jonathan had heard little of his aide's briefing on web statistics. No matter, he could talk Internet privacy and protection in his sleep.

"Well, that should be enough to keep Collins on track," Shane said.

"What else is on the docket today?"

Shane scanned a legal pad in his hand. "Lunch at noon. Television studio at two-thirty. Reception at six. There's that stack of letters for you to sign. You know how donors love the personal touch." He looked up. "And Mrs. Nelson wanted a minute on the phone to thank you for coming to her son's fundraiser. She suspects you had something to do with the therapy bills being paid."

"I trust you disabused her of that notion."

"Of course, but, sir, I'll say it. I'm not sure why you don't want them to know—"

"To keep you from putting out a press release on it."

Jonathan shot him a grin. "Some things have nothing to do with elections. And this is one of them." He stood and reached for his jacket, signaling it was time to move. "Snow still calling?"

"Yes, sir, I put him off as you requested."

Peter Snow had been the real reason concentration eluded Jonathan this morning. Christiana's father had been calling Jonathan's office every few hours the last two days—since the night Jonathan had danced with Christiana.

Since then Jonathan had tasked his personal assistant, Mark, with investigating Peter Snow. Mark had unearthed, in addition to the man's unwavering commitment to a reporting career, Peter's love of Dewar's and distaste for fatherhood. No wonder Christiana carried such sorrow in her pretty azure eyes.

"I didn't find a lot on her." Mark had handed over a thick file folder. "But, her parents were a piece of work. In particular, check out page fourteen. The death of Snow's wife left him to raise a seven-year-old child on his own. No reason to disappear into a bottle, but, well, just take a look."

Nor an excuse for making Christiana a designated driver after she grew up.

With every word on the page he read, an intense need to help Christiana built inside him. She didn't seem the type to ask for support. Christiana's working life—another fact uncovered by Mark—proved the point. She might as well unfurl a sleeping bag in The Oak's kitchen to keep up with her shift schedule.

Did she have many friends? That Avery Churchill girl couldn't be much support, unless it involved fitting a ball gown.

Surely Jonathan could come up with something to improve Christiana's circumstances. His mind returned to one thought, which he shuttered—quickly. Her age alone made his imaginings inappropriate.

He needed fresh air. "Lunch, on the terrace."

Shane glanced over his notepad. "I should handle some things here."

"I'm surprised. Giving up a chance to sit under an umbrella instead of a fluorescent light? We've got plenty of time."

They both required a reward given the morning's tedium. Plus Shane's presence in his car would ensure he didn't make a pit stop at a certain reporter's office and rearrange the man's priorities. Perhaps even a few body parts.

Christiana never appreciated seatbelts or ponytails as much as when she rode in Avery's blue Fiat. Avery yanked the gearshift into fourth gear and raced up River Road, squeaking through another yellow light as it turned red. The top was down and Christiana let go of the armrest long enough to peel stray hairs, whipped forward by the hot wind, from her lip gloss.

Avery's cell phone rang for the fifth time since they left her house.

"Man, that's Chase," she said.

"Still not over you?"

Avery shrugged and switched off her phone as she pulled into the country club entrance.

Madonna's love life had nothing on Avery's. Her collection of ex-boyfriends would rival any game hunter's trophy wall. Most of them lasted a few months. Lucky Chase had the good fortune to last her whole senior year in high school. Apparently, he wanted a repeat.

Christiana jogged behind Avery across the parking lot. Her heart skipped a beat as they walked past the empty Adirondack chairs where she talked with Congressman Brond. Avery hadn't grilled her anymore about her dance with him. That didn't stop Christiana from replaying the encounter in her mind a hundred times. She'd spent the last two days trying to shake his voice from her head. *You really are exquisite.* She scarcely believed she'd heard those words.

Avery dragged Christiana through the grand foyer to the pool area behind the restaurant and turned a lounger to face the sun. Christiana pulled its twin to settle underneath an unfurled umbrella. Tanned, thin women occupied nearly every chair and chaise around the pool, feet pointing east to allow maximum exposure to the rays.

Christiana dropped her stuff on the shaded table and collected her necessary accoutrements. Extra towel from the pool stand, bottle of water from the large barrel holding assorted drinks, and sunscreen to slather over every inch of exposed skin.

Her checklist completed, Christiana flipped her long ponytail over the back of the lounger and took in the view of the golf course. Acres of greens cascaded down a hill to surround a large lake at the bottom, water glittering under the harsh sunlight. Half a dozen men in red and orange polo shirts swung golf clubs and squinted into the air, their faces etched in silent prayer that their balls would land well. The landscape was manicured, groomed and pruned to perfection. Too perfect if anyone had asked Christiana. *Unreal. Artificial.*

Avery flicked through a magazine and Christiana let the sunshine lull her into a doze. She had worked a late shift the night before, and her feet still ached from running table to table at The Oak Room. The tips grew larger as the weather improved, but so did the work. If she wasn't serving impatient tourists trying to get to Ford's Theatre, she attended the locals dashing in between meetings at the White House or the Treasury Department.

Christiana's eyelids drooped shut. Time slipped to a dream, and heat from The Oak Room's kitchen pressed on her chest. She was back in the main dining area, a nineteenth century Edwardian room, with dark mahogany booths and shiny brass fixtures. A man with green eyes and gold hair smiled down at her. He opened his lips to speak and drops of ice hit her stomach.

Christiana lifted her head from a thick, muggy cloud.

Avery shook a wet Diet Coke can over her torso. "Hey, wake up. He's here."

"What?"

"Shhh, not too loud. Over there. And for God's sake, Chris, *don't stare!*" Avery put on her straw hat and stretched into a pin-up pose. "He's always been so elusive. But I hear he's been coming to the club more often lately."

Christiana scanned the table area. Her eyes found two tennis players, three older women playing cards, and *him.*

Congressman Brond sat under the diffused light of an umbrella with several men dressed far too formally for a summer poolside setting. Ties hung loosely around necks. Perspiration darkened khaki pants at the hips. Starched shirts wilted in the muggy summer heat. All sweat stained except the congressman, who sat silent and still in a crisp white shirt with aviator glasses masking his eyes.

Brond slapped both hands down on the table and stood. The other men rose hastily, scraping their chairs behind them and gathering papers. The congressman strode into the sunshine alone, his suit jacket hooked from a finger over his shoulder.

Christiana stared at his Roman profile as he slowly scanned the sunbathers around the pool.

"Man, he's something," Avery muttered. Of course she hadn't taken her gaze off him, either.

Christiana squinched her eyes closed. While her mind refused to acknowledge he stood mere feet away, her body tuned into his presence with a vengeance. Moisture tickled down her spine as she concentrated on calming the hunger threatening possession of her senses. She flattened her back into the towel she'd draped over her chaise longue, but today even the expensive Egyptian cotton proved unable to hide her response to the heat—or Congressman Brond's presence. She licked her lips and fought the restlessness in her legs, willing herself not to wriggle her bottom into the lounger seat. *Breathe, Chris.*

Jonathan stood on the blazing hot concrete longer than he cared to, but he needed to resolve the internal debate that had raged in his head since he sat down. The last person he expected to see here was Christiana Snow. Yet, there she sat, tempting him like a creamy delicacy.

A fall of blond hair cascaded over the back of the chaise and her long, elegant legs stretched out, glistening with sunscreen. Small breasts, barely covered in triangles of sapphire Lycra, rose and fell with her deep breaths. She looked more serene than he'd ever seen her, certainly more than when they plowed into one another at the Churchill fundraiser mere days ago.

Her rosebud lips parted on a sigh. His mind filled with visions of succulent kisses—and wet sucking sounds from her mouth encasing his cock. He hardened instantly.

Perhaps running into Christiana at the fundraiser—and

now here—was fated. He didn't believe in such nonsense, yet some kismet seemed at work.

The more voluptuous Avery Churchill perched beside Christiana. She wore the same expression he'd seen at the fundraiser. *Ennui and entitlement.* She irritated the fuck out of him.

It was strange seeing these women from two different worlds together, given what he knew of Christiana's family history.

And, he was from yet a third universe.

He should walk away.

Christiana stretched like a warm kitten in a slat of sunshine.

She's nineteen. Forget it. He had an election to win, a family legacy to restore, and a personal life that already skated the edge of respectability.

Walk. Away.

Her pink tongue swirled over her lips.

He turned toward them. Jonathan had an hour before he needed to be at the television station. He could at least say hello.

"Don't. Say. Anything," Avery hissed.

Christiana's eyes popped open when a shadow replaced the sun's warmth.

"Miss Churchill. Miss Snow." Congressman Brond stood taller than Christiana remembered.

Avery beamed. "Why, Congressman, how nice to see you."

"And you as well."

Christiana nodded, entranced by her reflection in his aviators. Her mind had blanked.

"Are you enjoying your summer break?" he asked.

Avery grinned up at him. "Oh, yes. That's what summer is for after working so hard, right?"

"I'm sure. Miss Snow, I trust you won't let The Oak Room monopolize your time."

"I'll try. Um, I mean I'll try *not* to." Christiana jogged her mind for something—anything—to add to the small talk. Jonathan Brond's shadow overlaying her legs did nothing to cool her overheated body. Instead a rush of blood flooded her core.

"It's a good day for swimming," he suggested.

"Oh, Chris doesn't swim. She hates the water," Avery cooed.

Ignoring Christiana's frown, Avery continued her barrage of flirtation—of course.

"What about you, Congressman? What do you do for fun?"

"I'm afraid I won't have much time for that this year. Election year." He regarded Christiana. "But I'll get away for a few weekends."

"The beach?" Avery asked.

"I prefer the mountains. Quieter."

"Too shady. I need sun." Avery stretched her legs out and arched her back.

"And, you, Miss Snow?" the congressman asked.

Christiana had never thought about it before. "Both, I think."

He laughed. "Spoken like a true politician. And I agree, if one can have it all, one should."

"I suppose," Avery scoffed.

The congressman turned to Avery as if he'd forgotten she was there. "Did you have a good turn-out for your family's fundraiser, Miss Churchill?"

"Oh, yes. I'm sorry you never got a turn with me on the dance floor." Avery dipped her eyes. She was one step away from waving a palm frond over the man's body and feeding him grapes. Christiana could see why. A man like Jonathan Brond serviced a harem somewhere.

Jonathan smiled at Avery. "I'm afraid you're too popular for me." Christiana had no idea why, but she felt a little better at the congressman's response to her friend.

As he squatted down on his heels, her whole body vibrated under his attention. He took off his sunglasses, and flecks of gold danced in his green eyes. Christiana could feel Avery's cold gaze drench her in jealousy, but she couldn't turn away from his face.

His lips twitched into a smile. "I understand your father wants to interview me." His eyes whirled with amusement, or was that annoyance? Sarcasm or mockery definitely, but she wasn't sure which. He rose and turned away before Christiana could absorb his words, much less respond. "Don't forget your sunscreen, ladies," he said over his shoulder.

"We promise!" Avery yodeled and leaned back.

He wove through the tables under the pergola. Stripes of sunshine lanced his broad back until he disappeared through the wide glass door.

"Oh. My. God." Avery said. "He came over to talk to me! And your Dad's going to *interview* him." Avery's voice dropped to a whisper. "He's thirty, one of the youngest people ever elected to Congress, *no wife.* And I couldn't find anything about a girlfriend, though there are enough pictures online with women. You wouldn't believe what you can find on Google."

Christiana took a lungful of stifling air. *Shit, Dad. Your timing sucks.* What if the congressman thought Christiana had blabbed every word about their meeting to her Dad? She hadn't breathed another word about that dance to her father since she'd blurted it out on Sunday. She knew better than to elaborate. But Congressman Brond wouldn't know that.

He'd think I was a little girl swooning. A wasps' nest of nervousness settled in Christiana's belly as if she'd been caught downloading porn. Well, lately her mind *had* resembled an X-rated film set. *Oh, God. What he must think!*

Avery's chatter impinged on her awareness. "The Bronds were big into mining before his grandfather got into publishing. Congress was later. They're like the Hearsts or something. His grandfather moved the whole family to Rhode Island. Can you imagine? That tiny state? I'd kill myself."

Her tidal wave of words only added to Christiana's shame. Avery wouldn't have smutty pictures floating in her brain. Avery wouldn't have sat like a stone while a gorgeous man talked to her. Avery wouldn't have her inner thighs catch fire every time his gaze landed on her face.

"Jesus, he's so damn hot," Avery swooned. "You don't think he's gay, do you? I wonder who I can ask. Not your Dad. Too obvious. What if he told him? *Mortifying.*"

Humiliation washed Christiana from head to toe at the thought her father might do just that.

"Maybe your Dad can get him somewhere, and we can just happen to run into them," Avery said. "Wait!" She glared at Christiana, aghast. "What if your Dad writes something to scare him off?"

Yes, what if he does? Her father would jump at the chance to interview a congressman and produce a piece that'd be talked about from the Capitol steps to the Pacific Ocean. What if Congressman Brond thought she was her Dad's *accomplice?*

"Avery, I have to get ready for work." She lied. But she had to retreat to her room to regroup. *To think.*

"But it's only one."

"I promised I'd come in early to help set up."

"Like I said, Chris. You work too much." Avery pulled her towel from under her legs, brows knit in concentration. Probably planning her wedding to him. The Congressmen Bronds of the world ended up with women like Avery. Refined, sophisticated, experienced. Avery didn't have an alcoholic father to compromise a man like Jonathan Brond. No, Avery would be the embodiment of grace and discretion.

6

Jonathan stepped into the late afternoon sunshine, provoked but containing his irritation. He'd spent thirty appalling minutes taping a segment for the evening news in a vain attempt to warn people how dangerous social media could be. The idiotic host, Collins, had no idea what he preached. People were sending other people over the edge with a touch of a button.

Fuck. Yes, he needed to fuck.

Jonathan had two hours before a mandatory reception. He couldn't go with his cock on fire. Fingering his phone, he ran through a list of women he could call. He shouldn't call any of them. *Damn election.*

Jesus, what he wouldn't give to have an agreement with a certain young blond woman. Christiana Snow hadn't been out of his thoughts since he ran into her for the second time in days—unheard of in Washington. But he must stop. He'd give an interview to Peter Snow and be done with it.

Jonathan pushed the image of her blue eyes and perfect round ass from his mind and dialed Christiana's polar opposite. Someone whose need for discretion exceeded his own.

"Yvette." She'd answered on the first ring. "Are you in your suite?"

"I'm having lunch with my *friends*." Laughter rose in the background.

"Can you get away?"

"I thought you had *fundraisers* to attend."

Ah, the brat he'd grown to expect. Well, he knew how to handle petulance. "I won't ask again."

"I can extract myself in another hour."

"Thirty minutes. Your suite," he directed.

"I'll try."

He steeled his voice. "Yvette."

"Yes, sir. Thirty minutes."

"Don't keep me waiting."

She would be late. She'd do it to force a spanking, her favorite punishment. Today, she'd learn attempting to top him would not result in anything she liked. God, he needed this. Someone who understood what he required and, in return, required what he could give.

Jonathan slipped behind the wheel of his convertible, heat seeping through his pants from the sun-warmed leather seat. If he hurried, he would beat Yvette to the Jefferson Suite and have time to prepare.

The light traffic allowed him to arrive at The Oak in twenty minutes. Rich hues of lush lawn and paler pastels of spring blooms colored the landscaping around the entranceway as he pulled up. The valet rushed to open his door.

Jonathan tossed his keys to the eager young man, who yelped, "Congressman."

The Oak's lobby didn't teem with guests. A sliver of suspicion ran up his spine—an automatic reaction to significant environmental changes.

As he ascended in the antique elevator, he wondered if

Christiana would work the restaurant later that night. *Stop it, Jonathan.*

Jonathan used his master key to enter the suite, a waft of lilac scent hitting him square in the face as the door opened. Yvette kept fresh flowers at all times. He smiled, knowing she likely had doubled her order this week. As long as Arniss DeCord dallied in their divorce settlement, she'd run up his tab. The worst thing she could do to the prick was spend his money.

Jonathan and Yvette had been friends since college. He'd warned her about marrying Arniss, and now his prediction had come true. The affairs aside, the man's greatest cruelty lay in ignoring her needs. Jonathan would do no such thing, could not. Yvette deserved better. He hated seeing her suffer —seeing anyone suffer.

His steps echoed through the marble entrance of the vacant suite. He flipped the wall switch in the master bedroom and recessed lights' soft illumination rose. His bag made a loud thump as he threw it on the bed. A quick glance at the clock soothed his earlier anxiety. Yvette had to arrive in the next ten minutes in order to avoid a punishment. She wouldn't make it.

He pulled out a short bamboo switch from his bag, ran his fingers over its knobby surface. He laid it on the silk duvet where Yvette would see it immediately upon entering.

Jonathan loosened his tie and fell into the corner wingback chair, facing the French doors, which he'd left opened to the main room. He needed to see her enter. Yvette didn't so much walk as sashay, hips rolling with each step. Her walk was his favorite part of the dark-haired beauty queen's manner and physique.

Of course, Yvette's brat nature wasn't his ideal for a submissive. Her hot temper blazed too quickly. But she acquiesced often enough to keep his interest and keep him serving her need for domination.

Jonathan loved seducing a female submissive, teasing the consent from her willing body. He loved the feeling of absolute control—control he had nowhere else in his life. His political career provided power. But nothing compared to the rush from earning a submissive's trust and consent. Dominating a willing woman provided him a unilateral authority. His will dictated every action without compromise —far removed from the *fucking consensus* that ruled his political life.

"Take off your clothes. Everything but the panties." Those would be his only words.

She'd peel off her bra slowly, letting her full breasts with dark-berry nipples pop free. He grew stiff at the thought of capturing each bud in the little clamps he brought. Pinching the firm tips, one in each claw, would be his first action. Then, he would connect the clamps' chain to a collar she'd wear.

He'd bend her over the dark-red leather bench at the base of the bed, ass displayed for his taking. The thin chain would pull each tip hard when he yanked her hair back—smooth, silky, dark locks that slide through his fingers and waterfall down her back.

Perhaps she'd earn that spanking then. He knew from experience her cunt soaked through lace in three slaps. A cane would brand her ass but draw out her orgasm. When her mewls stopped, she'd be ready. He would then take his time, lots and lots of time, to drive into her heated pussy, like plowing new earth with his rutting.

A snick sounded from the suite's front door. Yvette's high heels clicked on the hallway's marble floor. She was late. *Good.*

~

Christiana dropped her pool bag just inside the marble entranceway of Avery's home—if one could call the mansion a home. The echo of Avery's steps on the stone chilled her skin.

"Well, don't stand there like a servant in the entrance. Come in," Avery beckoned her to follow her up the steps leading to the living room.

"Uh, thanks, Avery. I've got to head out."

"Not even a minute? We can Google him!" Avery's eyes fired.

"No, I've got to—"

"I know, I know. Go to *work*." Avery sighed and picked at her cuticles. Her manicures hadn't lasted lately. "I just don't like being here by myself."

The Churchills had a live-in maid, cook and butler. It was unlikely Avery would ever be alone. Yet, Christiana understood. She supposed most people would find the Churchill home the epitome of success—a seven-bedroom Georgia mansion behind gates, a large C curled into the black ironwork. A long limestone drive led up to a white-columned portico, where an actual butler would emerge to see if you were friend or foe.

If someone made it through the house entryway, they learned Avery's mother, Coco, was no art dilettante but a true patron. A rare oil of a maritime war scene by Jacques-Louis David, a hedonistic view of three frolicking women painted by Jean-Honoré Fragonard and several peaceful pastoral scenes by Thomas Gainsborough hung in large, gilded frames, lining the oval foyer. A large, brass sculpture of a young girl holding a basket held court on one side; its twin statue, a small boy holding out a bunch of wildflowers, faced her on the other side of the vestibule. More paintings, including oils of the family together and single portraits, led the eye deeper into the Churchill manor.

The famed J.R. Robichaud had captured Avery's likeness. She hated the depiction, saying Picasso would have captured her more accurately. Christiana thought the portrait looked beautiful, albeit a little angry. Christiana often wished she felt like Avery looked in the painting—someone who didn't take any crap.

Avery fluttered her hand, dismissively shooing Christiana away. "Well, go serve your crab cakes and sirloins to Washington's elite. I'll be *Googling*." She winked, with a return to the old self-assured Avery.

She headed up the large staircase to the right to the *family rooms*, as Coco called them. The staircase on the left side of the entrance hall led to the *guest quarters*. Both sides looked the same to Christiana—straight out of Washington Home magazine—only nicer. Yet, despite Coco's impeccable taste, Christiana had always thought the house resembled a museum except no one who lived there ever stopped to admire the artwork.

As Christiana drove home, she realized she hadn't hugged Avery hello or goodbye once this summer. Those friendly embraces had been part of their routine—before they'd each headed off to their respective freshman years at different universities. She tamped down the thought that the lack of hugs meant something and concentrated on taming her untamed thoughts about Congressman Brond. She needed to regain her footing. The last time she ran into him, it took hours to reorient. Hell, days.

She mentally ran through her summer mantra to try to calm herself. *Make money, think about your future, money, future.* It didn't help recover her equilibrium or quell the shame that the gorgeous Jonathan Brond might think she was a complete idiot.

A cold shower when she got home didn't help either.

Christiana stepped out into the living room, her hair wrapped in a towel, as her father's key clicked in the front door.

He dropped the mail on the table by the door. "Hey, Chrissy."

"Hi, you're home early."

His face registered shock. "Oh, shit, I forgot."

"Don't tell me. You didn't file for that tax extension." Christiana sighed.

"Tomorrow, I promise. We've got that reception tonight. The Caucus Room. Gonna be big. You not ready yet?"

Great, she'd forgotten she'd agreed to be "his date," as he called it. *More like his chauffeur.* Her get-a-real-life agenda didn't include loitering around a bunch of legislative aides who either ignored her or looked down the front of her dress for hours—unless they fixated on her scar. *What fun.*

"See anyone in particular today?" She had debated all afternoon about just asking straight out if her father had used her as bait to get an interview with Jonathan Brond.

He cocked his head like he didn't understand. "I see lots of people. Got anyone in mind?"

"No, wondered about your day, that's all. So, what's this thing tonight?"

"Copyright issues, online privacy, cyber-bullying. Strange, but the Blanchard and Brond families called it."

Christiana froze. He *had* pestered Jonathan Brond—and probably aggressively. The man could forget the mundane, like *taxes* and *house payments*, but potential stories? They remained front and center in his mind. No wonder the congressman's eyes swam with displeasure earlier.

"I need twenty minutes." Christiana headed to her room to prepare.

She had to repair this situation. Here was her chance to

tell the congressman she hadn't told her father anything about him, apologize for her dad's forceful behavior.

Christiana slipped on her ivory sundress, another hand-me-down from Avery's regular closet purges. Wouldn't it be the nice thing to do to invite her to the reception? Avery would kill to be in the room with Congressman Brond, and it would make her father happy to see her together with Avery. It also might get their friendship back on track.

Christiana looped her pearls around her neck, a talisman against making any more social blunders. After tapping some Dermablend on her forehead, she checked her reflection in the mirror. Not too bad, but she'd always fade into the wallpaper standing next to Goddess Avery.

She changed her mind. It would be best to go solo with her father. She could then talk freely.

7

Black-suited attendants rushed the car when Christiana's father pulled up to the Russell Senate building. The reception would be large. Sponsors didn't spring for parking help on Capitol Hill unless they expected a strong turnout.

People streamed toward the reception area and Christiana jogged down the wide hallway, trailing her father. You'd think he was about to lose the story of a lifetime if he didn't get there before any other reporter. He only slowed down when they hit security. Her father had forgotten to empty his pockets of metal objects—coins, keys, an embarrassing nail clipper. His sheepish smile didn't stop the large African-American woman in uniform from sending them back to the end of the security line. Twice.

Once through the security protocol, Christiana took her father's arm in the reception room entrance and immediately wished she had known the dress code. Both men and women sported dark suits even though it was on the cusp of summer. Only the interns stood out in their khaki pants and polo shirts. In her sundress, she didn't look like any of them.

Light streamed in through large windows on the far side

of the cavernous room. Tall marble columns glowed a stark white with thick black and grey veins crawling up to meet ornate tops.

"Chrissy? Club soda?" Before she had a chance to respond, her father slipped his arm free and set off for the bar in the corner. A few of the khaki-clad aides moved away as he walked across the blood-red carpet.

Christiana edged through the doorway to stand on the periphery of clusters talking in hushed tones. She searched for people who stood alone, hoping someone could point out Congressman Brond's legislative assistant, while minimizing the risk someone might know she was asking for the Congressman himself. Everyone seemed deep in discussion. That didn't stop her father, who floated from one group to another.

Her father slapped a man on the back affably. The man retreated, and two other gentlemen nearby laughed loudly, only to edge away from Peter's outstretched hand. By the time her father made a third trip to the bar, Christiana gave up in her quest to find a friendly face. Her feet hurt from standing against the wall, so she crossed the room to retrieve a club soda her father had forgotten to order.

"Could I also have some lime, please?" she asked the bartender.

"Hitting it a little hard, aren't you?" Warm breath whispered through her hair.

She turned and blushed. "Hello, Congressman."

"Vodka. Straight up," Congressman Brond said to the bartender without turning his eyes from Christiana. "It must be my lucky day."

"Sir?"

"Third time's a charm?"

"Um, I'm glad I ran into you."

"Well, that's the best news I've had all day."

Christiana smiled and felt her cheeks redden more. Why did everything he said in that silky voice sound like a proposition?

"I–I wanted you to know that I didn't say anything to my father about us . . . talking, I mean—"

"I know you didn't, Christiana."

"Well, I wanted to make sure—"

"Gossip is not in your nature," he interjected before she could finish her thought much less her sentence.

"No. It's not." She smiled at his attempt to relax her.

"There's someone you should meet." He took her arm and steered her across the room toward a tall young gentleman, built wide and stocky like a football player rather than like the more slender congressman. "Christiana, this is Mark, my assistant."

Christiana hoped he didn't feel the pounding of her heart beneath his grip on her arm. His warm hand didn't stop a chill from running up her spine, either. She silently cursed her inability to stay composed in the congressman's presence.

"We were wondering what your generation felt about social media," Mark said.

"I don't have much experience with it."

"But you're on it, right? Facebook, Twitter . . . ."

"Sometimes. I never considered it that social."

Jonathan grinned. "I completely agree. Too removed from normal human interaction and rife with carelessness."

"Um, you're doing market research on Internet issues or something?" she asked.

"Perhaps." The congressman sipped his drink, his eyes scanning her flushed face. Another man, in the 'legislative aide' uniform of khakis and white shirt, sidled up to him and whispered in his ear.

Christiana scanned the room for her father. When she

inadvertently caught his eye, he abandoned the group of men he'd been chatting up and wove a boozy path her way. *Oh, shit.* Within seconds, her father circled her shoulders with one arm and dangled his empty glass from his fingertips.

"Congressman, good to see you," her father slurred.

"Mr. Snow."

"So, Chrissy, I see you've found the man of the hour."

Her cheeks colored anew. "Dad—"

"What can I do for you, Mr. Snow?" Brond asked. "My aide tells me you've been calling."

"Yes, well . . . ." Her father handed Mark his empty glass. "Do you mind? A double? The congressman and I need to talk business."

"Double what?" snapped Mark.

"Mark." The congressman kept his eyes trained on her father's face.

Her father held Congressman Brond's stare. "Bourbon. One for the congressman, too."

Mark stalked off, and Christiana wondered if she should leave, too. An invisible string of tension ran between her father and the congressman, as if they were two gunslingers striding toward one another, spurs clinking, along the board sidewalk of a town in the Old West. Little bullets of light bounced around behind her eyes and she concentrated on breathing in and out.

"This social media thing . . . ." her father said.

"Yes, Christiana and I were discussing it. You've got a smart girl on your hands, Mr. Snow."

"Yes, she is. So, this privacy bill you're backing. Severe, almost authoritarian."

One side of Brond's mouth quirked up. "Well, there is a time and place for authority."

"Not a fan of transparency?"

"Not everything needs to see the light of day."

"Such as?"

Mark returned and handed her father a half-filled tumbler.

"You forgot the congressman's drink, good man," her Dad said.

"No, Mr. Snow. I've reached my limit."

"So strict . . . and disciplined."

"You have no idea."

The young legislative aide murmured in the congressman's ear.

"Mr. Snow. We'll finish our conversation when things are more sane." The congressman strode away without looking back, Mark and his aide trailing behind.

A band of cold steel clamped around Christiana's forehead, and she grabbed her father's arm before she stumbled.

"Whoa, Chrissy, you been nipping at someone's drink?"

She took several more inhalations, listening to blood gush through her ears.

"I'll be right back." She hurried out a side door.

The cold ladies' room reeked of antiseptic. Thankfully, it was empty. She leaned against the marble sink. She had gotten out what she needed to say, even if she witnessed legislative aides parting like the Red Sea when she and her father walked in. Even if she had to endure getting her father back to the car after he turned brash, spitting Jim Beam on his targets. Even if she had to see Congressman Brond's expression harden and feel the very air around him close up like an umbrella.

Christiania pressed a wet paper towel to the back of her neck as she rested her forehead on the marvelously soothing tiled wall. The pricks of light stopped dancing and her heart slowed. It was time she and her father headed home. She shouldn't care what people thought.

She turned and took a last check in the mirror. At least

her make-up behaved. She pushed open the metal door and stepped into the hall, steeling herself for the extraction process. No matter what her father said or how loud he grew, she would get him to the car.

The tap-brush sound of feet on marble steps echoed through the deserted hall. It was *him*. Even his footfalls exuded confidence.

Congressman Brond appeared in front of her before she could duck away. Without a word, he encircled her waist and steered her into a room across the hallway. He caged her against the wall inside the door. His green eyes reflected how he felt about what had happened upstairs.

Christiana hated that look of pity.

Should she protest him stealing her away or apologize for her father's behavior?

Cupping one side of her face with his hand, his thumb moved slowly over her bottom lip, releasing it from the nervous clasp of her teeth. She gulped, startled, as his hand grasped the back of her neck. She inhaled his expensive linen and leather aroma. Her mind struggled to catch up to his hold when his knee slipped between her legs and parted them. He leaned into her pelvis.

Her heart pounding, she arched her back to meet his rigid erection underneath.

What was she doing?

His eyes narrowed in response, a little surprised, a little less sympathetic.

She wanted to know what his body would feel like under her hands. Her palms slid, almost as if under someone else's control, under his jacket until she embraced his waist. His jacket, now parted on either side of her, left only a thin shirt and her dress between her belly and the ridges she felt across his abdomen. She was right about what she'd imagined under his suit. She curled her fingers around his lower back muscles. The congressman's mouth was on hers before another thought had time to form. Soft lips moved over her mouth. His leg forced further between her thighs, parting them more.

A greedy yearning obliterated her thinking. She never wanted him to break away.

His tongue demanded entrance to her mouth. She moaned as she acceded to his command. He slanted his face to latch his firm lips onto hers more fully. She didn't know how long their tongues danced or exactly when she lost the distinction between her body and his, but she didn't care.

He finally broke their kiss but kept his face close. "Lovely," he murmured.

"Congressman?" Her voice sounded as weak as her knees.

"Drop the whole 'congressman' thing, Christiana," he said, his hot breath moving over her moistened lips.

"Yes, sir," she said softly.

She could feel his lips quirk into a smile, sliding over hers. "Call me Jonathan when we're together. At least for now."

He brushed a strand of hair from her forehead. The gentle glide of his fingers teased her skin, until his thumb faltered over her scar. Her legs sagged onto his knee, still firmly planted between them. The urge to rub her ache up and down his quad grew stronger.

"Come with me. I'm taking you home." He slipped his leg free.

She hesitated. "Home?"

He cocked his head, then smiled in reassurance. "Not my home. Yours." He grasped her hand.

She blushed like a schoolgirl and hated the naiveté that continued to display every time she ran into the Congressman.

As he guided her through the hallways, the rush of cooler air replacing the warmth of his body did nothing to shake her disbelief at what just happened. *He kissed me! Me?* She'd never had anyone take her mouth like he had. The taste of his lips lingered on her tongue all the way back to the reception. She wanted to grab his hand and pull him back. *Please. Kiss me.* Otherwise she wasn't sure she hadn't hallucinated the last five minutes.

Jonathan's tall frame wove through the throng of people. He marched to her father, punching the air with his hand emphasizing his point, a sure sign the alcohol had begun to take its toll. A sick sense of shame replaced her euphoria. Jonathan would never touch her again after witnessing her father's sloshed tirade.

"Mr. Snow," Jonathan said. "Call Shane tomorrow. We'll talk then. He'll set it up." The young man in khakis magically appeared behind her father.

Her father blinked. "Uh, 'kay. I'll be sure to do that."

"My driver is taking Christiana home. She shouldn't be out this late."

Jonathan noticed Snow had the decency to flush, realizing the unforgiveable situation he created for his daughter.

"Of course. Such a gentleman," Peter lifted his glass in a half-toast toward him.

Jonathan led her outside to an idling black sedan. Mark held open the passenger door as Christiana slipped into the back seat. Jonathan folded himself next to her.

"You said your driver was going to take me home." Christiana's eyes registered alarm.

"He is. He's taking me home, too. To my home."

"My Dad . . . ."

Her words evaporated when he patted her hand. Nothing she could say could possibly make up for her father's conduct. Peter Snow's boorish behavior wasn't her cross to bear though, by the look on her face, she'd likely had a lot of practice.

"Don't worry," Jonathan said.

Shane popped his head into the still open door. "Congressman, you wanted to see me?"

"Yes, make sure Mr. Snow makes it home safely after the reception, and go over some possible subjects with him for our interview later in the week, would you?"

"Yes, sir." Shane slipped from sight, and Mark closed the door. The partition rose between Mark and the back seat. *Finally some privacy.* Christiana slid across the leather closer to him as Mark smoothly made a U-turn in the street.

"I didn't know Mark was your driver," she said.

"Among other roles." Jonathan took her hand. "Christiana."

"Yes?" Her rosy lips parted on an involuntary sigh, and his imagination got the better of his intellect. It took every ounce of control to not crush her to the seat with his body and take her right then and there.

"I shouldn't have . . . ." He had no right to her. She had not given herself to him. He had yet to even ask, and he shouldn't. Washington was unforgiving in many matters and getting involved with a nineteen year-old would prove fatal. He already tested the boundaries with his sexual proclivities.

"No, please. Do it again."

Okay, so he hadn't scared her off completely. He laughed and then tamped down the ferocious protectiveness filling his insides. "I shouldn't have been so impulsive with you." He touched her face. She pushed her cheek into his palm, like a kitten might arch into an outstretched hand.

No mistaking, she would test his control. "You really are exquisite." He dropped his hand and leaned back into his seat.

"Thank you." Her cheeks turned a beautiful shade of pink, like the inside of a seashell. But, just as quickly, all color drained, and her lips pursed. Her hand went to her temple, and she massaged a small circle next to her scar.

"Are you feeling alright?" he asked. "I didn't mean to scare you."

"No, you didn't. Just a little headache."

"Give me your hand." Jonathan tugged her even closer to him across the leather seat. Her bare thigh rested alongside his leg. She didn't pull back at the connection. He pulled one of her slender, warm hands to his lap, palm up. He pressed his finger into the soft fleshy pad below her thumb.

"Acupressure," he said.

Jonathan had learned how to stave off headaches arising during meetings and hearings. Popping a pill in front of colleagues would be a sign of weakness and used against him.

Christiana's arm rested across his thigh. He stroked her delicate palm and then pulled on each finger. She took a sharp intake of breath as her delicate tendons stretched under his larger fingers. He tried to be gentle.

She leaned her head back and closed her eyes.

Jonathan massaged her whole hand, kneading and rubbing until her fingers fell open, splayed out wide, fully receiving his touch.

He pulled her other hand across his leg, and her blue eyes opened. He held her eyes with his own as his hands engulfed both her wrists. The tightness around her mouth released. His eyes fell to his lap, where his index fingers and thumbs grasped her pale wrists. He rubbed his thumbs across the sensitive thin skin, and she shuddered. *She likes having her hands held captive.*

"I'd like to take you to dinner. This weekend."

Christiana raised her head from the headrest and blinked.

"You want to take me to dinner." Her voice held astonishment.

"A gentleman never asks a beautiful woman for a Saturday and expects her to be free," he said. "But, you'll find out, I'm not much of a gentleman." He released her hands. "I know a little place about an hour outside of Washington. The drive will give us a chance to talk. And I promise not to keep you out too late."

"No, I—"

"No?"

"No, I mean, don't worry about being late."

Jonathan smiled. "I have an offer I'd like to discuss."

Though he had sufficient discipline to pass on this woman if need be, he believed in helping people. He could at least show an interest in her life and help her better navigate the obviously overwhelming situation with her father and the brat socialite. *Like a mentor,* a voice whispered in his brain. The brain in his pants responded, *yeah, right. Who are you kidding?*

The car slowed as it pulled up outside her house.

"Feel better?"

"Yes, thank you."

The color had returned to her cheeks. Jonathan thought of how pink he could turn other parts of her anatomy. His groin ached.

Mark opened the door and offered his hand to help Christiana from the car.

"I've got this, Mark," he said. The momentary blow of jealousy caused by the thought of Mark touching her startled him.

He eased himself from the car and placed his hand on the small of her back to guide her over the cracked and uneven concrete.

He laid a chaste kiss on the back of her hand. "Saturday

night. I'll pick you up at six." He waited for her to unlock the front door and step inside before walking back to his car.

Jonathan slipped into the back seat and took a few deep breaths. Mark eased the car away from the curb, and the privacy screen lowered in a muffled whine.

"Where to, sir?"

"Home. The Oak's not a good idea tonight."

"Very good, sir." The screen rose to separate them.

As they entered the parkway, the traffic sounds quieted. Jonathan's daydreams took advantage of the renewed silence. Christiana proved irresistible, a delicious smorgasbord of opportunities for pleasure.

So why am I fighting this? She's of legal age, a girl on the cusp of womanhood. How could I resist her? She's catnip in a den of lions.

At the reception, he'd seen how the men gawked at her. There were a few in particular he definitely didn't trust. Her response to his kiss showed how ripe she was for surrender to a Dominant will. If he was right about her submissive nature—and he hadn't been wrong yet—he'd ensure it was *his* will.

8

Gas lamps illuminated the pine-wooded drive up to the exclusive Lodge at the Point restaurant. Jonathan said the food would be worth the hour drive from Washington. Christiana didn't care. She would have driven to Texas to have dinner with him.

On the fifty-minute ride over, Christiana listened to him dictate legal language over the phone. It seemed his work never ended. She didn't mind. She'd listen to him recite the periodic table so long as she could be close enough to take in his scent and the energy that seemed to radiate from his body.

For days she'd thought of nothing but the touch of his hand, kneading away her headache in his car. No guy before had ever sparked such hunger in her. She had trouble keeping her legs still. It was like she'd morphed into a trollop who wanted nothing more than to straddle Jonathan's lap.

A valet hustled over to take custody of Jonathan's keys while another helped Christiana step from his BMW convertible into the unseasonably cool air. Christiana was thankful he'd put the top up for the ride over—her dress was backless but for a few straps. She'd rooted through the recesses of her father's closet earlier that day and found her mother's favorite little black dress. She'd hoped he kept it since nothing hanging in her own closet seemed right.

Christiana stood next to Jonathan in his elegant charcoal grey suit and blue foulard tie that screamed old money and hoped she didn't look like what she was—a girl wearing her mother's outdated dress and pearls.

Jonathan placed his warm hand on her back and guided her up the limestone entranceway shrouded in shadows of massive evergreens. The maître d' intercepted them at the door.

"Ah, Congressman, so good of you to join us this evening. Mademoiselle." Her shoulders relaxed a little under the older man's unforced courtesy.

Jonathan held her hand as they passed antique oils of pheasants in nature settings and foxhunting scenes hung on the faded wallpaper. She hoped he touched her often tonight. She hoped he'd do a lot of things tonight, like kiss her.

The maître d' smiled as he pushed open an unmarked white door. They entered the cleanest, most elegant kitchen Christiana had ever seen. Fading sunlight streamed through a bay window over two long Carrera marble counters and bounced off twin stainless steel refrigerators. A bored-looking, lanky man swirled a spatula in a gigantic copper pot.

They stopped in a small alcove housing an intimate table set for two before a pale stone fireplace. "Mademoiselle." The maître d' pulled out her seat. Christiana settled into the antique farmhouse chair.

She'd entered a fairytale. She hoped she'd never wake up. If she did, she might go back to wondering why a man in his position, with his looks, who could have his pick of beauty queens and trendsetters, had chosen to dine with her.

Two servers materialized from behind the maître d' and

laid crisp, white linen squares in Christiana and Jonathan's laps. She liked being on the other side of service for once.

It did seem strange they'd gone so far away, however. Christiana didn't know if she should be afraid of such privacy or thrilled they were dining alone. She chewed the inside of her cheek as uncertainty tainted her previous happiness.

Jonathan leaned closer. "Anything wrong?"

"Are we hiding?"

Surprise crossed his face but then comprehension. He chuckled. "Christiana, the kitchen table is the most coveted seat in the house. People wait months for a chance to dine with the chef."

"He's joining us?"

His grin widened, and her face heated at her gaffe.

"I certainly hope not. I don't think I'd be good at sharing you. Which is why I apologize for forcing you to share my work on the ride over," he said. "I told the office to hold my calls. But tell that to a nervous aide who thinks every call from a constituent is Armageddon. I'm turning *this* off for the rest of the evening." Jonathan tucked his cell phone in his inner jacket pocket.

A man in chef's whites emerged from behind a screen and nearly ran to the table.

Jonathan rose to shake his hand. "Chef Georges, please meet my date, Miss Christiana Snow." Christiana's stomach backflipped at his words. *He called me a date!*

"Pleased to meet you, Miss Snow." He held a hand across his middle and bowed. Then he clicked a small remote. Gas flames flickered around the 'logs' in the fireplace at their elbows.

Jonathan sat down and snapped his napkin back into place. "What delicacies do you have planned for us this evening?"

Chef Georges rubbed his hands together. "The loin of lamb with sauce Béarnaise is excellent. The filet of beef, superb! Vichyssoise and deviled scallops, and, of course, fresh lavender ice cream, your favorite. But, first, a cocktail, some wine?"

"Champagne. The ninety-seven Bollinger Blanc de Noirs." Jonathan looked over at Christiana.

"Ah, celebrating, I see! Excellent." The chef turned away immediately.

"Feel better?" Jonathan placed his hand over Christiana's.

Her insides warmed at his obvious attention to her comfort. Her feminine parts grew downright hot. "Sorry. I'm new to all this."

"Never apologize for what you haven't done yet, Christiana. I am honored to introduce you to a new experience. It reminds me not to be so cynical and jaded."

A man in black tie set a sweating silver ice bucket on a tall stand next to their table. After ceremoniously uncaging the cork of the chilled champagne bottle, he opened it with a muffled pop.

"Wonderful sound, isn't it?" Jonathan asked. Christiana smiled at his implication that she was familiar with the sound of champagne being uncorked. She could tell he was trying to make her feel more worldly than she was.

After the server filled two flutes, Jonathan handed Christiana a stem of shimmering bubbles. He lowered his voice conspiratorially. "I'm about to violate the alcohol laws. But they like me here." Jonathan winked.

Christiana touched her flute to his, held out for a toast. She took a small sip and wrinkled her nose in delight at the effervescence.

"You, uh, said you'd met with my dad. How was the interview?"

"Nothing too interesting. In my line of work, one cannot

be too careful, even around seemingly insignificant conversations." He reached over to the champagne bucket, holding his tie with the other hand. "I would rather talk about you. What do you plan on majoring in at UVA?" He refilled her glass to the brim.

"I don't know yet. I figure I'd explore. Try a little bit of everything." Her hair started to prickle her back, so Christiana pulled it over her shoulder to one side of her neck.

"Discovery is always a good idea." Jonathan twirled the stem of his champagne flute and stared at her shoulder. "I'm glad you wore your hair down, Christiana. It's beautiful that way."

"Ah, thank you." Her legs quivered at the sexual tension his innuendo brought.

His eyes searched her face. Could he see her vision of his fingers trailing down her spine to dip into the crevice between her butt cheeks? How she'd pleasured herself to the sound of his voice? She ducked her head slightly, worried he could read her thoughts.

"I'm surprised I haven't run into you at The Oak Room."

Oh, if he only knew how they almost ran into one another. An ache grew in her crotch at the memory of a silky voice followed by sharp slaps to skin and delighted moans in the Jefferson Suite.

"You work long hours. Is it because it's such a nice place?" he asked with a playful glint in his eye.

"No, it's because college is so expensive," she teased back. It helped take her mind off where she wanted his hands. Well, it did for about two seconds.

"When you're not working or studying, what do you enjoy doing?"

Daydreaming about you. "I read, watch movies, go to the pool, the usual stuff. What about you?"

"I sail. I have a thirty-two foot schooner docked at the

Washington Marina. I'll have to take you out on it some weekend."

"I'm a little afraid of deep water. But Dad and I used to go down to the Potomac on July Fourth to see the fireworks reflected off the river."

"Seeing them from the deck of a boat is a spectacle not to be missed."

"You don't get cinders dropped on you?"

"Hasn't happened yet." He laughed.

Renewed warmth spread across her chest. Jesus, she might as well wear a sign that cried "naïve ignoramus." At least he seemed amused.

A small beef filet surrounded by a creamy shallot sauce arrived, and a server opened a bottle of wine.

"This cabernet pairs nicely with the beef," Jonathan said. "And I trust you like medium rare." Christiana placed a small bit of tender filet in her mouth. "Well?"

"I've never tasted anything so delicious."

"Good. It's important to me to know what pleases you."

His words darted between her legs. He wanted to please her? He already pleased her. If what she had heard in the Jefferson Suite was an indication of what he required, she wasn't sure she could return the favor.

He ate in silence, keeping his eyes on her face. The movement of his mouth around the fork as he ate the savory beef in the rich sauce only fed more salacious imaginings of what his lips and tongue might do.

What had he done to make Mrs. DeCord so needy? In her mind, black straps wrapped around the woman's ankles, keeping her legs parted while Jonathan licked juices from her most intimate parts.

She took a swallow of red wine and winced at its acidic tang. It was much better than the chardonnay from the fundraiser, and it helped clear her dirty mind—a little.

Finally Christiana finished her last bite of beef. A small cocoa soufflé centered in a pool of darker melted chocolate replaced her empty plate. Her stomach complained in fullness. Yet she couldn't let good chocolate go to waste, so she took a small dollop.

"Christiana. Put down your spoon."

She slowly set her spoon on the rim of the plate and raised her gaze to meet his emerald eyes. Kitchen noises faded into the background as she stared into his eyes. The intensity of his stare and the thundering of blood in her ears drowned everything around her.

He leaned forward and rested his hand on her wrist. "I want to spend time with you. This summer."

"Spend time with me? I want to make sure I understand. Are you offering me an internship?"

"No." He chuckled.

She swallowed. "You want to date me?"

"Not exactly. More wine?" He filled her empty glass without waiting for her answer. "You don't have a boyfriend."

"No."

"How many relationships have you had, Christiana?"

Her mind raced for an acceptable answer. She didn't want to admit to the truth. She couldn't bear to even remember that night in Jeffrey Daniels' dorm room. She dropped her attention to her hands, wrapping her pearls around her index finger. "Not many."

"You don't need to be shy. Look at me."

She lifted her eyes.

"I realize this may seem unorthodox. But, I'm going to lay my cards on the table." He paused. "I enjoy the company of beautiful women. In *every* aspect of my life. And I'd like exclusive rights to your company until you leave for school. Late August, correct?"

Fragments of an unnamed emotion surfaced. His was no

ordinary offer. This was a proposition—for sex, for the whole summer. She teetered on a cliff, where fear wanted to push her over and desire begged her to jump. Either feeling, she wanted to go over.

He held her hand, and his fingers played on her palm. She prayed that when she stood, the moisture dampening her panties didn't breach the lace.

"I'll take you to Charlottesville next weekend. I have a house there, and it will give us a private place to discuss our arrangement. Of course, I'll book a room for you at the Hilton near campus in case you'd rather—"

"No, that's okay." What did she just say?

His lips twitched into a grin but then dropped back into a relaxed expression. "Of course, there is the matter of your father." He released her hand and leaned back in his chair. "Your father cannot know. Or your friend, Miss Churchill."

She looked up at the stern warning in Jonathan's voice. "I won't tell them."

Avery would murder her, and if her father found out she had gone away with Jonathan Brond, regardless what happened, he would try to use her to spy. Her father hadn't been home when Jonathan had picked her up. He'd said he had a meeting with an important legislative assistant. Had Jonathan arranged her father's absence?

"Um . . . ." She didn't know how to ask what she needed to know.

"I can't tell you details right now, but it will be a private, *exclusive* arrangement between us. I just need to know if you are interested."

"Yes, I am, but . . . Congressman Brond, what aren't you telling me?" *Is this real? What do you want with me? What did you do with Mrs. DeCord? Am I hearing you right? Sex, with me? Will it mean anything to you? Why me?*

His green eyes examined her face with rueful appreciation. "Smart, as well as beautiful. You have questions, fair enough. But, I need to *show* you. I promise you're safe with me. I'll never force you to do anything."

"Is it okay if I get back to you? About this weekend, I mean. I have to check with work." Her cheeks burned hot with embarrassment. How lame was that? She doubted Congressman Brond had ever waited for a woman's answer based on her work schedule. And who was she kidding, really? She'd trade every big-tip shift this summer if it meant she could get next weekend off.

"Of course. But, now, I need to get you home. I promised not to keep you out too late." He rose, and Christiana followed suit. His hand pressed against her back, steering her forward.

Eyes fell on them as they walked by the main dining room. So much for keeping tonight hush-hush.

On the drive home, neither of them said much, though he held her hand over his parking brake the entire way. Every time his thumb rubbed her hand, a little spark blotted out everything but imagining that hand between her legs. By the time they reached the final exit ramp, she worried she'd left a damp spot on his leather seat. Who cares that his proposal was vague? Whatever she'd agreed to over dinner, the arousal he called up by a single touch demanded she find out.

The sight of the familiar arts and crafts houses in her neighborhood brought her back to reality in a crushing flood. Jonathan turned into her driveway. No lights were on inside the house, not even a flicker of a television set behind the closed curtains. Her father hadn't come home yet. *Thank God!*

Christiana inhaled deeply before getting out of Jonathan's car. She hoped his musky, elegant scent would stay with her at least until she got inside.

Jonathan scanned the empty neighborhood street before stepping from the car.

At the door, she paused, uncertain, but lifted her chin anticipating—no, praying—he'd press his lips against hers, demand her mouth open to him.

He took both her hands and brushed his lips over each knuckle. "Christiana, thank you for this evening. I look forward to more." The last remnants of her brainpower vanished.

Back inside, she stood at the front window watching him drive off. Her mind spun from the alcohol, his voice, their conversation, and his proposition. The man whose voice, tinged with sand and smoke, stroked between her legs every time he said her name, wanted her for *a private, exclusive arrangement between us*. Six words that promised an answer to a prayer—one she'd never voiced, but somehow he'd heard. To be *someone's*, even if just for a summer.

9

A sliver of early morning light cut through an opening in the hotel curtains. Jonathan should have been more tired. He'd pounded into Yvette on and off all night. The temporary ownership of Yvette's body should have propelled him to something more. Yet the nirvana he usually gained from being buried deep inside a woman still eluded him.

Yvette writhed underneath him, grinding herself into his pelvis.

"Be still, Yvette."

"I want to move."

"Don't."

Twin tears trickled from her coffee-colored eyes. "Please."

The cruelty in having her hold back her orgasm for an hour was not lost on him. "Shhh. Hold on to the bed."

She grasped the brass rails, and he tied her wrists to the frame in half hitch knots. She squirmed, shifting her hips.

He smacked the side of her thigh, hard. "Yvette. Should I tie your legs?"

"No, I . . . ."

"Say it."

"I should not move."

"Good. What else?"

"I must not come until you say . . . sir."

He placed himself at her wet opening and thrust his cock in to the hilt.

Her eyes flew open at the sudden invasion, but her lips curled into a smile. As always, her need to yield was as strong as his need to claim. He raked his hands up the back of her tanned legs and pushed her slim ankles over his shoulders. Her insides pulsed farther open, and his balls slapped her cheeks as he lunged into her hot passage.

"Again," he said.

"Whenever. You say. Sir." Her words hitched in time with his stabs.

"Good girl."

"Yes. Yes, please . . . ."

"Yes, what?"

"Yes, sir, more."

He urged his own fire to build while she panted beneath him. He tried to feed off her appetite for him to open her, push her, and spear her deeper. A sheen of sweat broke out on his forehead.

Not working.

"You're released," he grated out between his teeth.

Yvette arched her back and cried out. Her lips twitched as relief swept over her face. Her body racked with convulsions. He rode the little waves inside her slippery cunt as his own release matched her orgasm.

When she stopped trembling, Jonathan let her legs fall to either side. Yvette exhaled deeply and he nestled his face in her neck. He inhaled her perfume, once sweet but now cloying. Something twisted in his gut.

Achievement, satisfaction, relief—all should have filled his body. But none did. He floated inside a void.

Damn, his concentration was off.

On Sundays, his phone didn't ring off the hook. He had planned to spend all day between Yvette's silky thighs, hoping to slake the surprising level of lust Christiana had provoked in him during last night's dinner conversation.

Jesus, last night was a night of heroic self-control. The way Christiana pulled her fork through her lips, waited for him to refill her glass, her soft small hand quivering in his grasp, all signals he knew too well in a budding submissive.

Jonathan unbound Yvette's arms. She tried to pull him back down, but he wrested free from her clasp.

"I've got to head out, Yvette."

"But you wanted—"

"What can I say? You wore me out." He wanted to be anywhere but there.

"Not yet, please."

"Don't you have a ladies' lunch to attend?" Damn, he should have gone to Charlottesville for a day or two, to regain his civility. His well of diplomacy had run dry.

She encircled his torso with her legs. Wetness smudged the small of his back. He rose, rubbing his forehead to ease the tension that spread across his skull, and turned to place a kiss on her forehead before heading to the bathroom.

Jonathan stepped into the shower's spray of hot water and leaned against the tiled wall to let the stream pound his back. He was grateful Yvette didn't follow. He wanted no questions, no small talk, and no interruptions. He needed time to gather his thoughts. Unhappiness wasn't his style, yet something inside twitched. Of late, his mind careened down paths he didn't normally tread, and questions arose where decisions once lived.

His shoulders relaxed under the hot water bathing his muscles in the heat but his cock lay heavy in his hand, slick with soap and hard. The shocking lack of discipline irritated him, his lust rising, no doubt, from his recent imaginings of a certain young woman.

Control, Brond.

Jonathan mentally called up his master plan, the exercise of running through his future steps akin to meditation. He continued to wrestle with one key decision. After another two years in the House, would it be better to go for a Senate seat or a gubernatorial position? Either job, held for a few years, would allow him to leave public life for good. He'd then find something in the private sector more suited to his interests and gifts, exit the spotlight and gain freedom for the personal life he craved.

First he had to get the Brond reputation back on track. He couldn't let his family's legacy end on his father's note—a messy divorce coupled with a shocking lack of interest in his constituents' wishes. His father had let his own needs overtake his office. Jonathan would not do the same.

Jesus, he could end up the same. Jonathan could easily bring yet another scandal down on the family if he wasn't careful.

A thousand images flashed before his eyes: television cameras capturing him and a certain blond through half-open curtains of his home; the House majority leader calling him into his office for the "sex lecture" delivered too often to his colleagues lately.

What the hell had he been thinking, asking Christiana to go away with him, dallying with someone so young? If Peter Snow got wind of his intentions in regards to the man's daughter, Jonathan's reputation would be irretrievably lost. He'd arranged for Peter to be at another event when he picked her up last evening, to guarantee they wouldn't cross paths. How could he cover up an entire weekend?

He should cancel.

He knew he wouldn't.

Christiana's honesty and utter lack of agenda enticed him like no other womanly delight set before him. She had no idea who he was or where he came from. No questions about his father arose, no support of some cause was requested, and none of his family's connections were entreated. Every time he ran into her, her innocent eyes bathed him in undeserving, albeit welcomed, admiration, her face flushing a rainbow of pinks and corals. God, what she'd be like, once unbridled.

He had to be careful with this woman. She could lead him speeding down a path he wasn't ready to tread. She'd make him forget why he'd sold his life to the people of the United States.

Was that so bad? Jonathan held his face up to the cascading water and steeled himself for a rare indulgence. He would permit—just this once—the romantic notion of following his heart instead of his plan. No one had to know. He'd ensure extreme caution this week, make everyone believe he was enthralled with work and not the image of soft white legs clutching his torso.

His shoulders softened while his cock grew stiffer. He inhaled the thick, misty air and let an image of small hands running up his shoulders and milky white skin pressing against his legs step into the steam with him. Pink lips touching his chest. Soft sighs released into his mouth when he entered her lower lips. Sweet. Pure. *Christiana*.

Christiana threw two dirty plates into the plastic bin, and barbeque sauce splattered onto her white button down shirt. "Shit."

"Wow. Chris can swear." Henrick handed her a towel. "Working so many double shifts will do that to you."

She shrugged. "I'd rather earn money than sit around an empty house. Dad's still on the road. Election year and all that." *Plus I'll get my weekends free.* She wouldn't mention that last part in case he got the idea to ask her out.

Brian clapped loudly and yelled for everyone to move faster—as if they could.

The Oak Room burst at the seams with a larger than normal Wednesday lunch crowd, lured out of their fluorescent lit offices by the good weather. Even the dining room lighting, usually kept low and dark for gravitas, was augmented by the sunshine that poured in from the tall windows by the revolving door.

Christiana wished her mood matched the sunbeams streaming inside.

Sunday. Monday. Tuesday. Now, Wednesday, and Jonathan still hadn't called. She had almost requested room service detail to see if he revisited the suite for a rendezvous with Mrs. DeCord. She wisely rethought the idea. What if he was there? *Hey, you, hot Congressman, why haven't you called me?*

He must have changed his mind. A memory of his hands holding hers, the promise of sliding his fingers between her thighs, asking her to part them, *for him . . . for the summer.* The fantasy disappeared as quickly as it bloomed. The tingling from his fingers as he played with her wrist became only the flow of barbecue sauce trickling into the bus tub.

When the stain on her shirt reached an acceptably diluted level of orange, Christiana headed back to the floor to do what she knew she was good at—serving others.

The hurried lunch crowd morphed into the demanding dinner crowd, which segued into the happier bar crowd. By eight o'clock, The Oak Room's long mahogany bar teemed with laughter and backslapping,

Christiana straightened silverware at an empty table for the next party. Loud giggling at the front entrance drew her focus. Avery swung through the revolving door, trailed by Jessica, a girl from high school whom Avery swore she hated, but then Avery had declared she wouldn't be caught dead at The Oak Room.

Avery tossed her long hair and settled onto a bar stool. The bartender, Josh, examined her driver's license. Maybe Christiana should speak to him about the fake ID he'd been handed if she were willing to risk the wrath of Avery Churchill.

Christiana steeled herself to walk past their laughter. Avery threw Christiana a practiced smile. "There she is, waitress extraordinaire. Really, Josh. You guys should give this girl a raise. All she does is work."

Josh poured red wine into a glass before Avery, who sipped her illegal beverage. "Have a drink with us, girlfriend. We're celebrating our new freedom."

"I have to go back to work. Have fun." Once through the doors, the whooshing of hot water from the hoses at the washing station drowned out the girl's cackling. Could her day get any worse?

Every few minutes, Christiana had to walk by them. With each pass, Avery's laughter grew louder. By the third glass of wine, she began grazing Josh's arm with her manicured fingers. He smiled. If he only knew the hundreds of men Avery had touched in the same way, payment for a free drink or advancing a place in a long-waiting, slow-moving line.

On her break, Christiana stood out by the hostess stand to clear her aching head and watched customers shake out umbrellas as they stepped inside. The day's sunshine had been swallowed by a summer shower and the fat, slow-moving raindrops of summer pelted the tall windows framing the door. So what if the famous, elegant, hot-as-hell congressman had forgotten her? She had the summer ahead to shift her world. Regardless of his empty offer, she'd move forward.

Avery's voice hit her from behind. "Come with me, Snow. We gotta talk."

"I can't, Avery." She tried to scoot around her friend, but Avery gripped her arm and led her toward the stairs.

"You can take a minute," she slurred.

When they stepped inside the ladies' room, Avery drew Christiana close, her breath reeking of red wine. "Working a lot lately? Or you just trying to avoid me?" Avery's glazed, unhappy stare cut into Christiana's heart.

"No, Avery, I'm not—"

"Cause you know friends aren't easy to come by." The corner of her mouth turned downward, and she swayed a little.

"Neither is tuition." Christiana regretted her tone immediately. Avery didn't deserve hearing about the tension of her day even if Christiana didn't deserve Avery's drunken, self-absorbed drama, either.

Avery turned to the sink and laid her hands on the marble counter. "So, who've you been hanging out with then? I know you're not always here."

Shit. Avery's mistrust was firing on all cylinders. Did she know about Christiana's sudden social life? If so, she'd be pleased to hear it had ended before it ever began.

"You mean besides the customers at The Oak?" Christiana's laugh sounded fake. *Like the friend I've become.*

"Well, you'll never change your life by working all the time, Chris. Speaking of getting a life, I heard your dad met Congressman Brond at a reception last week."

For a brief second, Christiana felt the floor give way under her. Had someone mentioned her attendance at the event also? Death at nineteen at the hands of a socialite. What a plot for CSI. She should just confess. Her secret-keeping ability ranked alongside an ability to perform brain surgery.

Avery re-applied her lipstick. "So, I need your help. I need one more run-in with Jonathan—"

"Jonathan?" A colony of fire ants crawled under her skin at the sound of Avery slurring his name.

"Yes, *Jonathan*. When your dad interviews him, you tell me when. And *where*."

"That's not a good idea."

"How would you know? Jonathan would love to see me. Our families have been friends for years. I'm shocked we haven't run into each other more. And don't do that." Avery pulled Christiana's hand away from her scar. "You won't catch any man by drawing their attention to that."

"I can't ask my Dad—"

"Yes, you *can*." Avery gripped her arm. "Unless you aren't my friend anymore."

"I am your friend, Avery. But—"

"But, what?"

So what if Jonathan hadn't called. She wouldn't let Avery use her to get closer to him.

"Promise me you'll do it. For me," Avery said.

"No." Avery's shocked face told Christiana she'd said the word out loud. She'd meant to delay Avery's demands, not ratchet up the anger simmering under her friend's skin.

Avery's eyes blazed. "So, that's the kind of friend you are?"

Christiana crossed her arms and met her gape.

Avery matched Christiana's stance. "Wait, don't tell me. Timid little rabbit afraid to ask her drunken father for some help?"

Irritation warred with embarrassment. Shame won. Unable to marshal a counter defense, she turned on her heel and left Avery swaying by the sink. Aching feet always did prevent Christiana from conjuring up more patience.

Christiana entered the kitchen, smoothing down the front of her apron. Before the door swung shut behind her, she glimpsed Avery stumbling out the front door of the restaurant into the street, Jessica jogging behind. *Back to planning her perfect future as Mrs. Congressman Brond no doubt.*

But how was she any different? She'd spent days spinning fantasies on the strength of one dinner date with a man so far out of her reach, she was no more grounded in reality than Avery.

Still, her heartbeat quickened as Jonathan's face, certain and beautiful, rose up in her mind. Christiana would go to the grave keeping her dinner with Jonathan secret, a treasured moment in time tucked away, something just for her, something Avery could never touch.

Christiana didn't bother to turn on the lights when she entered the Cabinet Room. She let the dim, soft light from the opaque glass in the French doors submerge her in cool dark. Somehow the room made her feel both adventurous and safe.

She often escaped here during her breaks. Her fellow workers called The Oak's private dining room "the tomb," given its windowless walls and soundproofing to screen the most secret meetings. Several of the wait staff held low-level security clearances to allow them to wait on these gatherings; Christiana wasn't one of them. She felt if the Cabinet Room walls could talk, they'd erupt with CIA secrets and congressional deals and compromises that no one in Washington would admit to.

She perched on the large mahogany dining table and dangled her legs over the edge. She needed a moment to regroup. She wasn't quite ready to shelve the awkward conversation with Avery if you could even call it a conversation. *More like yet another opportunity to be Avery's wingwoman.*

Her cell phone vibration broke the silence. *Avery always wants the last word.* Well, Christiana was sick of her diva behavior. She answered with a snarled "What."

A soft chuckle warmed her belly. "Hello, Christiana."

She drifted off on a wave of happiness. "I thought you were someone else, sorry. I'm still at work."

"I see the election year has us all running. So, regarding this weekend—"

"Yes, I'm ready." Her back straightened.

More laughter washed over her. "You should know I spoke with your father today. He called with follow-up questions. He then promptly offered you up as an intern. Said you were smart."

Her next thought shocked her. She didn't want to be smart. She wanted to be something wholly unsmart—to be Jonathan's lover, even if only for one summer. "What did you say?"

"I agreed with the second point. You are smart. But I don't need an intern. I have an entirely different position in mind for you." Jonathan voice dropped low. "I did not mention this weekend to your father. I need to remind you it's imperative that no one else knows."

"I understand. I won't tell anyone."

"*No* one," he said.

Christiana's stomach fluttered. His dedication to keeping their acquaintance secret promised something she couldn't name. The mystery bathed her in an exotic, grown-up feeling, like she had been admitted to a mysterious clandestine club.

His voice lowered to a whisper. "Where are you?"

"I'm in the Cabinet Room, taking a break."

"Are you alone?"

"Yes."

"Good. I don't like the thought of all those Washington business men looking up your waitressing skirt."

"Oh, yeah, I'm so sexy in my apron."

"Yes, you are. They're all wondering what's under it."

"Cotton." Jesus, did she just say that?

"You should be in silk. What color?"

"Um, blue."

"Hmm, if I was there, I'd make you prove that."

Any doubt about Jonathan's proposal not involving sex dissolved.

"Until Friday. Four o'clock in front of The Oak. Good night, Christiana." The line went dead.

Christiana closed her eyes. The remnants of remembered scents—leather, wool, man—flooded back as recollections of warm arms holding her on a dance floor sent a thrilling ripple up her spine.

She eased her butt off the table. Fingers shaking, she reached under her skirt and pulled her panties down. They slipped easily down to her ankles, cooler air hitting her damp crotch. She pictured Jonathan watching her do it, smiling and beckoning her forward.

She scrunched the slip of cotton in her hand and stuffed the panties into her apron pocket. *A gift for Jonathan. Friday.*

10

Christiana pushed through The Oak Room's revolving doors into the oppressive summer air. Mark stepped from Jonathan's black SUV, idling in the valet parking area.

"Miss Snow, please take a seat in the front," he said, as he picked up her duffle bag.

When Christiana slipped into the front seat, a swarm of butterflies flew up her middle. Jonathan, in the driver's seat, gave her a broad smile, crinkles forming around his eyes, now more blue-green against his light grey suit and cobalt shirt. *His looks should be illegal.*

"Ready to leave Washington behind?" he asked. "If we hurry, we'll beat the traffic."

Mark slammed down the back hatch door and knocked on the roof.

"Do you go away every weekend?" she asked as Jonathan made a U-turn across Fifteenth Street.

"Not as often as I'd like. It all depends on the company." Jonathan winked.

Down, butterflies, down.

They turned onto Constitution Avenue, and Christiana

glanced at the long line of tourists snaking around the Washington Monument. The Oak would be packed over the weekend. She sent a silent thank you to the heavens she wouldn't be there.

Jonathan stayed silent as he wove through Friday afternoon traffic over the river to ease into the steady stream of cars out of the city.

"Have you had your house in Charlottesville long?" she asked.

"Built it three years ago. It's a haven away from the madness. Important for intimate conversations, like what we'll have."

"You said you wanted to show me something."

"Not while I'm driving." Jonathan rubbed his thumb, feather-light, along her wrist.

"Will you show me when we get there?"

"Yes."

"Can you tell me *anything* now?"

"No."

"Not even a little?"

"So inquisitive, Christiana." He smiled over at her. "You sure you aren't going to be a reporter after all?"

"I've been . . . curious. About you. About what you wanted to show me."

"That's good, Christiana. That's very good." The intimacy of his deep voice stroked her impatience. He slid his hand up to the back of her neck while lazily draping the other over the steering wheel.

"Um, when you called the other night, you were wondering something, too."

He appeared thoughtful, and then his mouth stretched into a grin. "Yes, I was."

His eyes darted to her legs, barely covered by the hem of her sundress.

"I have something for you." She wished she'd left her work uniform on, just to accentuate the effect of pulling from her purse the blue panties that Jonathan's seductive voice lured her to shed the other night. He stopped his light massage on her neck and presented his open palm. His eyes never left the road as she laid the panties in his hand.

"Good thing I didn't know about this." Jonathan stuffed them into his inside suit pocket. "My concentration during meetings would've been shattered."

Christiana clasped her legs closer together. A deluge of new yearning soaked her current panties with the realization he'd thought about her nude.

He reached over to knead the base of her head. "Any more headaches?"

"Nothing serious." *Okay, maybe.* Even in her state of constant, simmering arousal, she'd fought an impending migraine all week—first from worry Jonathan wouldn't call and then worry someone would discover he had.

As soon as she'd emerged from the Cabinet Room, panty-less, aroused and smug, her cell phone had chirped, blinking Avery's name. Christiana had let her stew. Ten calls later, Avery had left a voice mail message in which she declared wine wasn't her drink because it made her say things she didn't mean. Christiana knew that explanation was the best apology she'd ever get out of Avery Churchill.

Jonathan's brows knit together. "You'll tell me if a headache starts. I can help."

"They're never bad enough to need medication."

"That's not what I had in mind. There are other ways to relieve pain. And help is my specialty." He grinned.

Christiana's neck and shoulders relaxed under his deft fingers while all her nerve endings crackled. The thought of him moving his hand lower and cupping her breast made her grow wetter. Jonathan pulled his hand away to press the Bluetooth button on his steering wheel.

"Yes, Shane. I'm not alone." Jonathan gave Christiana a side look and whispered, "I'll make this quick."

Christiana nodded and shifted to look out the window. As Jonathan launched into a barrage of dictation, the lightning between her legs lessened. But only a little.

The urban landscape thinned. Soon farmland stretched out on either side, and warm sunshine streamed into the car. Christiana grew drowsy.

Jonathan's voice broke into her stupor. "Hey, sleepyhead." They had pulled up to a gate made of pale smooth wood. It cracked open when Jonathan punched in a code on the greeting console. A brass sign on the left-hand post read *Covil Sereia*.

A modern Asian Minka home nestled among red oak, and chestnut giants came into view as they drove up the curving drive beyond. Its rustic, dark cedar exterior blended into the forest landscape as though it had risen from the earth itself.

Jonathan released his seat belt as he opened his door. He seemed springier, almost buoyant with happiness at having arrived. A smile tugged his lips as he helped her out of the car. He carried her bag in one hand and pressed the other against her back.

Christiana took in a lungful of the woodsy, clean air. A light breeze swayed the tree branches, and birds sang from somewhere deep in the coppice.

She followed Jonathan into a small dim foyer. A red Buddha smiled from atop a small, round-topped teak table. Christiana wanted to linger and study the hallway paintings of koi, glittering with red and gold scales and swimming among lotus blooms. But Jonathan towed her forward into a massive room.

Cathedral ceilings rose high above them, and two long hallways trailed off in opposite directions. The hall's polished wood floors mirrored vague images of the artwork hanging on the walls. A painted mermaid held court at the end of the hall. Christiana shuddered, noticing the siren's distorted reflection swam toward them along the gleaming oak hallway.

In the main room, a white couch and several modern leather chairs were placed in front of a large fireplace that dominated one wall. Floor-to-ceiling glass sliding doors opened to a light wood deck.

"It's like an *Architectural Digest* spread," she said.

"I'm glad you approve." Jonathan smiled.

The fragrance of something spicy drew Christiana's focus to the kitchen area to the left. "What is that wonderful smell?"

"Blanca, my housekeeper, always leaves something delicious cooking for me when I arrive. We'll eat soon."

Jonathan took her hand and led her down the two steps into the center room and out onto the deck, seemingly suspended in mid-air by steel cabling. The house clung to the mountainside, thick with trees cascading down the slope. A cardinal flitted from branch to branch as the limbs parted in the wind and revealed glimpses of a valley below.

Christiana held her face up into the breeze. "The air's so fresh. Nothing like Washington." She took another lungful of pristine air.

"I'm getting out of this suit. Come." He took her hand and led her down the hall to an open door at the far end. "The guest bedroom. Feel free to freshen up in here. I'll meet you in the living room."

He set Christiana's duffel bag atop an expensive-looking green duvet on the queen-sized bed and left her alone.

Christiana smoothed the front of her sundress, glad it

held up, so she didn't need to change it. Her panties were another matter. She also was desperate to brush her teeth.

The guest bath was small yet anything but ordinary. The walls glimmered with gold metallic paint, and the floor was the same light polished wood as the hallways. A black granite countertop held a blue glass bowl for a sink. Christiana found a blow dryer and moisturizer in a drawer that clicked back into place with a gentle push.

"Fancy," Christiana said to her reflection in the mirror, noting the dark circles under her eyes. She brushed her teeth and splashed cool water on her face. Even after the nap in the car, her legs still wobbled from working all day. After applying more concealer, she slipped off her sandals. Her feet needed a break. She also changed her panties.

Christiana found Jonathan on the deck talking on his cell phone. He paced, also barefoot, in a white linen shirt and faded jeans. His broad back flexed when he rolled his shoulders back and stretched. He laughed. He looked happy. *And hot as Hades.*

Jonathan put his arm around Christiana when she stepped outside. She smiled up at him, her eyes laced with curiosity. Her questions in the car were a nice surprise. When she'd handed him her panties, he'd nearly risked a charge of indecent exposure and public sex. Christ, she was eager.

She looked tired, presumably from that ridiculous work schedule he had yet to correct. He vowed to take her to the Hilton tonight no matter how many times she bit her rosy bottom lip. It had taken Jonathan all week to regain his sense of control when it came to Christiana Snow. He would not lose it now. He could wait at least until tomorrow, let her get settled. A delicious anticipation would build for them both, make his plans that more sweet.

"You must be starving."

"Food sounds good," she said.

Jonathan led her to a small table she hadn't noticed on the deck before, set for an alfresco dinner with a small pillar candle flickering in the twilight.

"Blanca is a wonderful cook." He pulled out Christiana's chair. "And she's made her signature stew."

"Is she here?"

"No, I wanted us to have some time alone." Jonathan retrieved a bottle of sparkling water, dripping with condensation, from a silver ice bucket and sat down.

"No champagne?"

"Not tonight. We both need a clear head. I love eating out here. But let me know if the mosquitoes start biting." Jonathan poured the cool fizzy water into large goblets.

"They do tend to go after me." She tossed her hair over one shoulder and bared skin. His jeans pulled against his cock, now swelling to life.

"To an evening with no bloodshed." He raised his glass in a toast. "Try the stew. Feijoada. Blanca's specialty."

Christiana slipped a small spoonful between her lips. God, he loved watching her mouth. His cock would slide through those lips so deliciously. He shuttered the thought away. They would never get through dinner if he didn't.

"What does *Covil Sereia* mean?" she asked.

"Mermaid Lair. It's Portuguese. My mother's family was from Brazil." The words tasted strange in his mouth. He hadn't spoken of his mother to anyone outside the family in years.

They ate a few bites in silence, as wind rustled through the trees, and the drone of cicadas filled the quiet space.

Christiana didn't eat much. When she leaned back, apparently sated, he pushed his own plate away.

Jonathan picked up his glass of bubbly water and caught Christiana's eyes. *Still simmering with questions.* Jonathan prayed she would never lose her inquisitive nature. It would make things so much easier.

He brushed his foot over her bare feet. She pulled back but didn't break his gaze. *Not so fast, lovely.* He captured one of her feet between both of his and held it. Her lips parted in surprise but her eyes stayed locked on his while he rubbed her softness between his larger feet. She quieted. A sliver of understanding clicked into place in his mind. *She needs to be touched. Often.* His imagination kicked into high gear. Given the velvet-smooth skin on her tiny foot, silk and satin must lie between her thighs. If she granted him access, he'd ensure she'd have trouble staying still.

11

Christiana willed herself to keep breathing. It was difficult, given his larger feet held hers captive, the gesture over-whelmingly intimate.

As if reading her mind, he released her foot, rose and disappeared inside. Maybe he was finally going to show her what he meant earlier—*show me what?* Christiana took a few more sips of her sparkling water. Jonathan returned to the table with a manila folder. Her heart wobbled at his solemn expression.

He sat. "You know I'm a member of Congress. And, my family is . . . well-known."

"Yes." She let out a half laugh at his understatement but stopped when his eyes narrowed.

"Forgive the formality, but I'm an attorney at heart, and it's my job to foresee anything that might arise." He handed her the folder.

Inside, Christiana found a single sheet of paper with "Non-Disclosure Agreement" typed at the top.

"My Dad never signs these."

"Nor should he, given his line of work. He has to be free to report things as he sees them."

She scanned the text of the NDA. "So, I can't discuss with *anyone* what happens between us."

"That's correct. Not your father. Not Avery. No one. Even the slightest joke or slip about the subject of our discussions, or what we do, could give the wrong impression."

"I understand." *Sort of.*

"What we do here cannot ever leave here," he added.

His last statement unsettled her nerves, as if he silently underlined the temporary nature of this arrangement. That *this*—whatever it was—was to be a *liaison*, straight out of an old French movie.

Did she even care?

Christiana took a large swallow of water, which went down in a fizzy lump. She stared at the piece of paper now weighing more heavily in her hand.

Of course, it wouldn't be fair to talk about him to anyone. Aren't members of Congress hounded enough? The gossip rags must be relentless about who he's dating to find some indiscretion they could report. Lord knows her father circled a room like an eagle, talons open and ready to grasp any shred of personal data to color a story. Jonathan had obviously worked hard to maintain some privacy. Even Avery couldn't find much on him.

Avery! If she ever found out anything about her being with Jonathan, Christiana could play this NDA card.

Caught, what a funny thought. She'd never so much as snuck an apple from The Oak Room. Now she sat where Avery would *kill* to be, being asked to hold a man's secrets, a man whose voice . . . .

Her mind stopped. Jonathan's warm, powerful hands had enveloped her shoulders, sending prickles of sensation down to her fingertips. She hadn't even seen him get up. He leaned down and placed his soft lips to her neck, trailing kisses down to her shoulder. Every nerve in her body fired as his hands slid down her arms. He whispered in her ear, "Please. I want to protect you. And I need this in order to *show* you."

She dissolved into a puddle of lust. "Do you have a pen?"

Jonathan laid a silver pen next to the paper. "You should read it first."

"I trust you." She scribbled her full name across the bottom and slipped it into the folder.

Jonathan twisted her hair in his hands and then set the coil free, running his fingers through its length. Shivers ran down the base of her skull, down her back and her legs. She made a mental note to always wear her hair down around him.

"Now can you show me?" His touch lulled her into a courage she didn't know she possessed. But then Christiana had grown tired of being in the dark, and if this was her moment to indulge in a little fantasy, she wouldn't punch the universe's gift in the mouth.

"Yes," he said. "I want to show you."

Jonathan ran his hands down her arms and pulled her up. "Let's take our drinks inside. The vampires are out." She raised her eyebrows in question. "The mosquitoes. They can't have you. You're mine." He tucked the folder under one arm and opened the door, gesturing at the couch inside. "Sit."

Christiana curled her feet underneath her butt on the cool, white leather loveseat. Jonathan stood a few feet away in front of the fireplace. Soft recessed lighting shone down on his gold hair and accented the angles in his face.

"I mentioned I have short relationships." Jonathan paced.

Christiana sat up straighter. "When you said you wanted me to be—."

"Mine. If you agree, you'll be involved solely with me. Until you leave for school."

"That won't be a problem."

He smiled. But then his face grew serious. "I need to know you want to spend time with me the way I want to spend it with you."

"You want to sleep with me."

"I would like to do more than sleep. Would you like that?"

"Yes." Being with Jonathan was all she'd thought about since meeting him. She would let this man do anything to her tonight, including things requiring a non-disclosure agreement.

"I'm a sexual Dominant. Do you know what that means?"

"Sort of." She had *no* idea.

"I will dominate you. And you will submit to me."

"Submit." She measured the word in her mouth. "You want to control me?"

"Not exactly. You'll tell me what you like. From there, I'll say when and how those things will happen. I will direct you. Ultimately, I want you to lose all inhibition with me. If you do, it shows you trust me. I require that."

"You want me to be a sexual dynamo?" She hoped her joke would lighten him up a bit.

He smiled. "Well, if you are, that would be a side benefit."

Jesus, she walked right into that one.

"You're a sexual submissive," he said. "You've already proven to me you feel better when I take charge. You've needed someone to take control of your environment for a very long time."

"I don't know about that."

"You handed your panties to me without my having to ask. You wanted to please me."

"So?" Indignation rose in her chest as her eyes held his smirk. True, she'd never had anyone take such command—or care—of her. It felt good. But, panties or not, she wasn't a doormat. "I've been taking care of myself for quite some time, Congressman."

"I know." He sat down next to her and stroked the back of her neck. Her irritation stalled, though his eyes projected an empathy that put her nerve endings on high alert.

"There's nothing wrong with being submissive, Christiana. In fact, it's a sign of great strength. When you give up total control to me, it's a gift, one that I don't take lightly. It shows you trust me to take care of you. You haven't had enough of that, and I'm correcting your situation now.

"It's difficult to explain in words. The exchange of power between two people in this sexual dynamic is special, sacred. When you put yourself in my hands, it's a great honor."

The apex of her thighs twinged at his words. She wanted his hands, everywhere. She wanted Jonathan, period. But him? Jonathan wanting her made no sense.

"You're a powerful man. A member of Congress," she said. "I'd think women would line up."

"It's not a matter of showing up, Christiana. You must give me your whole heart and mind for it to work. You've never been asked to trust anyone the way I'm asking you to."

"What do you want me to do?"

"First, You must promise you'll always be honest with me."

"Of course."

"If you're ever dishonest, I'll administer a punishment."

"Like what?"

"That's for me to decide."

She gasped.

"I won't hurt you, Christiana. Not ever." As he brushed his knuckles over her cheek, her nerves settled. "But, I do mean it when I say discipline is part of this dynamic."

"I-I promise to be honest."

"Eventually I'll learn your cues. But in the beginning, you must be open to extensive communication."

"Define extensive."

"You know what it means, though you're not used to it." His lips twitched into a smile. "You're the strong silent type. I can tell."

Her face broke into a return smile. "Okay, I can talk more."

"Next, tell me what you like. What you don't. Everything we do must be consensual."

"With sex . . . I'm afraid to tell you."

"You can tell me anything. I'm sure you had your share of grabby boys joking about their supposed experience and then not delivering."

If he only knew.

"Yes. It was all so . . . ."

"Dispassionate." He'd completed her thought, precisely.

"Christiana, there's nothing you'd like to do or try that I probably haven't—"

"You may not want me."

"Nothing could have me not want you, Christiana."

"Are you sure?"

He chortled. "I'm sure."

"I'm going to disappoint you."

He lifted her chin with his hand. "You could only disappoint me if you say no."

"I-I haven't done this. Not very much. Um, I mean, my experience is a little . . . ."

"Christiana. Considering your age I don't expect you to be Mata Hari."

She almost laughed, but the embarrassment of her one encounter washed her in shame. "It was only once, and it was—"

"Disappointing?"

She looked into his concerned face. He deserved the truth. "Boring."

He sat back at her word, even though it fit her encounter perfectly. Losing her virginity was honestly one of the most uninteresting events of her life and that was saying something. Before that night, she thought society events were the most dull events of the century. She'd been wrong.

An intense burn spread across her chest, as if she'd taken an overdose of niacin. Being so inexperienced was embarrassing enough. The last thing she wanted to do was tell Jonathan Brond how she let Jeffrey Daniels from her English composition class take her virginity in her dorm room after they'd run into one another at a party. She hadn't cared for him. Given how he looked right through her in class the next day, he hadn't either. To this day, she couldn't understand what she was thinking that night she spread her legs for him.

She kneaded her palm with her thumb. "You're not going to ask me about it, are you?"

"It sounds like there wouldn't be much to say. I'll try my best not to be . . . boring." He grinned widely, and the burn across her chest darted between her legs.

She could barely think about the right words, let alone speak them. She had wanted something larger, more *life altering.* Instead, the next morning she stuffed pink-stained sheets into the washing machine in her dorm room laundry room and listened to the same whooshing of water and clanking motor the same way as she had so many times before.

Jonathan Brond couldn't be anything like Jeffrey Daniels. He promised an experience wholly incomparable.

Thanks be to Christ, Allah and all the Greek Gods. Jonathan hadn't dared to believe it was possible. No woman who looked like Christiana could have made it through the hallways of high school, let alone a full year at college, without falling into the backseat or dorm room bunk of some football player. So, she'd given some idiot the pass of a lifetime, and he'd fumbled. He didn't feel bad for the prick—only remorse she'd somehow shouldered the blame for the outcome. For some reason, he wanted to cuff her father—probably the first male influence to show her anything that happened to her might be her fault.

Jonathan took a deep breath and reassessed the situation. Short of the usual young girl's romance novel fantasies, her naivety guaranteed she had few preconceived notions of what sex should be like. *Uncorrupted. Simmering with potential. Mine to shape.*

Christiana had lowered her eyes to her lap, and her bottom lip trembled. *Oh, my sweet girl. So shy. When she opens up . . . .* He tucked his hand under her chin and lifted her blue eyes back up to his.

"You have nothing to be ashamed of, Christiana. Your innocence pleases me." Pleased didn't touch what he felt. Her confession thrilled him. His cock throbbed in anticipation of being the first to fuck her into total abandon.

Her eyes filled with wonder. Her expression sent the remaining blood supply from his brain to his cock, already impossibly tight under the rough denim. Christ, he was going to need her soon.

But he'd have to go slower than anticipated. For her. The thought he'd do almost anything for this girl shocked him. All his former liaisons hung like paintings in his mind—beautiful, each unique, treasured, but all so flat and two-dimensional, especially compared to what lay before him now.

"Do you have any idea how rare you are?" He brushed her hair back over her shoulder, and she quivered as his fingers trailed down her back. "This means you'll really be mine. Do you want *me*?" he asked. He knew the answer, but she had to speak the truth vibrating from her body.

She nodded slightly.

"You have to say it," he said.

"Yes, I want you." She barely whispered, but it was enough.

"Then close your eyes."

Jonathan inhaled vanilla from her skin and spices from the stew they'd eaten for dinner still on her breath. He took her face in both hands and joined his mouth to hers. She leaned into him. He relished the smoothness of her lips, a constant thought ever since he pulled her into the empty conference room and leapt into this thrilling, dangerous obsession.

Jonathan tried to be gentle, but he couldn't. He circled her back and crushed her against him. She yielded completely.

He speared her mouth with his tongue. Forced her to straddle his lap. When his erection pressed into her mound, she gasped into his mouth. The graze of tiny nipples into his chest through his thin shirt made his balls ache.

Jesus, he couldn't wait until she took his cock between her lips.

Jonathan wound his hands in her hair and pulled her head back, releasing her mouth. Her dress had hiked to her hips, revealing pale skin against his lap. He ran a hand up her bare thigh and traced the crease in her hip with his thumb. She quivered but didn't break her gaze. Her wide blue eyes showed surprise yet glowed with uninhibited, pure want.

"Christiana, you have to be sure—."

"I'm sure."

If she had pulled back even an inch, he would have

packed her up to the Hilton. Her face flushed a deep crimson, but her lips and eyes revealed her decision. Now Jonathan wasn't about to let her go anywhere tonight except his bed. *Fuck the hotel.*

12

Christiana licked Jonathan's kiss from her bottom lip. Sweet Jesus, his kissing was an art form. His hand crushed hers as he led her down the hall and through a set of double doors. Mahogany furniture surrounded a king-sized bed, ivory and taupe pillows scattered at the top. The room was drenched in masculine elegance.

"Get on the bed." He turned his back and opened the top drawer of a tall chest.

She climbed onto the silk duvet, mesmerized by the shifting of his back muscles. What would it be like to rub her breasts along his back? Hundreds of women have probably gotten the chance. A jolt of insecurity stabbed her courage. She hadn't the first idea how to satisfy this man.

He lifted a slip of black fabric. "I'm going to blindfold you."

The little butterflies in her stomach were zapped dead by little lightning bolts. "Do you have to?"

He pulled her legs forward, so she sat on the edge facing him. God, how he moved her body around with such ease.

"Yes. If you can't see me, your reactions will be more

honest. Then I'll be able to distinguish between what you truly want and what you're willing to do simply because I ask."

"Isn't that the same thing?"

"Not at all." He cupped her chin. "You want to please me. That's very good. But I won't be able to please you if I don't know what honestly works for you."

Jonathan fastened the blindfold around her head. He cupped her cheeks and tipped her head to his voice.

"Trust me, lovely. Your body will not lie. Concentrate on feeling the sensations that arise." He rubbed a thumb over her lips. The darkness made his hands larger, rougher, and her imagination ran wild envisioning what he would do to her with them.

"But—"

"Christiana. Trust." His voice, sharp and smooth, impaled the last surviving butterfly.

"Is this what you wanted to show me?"

"Part of it."

In the absence of sight, her own shallow breathing rushed louder in her head. Woods, honeysuckle, and his male scent rose under her nose.

The bed dipped. Jonathan was behind her. His legs hugged hers, his broad chest connecting with her back. She gasped when his cock connected to the small of her back. He slid the straps of her dress down to her elbows and kissed her lightly on the shoulder. Then he gathered her hair with both hands and ran his fingers through the long strands. Her head fell back onto his shoulder.

"Feel good?" he asked.

"Mmm-hmm." She couldn't stop feeling his hardness against her tailbone.

He peeled her dress over her breasts and snapped off her

strapless bra. Before she could think, he palmed her flesh and rubbed his thumbs over her stiff nipples.

"So soft, Christiana," he murmured into her neck. "And so hard. Do you like this?"

Words tumbled from her grasp, even the most basic vocabulary blocked by his pinching and twisting the tips of her breasts. Dragon wings had replaced the butterflies.

"Tell me everything you like." His voice was edged in a rough lust.

"Oh, okay."

His hands and legs left her side, and the bed shifted upward, relieved of his weight. *Where did he go?* Sound of a zipper, of jeans dropping to the floor. Then more fabric rustled near the foot of the bed. He was right to blindfold her. The sight of a naked Jonathan would overwhelm her senses. At the same time, she was desperate to *see* the chest she'd felt.

Jonathan climbed onto the bed behind her. He put his arms under hers and laid her back.

Christiana's sundress pooled at her ankles, but she didn't dare move. He positioned himself alongside her, the hair on his legs brushing her skin. He lifted her arms up over her head and placed her hands on the low headboard.

"Hold on to the bed." Obediently, she gripped a smooth wood rail.

"I will tell you everything I'm going to do. You can stop me at any time. Do you understand?"

"Yes."

"Good girl."

Jonathan's whole body drew closer, his cock—steel and velvet—lay heavy against her hip. He kissed her neck and then trailed his lips lower. He latched onto her bare nipple, and her back arched into his mouth. *Oh, God.* His chest hair, not rough but not soft, brushed her skin, and his thick erection pressed into her thigh. He suckled and pulled at her nipple peak until a raw unbearable ache settled below the surface.

"You pink up so easily," he said into her skin. He fixed himself onto her other nipple. Her ass wiggled on the silky fabric, and a hand forced down her hip.

"Be still, lovely. Now talk to me," he said. "Tell me if you like this." His wet mouth took small bites.

"I . . . like it." She surprised herself with her ability to speak.

Fingers crept under the elastic of her panties and rested on her down.

"What else do you like, Christiana?"

"I don't know." Her whole body flushed, and he laughed.

"Oh, I think you do." His rough chin brushed across her belly, and he laid a kiss on her navel. He dipped his fingers lower and rimmed her clothed folds.

Christiana inhaled sharply and gripped the bed frame harder, afraid if she let go she might try to push him away or seize the back of his head and pull him closer. *Just feel, like he said.* She tried not to moan as his finger traced her crevice, down and up, barely reaching her clit. Her knees rose, and he pushed them back down.

"You need to be naked." His voice coiled around the tension welling up inside her.

Her panties were whisked down to her ankles. The absence of her dress and the slip of cotton sent a renewed rush of inhibition to the core of her being. Startled, she released the bed and reached her arms down to cover herself but contacted only his back. *Smooth. Solid. Hot skin.*

He grabbed her wrists with one gentle hand and lifted them back above her head.

Her body had to be crimson, there was so much blood rushing everywhere. "Please."

"Should I restrain you, Christiana? Tie your hands to the bed?"

Like the Jefferson Suite. She shook, and a tear escaped from the blindfold, its warm trickle trailing down her cheek.

"Shhh, lovely. You're safe. Remember what I said. I'll tell you everything I'm going to do." His voice both soothed and electrified her nerves.

He moved his lips over hers in a soft and gentle slide.

She panted into his mouth.

"Christiana. Breathe," he said, releasing her mouth. "I won't let anything bad happen to you. Accept that."

She took a lungful of air. "I-I do."

"Show me. Keep your hands on the headboard."

Jonathan slipped a small pillow under her head, and his arm snaked under the cushion. She vowed not to let go of the bed.

He murmured into her neck as he ran a hand down the length of her body. "I'm just going to touch you . . . for now."

She concentrated on his caresses though driven to distraction by his large cock, prodding, iron hard and hot. *So big.* She couldn't stop focusing on how this was going to work.

"Open your legs," he said. "Don't move, lovely. I'm going to put my finger inside you." Jonathan cupped her sex and dipped his finger deep into her folds. Her fingers dug into smooth wood.

I want to move. Please let me move.

"So wet," he said.

Christiana shifted under his hand, the feeling overwhelming.

He clucked his tongue. "Still, Christiana. We're going slow. Am I hurting you?"

She shook her head slightly.

Jonathan's finger moved deeper inside, and he swirled his

thumb over her clit. Ripples of sensation coursed through her whole body. She strained upward, riding the waves of sexual electricity that coursed up and down her thighs.

She whimpered. "I want to see you."

"No."

A second finger entered and stretched her insides. She gulped more air. His probing was not quite painful but not quite right. *Keep going.* She spread her legs wider, one leg slipping between his knees.

"Christiana. More?" His hot breath moved over her neck and face.

"Don't stop. Please." God, she begged.

His lips pulled into a smile against her shoulder, and she sensed a subtle shift in his energy. Though she couldn't see his expression, she felt she had pleased him.

Jonathan circled her sensitive nerve center. "I'm going to keep doing this until you come." He quickened his fingers, plunged in and out. He was not gentle.

Oh, harder.

Jonathan covered her lips with his own. His hand plundered her most private parts while his tongue, wild and demanding, mated with her mouth.

Harder.

She strained and arched, unable to keep still anymore.

He released her mouth and latched on to her breast. He gently bit her nipple and thrust his fingers inside her, impossibly deeper. Her sex convulsed around his piercing hand, and her legs twitched. Her inner muscles clamped down on his fingers, and his mouth returned to hers to swallow her cries as she came.

The spasms subsided, but she couldn't catch her breath. Jonathan released his kiss, and she took big gulps of air. He slipped his fingers from inside her enflamed tissues.

Two wet fingers were stuffed into her mouth.

"Taste yourself," Jonathan said. Her tongue swirled around the salty flavor she'd left on his working hand. She sucked his fingers gently.

"Mmm, that's it, lovely. Show me how well you suck."

He withdrew his fingers and dragged the blindfold down her face to her neck. Twilight had turned to night outside the side window. How long had it been?

"Very good, Christiana. That pleased me." His hungry eyes told her he meant it. "And, you?"

She nodded and flushed anew. She didn't take herself for a screamer, like those women in the movies who thrashed and begged for whatever their heroes dished out. What else would she end up doing tonight? *Please don't let me humiliate myself.*

He straddled her torso. "Your body is quite responsive."

Christiana swallowed at the sight of Jonathan's nude torso, ridges and planes across his abdomen. Her gaze followed the fine trail of gold hair running down his chest to his thick penis, a deep fleshy red, swelling straight forward. She knew then how a man could be called beautiful.

"Let's see what else you like," he rasped.

The tingling reaction to what she liked trickled down her labia to her butt crack. His hard cock bounced on her belly as he leaned forward to bring her arms down. He turned her palms over and rubbed the aching skin. "We'll have to be careful with restraints, I see. You already have marks from the headboard."

Jonathan removed the blindfold from her neck and lifted himself off her.

Christiana scrambled backwards to the headboard and drew her knees up, intensely aware of her nudity. But Jonathan yanked the duvet down and off the bed and drew her ankles toward him, so she slid down onto her back.

"Trying to get away?"

She shook her head. "No, I don't want to be anywhere else."

He settled himself between her moist thighs and slid a pillow under her head. "Good, because we've just begun."

She stared at his cock and then blushed scarlet at being caught examining his impressive virility.

He took one of her hands and brought it to his erection. She wrapped her fingers around the velvety smoothness that covered his steely length. Her hand shook—she had never seen a naked man in broad daylight. She decided pictures didn't do it justice. Certainly her one encounter with a penis poking her in the dark didn't come close.

He stilled her shaky wrist. "Perhaps I should've kept the blindfold on." He looked so comfortable between her legs. His confidence quieted her nerves.

"No, I want to see everything." She didn't want the sight of him stolen from her.

"Good. You have every right to look." He inhaled abruptly. "Mmm, easy, with the fingernails. It may be hard, but it's sensitive."

His strong hand encircled her fingers and moved them up to the head and down the long shaft to his balls, drawn up tight against his body. His head fell back slightly as she played with his sacks, lightly dusted in soft hair. When a long sigh left his mouth, a renewed rush of hunger took her over. She wanted this man to do things to her, things for which she didn't even have words.

Jonathan searched for his center of self-control, surprised such tiny fingers could elicit such a strong response. Her fingers played on his shaft. Up, down, up, down, even as she regarded him with those inquiring eyes. He also recognized the raw need behind them. *How long has she needed?*

Christiana had come fiercely under his coarse treatment, meeting his impatient handling with a surprising level of arousal. Her sheath clenched tightly around his fingers when he drove her over the edge. God, what would she do to his cock?

He couldn't wait any longer. He had to be inside her. Driven by the excitement to claim her at last, he rolled a condom on his cock in one swift slide.

Without a word, he lifted her knees and spread her farther apart. She didn't resist though concern replaced the wonder in her eyes. He arrowed the head of his covered length along her creases, spreading her post-orgasmic fluid around her opening. He had enough control to make one last check before he took his fill.

"Christiana, I'm going to fuck you." He held her wide blue-eyed stare.

The tacit permission of her half-nod was all he required. He met resistance, but he surged forward and breached the main muscle. His desperation to claim her completely reached a crescendo. He thrust, hard.

His mad lust for Christiana cracked a little when she cried out underneath him. He was only half way in, yet her small hands pushed against his chest.

Her blond hair splayed out on the pillow as she panted. Her pussy clenched him firmly, and his cock throbbed painfully, so close to possessing the girl-woman. *So narrow, so hot.*

"Shhh." He pressed soft kisses along her neck, across her cheeks and mouth. "Try to relax."

She whimpered, and his mind interrupted his body's mad demand for the girl. He pulled out.

He leaned over to the nightstand and popped open the

drawer. She may have technically not been a virgin, but her inexperience meant even after her climax, they'd need more lubricant.

After applying a thick coat of lube to his demanding cock, he gently pushed an oiled finger inside Christiana, who hadn't moved an inch. "There you go, lovely."

She smiled as he stroked her insides, coating her channel.

He hovered over her quaking body as he slipped his sheathed cock into her, an inch, two inches, more. He took her mouth, tangling his tongue with hers—so sweet and addictive. Her inner muscles released a little more.

Jonathan lifted himself up, a sheen of perspiration left on her chest. He hooked her smooth thigh under his arm and pushed the knee higher, opening her body more for his access. His thumb found her clitoris, and he coaxed more juices to flow. His cock slipped into her slick tunnel, further, deeper.

She moaned and dropped her hands to his hips and pulled. She wanted him.

"Yes, Christiana. Let me take you."

Christiana tried to relax around his thickness, but, even with the additional lubrication, pain gnawed on the edge of ecstasy, compromising her complete surrender. An avaricious longing fought her nervousness.

Inside. Jonathan's assertive thumb had added to her frenzied longing. Now nearly impaled and so close to being taken by his virile needs, Christiana rotated her hips around his cock, rocked her pelvis, desperate to ease his entry. Flames lit in his eyes, and his lips curled in response. He grabbed her hips and pulled her burning insides deeper over his cock.

"Do you want me, Christiana?" She squirmed underneath but only nodded. "Say it." He smacked the side of her ass cheek lightly. "Speak."

His lascivious craving fed her own hunger to have him, be claimed by him and his cock. "I want you," she whispered.

"How?"

"Inside me."

"More."

"Deep inside me." She needed him to take full ownership of her body.

He drove into her core with an animal-like snarl.

Christiana cried out as her insides pinched against the invasion. It wasn't like anything she'd experienced before. *Want more.* Her arms constricted around his back, her nipples tightening. *Closer. Come closer.*

"Fuck, you're sweet," Jonathan said into her neck. He stayed inside her for a minute, face buried in her hair—she could tell he waited, as if getting her used to the penetration. "Christiana?" His question whispered over her skin.

Christiana clenched her inner muscles, testing and checking on her state. He felt . . . right.

"Jonathan, please. *More.*"

He seemed to understand. He pushed into her with tight strokes so deep the pressure reached her chest and up into her throat. He filled her so completely she knew she'd feel empty whenever he wasn't buried inside her.

He grunted with each drive forward, adding to her growing need to get him deeper. She wrapped her legs around his hips and matched his assaults, liquid heat trickling from awakened nerves.

She heard herself moaning into his shoulder. He circled her body in a hug, raising her off the bed slightly to crush her to him. *Yes, closer.*

Christiana sucked in her breath when he craned his neck

down to lick her nipple and then took her breast deep into the heat of his mouth. He pulled back and nipped the firm peak only to encircle her breast with a wet sucking sound. He matched the rhythm of small bites with his thrusts, pushing her deeper into his arms and the mattress all at once.

Jonathan's strokes grew longer; he withdrew almost all the way and then pitched inside. His balls slapped her ass as his pelvis banged into her swollen nerve center. Bolts of pleasure spiked through her whole body. *Please, don't stop.*

He spread the lips of her labia, ground his pelvis, and ignited deeper inner nerves. Sensation shimmered through her aching pussy. Despite the sparks of pain, she'd never felt this good.

More savage pounding raised her to yet another, higher precipice. She lay splayed open for his taking, and he took, relentlessly.

Uncontrolled cries rose in her throat as she disintegrated into pure sensation. Her inner channel convulsed as her mind separated from her body. She heard Jonathan cry out, as if from an unimaginable distance. She felt his release pulse inside her tender flesh. Panting heavily, she suckled his shoulder and held onto his back. His hot breath moved through her hair, as he held himself over her quaking body.

After long minutes he raised up to his elbows, putting his hands on either side of her head. "Are you okay?"

Christiana nodded. *More than okay.* She knew she'd never want to be anywhere else, ever.

13

Jonathan paced on the outside deck and fingered his cell phone, waiting for the callback from Carson Drake. Between re-election commitments and Christiana's training, he didn't have time to spare. He had to unload his obligations and soon.

Yvette's three increasingly erratic messages since Jonathan and Christiana departed Washington reminded him of her requirement for a strong hand. Even though they'd agreed to a temporary affair, her need had grown. Now, he couldn't leave her unattended. Left to her own devices, Yvette could make trouble for Mother Theresa in heaven. Carson would be a good replacement for him.

He looked at his phone when it vibrated with a new text from Shane. Avery Churchill had called. She'd left a message late Friday trying to set up an appointment with him this weekend under the guise of some "fundraising opportunity." Jonathan knew better. He'd been offered such opportunities before. The only female who now held any interest for him slept in his bed down the hallway.

After their aggressive evening, Christiana had fallen into

a deep sleep, twitching from a dream he hoped involved him lying between her legs, still vibrating from an orgasm.

His cock tightened, remembering Christiana's responsiveness. Her commitment wasn't yet firm, but he was sure she could be convinced. She had not only unhesitatingly spread her creamy thighs when he asked but also matched his thrusts. He hadn't been polite, taking her with no uncertainty, and she'd responded.

Jonathan now knew what she needed, and he wouldn't be anything less than that from this moment forward—a lover who understood desires her mind had yet to comprehend and express. The gift of being the man to liberate that spirit behind her cool sapphire eyes was not something he could take lightly. He would not betray the trust she had shown.

The vibration in his hand broke his thoughts.

"Drake, you got my message," Jonathan said into the phone.

"I wasn't sure I heard you right. I've never known you to share," the deep voice said.

"Not share. Take over, if she's willing. I'll send her to you." *If she'll go.*

"If it's that blond lusciousness you were with at the reception—"

"Not her. Yvette DeCord."

"Ah, yes. Former Miss Dallas," Carson said. "Shame about her prick of a husband."

"Almost ex-husband. So you know her. You won't require my referral." Jonathan knew Carson would take the challenge.

"I'll listen to what you have to say."

Carson Drake had been fairly honorable during the handful of stand-offs they had back at Club Accendos. Jonathan and Carson were standing members of the private club's executive team. But since he'd come into the public eye, Jonathan rarely visited outside of occasional meetings. Though the club's secrecy and discretion remained legendary, moving personal activities to Charlottesville proved more prudent. He needed to ensure Yvette didn't return to Accendos either and that she find more discreet, careful hands. The networks spoke highly of Drake, so he was the logical choice.

"She needs a firm hand, Carson."

Carson grunted.

"Also, be careful of the prick. Arniss DeCord is rather sadistic."

"More than us?" Carson chuckled. "Tell me about our Texas flower."

Good. This would give Carson a reason to be occupied far away from Christiana. At the Hill reception last week, he'd run his eyes over her so ravenously Jonathan had almost dropkicked his ass into the hallway. They'd made a pact long ago not to cross territories, but Christiana posed the kind of potential that made alpha wolves forget deathbed promises to their sainted mothers. He wouldn't risk Carson finding some loophole in their longstanding agreement.

Jonathan stretched his long legs on the chaise lounge and spent a few minutes telling Carson the basic facts a Dom should know about Yvette.

Christiana awoke to the sight of Jonathan standing in the bedroom doorway. His eyes sent questions her way.

"Sleep well?" he asked.

"Yeah, I guess I needed it." She pulled the sheet back and sat up. How had she ended up wearing his T-shirt? She wondered if she could wear it every night. It smelled like him.

His mouth quirked, and he held out his hand. "Ready for a shower?"

The idea appealed. The sheets clung to her tacky legs.

Jonathan's bathroom was as modern as the rest of the house. Soft lighting suffused the entire room from recessed track lighting in the ceiling. A suspended piece of polished teak wood held matching green glass bowl sinks. A voyeur's dream shower stood in a corner: floor to ceiling windows revealing poplar trees that winked their silver leaves to anyone inside the shower stall.

After stripping off his clothes, Jonathan pulled the t-shirt over Christiana's head and towed her under a warm stream descending from an oversized showerhead. She hadn't realized Jonathan had meant a shower *with him*. Christiana held her face up into the water and tried to forget her nudity in broad daylight.

"Turn around," he directed. A bottle squeaked, and an orange-ginger scent rose up in the steam. She finally dared to open her eyes when she felt his chest against her back. Jonathan vigorously fingered her scalp, soap crackling in her ears. *God, he has talented hands.* He pulled her head back, and silky ribbons of shampoo foam snaked down her back and butt.

Slick with soap, Jonathan's hands circled around her chest to fondle her breasts. He rolled her nipples between her fingers, and Christiana pushed backward into his growing cock.

"You'll never hide this body when you're here." Jonathan's rich voice rang against the tile, echoing only slightly. His lips grazed her shoulder as his hands explored her back.

He leaned her over his arm while he slipped his other hand's fingers, parting her tender inner lips. She gulped as pain like burlap scraping sunburnt skin erupted. Warm soap-suds laved her raw tissues.

"You're sore," he said.

"Not too much." Her bruised insides disputed her half-truth, but she wouldn't chance him stopping that luxurious, lascivious motion.

"Hmmm. Spread your legs." His breath, hotter than the steam, moved over her ear as he rested his chin on her shoulder. His chest glided over her back, slippery with soap and water.

Christiana hooked her hands over the arm holding her ribs and pushed her ass backward into his cock, urging it deeper into her crevice.

She startled when his finger dipped inside her slit.

He withdrew. "I think you're more than a 'little' sore."

Christiana held her breath at the soft correction in his voice, then released it in one pant. "But I don't want you to stop."

"There's little chance I could ever stop with you. But I insist you always tell me the truth."

"I will. I-I am." She pushed against his erection.

"Hmmm. I know how to make you feel better." He returned his hand, his fingers intruding and moving slowly in little circles until all the consciousness in her body coalesced into that one spot. Her legs weakened, and his arm tightened in response.

Christiana spread her legs to rest astride his muscled quads and fell deeper into his thrumming fingers.

"Christiana, let go."

Her name, spoken in his voice, drove all remaining awareness to her clit. He pressed the tip of his finger inside her and his thumb on her nerve center, just firmly enough. Her bruised interior squeezed his finger, and he gently nipped her shoulder. Peak followed peak until the tidal wave of ecstasy tipped her over into a waterfall of spasms, her knees buckling. A moan escaped her throat and echoed off the tile.

As her orgasm subsided, she took big gulps of thick, steamy air, her muscles milking his fingertip in a final shudder.

Jonathan slipped his hand from between her legs and spun her around. He scooped her up into his arms, and his rigid cock ground into her belly. *Should I do something for him?*

But he only pulled her head back by her wet hair and grinned. "So, now that you know more, perhaps we can continue our conversation?"

Conversation . . . now? "There's more?"

"We've only just begun, lovely."

Christiana wondered what else she didn't know. Jonathan seemed to be alluding to a depth of sexual knowledge she'd never imagined existed.

Jonathan handed her a fluffy white robe after turning off the shower.

"There's a blow dryer in that second one." He pointed to a set of recessed drawers and wrapped his middle with a large blue towel.

Christiana bent over to towel dry her hair and when she threw her head back, he was gone.

Twenty minutes later, clad in jean shorts and a plain white t-shirt, hair dried, she stepped out to find Jonathan. She blushed at the thought of running into his housekeeper.

Christiana tiptoed to his office. He was on his phone, his voice sounding pissed, so she retreated to the deck to check her phone. Avery had been texting all night. She also had missed two calls from the dishwasher repairman. After listening to one slurry voice mail message from her father, she laid the phone down. She wouldn't let reality encroach further on her fantasy weekend.

∾

"Yvette. It was simply a referral." Jonathan rubbed his forehead. Shit, the hand-off wasn't supposed to go down like this.

"Fuck you, *Congressman*. No real man has another guy call me to pick up pieces that haven't even fallen."

Her words arrowed through his heart. The last thing he'd meant to do was add to the hurt Yvette had amassed over the last few months.

"I'll see you on Sunday, as planned. But with my re-election coming up, Carson is better suited for you." A little bit of truth mixed with a small white lie.

"Like hell."

"Our time was always to be limited, Yvette."

"Why now?"

"Yvette." Jonathan didn't need to see her sit down. He knew her—and himself well.

"Sir." She sounded like she might cry.

"On your knees." Jonathan heard her breathing. "I'm warning you." He'd wanted to soothe her, but he'd known Yvette long enough to quickly assess what she required at the moment.

"I am."

"Good girl."

"Jonathan?"

"Yes, baby." He'd let the informal address slide.

"You'll always be my friend, right?"

"Always."

"Because I'll always be yours. I've always wanted to-to . . . help, too."

"You do help me, Yvette. We'll always be together, just differently." He meant it. His loyalty—once given—was *never* withdrawn. "Now suck on a finger."

"Jonathan, please—"

"Yvette."

Wet sucking sounds. *Very good.* She was hurt but wasn't pissed.

"Put your finger inside yourself," he said. "Good. Now I want you to stay that way for ten minutes. You'll not move your finger in any way. Do you understand?"

"Yes, sir."

"When ten minutes are up, you will get dressed. You will not make yourself come. I will see you Sunday—to *talk*."

Christiana dangled her legs off the edge of the deck and leaned her back onto the wooden surface. She centered her mind on the speckled sunlight squares that filtered through the tree limbs to blanket the deck and dance across her torso. She needed to think. First she needed to wrest control away from the stupid cheerleader girl dancing about and shouting, *you had sex with Jonathan Brond!* She had so many questions.

Was sex supposed to be like this? Was it strange she liked it when he held her arms down? Would her body now obey any command Jonathan's spoke?

She couldn't get answers from Avery. Avery coveted Jonathan and would kill Christiana for *talking* to him. But just because Avery wanted Jonathan didn't mean he was automatically hers, right? Who said Avery had rights to every man who struck her fancy? Besides, Christiana didn't want to stop. Despite her soreness, her female parts jumped into readiness at the mere thought of what his advances led to.

But now what? It was the *after* part she hadn't quite considered.

Christiana's eyes snapped open when Jonathan's bare foot nudged her leg.

"Still jumpy, I see. Come, you must be hungry." He held out his hand to help her up.

A tray of fruit and croissants, butter and jams, and two glasses of orange juice waited for them on the kitchen counter. Roasted meat scents rose from the oven, where juices spit and sparked inside.

"Blanca brought us a roast for later. For now, would you like some eggs and fruit?"

When did Blanca arrive? She slipped in and out like a ghost, even in broad daylight.

"No, fruit is great," she said.

Jonathan watched Christiana intently as she nibbled on a piece of melon after consuming a croissant loaded with butter and jam. "You finally look rested," he said.

"Yeah, I feel pretty good." She was more than good. The sugar from the breakfast treats coursed through her limbs. Or maybe Jonathan's company made her jittery. She didn't know how to interpret her body's reactions anymore in his presence. The man unleashed a torrent of craving with one glance.

He pulled her off her stool into his arms. "I'm glad you let me make love to you, Christiana." He smoothed her hair off her forehead and ran his thumb over her scar.

She instinctively pulled back a little.

He only held her more strongly. "I think you've been waiting for someone to understand you. You haven't always had it easy."

Her stomach lurched. She hoped he wouldn't tread into hazardous territory, like anything about her father—or ask about her forehead. *Talk about a downer after last night.*

"This summer, when we're together, I'll take care of you." Jonathan released her head and ran his hands down her arms to encircle her wrists, ran his thumbs over the thin skin. "But we're going to go slow. Yet there's much to get in order, quickly."

Jonathan pulled her to the couch and sat her down on the snow-white leather.

"First, we'll start with the basics," he said. "You should always know the medical condition of anyone you're sleeping with. I'll show you my medical records later. Do you have a gynecologist?"

Okay, she had wanted the conversation to turn away from her past . . . but perhaps not in this particular direction. She shook her head. She hadn't seen the need for a gynecologist before.

"I'll make an appointment for you. Dr. Bethany Jevicky. Discreet. Tuesday morning since you don't work that shift. Depo-Provera should work nicely."

Irritation ran up her spine when he mentioned her work shift. But birth control? She didn't argue. She wanted to feel his hardness deep inside, naked and unfettered.

"I want to make the most of our time together, and for that, you need more sleep."

Christiana couldn't fathom choosing sleep over Jonathan buried deep inside her most intimate core. Besides, she'd slept more last night than she had all week.

"You need to stop pulling double shifts, wearing yourself out."

"I'm not quitting work. If I don't work a lot, I won't make enough money for school. I also won't be able to take time off to be with you."

"I'm not asking you to. I can help."

"Please. Don't. I know I'm naive about sex. But I've been taking care of myself for a while." She dipped her face from the concern coloring Jonathan's eyes. "I can handle my schedule at work."

He frowned. He didn't believe her?

"I'm not afraid of hard work." She sent him a small smile, and his mouth relaxed.

"That's what I'm afraid of. Doing too much." He pulled her to his chest. "I want to do so many things with you, Christiana. We'll come back here next weekend." He placed a soft kiss into her hair, and she relaxed into his body.

"But now I want to get you out of those jeans." He dipped his fingers to the apex of her denim-clad crotch and rubbed.

"Whatever you want."

Jonathan had her back in the bedroom and naked in seconds.

14

Birds. Screeching, twittering, calling. Christiana's consciousness arose from a sleepy cloud. Jonathan's arm draped over her torso, a sheet covering only their lower halves. She stretched under the heaviness on her ribs. She felt stiff, wooden, and a fire sizzled between her legs.

Christiana marveled at Jonathan's ability to grow hard within minutes of taking her. She could tell he'd restrained himself last night, slowing down, moving into her gently and steadily until she came several more times. Finally, as light rose in the sky, he cradled her worn-out body with his own, succumbing to sleep.

She loved every second of his demanding hands, lips and tongue—pulling sensations from her she didn't know her body could produce. Now she understood what she heard in Yvette DeCord's voice that day at the Jefferson Suite. In seconds she moved from longing to begging to *rapture*.

Even sore and aching, she wouldn't have stopped Jonathan last night if Avery Churchill, herself, sat in a corner, watching.

Christiana slipped from under Jonathan's embrace and twisted to face him. His breath ran between chiseled lips, and the gold hair on his head lay tousled in little waves. *Like a men's cologne ad, of course.*

The clock read seven a.m. She'd been in bed for twelve hours. She'd never had so much sleep or activity in her personal life as in the last two days.

Jonathan stirred. He rolled to his back, stretching his arm out over his head, but remained asleep. He presented the perfect classical profile.

Christiana pulled the sheet down his body, inch by inch. She didn't want him to wake. Her insides still pulsed with his use. She couldn't afford to start something she'd have to stop. Yet she wouldn't disregard the opportunity to study the man. Muscled planes and angles landscaped his arms and chest. He had to lift weights all the time, she thought. Blond hairs dusted his pecs and trailed down his torso into a triangle that disappeared under the drape. She wondered how many elections he'd win if he used this shot on his campaign poster.

Christiana lowered the sheet, and her eyes followed the track of blond hair from his chest down to his . . . Jonathan moved. *Please don't wake.* He sighed and turned his head on the pillow to face her, but his eyes stayed closed.

She scooched closer to his hips and pulled the sheet down to his knees. Even limp, his penis was huge. It explained how raw she felt. She wondered how his slack flesh would feel cradled in her hands.

Her phone vibrated in her jeans, draped over the chair in the corner. She glanced up at Jonathan who slumbered despite the insistent shuddering. Christiana knew who wanted to connect with her this early. *You go back to sleep too, Avery.* Finally, the phone silenced.

Seeing Jonathan like this provoked an overwhelming

sense of ownership within her. *She* lay next to this god, not a certain member of high society. She had squatter's rights. Christiana kissed the velvet skin of his shaft and took in his musky warm scent. She placed her mouth on the tip and ran her tongue around the rim. *Salty*.

He moved underneath her lips, and his hand came down on her shoulder.

Christiana looked up. He still slept. She crawled between his legs and took more of him into her mouth. His cock stiffened, and his hand knotted her hair in a fist.

"Christ," he hissed.

Her mouth released its hold, and her eyes shot to his face. He stared down at her as if he didn't quite recognize the girl holding his hardness in her hand.

Without breaking his gaze, she sheathed her teeth within her lips and slowly sucked him inside her mouth, running her tongue on the underside to wet his entry. She swirled her tongue around the head. Then she pushed down on him, taking as much of his cock inside her throat as she could. For a moment she fought a gag reflex, quelled it, and moved him out and then back in.

"Easy," he said. "Christ, you're eager."

She looked up.

His eyes were unreadable as he pulled his hips back. His cock slipped from her mouth. "You didn't tell me you knew how to do this."

"I don't. I'm experimenting."

"You've never gone down on a guy before?"

"No, I, um, never got that far. I told you I really have no experience at all. But I've always wondered."

His eyes said he didn't quite have confidence in her words, but he only answered "Good. I want to be your experience. Do you like this?" He arched one eyebrow to indicate the blowjob.

She nodded because, actually, she did. It felt strangely powerful holding his most intimate part in her mouth.

"Well, don't let me stop your fun." He pushed her head back down toward his rigid, slick cock.

Christiana trailed fingers through the fine, soft hair covering his balls. She pulled his hard rod in and out of her mouth, running her tongue up and down, rising and falling, circling and lapping.

His breath caught. "Mmm, you're good," he said.

Heady elation blossomed in her heart. *He thinks I'm good.*

His hands twisted in her hair and pushed her head down until his cock, now rock hard, hit the back of her throat. She fought another gag response. When he released her head, she pulled out only to reclaim him. She sucked as firmly as she dared.

Jonathan's balls tightened under her other hand. A shot of warm, salty liquid hit the back of her throat, and she eased him out a bit so she could swallow. When his length went limp, he released her hair.

Christiana slipped her mouth free. A mildly victorious feeling spread across her wet face. She did something he hadn't asked for. She'd pleased him.

Maybe.

She glanced up to check.

His face was inscrutable, but he pulled her up into a waiting kiss. "You're a fast learner."

She sank into triumph.

He brushed her hair out of her face and smiled. "And I do believe you are a morning person, Christiana."

"Sir, I'm doing my best. Your father is rather difficult to, uh, redirect, especially in person."

Didn't Jonathan know it. An image of Shane being bent over backwards on his desk while his blowhard father barked orders raised some sympathy for his legislative aide.

"He's just pissed I didn't make that floor statement."

"Well, making it part of the congressional record—"

"Is not what I'm going to do. Shane, next time he shows up uninvited, just say you don't know where I am."

"When can I tell him he can reach you?"

"You can't. I'm out of town, and he'll have to figure out someday I'm not eleven anymore." The roiling in his gut belied the humor he'd peppered into the conversation. Shane's loyalty deserved more than he was getting from Brond Senior. Dammit, why can't the man leave well enough alone? Showing up at his office on a Saturday when his over-worked staff toiled their weekend away took nerve. While he, himself, had burned plenty of midnight oil, Jonathan frol-icking between a woman's legs while they labored at this critical juncture probably wasn't much better.

"Sir, if I may, I think he just likes being here."

Jonathan sighed heavily into the phone. "I know he does. Giving up that kind of power is . . . hard."

"I can only imagine."

His father's obvious dismay at being dethroned from his beloved political post only added to the mystery around why he'd let things get so out of hand in the first place. The messy divorce from his mother, the stupid public remarks, and then his ultimate betrayal . . . . He shook the memories that dared to arise from his head. Nothing good came from visiting the past.

He had a future to focus on. Jonathan had worked hard to get elected and even harder to ensure his promises to voters did not go undelivered, especially on his platform of mental health reform and personal privacy. Perhaps his father would have still been in office if he'd followed a similar plan.

Voters hadn't appreciated Brond Senior's last few speeches about mental health care funding, saying people just needed to pull themselves up by their bootstraps and stop bleeding the system dry. Well, they took his advice and offered his father a chance to do just that—go home and stop draining their tax dollars with his Senate salary.

Jonathan heard quiet footsteps in the hallway headed to his office. He swiveled his chair just as Christiana appeared in his doorway.

"Shane, enjoy your weekend. Stay out of the office. That'll ensure you won't run into any more ex-Senators who wish they could turn back the clock."

Shane chuckled, finally. "Yes, sir. You do the same."

"Oh, I will." Jonathan had no intention of letting news of his father's untimely visit to his office eat into his weekend. Not when the beauty shyly shuffling from foot to foot in his doorway, silently questioning if it was okay to enter, stood mere feet from his growing hard-on. When Christiana was anywhere near him, his cock took over.

Jonathan loaded the car and debated how to discuss next weekend's potential activities—there was so much more to show Christiana. Waking to her pink lips encasing his cock had almost caused him to lose the final shred of self-control he'd been hoarding since releasing her from her inexperience over the last thirty-six hours. If she had had more practice, he'd be buried inside her right now. But he'd already availed himself of her body far too often this weekend.

He'd left her at the breakfast bar, swaying as she shifted gingerly up on the stool. The aftermath of the weekend's activity had to be akin to sliding down a concrete banister. He hoped she'd recover before next Friday.

Jonathan silently berated himself for the loss of his prized control. Something about her hit a vulnerable place inside him—a most undisciplined place where the only rule was seize and conquer. A mere inhalation of her honeyed skin impacted his judgment, the loss of which neither of them could afford. Until he got that weakness under control, it was better for Christiana that he couldn't see her this week.

Next weekend would be pivotal to their agreement, and he had to plan it carefully. So much more awaited them both. But facing a week ahead of meetings and conferences, he had little time to coddle a newbie. Such succulent innocence came with a price—even as eager and quick as Christiana proved herself to be. Hundreds of questions would arise after he showed her what was possible.

No, it would be better to sequester her here next weekend and introduce his plans for her all at once. With her submission as the prize, he had to be sure he'd win.

"Ready, lovely?"

Christiana winced when Jonathan helped her into the front seat. Yes, they needed to be separated for the next five days. The uncanny passion lying underneath her quiet demeanor would slow her much-needed recovery. She'd be her worst enemy, her thirst now easily overtaking her capacity. It was the curse of a true submissive, always seeking to do more for her Dominant.

The gates of *Covil Sereia* closed behind his car.

On the slow drive home, Jonathan talked about mundane things—movies, books, current news—as he caressed her tiny hand. The small talk helped keep his hard-on at bay. Sort of.

He'd thought about asking about that scar across her forehead. What he knew about her past—and present—caused him great concern. Instead, he filed away the undisciplined emotions that came with the thought of anyone hurting Christiana. In the long run, it wouldn't help her if he indulged in the feeling he hadn't humored since he was eleven—wanting to kill.

15

Christiana exited Dr. Jevicky's office building into the thick wall of Washington summer heat, like swimming through a haze. Still, nothing could quell Christiana's euphoria.

She hadn't expected the physician to make her feel so at ease, even with her feet up in stirrups enduring cold, prodding instruments. Now, graced with a clean bill of health and fully inoculated from pregnancy with Depo-Provera, Christiana nearly bounced out onto the street.

New York Avenue teemed with men in business attire and pencil-skirted-women, all weaving through the throngs of tourist families.

Christiana passed a café where women sat, lunching under an umbrella despite the sizzling temperatures. Clad in elegant high heels and skirts, they lifted sweating glasses of iced tea in a toast and laughed lightly. One of the women glanced at Christiana as she passed and smiled warmly. Even though dressed in her nicest sundress, her clothes were not on a par with what they were wearing. Christiana wondered what the woman saw in her to warrant such an open acknowledgement. Was one weekend with Jonathan enough to admit Christiana into the world of preferred women—women who had men who savaged them in dark, leather-scented rooms?

Christiana slowed her pace and lifted her chin to a few passers-by, clad in business suits. They responded in kind. Perhaps she not only felt different, but looked different too. Would Avery notice when they met later?

Buoyed by her weekend of very adult activities, Christiana finally had broken down and returned one of Avery's messages. Avery acted like nothing happened in the ladies room at The Oak, which suited Christiana fine. Avery simply said she and her mother had gone to California for the weekend—and didn't she get any of her texts over the weekend about the hot surfer guys? Christiana hoped Avery had moved on to her next potential conquest and abandoned her designs on Jonathan. He was *hers* now.

A sheen of perspiration covered Christiana's body when she finally flopped on the lounger next to Avery at the club. "Thanks for saving me a seat."

"Yeah, well it wasn't easy. Mrs. Darden kept asking for it. Where were you anyway?"

"Errands. Hey, you got a phone charger with you?" Her phone died before she had a chance to call Jonathan. Her father had conveniently borrowed her phone charger for his road trip, and she hadn't had the chance to pick up a new one.

"Nope, but someone here might. Ask the front desk. Expecting a call?"

"Oh, uh, no. That's okay. I'll get it later." A dead cell phone might be better than Avery checking her recent call list or getting an unexpected call from Jonathan. Christiana still wasn't sure how to broach the subject of Jonathan with Avery. She couldn't figure out how to tell her and live.

Mercifully Avery steered the conversation to her favorite subject—herself.

"I don't know, Chris. Chase is cute and all and, man, he's on me all the time."

She'd heard those words from Avery a hundred times, but never responded so physically. She let her mind wander. Jonathan pushing her deep into the mattress with his weight. Jonathan kissing her into utter stupidity. Jonathan's clever tongue dancing around her clit. Jonathan doing anything . . . and everything.

"What do you think?" Avery asked her question to the sky.

"Me?" She was asking Christiana for advice? "I think you should do whatever your heart tells you." Was it bad she hoped she'd get back together with Chase? Or with anyone *not* Jonathan.

Avery snorted. "I don't have time for that lovey-dovey stuff. I need to choose wisely. I need someone more settled, stable. Like—"

"You sleeping better now?" She couldn't chance Avery saying *his* name.

"My internal clock is messed up. I'm out so late at events these days. Jesus, you'd think my mom was afraid to go out alone."

"There must be some cute guys at those events."

"Oh, yeah, married men who can't keep their eyes off my breasts, and old geezers who can't get it up anymore. Hey, you want to go out this weekend, the two of us? We can go trolling in Georgetown or that new club in Adams Morgan."

"Oh, um, sorry I can't."

"You're acting like you're thirty or something. Hey, speaking of thirty-year-olds, has your father said anything about Congressman Brond?"

Christiana's heart skipped a beat. "Um, Dad's on the road." *There. Not a lie.*

"Oh, man, score! I can come over for a sleep over."

"Let me check my work schedule."

"This weekend!"

"I'm pretty sure I'll be all tied up. But, hey, how was California? You didn't tell me about your trip."

"The Dean wants to sleep with me."

"You're kidding, right?" Christiana leaned up on her elbows. "Is he harassing you or something?"

"No, I'm fine. Look, we need to go out soon. I don't care if I have to march into The Oak Room and suck off your supervisor's cock to gain your release." She let out an awkward laugh.

Christiana stared at her friend. Avery had shadows lining her eyes. She looked older. Perhaps they both had unwittingly moved into a new stage, like crossing a state border and not realizing it until the road filled with cars bearing new license plate colors.

Avery dropped her chin onto her bent knee and picked at her already chipped red toenail polish. Christiana had never known Avery to miss a pedicure.

They didn't talk again, but kept their faces turned toward the bright sunshine. Christiana didn't try to fill the empty space, and Avery didn't ask any more questions. Instead, Christiana let the strange new secrets settle between them in the heat.

Shane droned on about Congressman Blanchard's offer to support the Internet privacy bill. Jonathan couldn't take his eyes off his phone. Christiana hadn't called back.

"So, that's my summary of the issue," Shane said.

"Whatever you think's best. I trust you."

Shane's shock registered Jonathan's break in protocol. Jonathan rarely relegated decisions.

"You know Blanchard as well as I," Jonathan explained. "Call him today. Make it short. Don't let him prattle on."

"Yes, of course." Shane retreated to the back room where the interns crouched over tiny desks, opening mail and answering the phone.

Jonathan turned his phone over in his hand. Christiana couldn't still be with Dr. Jevicky, and she knew to call him right after her appointment.

Yvette also hadn't called Jonathan since he'd met with her on Sunday. She had fussed and preened, but all her attempts to provoke some much-desired discipline had failed. Jonathan was singular in his sexual relations, not at all interested in the promiscuous play that too many in the scene called "practice" and "education." He'd have his hands full with Christiana.

He hit Christiana's number on his speed-dial. Hadn't he told her there would be consequences if she didn't communicate with him? Perhaps she didn't believe his conviction around such matters. He would be happy to exact a reminder —and prove his position.

After picking up a new phone charger, Christiana barely made it to The Oak in time for the four o'clock shift. Tuesday was not her usual day, but she had managed to convince Brian to let her serve the dinner crowd. Her time with Avery was peculiar, and nothing shook strangeness faster than working. Plus she needed to stockpile as many tips as possible. Weekend work was jeopardized by Jonathan's super seduction skills.

The Oak crowd thinned early so she was let go at nine-thirty. As she drove home, she fingered her useless cell, eager to get it charged, so she could connect with Jonathan. She had no privacy at work, especially not with Henrick's constant hovering every time she had a minute to herself. And Brian refused to let staff plug their phones in around the kitchen.

When she turned onto her street, Jonathan's SUV idled in front of her house, Jonathan waiting inside the vehicle, as if that would make him go unnoticed. His car alone was enough to draw suspicion in her neighborhood.

He stepped out of the driver's seat. "Where were you? I've been calling." He sounded livid.

"I was at the pool with Avery and then work."

"Why didn't you answer my calls?"

"My battery died. I didn't have my charger and—" He grasped her arm and led her up the walkway. At the doorway, he took the keys from her hand and opened the front door.

She turned to him in the entranceway. "I'm-I'm glad you're here. But I smell like sunscreen and fry grease." She stepped backward when he tried to embrace her. "I'd really like to take a shower before we talk."

"Trying to avoid me already?"

"N-no, not at all. I just feel icky."

He brushed a strand of hair behind her ear. "Go on. I'll meet you in your bedroom."

She scooted around him. After stripping off her clothes, she stepped under the warm water and took a few steadying breaths. She'd never handled anger well, and she needed a minute to regroup. Okay, she'd promised to call and didn't. Why the big deal?

She scrubbed her head vigorously with shampoo. It felt nothing like Jonathan's fingers digging into her scalp. Her insides jumped to attention remembering the way he'd handled her in his shower at *Covil Sereia*.

When she stepped inside her bedroom, wrapped in a towel, wet hair trailing down her back, her body hummed with anticipation.

Jonathan sat on her bed, fingering a photograph Christiana had on her bedside table, of herself with her parents on the sands of an Outer Banks beach—North Carolina, she thought. She had only vague memories of the vacation, but the photo comforted her. Like she had a family, once.

"You didn't tell me how it went with Dr. Jevicky."

"Fine. She gave me Depo-Provera."

"Good. We're going to need it."

Her heart fluttered. Had he softened? Christiana plugged her phone into the wall jack and then sat on the bed next to him. Her legs ached, and she felt like several days had passed instead of one.

"Today I didn't know how to get in touch with you. I didn't know where you were. If you were ignoring me, or if, God forbid, you were in the car with your father—"

"No. It wasn't like that. My phone died."

"You couldn't borrow one? Surely The Oak or the club have telephones you could have used."

"I didn't have a . . . secure line. There were people around. I was keeping our secret. Besides I would have called you later."

Jonathan's chin jutted upward sharply and his nostrils flared. "I see. You're not taking our agreement seriously."

His words didn't make sense. She'd never taken anything so seriously in her life.

Jonathan placed a knuckle under her chin and lifted her face to look at him. "It's simple. If you cannot keep the lines of communication open, then our agreement is not important to you. And if you are playing games with me . . . ."

She immediately regretted the heavy sigh that escaped her lips.

He dropped his hand and stood. "You are failing to grasp the most basic tenet of our arrangement."

Christiana reached out and grabbed his wrist. "I'm sorry. I didn't mean it like that."

He peeled off his jacket and laid it on the chair in the corner. "You remember what I said about discipline, if you didn't do as I asked?"

"Yes." The word almost got caught in her throat. Someone else seemed to shine through Jonathan's eyes, smoldering with some unnamed intent.

He tossed her towel back on to the bed. "I want to look at you."

She flushed a little, even though the man had seen her naked before—*very* naked.

He grasped the back of her neck and pulled her into a kiss. His tongue reached inside and studied her mouth. Fingers tweaked her nipples, and his hold on her neck grew stronger. His hand slipped lower, between her legs. Christiana dampened when he drew a finger up between her folds.

He sat and snaked his arm around her waist. His strong arms pushed her down over his lap, facedown.

"Jonathan, what—"

"I'm going to spank you."

She tried to lift herself off, but he pushed her back down. She grabbed the bed frame to steady herself, even though he held her firmly, one hand on her lower rib cage and the other on her neck. Her wet hair trailed down the side of her face.

Fingers ran up and down her spine and then cupped an ass cheek. *Smack!* A sharp slap stung across her butt. She gasped and twisted on his lap, but he held her neck down with one hand.

"Wait," she whimpered.

"No." His fingers brushed her stinging backside for a few seconds and then another slap.

Smack! Smack! Pain spread, followed by a warmth and a strange tingle down her legs.

"You won't make me worry about you. Do you understand?" He caressed where his hands had fallen.

"Y-yes," she sniffled. Tears pricked her eyes, not from the sting but from something else. The bite across her backside threatened to loosen something inside her, something she'd been repressing.

His hands came down harshly on her ass twice more, and she let out a moan.

"Do you want me to stop, Christiana?" He leaned down and sent his hot breath over her neck.

"I . . . ." she started.

"You what?"

"I . . . don't know."

His hand lightly stroked her smarting ass. "Such a lovely pink." *Whack!* The loud smack reverberated in her ears, and her pelvis ground into his erection.

Damn, her crotch moistened in response to the blows. She willed herself to stop wiggling. From the second Jonathan had first parted her legs, her body responded whenever he touched her, any way, anywhere. Even when spanking her backside.

"If anything ever happened to you. . . ." His words came out tight, focused, as if through gritted his teeth.

Another brisk swat, hard and focused, landed on her ass.

She cried out, frantically sifting through the conversation in which Jonathan had revealed what he wanted. What words did he use? *Submission.* She had agreed? Yes, she had. What else? *Be his.* Yes.

Jonathan stroked her hair and then cupped his hand under her chin to lift her head. He leaned in to whisper in her ear. "You will not make me wonder where you are. You won't make me worry about you. Not ever."

"I won't make you worry," she whispered.

"Good girl." He let her head drop down. He ran his fingers over her sore behind and kissed her shoulder. "Mmm, nice and hot. Sit up."

The comforter cover felt rough across her chapped ass as Jonathan dragged her across the fabric to sit on his lap. "My beautiful, Christiana." He swept her hair aside, cupped a breast and tugged on the nipple.

She arched into his hand, her body betraying her mind, still stunned by his harsh treatment and the bewilderment over how aroused she'd become.

His hand snaked between her legs, and he inserted a finger inside, roughly but easily. She inhaled sharply.

He dipped his head so their foreheads connected. "If you are not interested in—"

"No, I am." Christiana placed her hands on either side of his head. "I want to be with you. I-I . . . ." Words stuck in her throat, and her eyes pricked. *I know what it's like to wonder where someone is. If they'll ever come back.*

"Good."

She barely caught herself with shaky arms when he pushed her facedown into the comforter. His zipper sounded and pants hit the floor. A loud clunk of a shoe falling. Shirttails brushed the back of her thighs when Jonathan pulled her hips up. He parted her knees.

Pearls zinged out of the jewelry box on her bedside table, and cool beads touched her back. Jonathan trailed them up her spine and around to her face. "These are important to you."

"They were my mom's."

"Up on your knees and palms together."

Jonathan slowly wound the long white strands around

each of her wrists, their length wrapping around several times. He continued coiling them up the back of her hands to her fingertips until they were pearl-bound in prayer pose. He slipped a final loop around an index and middle finger.

"Hold them there." He pushed her face and bound hands down to the mattress, pulled her hips back until his cock nestled in the cleft of her ass. He caressed her cheek. "Fuck, I can't wait to own every part of you, Christiana."

She didn't try to rise up, her face afire against the bedcover, self-conscious but edgy with lust, pearls digging into her sternum.

He pressed the thick head of his cock into her wet opening and held it there, stretching her. He moved an inch into her and pulled away, teasing and tempting her entrance with possession.

An overbearing need for him to be inside overtook her senses. She pushed her hips backward, trying to capture his fullness.

His hands stopped her advance.

"Not until I say so." Jonathan held a hip with one hand and ran his fingers over her stinging ass. The signal was clear. He was in charge.

In the corner of her eye, she watched fabric float by. He'd taken off his shirt.

Jonathan reached around her waist and spread her labia with his fingers, finding her clit. His fingers caressed and circled, making her unbearably wet. His manliness lording over her smaller frame reminded her of his power and his virility. She'd never felt so female as when the hairs on his taut abdomen brushed her back.

"Please, Jonathan." She spread her knees more, chest heaving as she panted. The pearls clicked as they resettled under her breasts.

He placed a warm kiss to her flushed skin, his erection resting on her cleft. "What do you want, Christiana?"

"You."

"What will you do when you get me?"

"Whatever you want."

He withdrew his taunting fingers from her nerve center. "Yes, because I will take care of you." She heard something like rubber snapping. *A condom?*

"Please. I need you—"

"You do need me, and, you're going to get me."

He thrust his cock inside her, stretching and filling every millimeter of her inner parts. She tried to push back, so she sat on his legs, her only focus to drive him farther inside. She needed his rock-hard cock, deeper. She *needed*.

Jonathan, sheathed tightly inside her nirvana, nearly let her take control. Fuck, she was going to kill him. He grunted and pressed her upper body back down to the mattress.

He strained to withhold his release. She folded forward, impaled on his aching cock, and his mind searched for words, lost in his lust for the slender body stretched before him.

"Christiana. Still."

"I can't."

"Tell me you're mine." It was too soon for such a declaration, but her pussy muscles clenched around his shaft, unleashed his most base dominance. Each woman felt unique and special. Yet Christiana's channel presented a valley of lushness that some god had designed for his pleasure. She gloved his thick length so sweetly his mind would never win the battle over sensation. He wanted to own this woman.

"I'm yours." Puffs of air accompanied each word from her sweet lips.

His eyes grazed her pinkened backside, propped up for his pleasure. A series of detonations fired in his head. Her pose taunted his cock, now aching to bury himself in her ass. Jonathan dug his fingers into her hips. They would leave bruises, marks of his impending ownership of all her untouched parts.

With a carnal grunt Jonathan pulled back and then hilted himself.

Wild and unconstrained, he began fucking her. Her core grew slicker, hugged him tightly even though he ravaged her insides. His cock seemed filled with new nerve endings threatening to consume his rational thought.

Her submissive pose wouldn't permit him to continue much longer. He spun, quickly reaching that peak where senses overcome and time suspends. His world narrowed to her heat squeezing him.

Christiana's squeals cracked the blank space, breaking his focus on his own pleasure to pull his awareness back to her body. Her contractions massaged his torment, and hot liquid gushed around his cock. He released and flooded the condom with his own fluid.

Jonathan unclenched his hold on her hips. She fell flat to the bed, and he laid himself half-way across her prostrate body, careful not to crush her slender frame. His arms folded around her, all words and thoughts drained.

Wisps of damp blond hair across Christiana's face fluttered from her quickened breath.

As they lay together, letting their heated skin cool, his mind crept back into focus. He should say something, but nothing came. He shouldn't be here, half mad with lust over a woman who never left his mind. *Christ, it's been one week.*

And he'd broken a cardinal rule. He'd disciplined her

under anger. He should have walked away. But his usual finesse had retreated in the face of his primal needs. His mind had spun too many tales, imaginings that Christiana would somehow get away.

Jonathan hadn't laid such an animalistic claim on a woman ever. He knew Christiana could own him if he wasn't careful. She was woman incarnate, presenting him with treasure he'd never refuse.

"Jonathan?" Her voice, soft and hesitant, broke through the silence.

"Yes, baby."

"I am yours. I promise."

"I know." He nestled closer to cover as much of her warm, satiny skin as he could reach.

He had to regain his composure, and stick to the blueprint he'd written for their time together. He couldn't let emotion get the better of him. Work the plan, he told himself. He'd regain control. He'd count on his strategy. It always worked before. And never again would he let his temper overcome him.

Christiana stirred, and he brushed hair from her cheek. *So soft.* He murmured assurances in her ear until her breathing slowed. She soon fell asleep.

In the stillness only broken by a car passing on the highway behind her house and her gentle breath, he made a vow. He wasn't a praying man, but he made a promise to the heavens. *I swear I won't destroy the very thing I can't get enough of—her innocence.*

16

Christiana winced when The Oak Room's kitchen door smacked her on the butt. A quick pat of her apron pocket assured her phone lay nestled safely inside. She hadn't quite processed that Jonathan had spanked her like a little girl.

Jonathan's turn from passion to unyielding taskmaster back to passion left her dazed. But she'd learned something about him last night. He seemed to need her, which was so strange given how needy she felt around him.

Memories of the night slipped and rearranged themselves strangely. She'd been a worn-out dishrag after he took her so ruthlessly last night, her knees giving way as she came intensely in response to his pummeling from behind. Then Jonathan's soothing voice filled the space. He praised her as he rubbed her back. Pearls unwound from her wrists. The hall closet had squeaked and then cool lotion, like the aloe vera she used on sunburns, was rubbed into her tanned ass.

When the thick dark wave of sleep overtook her mind, she dreamt. Fragments surfaced. Avery laughed and offered her a glass of red champagne. *Poison*. Mrs. DeCord took it from her and downed it in one gulp. She'd smiled at Christiana.

Christiana had woken with a sticky towel between her legs, a man's arm draped over her ribs and a vivid mental picture of what had gone on in The Oak's Jefferson Suite a few short weeks ago. Before leaving that morning, he'd kissed her until her lips were bruised, which did nothing to stop her mind from spinning.

She'd have to look up the term *sexual Dominant* on her phone when she got home. She certainly couldn't do such a thing at work.

She admonished herself for not Googling the term the second she got home from that first weekend together. Jonathan clearly liked rough sex, and she wasn't sure how much rougher it would develop under this "power dynamic" he talked about. She didn't want to be caught off guard even if she did like how he moved her around with such confidence. His heady craving for her infused her with a strange power—like a delicious cyclone spinning uncontrollably inside.

Christiana went to work clearing a booth littered with reminders of a family's presence, complete with coffee cups stacked by bored children and red wine stains on the linen. At least it wasn't room service duty. She didn't think she could handle seeing Mrs. DeCord. The socialite might deflate her strange—and unexpected—high.

"Snow, snap out of it," Brian said. "We've got big crowds coming in. Let's motivate."

Christiana picked up the tray of dirty dishes and headed to the kitchen. She nearly threw it at a surprised Henrick when her phone vibrated alongside her hip. She fumbled a little bringing it to her ear.

"Christiana."

Her knees almost gave out. No one said her name the way Jonathan could.

"Hi," she said softly.

"You're running yourself ragged, aren't you? We'll have to introduce more recreation into your life."

"Have something in mind?"

He laughed. "Be careful what you wish for. Are you okay?"

"Fine," she said, warmed by his concern.

"I leave for Rhode Island this afternoon. Meeting with constituents. The usual. No one as interesting as you."

His voice penetrated every molecule of her body, and moisture pooled between her legs. She needed to sit down, but her sore ass protested the thought.

"I'll pick you up on Friday," he said.

"Um, I can't leave until Saturday morning. My manager says I have to work." Would this merit another spanking?

He sighed. "Saturday, eight a.m. Take care of yourself 'til then." He ended the call abruptly.

Mark closed the office door and turned to Jonathan, his face grave.

"Who's been following me for the last few days?" Jonathan asked.

"We're not sure, sir. The car's plates aren't traceable. The records are listed as private."

Mark folded his arms behind his back, an automatic signal from his military background that he required orders. Jonathan and Mark understood one another perfectly. Plausible deniability was crucial to their arrangement.

Jonathan deliberated for a few seconds. He had to know who'd been following him before he took Christiana back to

Charlottesville. If he gave the word, Mark would call on favors and could open any records.

"Can you crack them?"

Mark shifted his feet. "Yes, but I didn't know how far you wanted me to take it."

"Do what you need to do. Discreetly, of course."

"As always, sir."

"Let's go. I'm ready for the airport."

He hadn't been to Rhode Island in over a week, and he couldn't dodge any more speeches in his home state. Making a quick trip home also would distance himself from his stalker, not to mention Christiana, who was quickly eating into his daily concentration. Saturday couldn't come soon enough.

Christiana waited just inside the timeworn wooden door of Ireland's Four Provinces, letting her eyes adjust to the dim light. She scanned the room for her father's familiar form.

She'd had to beg Brian to let her leave work early, then cursed the whole way to the Irish bar for losing a night of tips and wages and earning a black mark on her work record.

The nearly empty room smelled of stale beer and dust. A bartender rinsed glasses behind the long, worn wooden bar, and a man shuffled through papers at a table by the door. Her father, slumped on a stool, fiddled with a shot glass.

When he had called, his words didn't make sense, but included something about a "fucking bureaucrat forgetting how to pour." He'd been cut off by the manager and wanted Christiana to clear it up, as if she had bartender clout.

She took the seat next to him. "Dad, you just get back?"

"Chrissy, my Chrisseeeee. Tell 'em I'm fine." His slumped posture and glazed eyes said otherwise. The bartender threw

Christiana a sympathetic look and whispered "Been here a while."

"I've got this." She looped her arm around her father. "Let's go Dad."

Peter pushed himself off the stool and slumped into Christiana's arms like a flounder.

The bartender hopped over the end of the bar and reached out for the other side of the man.

Christiana mouthed, "Sorry," over her father's hanging head.

He gave her a weary smile. "No problem, miss." He'd surely seen worse.

Peter shuddered, a spasm of recognition that he was being led away from the bar. "Chrissy, you're so like your mom."

She tried not to grimace as the stench of stale liquor wafted over her face. "Gee, thanks, Dad."

By the time she and the bartender got him into the front seat of her car, his head bobbed up and down, fighting sleep.

"Can I do anything else?" The guy seemed too young to be a bartender, more like a college student himself.

"No, thanks. Really, I appreciate your help."

"I'm sorry to tell you this, but he can't come back."

Christiana looked up over the hood at him. Why was she surprised?

"I mean, this is the third time and—"

"No, don't worry. Like you said, it isn't like this hasn't happened before." She forced out a huffed laugh as she opened her door and slipped inside. Her father's head hung down in a dead sleep. What did Jonathan say about discipline? Maybe it was time for her father to receive some. If her dad was still out of it when they got home, she'd leave him in the car.

"Anyone tailing?" Jonathan didn't look up from his phone, as he deleted two e-mail messages from Yvette. *Too many damned e-mails.* Carson had messaged she'd acquiesced to a coffee meeting, and Yvette later reported him "adequate." Jonathan chuckled to himself. Carson would serve her needs soon, and, in fact, probably better than he ever could.

"Mark?"

"No, sir." Mark pulled into the drop-off area in front of Reagan International Airport. "Wait. Don't get out."

Jonathan snapped his head up to glimpse a black sedan with government tags creep by. Hundreds of such cars rolled through Washington's closest airport. Still, the way it slowed had been suspicious.

"Is that our man?" Jonathan asked.

"Hard to tell."

"Well, try to catch up with him. See what you can find."

Jonathan swung his long legs out of the sedan and slammed the door shut as Mark pulled away, cutting off a taxi, earning a horn blare of outrage.

Jonathan headed into the crush of humanity. Even though he had to fly commercial, it was better than risking the black sedan following him all the way to Rhode Island or later to *Covil Sereia*. Few people knew about his Charlottesville home. He intended to keep it that way.

Christiana scrolled through her phone, viewing pages of Google references to Jonathan Brond. The mystery of his life scratched at her insides like poison ivy. She needed answers, though she wasn't sure of all the questions. She finally had time to explore, having the night off unexpectedly, thanks to her father. Her Dad had passed out in his room down the hall. He wouldn't bother her until morning.

The small screen filled with pictures of Jonathan at fundraisers, giving speeches, and standing in crowds in front of the capitol building. Shots with other women flew across her phone screen—more than a few.

She wondered how many of them signed his NDAs, got the chance to sit on his deck in the mountains or slip between his bedcovers? A bolt of envy arrowed through her heart. She couldn't imagine any woman fighting a craving to lie down for him. Was she a freak to yearn for his rough hands and commands to open for him? Hell, right now she inched her knees apart under the simple memory of his warm palm coming down on her tender backside.

How many other women did he spank like a child?

Christiana reminded herself of their exclusive arrangement and struggled to stem her rising jealousy.

At the bottom of a long list of image thumbnails, Christiana found one lone picture of him as a boy, standing next to a dark-haired woman, identified as his mother. Even through the low resolution of the screen, her eyes smiled a deep green, like Jonathan's. His hair shone almost white in contrast to his tan. *Adorable*. Then she found more pictures of him with a different older woman with short hair swept into a bob, simply identified as Mrs. James Brond.

Jonathan's bio was typical: education, committee posts, and bills he sought to pass.

Christiana typed in *sexual dominance*, but her phone chirped before anything downloaded. *Shit, I didn't call the dishwasher guy—or Avery.* Avery's barrage of text messages had grown increasingly nasty, accusing Christiana of avoiding her. Her accusations were true. Yet if Avery knew why, the occasional mean text messages would turn into an avalanche burying Christiana alive. She'd better answer this one.

"Hi, Avery."

"Jesus, Chris. Don't you ever look at your phone?"

Oh, if you only knew. "It's been a tough day, that's all."

"Yeah, well, we need to start talking about the Fourth of July. The fashion show isn't going to plan itself."

Shit, she forgot she'd promised to help backstage at the club's annual fundraiser. "No, of course. What are you modeling this year?"

"I'm done with that. I'm picking the models and showing them how it's done."

Christiana couldn't believe Avery would give up the spotlight. But maybe Christiana wasn't the only one who'd been evolving.

"So, it's time we went out, girl," Avery said. "You don't work Tuesdays, and we can plan then."

A spear dipped in toxic shame and guilt pierced her heart. "Of course."

"Good. Chase's brother is the bouncer at Ireland's Four Provinces. We're so going to check out the rugby players."

"What if we get caught?" *What if they recognize me?*

"We won't. Chase has it all set up."

Of course, Christiana ended up agreeing. Avery had a way of making Christiana do things—not unlike a man named Jonathan Brond. She'd spent three years wearing Avery's clothes, going to Avery's country club, and trailing after her from event to event. Never once did she want to do any of it. She'd just wanted a friend.

After hanging up, she returned to Googling to distract her from guilty thoughts. She felt awful, lying to her friend, not being around for her father, and missing out on work too much.

She erased "sexual dominance" and put in Jonathan's

name. His picture smiled from her phone screen, white teeth set in impossibly smooth, tanned skin. Green eyes reached inside her, even from a dated photograph.

Wait, something wasn't right.

The web revealed hundreds of articles and pictures on Jonathan. Her father's voice rang in her head. "Look beyond what you see, Chrissy. What *isn't* there?"

Recreation. It was mostly related to work. Jonathan Brond did a good job of keeping his private life, very private. Nothing about golfing and fishing trips, common public pursuits of other members of Congress. No picture of his boat. His house in Charlottesville was nowhere to be found. Surely someone would have mentioned his private residence. Yet thirty-six pages deep into Google, not even a single mention existed. The weight of the NDA she'd signed pressed down on her chest.

17

Christiana answered the door before Jonathan had a chance to ring the bell. Her father had hit the road last night, but she didn't want to chance even a neighbor might hear.

Jonathan held a too-small umbrella though she recognized it as a Hermes pattern similar to Avery's collection. Though his loose blue linen shirt clung wetly to his torso in the downpour, he still looked like a magazine model.

"Jesus, Christiana, you look like hell."

"Well, good morning to you, too."

"Do you have a pillow you can bring? You need to nap in the car."

She had already swiped concealer over her dark circles and drunk two cups of coffee. Friday evening shifts were late nights, but the tips made it worth the five hours of sleep.

As soon as they were settled into his car, the wisdom of the pillow hit. She bunched up the pillow in the doorframe and drifted off. Windshield wipers squeaked across the glass, and Jonathan's fingers tucked some hair behind her ear.

The door gave way under her head, and she startled. They'd arrived. She barely managed her seatbelt before

Jonathan lifted her from the front seat as if she weighed no more than a dried leaf. She let herself snuggle deeply into his chest all the way into the house. With each step forward, his strength awakened her insides even though she stayed relaxed in his arms.

He carried her straight to his bedroom. While still standing, he moved her back into a wall and swung her so she wrapped her legs around his waist. His tongue twisted deep inside her mouth, as he raked his hands up under her t-shirt and cupped the side of her breasts, mashed against his hard pecs. Christiana pushed into his massaging hands and groaned into his kiss, tugging fruitlessly on the buttons of his shirt.

Jonathan pulled his mouth from her buzzing lips and drew her legs down until she stood. He stepped backward. His eyes blazed a trail down the length of her body. He ripped his shirt over his head, buttons popping and skittering across the floor.

Christiana pulled her t-shirt from her body and kicked off her jeans and panties in seconds. It still felt like it took too long. She had craved this moment, and now, rested from her car nap, she couldn't wait another minute. Christiana's need to feel him between her legs decimated any leftover inhibitions she may have harbored.

He pressed her whole body deep into the bed with his own, his erection hot marble digging into her pelvic bone. His hands dug into her plump butt cheeks, and his mouth devoured her moans. His rough, possessive treatment held no hesitation.

When he released his kiss, his eyes suffused her in heat. "Stay down. Lie back." He crawled down her body. His fingers gently breached her folds and before she had time to consider what he saw, his mouth greedily kissed her slick opening. Startled by the attack, she started to jerk her knees away, but his strong arms held her legs open.

His tongue lashed her center, drawing small circles, then larger, assaulting her sensitive nub. Unable to lie still, her thighs clamped his head, and she cried out at the intensity of his mouth tormenting her clit.

Jonathan grabbed both her wrists and held them down by her side. She fisted the silky fabric, arching from the sensation. *Too much. More.*

She exploded.

He gripped her forearms as she convulsed, squirming and bucking. Comets of firework rockets ran the length of her body as she panted. As the flash inside subsided, her breathing slowed in time with his mouth, which stilled to soft kisses on her shuddering seam.

Jonathan climbed up to cage her underneath him. His thighs spread her wide. When his cock speared her, hard and fast, she bit a cry into his shoulder.

He pulled back and lifted her hips, so they rested on his quads. After grasping her legs, he pulled her back and forth over his cock.

"Oh, Christ, *fuck.*" He scooped her up by her butt until she sat on his lap. "Hang on to me."

Christiana ground her pelvis against every downward stroke. The tip of his cock banged her inner most nerves, and pleasure-pain burst throughout her body. Puffs of air escaped her lungs with each spear forward. *More.*

"Jonathan."

His sweaty, rough chin scratched her face. "You are so wet and tight."

Another orgasm ripped through her, and still he didn't stop reaming her insides. Ten minutes? Thirty minutes? An eternity? She didn't know. She didn't care. Jonathan lay between her legs. *My legs.*

∾

Jonathan stood at his office window watching a starling flit from branch to branch. He'd let Christiana catch another hour of sleep. He could afford to wait a bit longer because he now knew the approach he'd take to solidify Christiana's sexual submission.

On the drive down, Christiana had huddled in his front seat, clutching her pink pillow more like an infant cherub than the woman-girl now set free. How quickly she morphed into a feminine temptress when they arrived, her eyes smoldering with uninhibited want and devotion. She responded with gusto to his inability to hold back.

She was ready for the shorter, sharper introduction to his dominance. Some women required a more sensual persuasion to join his brand of sexual fulfillment. Christiana was not that woman. She relished being taken. She'd surrendered her body fully underneath him, even after her discipline earlier in the week.

The whooshing of the fax machine spitting out page after page of endless legal documents masked her entrance to the room.

"The rain stopped." She crossed the room and engulfed his torso in a hug. A waylaid strand of blond hair, still wet from the shower, trailed over one cheek. She looked so fuckable. But, then, when had she not?

"You look good in my shirt."

"It smells like you." Her rumpled hair and sleepy eyes radiated an innocence that nearly overwhelmed his resolve. *Almost.* She pulled back, little creases between her eyes deepening. Something dark plagued her thoughts.

"Tell me what you're thinking, Christiana."

"Oh, it's nothing."

"Christiana." He hoped she caught his warning tone. He

wouldn't tolerate a repeat of her radio silence earlier in the week.

She dipped her head. "I've been meaning to ask you something, that's all."

He sat in his chair and pulled her into his lap. "Go ahead. You can ask me anything."

"Did you ever bring Mrs. DeCord here?"

Ah, The Oak. Where she worked. Jonathan tamped down the flicker of suspicion that Yvette herself may have breached their confidentiality. Not possible, he admonished. Yvette had as much to lose from their liaisons as he did.

He ran a fingertip along the shell of her ear. "How do you know Mrs. DeCord?"

"She rents The Oak's suite upstairs sometimes. And, I, ah . . . deliver room service sometimes. I didn't really *see* anything. I thought I heard—"

"What?"

"You." She lowered her gaze.

"You might have." Jonathan learned long ago that honesty could derail the most heinous gossip, if handled properly. "Did you know what was happening?"

"No. But will you show me what you did with her?"

Jesus. So unexpected. "I never talk about my other submissives."

"More than one? How many have you had?"

"Mrs. DeCord and I are no longer involved in that way. Remember, I said we'd be exclusive."

"You also said I could ask you anything."

"Generalities only. No personal details about others. But, to answer you—about a dozen."

Her jaw went slack.

"I do like that you're jealous, however," he said.

She crossed her arms. "I am *not* jealous. I'm curious."

"About?"

"What you did together. I mean, if it was more . . . ." Her inquisitive look went straight to his loins. God, he loved that look of craving coupled with the will to please.

"Nothing more than what we're going to do together. If you trust me," he said.

"You keep saying that. I do."

"Hmmm. Well, trust is new territory for you." *The understatement of the century.*

Her eyes flashed. "I. trust. you."

"Okay, little firebrand. I'm going to hold you to that." He set her on her feet and stood himself. "Now you must be starving."

"Sorry I slept so late." She followed him out of his office.

"You needed it."

She required more than sleep. Her life as caretaker to an alcoholic father and ego-booster to a diva offered little room for expectations that her needs might come first. He vowed she'd experience that first from him, even temporarily.

Christiana took a large bite of her sandwich, the avocado squeezing from either side of the bread. Apple-smoked, crispy bacon. Cilantro-marinated shrimp. And the mayonnaise was handmade with just the right hint of tart lemon. *Yum.* She couldn't remember the last time she'd eaten.

"I think you like the sandwich," he teased.

"Mmm." She licked avocado that had escaped.

"You look better—rested."

She laughed. "I've snoozed more here than I did all week."

"We'll need to change that."

She wasn't sure whether he meant sleeping more at home or sleeping less with him. Everything that came out of his mouth sounded suggestive.

"You like sex," he said.

She looked up at him and swallowed the lump of sandwich.

"You like it a little rough too." He took another bite.

"Um, I don't know."

"When I spanked you the other night, you were wet. Then when we got here . . . ." He wiped his hands on a napkin. "You responded immediately to my taking you."

She sipped her milk, not sure how to respond. Ever since Jonathan pushed his cock inside her, she got the big deal. "I did what you asked. I just felt."

"Pleasure, pain. It's all sensation, no? There's a fine line between the two."

"I don't know about that."

"I do." He swiveled her stool to face him and encircled both her wrists with his warm, large hands. "Tell me, Christiana, when you thought about being with a man, what did you imagine? Your ideal, your fantasy." His eyes told her he really wanted an answer and that he would know if she lied.

An image of Jonathan making love to her forever, the smells of *Covil Sereia*—cedar trees and honeysuckle and leather wafting over her body—shocked her insides as much as her next thought. The exhilaration of his wild, sexual energy, holding her down and spearing her to the core had colored her fantasies the entire last week. Being worked over by his fire made her brave.

And then there was the strange sensation of his hands coming down hard on her ass when she worried him by not being available? She'd never had anyone worry about her like Jonathan.

"Like what we've been doing," she said. At least that was part of it.

"You've liked what we've done so far?"

She nodded.

"When I told you that I have specific types of relationships, that I'm a sexual Dominant, it didn't scare you." It wasn't a question.

"No. I didn't really know what you meant." She looked down at her hands, still held captive by Jonathan's grip. "But then I looked it up. Online, I mean. That's when I got more . . . concerned. You said I always have a say, right?"

She'd been trying to forget the images she finally Googled last night in the Cabinet Room on a break. People clad in black leather and latex, tubes jutting from their faces had set her heart racing. Then it got worse. Ball gags lodged in women's mouths, their eyes open wide in frightened desire as men lorded over their backsides, doing things she'd never entertained.

"I should have been with you." He released one wrist, raised her chin with his index finger, and then tucked a stray piece of hair behind her ear. "What bothered you the most?"

"The women, in pictures. They looked, I don't know."

"Afraid?"

"Yes, and in pain." Damn, her eyes misted. She didn't understand why she liked it when Jonathan had held her down, but seeing someone else? She knew Jonathan wouldn't really hurt her. She wouldn't be here, if so. But she also knew he hadn't told her everything.

No matter. She wanted more, not even knowing what *more* might entail. She'd dance on the edge of this addiction, this obsession named Jonathan Brond, until she bled.

He puffed out a burst of air, agitated. He shook his head slowly back and forth. "Damn Internet. Why didn't you call me that night? You should always call me immediately whenever anything, and I mean *anything*, arises that causes you discomfort."

The sides of Christiana's mouth quirked up in a half-smile. Jonathan's chivalry was beyond anything she'd ever encountered. He cared. Not like the false niceties she'd received from the legislative aides, politicians and society ladies who oozed unctuous praises and commendations. Christiana was sure Jonathan rarely said anything he didn't mean.

Jonathan captured her eyes. "What you didn't see was the consent behind those activities. In our world, it's an egregious act to do anything whatsoever to a person—anything at all—if they don't want it, if they don't permit it. That's why I asked you from the beginning, at each step along the way, to tell me what you're thinking."

"So, you won't—" she started.

"I won't do anything you don't give permission for, willingly and eagerly. You can stop me at any time. Remember that." He captured both wrists.

His words soothed her inner parts, the truth washing away any doubts. Yes, he had asked for her assent along the way. *Repeatedly.*

"Okay," she said.

"I will only give you what you really need, Christiana." Jonathan's fingers played with her wrist line, and it was oddly comforting to have her hands held down in her lap.

"What I need?"

"Yes, my lovely. You have a lot of need. You're overwhelmed with responsibility and starved for passion. This summer I'm devoting myself to showing you a different way."

"I'd like different. I like . . . ."

"What?"

"What you do to me."

When he released her wrists, an empty feeling crawled up her arms.

He stood. "Good. You're ready for more education."

18

Christiana perched herself on the edge of the bed. Jonathan stood in the open doorway, silhouetted by the dusky light streaming from the hall's skylights. His imposing stance only added to the uncertainty. She straightened, her body on high alert. Something serious was about to happen.

Jonathan hit a switch near the door, and she gasped. Soft red lights shot up from unseen areas near the floorboards and down from recessed lights in the high ceiling. The room seemed to change shape, glowing a deep cerise with tall shadows cast up the walls by the bed's richly carved posts. She hadn't paid attention before to the profound incisions forming filigrees and vines along the columns. Now their dark shadows snaked up the posts in the menacing crimson light.

Jonathan stepped inside the room and wordlessly stripped off his blue t-shirt, baring his muscle-honed chest.

He glanced to the bed, his green eyes darker in the rosy glow. "Three years ago, when it looked like I was headed to Congress, I built this house. The builders were told it was for an elderly couple, one of whom was paralyzed from the waist down and, hence, required certain adaptations."

Jonathan's deliberate tone stilled her heartbeat, stopped her breath. She got the distinct feeling he shared something important, and she didn't want even the sound of her own inhalations to mask her hearing.

She couldn't make out the details of his face, but she knew he stood appraising her, only his determined eyes piercing the dark. He fingered a small remote and a length of black fabric. Would he blindfold her again?

"Only seven know of the modifications of this house. That includes a master craftsman, an electrician, Blanca, Mark, and now you," he said.

He aimed the remote toward the ceiling. Two large panels recessed into the wall, revealing built-in drawers and cabinet doors. Instruments hung from brass pegs above them. Before her eyes and brain could interpret what she saw, whirring sounds tore her eyes upward from the secret closet.

Panels above the bed pulled back, exposing a lattice of steel grids and tracks. Flecks of red light glinted off hooks and carabineers tethered to thin girders. Bunches of dark blue fabric unfurled around Christiana, and she jumped, shrinking into the pillows.

"What is all this?" Her eyes darted back to Jonathan. "I-I don't think I like this."

Jonathan came around to stand next to the bed. He beckoned to her. "You needn't be scared. Nothing in this room is going to hurt you. *I* will never hurt you."

She took his hand and eased herself down, her shoulder brushing one of the swaths of silk that hung from the ceiling. As soon as her feet hit the floor, the smell of leather engulfed her senses.

Jonathan's hand released her trembling fingers. He spun her, so she faced the bed. He slipped the shirt off her shivering frame and whisked her panties down her hips. "Step out of them," he directed.

She obeyed.

Jonathan's warm arms encircled her body, holding her almost too tightly. But she didn't want him to let go. She dug her fingernails into his forearms to feel his hardness and reconnect with his protective male presence. His familiar scent, coupled with honeysuckle and leather, permeated the room. *Expensive* leather, she corrected herself mentally. *Like the tack room at the Washington Rosemont Country Club stables.*

Jonathan breathed heat on her neck. "Ever since I ran into you at the club that first time, I've wanted to share this with you, Christiana."

He held out the remote and pressed another button.

Her brain couldn't catch up with her eyes. A wide upholstered beam, suspended from four wires, lowered from the opening over the bed. Blood coursing through her ears shut out the electrical sounds of its descent. Finally the device hovered a few inches above the bed, revealing its true shape —an isosceles triangle, three feet on a side, covered in a deep blue suede.

"The suspension bench is connected to the grid above, so it can be maneuvered around the bed. It even swivels 180 degrees for more access options." Jonathan moved her toward it. With one arm, he pulled the triangular bench toward them, swinging it in front of her legs.

"What?"

"It's a device to restrain you, make your body available to me."

Available?

Jonathan released his hold and pulled her hands behind her back. Fabric swished as Jonathan wrapped something around her wrists, securing them together. She yanked at the binding, and he clucked. "I'm simply restraining your hands."

All the new sensations, the scent of leather mixed with Jonathan's musk, the electrical sounds, the red lights, Jonathan's voice, laden with intent, crammed in on her until she had to concentrate on breathing. Christiana was more than in over her head. She sat adrift in an ocean she didn't know existed. The Internet hadn't, *couldn't,* prepare her for this.

"What if I can't, if I don't want to?" She stared at the blue swing.

His hands stopped and the fabric slipped away from her wrists. "Then you don't have to," he said softly behind her. "We can leave here."

Her hands fisted on either side of her legs. "Can we just be here without all this?"

Jonathan stepped backward, his skin leaving her skin. "No." The loss of his body was immediate and unbearable.

She turned and looked Jonathan square in the face. His features stilled, as if waiting for her response. The pivotal moment hung heavy in the space between.

"This is what I meant by sexual dominance, Christiana. This is part of who I am."

Jonathan's gaze softened, as if understanding the weight of what he asked. But his features remained resolute. She knew he needed this—whatever it was—and he wouldn't change his mind.

The next thought nearly broke her heart. *If I don't do this, he'll let me go.*

If she wasn't brave enough to try whatever he had in mind, she'd return to her life, and he would return to his. *Apart.*

Images of her world flipped through her mind, a deck of life cards showing her the same options over and over. She could go back to her old world. Relive the summer she'd had each of the last three years. Long weekends waitressing, afternoons by a county club pool with Avery, and events with her father to make sure he got home okay. Then she'd go back to school: classes, exams and the occasional frat party with drunken boys ogling her breasts, sending beer breath over her face as they swayed in house hallways. More Jeffrey Daniels clones.

It wasn't what she wanted. What did she want?

Jonathan took her hand, the only contact he allowed. His thumb brushed over her knuckles and with that touch, a simple truth surfaced. Nothing else mattered but Jonathan.

She could not unknow Jonathan Brond. He would forever be a presence—a model of what she would crave. A primal need to please him rose up. She would deny this man nothing.

Christiana turned back to face the bed, crossing her wrists behind her back.

"Good girl." Jonathan's breath wafted over her neck as he wound silky fabric around her arms, binding her hands, one crossed over the other. "I'm just asking you to try. Remember, you can quit at any time."

She knew she wouldn't.

Jonathan placed his hands on the back of her thighs. She parted her feet, giving him access without thought. She pushed her ass against his crotch, his hardening manhood.

"You're more than ready. You need to trust yourself . . . and me."

He swung the wider end of the upholstered bench seat so it connected with her skin.

"I'll help you lower yourself." His hand pressed her bound hands into the small of her back while his other arm circled her chest.

She settled face down on the bench, the soft suede connecting with her quivering torso. The beam's length ran from above her sternum to her pelvic bone, leaving her head to hang over the blunted, narrower end. Her breasts hung down on either side of the board, her hips on the wider part of the bench, leaving her legs to dangle off the base. A notch in the wider end ensured her pussy would be as exposed as possible. She flushed at what he could see. *What he's already seen.*

Jonathan's hands gently lifted each breast to check if they were caught, grazing her nipples against the silk. She wiggled. Her heartbeat punched at the light padding under her chest, and her harsh pants rasped.

"I had this bench made specifically for your body length. It should support you well." He reached under the bench, and with a sound of Velcro separating, he pulled two large straps from underneath.

"These will hold you on more securely." One thick soft strap went round her lower back. The other secured her to the bench under her bra-line, if she'd been wearing one. She did feel more stable, as the bench was not as wide as she originally thought.

"The bench covering and fastenings are made of the softest materials available. Your skin is so delicate, any marks will come from my own hand and nothing else."

Next, he wound a loop of midnight-blue silk fabric around one thigh, tugged, and suspended her leg outward, frog-like. He did the same with her other one. More adjustments drew the fabric even tauter.

"Is that too much, Christiana?" He caressed her ass as he spoke. "You need to have good circulation. You're going to be here a while. Anything pinching? Any numbness?"

"No, it's fine." *Fine?*

"Good. This is parachute silk like they use in Cirque du Soleil. It'll burn if rubbed too harshly. You tell me if that begins to happen."

She nodded, her ability to speak departed. Her mind

offered images of circus performers nimbly flipping over hoops and adroitly gliding through the air. Those images did little to make her feel graceful.

Another whooshing sound and her body spilled forward so her head hung lower than her ass. Her pussy lay bared for observation. She blushed anew.

"You're beautiful. Glistening with need already." His breathing grew raspier.

She couldn't suppress a faint moan when he ran a finger up her inner folds.

The bench suddenly pivoted, and her head faced his crotch, bulging with an erection. Thin straps were drawn over her forehead and across her chin, lifting and supporting her head. "We don't want your neck to strain. Good?"

"It's . . . good." She surprised herself she could speak that much.

He made more adjustments, checking the silk fabric. She hung semi-suspended, bound and helpless, open to anything he wanted to do to her.

Jonathan pulled fabric over her head, covering her eyes, though he secured the blindfold with a gentle touch. Her descent into blackness nearly swamped her with panic. But then his hand lay lightly on her head, and she tuned into his presence. An odd calmness settled over her as a peculiar arousal surfaced. The desire to resist faded.

"I'm going to lift you a little higher, lovely." Another whirring sound and the bench rose a few inches. It spun. His hand disconnected from her skin. Where was she facing?

She lost her orientation until Jonathan's rich voice filled the room. With no other distraction, her attention narrowed on him with the total dedication a hunting dog gave to a fox. Maybe that was the whole point?

"Now, I'm going to reiterate our agreement."

He let silence settle between them, ostensibly giving her time to catch up to his words.

"When we are here, you will surrender the control of your body to me. I will take you, hard and often. You will come only with my permission. You will not protest. If you do, there will be discipline. If you accept, I will service you well."

His voice circled. He must be pacing.

"You will not be hurt or harmed in any way that is permanent. The most you'll suffer is discomfort and sore muscles."

She felt his hot breath near her face. "You'll also find ecstasy." His hand connected with her cheek. "Do you accept?"

"Y-yes, Jonathan." Her ability to say "no" had long left.

"You will address me as 'sir' and nothing else while we're here."

She nodded as well as she could with her head restrained.

"Let me hear you say it, Christiana."

She swallowed. "Yes, sir."

A lump of fabric settled into the open palm of her bound hands. "These are your panties, the ones you gave me the first night I picked you up at The Oak."

She fingered the wad of cotton in her hand. "Oh."

"Hang on to them. If anything gets too much, drop them. I'll stop everything and get you out and in my arms within seconds. Do you understand?" His voice had softened, but she had a feeling it wouldn't last.

"Yes . . . sir."

A motor sound engaged and vibrations coursed through her limbs, now strung tight from the bonds. The bench moved. She flinched, instantly disoriented.

"You're safe. I'm moving you further onto the bed."

The movement stopped. Jonathan ran his fingers through her hair and began twisting it, as if putting her hair into a braid. A moan escaped her lips. The pulls on her scalp felt too good.

"What have you liked about our time together so far?" he asked softly.

Christiana knew what he sought. He wasn't talking about dining al fresco on his deck, waking up in his arms, or even the pounding sex that made her climax within minutes. He wanted to know what she would allow and might like right now. Did she have a choice?

A shameful tear slid from her eye, escaping from the blindfold.

"You can tell me," Jonathan said.

"I like it when you pull my hair," she whispered.

"What else?"

"And when you slapped . . . ."

"Your ass?"

"Yes."

His hands left one plait against her back. "Never be ashamed of how you like to be pleasured, Christiana."

Long minutes passed of trialing kisses along her back. His chest hair tickled her bottom as he bent over her bound and helpless body. Her shame quieted. He ran his hand down the length of her spine to rest on a bare ass cheek.

"Tell me, right now, what is exciting you?" he asked. "What is making you wet?"

"You." She shocked herself with her own honesty.

The mattress dipped, and her nipples brushed the bed. His hand palmed her breast. He must be lying next to her.

"You like being bound? Knowing I can do anything I want to your succulent pussy, your mouth or your ass?"

The effect of his words bewildered her for a second. But then her arousal spiked as his hands ran down the length of her body. She should be scared. Terrified. She'd never relinquished control of her life to anyone. So why was she doing so now, being restrained so completely and thoroughly, and why was it making her whole body quake with need? She could barely understand who she was at that moment.

She heard denim rustling, then the clink of a belt hitting the floor. His strong quads leaned into her, hairs prickling the small patches of skin exposed between the parachute silks. His thick cock lay nestled up her butt crack.

His voice came close to her ear. "I'm going to help you let go. To bring down that carefully constructed wall you've built. Tonight you will come hard and often, on my command."

Christiana couldn't suppress a whimper of indignity—or was that hunger?

"Now, open up lovely." His hand cupped her jaw, and his index finger slipped between her lips. She opened up her mouth, and a long thick cylinder covered in terrycloth fabric slid between her teeth. She bit down, testing the give of the rubbery interior.

"This will muffle your screams," he said. "Now you know you can let go completely, not feel inhibited in any way. When you do, I'll remove it."

"Mmmnnnn…" She shook her head.

"Shhh, yes, Christiana. Relax into it."

She settled her lips over the cloth. It instantly moistened with saliva. She pulled more air through her nose, willing herself to calm, sending her awareness through each part of her body. Long seconds passed as he rubbed her lower back, as if lulling a baby to sleep.

"You ache for my command, don't you? Your need to accept my control is as strong as my need to deliver it."

Jonathan's voice wound inside her, and she trembled at his words. She didn't want to accept his words as true. What did that say about her? Yet her grip on her panties hardened.

His torso left her back. Then his hands wrapped around

either side of her inner thighs. Her whole body jumped when his thumbs reached her swollen lower lips, spreading them open more. Warm, firm lips closed over her needy slit. She shook as his tongue trailed up one of her inner lips and down the other. She moaned into the gag.

His breath caressed her splayed-out pussy. "You're delicious. I'm going to savor the taste of you with my tongue, before letting you fall to pieces."

Air rushed through her nose as her heart accelerated. Her legs wobbled in the silk bindings, and Jonathan steadied her with his hands. She tried to be still but his mouth joined her clit, his tongue working her like a juicy delicacy. Her whole world shrank to that contact. She careened off a cliff into wild pleasure in seconds. She screamed her orgasm into the gag, bright lights dancing behind the blindfold. A rustle of fabric mixed with her moans. Her back strained against the straps and bindings, as tremors rocked her inside and out. Jonathan's arms circled her legs and held them as he lapped at her juices like a starving man, making no effort to hide the wet sucking sounds.

His wicked tongue brought her body back up. A desperate sound erupted from her throat. Jonathan stopped his assault on her overwrought nerves. She teetered on a climactic precipice. A strong breeze would tip her over the edge.

His moist kisses left a damp trail as he worked his way up her bound limb. He smacked her ass with a chuckle. The suspended bench swung forward, her nipples brushing the bedcover.

"God, you come like a lioness. But next time, lovely, you'll wait for my permission. No matter what I'm doing to you."

His permission? Was he kidding?

"Yes, only by my command," he said.

Mind reader.

Jonathan released the mouth gag. It hit the bed with a soft plunk.

His voice grew clipped. "You'll learn to obey my every demand, no matter how slight, won't you, little one?"

He reached around to her breast and pinched one of the rosebuds. She captured her bottom lip in her teeth as a cry broke from her throat. "Y-yes, sir."

Without warning, Jonathan slipped his cock into her wet opening, sending her forward a few inches. She groaned as her nipples reacted to the subtle scratch across the duvet.

He stayed inside her, unmoving, for several minutes, even when she began whimpering like a lost puppy.

She clenched her internal muscles, trying to create friction. "J-Jon . . . Please. Please, sir."

"You didn't wait for consent, so you earned a punishment. What is your favorite number?"

"W-what?" Was this a distraction technique?

His hand slapped her ass once.

"Forty-two," she said quickly.

"Very good. You will count each of my strokes. You aren't to come until we reach forty-two."

He had to be joking. She would explode at any moment. He withdrew and pushed back in slowly.

"One," she said as his cock arched into her and hit the most delicious spot, dragged back inch by inch until his head teased her opening. His cockhead then slipped back in, along the topside of her passage.

"Oh, God. Two."

She tried to time her breath with the next eight but found the rhythm only brought her closer to her peak. Concentrating on her inhalations didn't help. Neither did sending her focus to his hands, clutching at her hips, reminding her of his control and possession.

The more she thought about not coming, the more she wanted to release.

"Oh," she moaned. "You're too good."

He chortled. "Flattery won't lessen your punishment, Christiana. Now, be good . . . for me."

She wanted to be—good and bad and feel like this, always. She clenched her inner muscles in hopes of causing her orgasm to retreat. A prick of perspiration across her forehead gave her something else to think of for about one second. Then it was back to Jonathan's cock drawing through her cream.

At twenty-three, her throat released cries each time he sunk into her. Her legs quivered in their silk prisons.

Jonathan growled behind her, making his strokes longer, sending his pelvis to join her behind.

"Twenty-nine. Please, please. I really can't."

The wicked man sped up his pace. "Yes, you can, and you will." His breathing labored like a marathon runner. He seized her hipbones, raising her up. He rocked her slightly forward, her nipples grazing the silk underneath. "Count," he growled.

"Thirty."

The distance between relief and his relentless jackhammering grew longer, not shorter.

"Thirty-one."

She couldn't swallow, just pant. She gripped the fabric in her hands, now dank from her clammy palms. A wet stain must be spreading near her cheek on the coverlet. "I'm going—"

Jonathan grabbed her hair and pulled her head up slightly. "You will not."

"I-I won't," she breathed.

Thirty-eight, thirty-nine, forty.

"You'll come with me, Christiana." He slammed forward.

"With me." He sent his cock crashing into her swollen, desperate insides.

"Forty-one." Her raw voice gave out, her number barely audible.

He thrust one final time. "Now," he grated between his teeth.

She released a hoarse cry. Sparks flew down her legs. Streaks of light obscured everything, but the convulsions that shattered her consciousness. Her contractions milked Jonathan's cock, hilted inside her. Pulsing, sporadic jerks of his cock prolonged her orgasm. She let go and rode the sensation down a seemingly endless mountainside. She landed at the bottom, spent, sated and filled.

Bit by bit, her skin tuned into the drapes encasing her and Jonathan's hands clutching her hips.

Her blindfold disappeared, and she blinked in the low red lighting. He lay down next to her on his back and stared up at the ceiling. His nostrils flared in time with his chest rising and falling. He placed one large hand on her shoulder, connecting with her skin. Her body instantly silenced, tremors from her orgasm stopping under his touch.

They both panted, wordlessly, for some minutes. Christiana didn't move—couldn't move—even when Jonathan's fluids leaked between her legs to the bed cover. The heat from their lovemaking faded, and a chill ran over her damp skin.

"Forty-two might be my new favorite number," he said.

She snickered. It certainly would remain hers.

Jonathan unwound each leg from their silk bindings, slowly, deliberately.

Her head hung down fully, neck muscles elongating deliciously in the stretch. When he ripped the thick black straps from around her middle, she took in a large, opening breath.

Jonathan rubbed her shoulders and sent a trail of kisses

down her back. Each movement, slow and cautious, combined with his whispers, solidified his lesson: Patience came with great rewards. When he lifted her off the suspension bench, a small tremor rumbled through her core.

He untied her wrists, and only when he held out his hand did she release the panties into his open palm.

19

Christiana leaned against the warmed shower tile walls and let his touches mix with the water streaming down her torso. Jonathan ran his fingers through her hair. Sparks erupted within her scalp.

They stood cocooned in the shower. Steam clouded the glass until the trees through the corner window walls lost all detail and morphed into blots of dark, waving masses. She wished she and Jonathan could never leave.

Somber thoughts invaded from corners of her mind. She could feel their weight squeezing out the euphoria she'd felt from the last few hours.

"You're conflicted." His whispered voice echoed against the glass and tile.

"Very." She exhaled heavily, releasing the strangeness that had settled within her after being so delicately unwrapped from Jonathan's sex cradle. "Suspension bench" wasn't close to how it made her feel, though time did suspend. Now unbound, her logical side made an ugly reappearance.

Her father, Avery, the Churchills, all of them peered down at her from some unnamed plane, faces stamped with disdain for allowing such blatantly wanton behavior as she'd displayed in the last twenty-four hours. Hell, the last few weeks. She could have said "No" to Jonathan. She should have said "No." It would have been the correct thing to do.

The weekend's events bore witness to what she'd always suspected. Her life had never been normal, perhaps because *she* wasn't normal. Regular nineteen-year-old college girls went to football games and flirted with frat boys or their twenty-something bosses during internships. They didn't sneak around with famous people doing . . . what had they been doing?

Jonathan turned her and drew her into his arms.

"Tell me." His voice reverberated from his torso and into hers, held captive by the muscled planes of his chest. She couldn't deny she loved being like this, so close to his strength. His words moved through her whole body. His power was never so evident as when he spoke.

"It feels, oh, I don't know." Of course, she didn't have the words to match, as usual.

He pulled back a little. "Deviant?" The corner of his mouth quirked up.

She nodded.

"Remember what I said. Never be ashamed about how you like to be pleasured," he said.

Christiana laid her head against him. She wasn't in the mood to talk, her black thoughts sapping any remaining good mood.

"Talk to me, Christiana."

Talking. Always talking. "I don't know what to say. It's just—"

"What, lovely?"

"I'm neglecting things at home . . . work . . . I really should be . . . ." She actually didn't know. "Can we change the subject?"

Jonathan stroked her hair and placed a kiss on the top of her head. "Okay, tell me how you got that scar across your forehead."

No way. She'd never tell the perfect Jonathan Brond about her damaged childhood. No words could describe what happened that day anyway—or any of the other days.

"I don't remember. I know it's ugly."

"Nothing on you is ugly. I worry about your headaches." He put his hands alongside her cheeks and lifted her face. The kindness in his eyes cracked her humiliation.

"I was really young. All kids have accidents."

"Hmmm."

"Didn't you ever get into trouble as a kid?" she teased.

"Repeatedly."

"Tell me something about when you were little." Christiana hugged his middle tighter. If she could stay here for the rest of her life, she would. Forget about dishwashers and measuring the liquor in her father's bottle and even feeling abnormal. He had a way of calming her quickly, even if he did try to extract things better left buried.

"I'm afraid that's classified," he said.

"Oh, please? Your stories have to be more interesting than mine. Where'd you get this?" She rubbed her finger over a small crescent shaped scar on his abdomen. It was so light it was barely visible.

"When I was twelve, I got into a fight with some other kids. They were stoning a bird – a blue-jay that had broken its wing. That's why my father calls me 'jay.' He told that story for years, though the number grew from two bullies to fourteen over the years." He chuckled.

"Your dad sounds like he's really proud of you."

Jonathan frowned. "There is something I'd like to talk to you about. *Your* father."

"You didn't bring up his FBI file?"

He smirked. "I was far more interested in yours."

"Oh, yeah, a best seller. Waitress, college student, designated driver." She ran her fingers along his pecs and then over his arms, touching the blond hairs and enjoying the definition of muscle. His strength amazed her, given his life was filled with so much talking and paperwork.

"You must work out all the time," she said.

"Mark works me out pretty hard."

"Mark? Your assistant?"

"He's many things. No one could ask for a more loyal associate and friend. I let him order me around at the gym four times a week for putting up with me."

"You're close to him, I can tell. He knows about . . . this?" She hadn't a clue how to label what they'd been doing.

"Yes."

"You said seven people know about this place, including you. You only mentioned six."

He smirked. "Well, you've proven you can count—twice today."

She angled her arms against his chest, so she could keep his eyes. "Did you ever bring Mrs. DeCord here? Was she the seventh?"

He sighed heavily. "The seventh person is my sister."

Hearing he had a sister, one he was obviously close to, quashed the second of pride she'd felt from hearing she'd been invited where Mrs. DeCord had not. "I didn't know you had a sister. I always wanted one."

"I'll bet you did." Seriousness colored his eyes.

More dangerous waters. She needed a distraction. Christiana trailed her hands down the ridges on his stomach to the soft triangle of damp hair. She pushed her pelvis into his semi-hard cock. His response was immediate and welcomed.

Jonathan kissed her neck, his free hand claiming her breast. He hardened when she arched into the tug on her nipple. He stepped back and leaned against the opposite wall and appraised her. Mischief danced in his eyes. A wordless understanding passed between them, a faint whisper of what was expected.

"Sir?"

"Yes, Christiana?"

"May I do something for you?"

His lips twitched into a smile. "On your knees in front of me."

She knelt between his feet. She put her small hands on his thighs, corded in muscle and strength. The water cascaded down her back.

Jonathan lifted his semi-erect penis, holding it heavy in his hands. He ran his thumb along the dark purple vein running on the side.

"Raise your eyes to me," he said.

He didn't have to say anything more than that. She wanted to serve him—and stop all the serious talk, all thoughts of family and former subs and anyone else who might slip into the steam with them. She ran her tongue over her lips, wetting them in anticipation of encasing the purple mushroom head with her mouth.

Christiana lifted his soft full length, now curving upward toward her face. She ran her tongue along the crown. She sheathed him, not stopping until she reached the thicker root. She traced that same vein as she pulled him back out.

"Look up at me, Christiana. I'm going to fuck your mouth," he growled.

Her eyes migrated north, capturing the desire tinting his emerald eyes. She dipped her tongue into the salty slit of the head, watching his reaction, then sucked down until her nose touched his low belly. He groaned and fisted her hair in both hands. When he pushed her head back, she encircled himself with one hand.

"Hand away." He nudged forward.

She gagged when he hit the back of her throat. He held her head fast, as she tried to back away. Slowly pulling back, he let her adjust and then pumped half his length between her lips.

She swirled her tongue as he used her mouth, keeping her gape locked on the feral lust filling his eyes.

He grew rigid and bucked his hips forward as a shot of liquid burst into her mouth. Jonathan pulled out and wiped the side of her mouth with his thumb.

"Very nice, lovely."

She smiled up at him through the steam.

"You may stand." He pulled her up to him.

He ran his thumbs up and down the crease where her legs met her hips. He studied her face, for what? He looked sad, not like a man who'd just gotten his rocks off.

"Did I do okay?" she asked.

His face relaxed, returning him to the in-command man she knew. He switched off the water. "More than okay. Let's go. I have a reward for you."

While Christiana dried her hair, Jonathan headed to his office. One glance and he saw insistent notifications of voice mails awaiting his attention threatening to vibrate his phone off the desk. Before he could even see how many messages had been left, it rang in his hand.

"Brond."

"Where the hell are you? It's not like a member of Congress to miss a chance to rub shoulders with the Majority Leader."

"You always told me scarcity ensures mystique." Jonathan sat in his chair and looked out at the swaying trees. He didn't need to be reminded that skipping a party fundraiser that weekend had consequences, but spending time with a certain blond woman was the best way to recharge his flagging spirits from the re-election mayhem.

"You've been a little too scarce lately."

"Father, I appreciate your concern—"

"I'm not concerned. I'm downright panicked."

"About what? Shane tells me the numbers—"

"Are pitiful. You've got to get out there. You had your chance on Collins' show, and all you could talk about was privacy, and during one of the most god-damned financial lows in our nation at that. Privacy! Jesus Christ. Who the fuck cares? You're going to the July Fourth benefit?"

"Of course." *Tell me you're not.*

"Good. Your mother—"

"Stepmother."

"—and I will be there. Do *not* bring a date. You need to focus on your job, not on some bimbo who'd love to bag a wealthy—"

"I don't get involved with bimbos."

"Oh, really? How's The Oak?"

"I hear the crab cakes are quite good."

"Clearly. You've been seen frequenting it enough."

"I thought I wasn't seen enough."

"Don't play games. The Bronds always did have a penchant for the ladies."

Jonathan fought the queasiness in his stomach. "Father—"

"I'm just saying you have to choose wisely. You're going to need a woman who can hold her own, not need a lot of baby-ing. I should know."

Anger replaced Jonathan's nausea. "I'll see you at the dinner. I have a dozen messages to handle."

"About the Blanchard brunch today—"

"I won't be there. I have plans."

His father sighed heavily into the phone. "Jay, what the hell's going on? The party is counting on you."

"Why?" Jonathan rubbed his forehead. "What is it you're really worried about?"

"I'm concerned you're about to throw away the only thing you're good at."

"Father, I'll see you next Thursday." Jonathan didn't wait for a response before killing the call. His father's aim was impeccable as always—straight to the gut.

Jonathan parked his SUV in an inconspicuous corner of the empty parking lot of Saks Fifth Avenue.

"It looks closed," Christiana said.

"We have an appointment."

Jonathan had declared they were heading back to Washington early, that he had a surprise waiting for her, a reward for her service. She hoped it involved sex. He hadn't touched her since the shower, and her "morning service" did nothing to abate the bonfire still blazing inside her, ignited by the weekend's activities. Conflicting as Jonathan's most recent sexual adventures proved to be, she was helpless in the face of the excitement it brought.

A stylish young woman in a cream-colored suit waved from an unmarked side door. Jonathan's face cracked into an ear-splitting grin. He walked up to her and kissed her on both cheeks. "Sarah. Thank you for the off hours."

"Of course, Jonathan. Anything for you."

Christiana took the smooth, cool hand offered by the polished woman.

Sarah turned to Jonathan. "You are quite right. She's lovely."

Christiana bristled at the endearment coming from

Sarah's mouth.

"Christiana, this is my sister, Sarah."

She smiled warmly. "Technically step-sister, but I'll admit he's a good brother. Come inside."

"Hi." Christiana's shyness returned in the face of his sister's diplomacy. She regretted the moment of jealousy she'd conjured seeing Jonathan kiss her cheek.

Jonathan gripped her hip and led her through the doorway.

Sarah led them down a hallway, clearly designed for deliveries—garment racks with plastic-encased gowns lined the walls, and wedding veils hung off a series of hooks. She pushed open a door at the far end. Floor to ceiling mirrors lined the large, eight-sided room. Christiana's image accosted her from every angle.

Sarah walked to a rack with a variety of dresses, gowns and other garments hanging from the silver rod. "I found everything except the Missoni." She lifted the skirt of a long navy blue gossamer gown toward Jonathan. "This will be perfect for the July Fourth benefit with your father." She regarded Christiana with such certainty that it felt like an order.

"I-I don't know."

Jonathan touched her shoulder. "Yes, I've arranged for it. Your father should have received his invitation from Shane by now."

"My dad's on the road," Christiana said.

"He'll be back." Jonathan inspected a few of the dresses.

"I might have to work the show." Shit, why did she say that? Maybe because she stood in a room that only reminded her of the society she'd always tried to avoid.

"We'll see," Jonathan said.

Sarah ran her hand down a long, silky black garment. "We have a few choices. The Oscar de La Renta, Marc Jacobs, and, of course, the Lise Charmel and LaPerla." She lifted a triangle of lace in her slim fingers.

"We'll start with this one." Jonathan touched a black cocktail dress.

"I see your taste hasn't wavered, Jay." Sarah slipped the garment off the hanger.

Jay? Renewed jealousy spread across her skin. She tried to tamp it down.

Jonathan winked at Sarah. He sat on a wooden bench lining one of the mirrored panels, stretched out his long legs. He leaned back like he was waiting for a show.

"We girls have some changing to do." Sarah took Christiana's arm and walked her over to an accordion screen. Once away from Jonathan's appraising eyes, Sarah leaned close to Christiana. "I know how to dress women, Christiana. Trust me."

She'd heard those words before. But Christiana wasn't sure she wanted to look like Avery. The clothes draped over Sarah's arm belonged to her friend's world, not her own.

"Now, off with that t-shirt. It does nothing for you."

Christiana sighed and pulled her shirt over her head.

Sarah frowned at Christiana's plain cotton bra. "Hmm, I'll be right back."

Her heels clicked across the hardwood floor as she disappeared into another room and returned with a handful of silky bras in various colors. Before Christiana could object, Sarah had snapped off Christiana's bra and handed her a black strapless one. The cups looked half the size they should have been, but she hastily put it on. She wasn't used to undressing in front of a stranger, even if she had spent the last twenty-four hours with fewer clothes off than on. She had to admit the demi bra fit perfectly. It also pushed her breasts up in such a way they looked larger.

Sarah slipped the dress over Christiana's head and zipped

it up the back. She smoothed down the fabric over her hips.

"Good." Sarah stood back to admire her work.

"Let me see you, Christiana," Jonathan's smooth voice beckoned.

"In a minute, Jay. Beauty can't be rushed."

"You call him Jay . . . too?" An urge to know everything that had ever happened to Jonathan in the past overwhelmed her senses. *He's done so much—without me.*

"Yes." Sarah bent down at her feet. Christiana lifted her foot, and Sarah slipped on a black heel that Christiana was sure she couldn't stand in, let alone walk a single step.

Sarah stood. "Louboutin's. They elongate the leg so nicely. Take a look."

Christiana stared at the young woman in the mirror. Her legs indeed looked impossibly long. The black dress hugged her body, but didn't feel tight. The woman reflected in the mirror looked at least twenty-five. She looked like she might belong with Jonathan Brond.

"Now you're ready." Sarah motioned for her to step from behind the screen.

Jonathan nodded as Christiana stepped forward. "This is how you should always dress."

"Yeah, it's perfect for delivering room service." She ran her hands over a small strip of black leather at the waist.

She hobbled toward Jonathan who stood to take her hand. "You like it?"

"Christiana, I like any dress that makes me want to take it off you."

She blushed, knowing Sarah overheard.

"The Herrera next," Jonathan instructed Sarah. "Skip the Gucci. No red."

"Yes, I agree. Too overpowering. But, this . . . . " Sarah held up the dark blue gown, the crystals twinkling in the bright light.

Jonathan cupped Christiana's cheek. "Will bring out your eyes, lovely."

Christiana wobbled back to Sarah, who ushered her back behind the screen.

Sarah unzipped the black strapless form-fitting dress. Christiana slipped her legs into the open back of the gossamer gown and Sarah pulled the sides together to zip it up.

Christiana searched her mind to say something to Jonathan's sister. If Avery were in her place, she'd know the appropriate small talk. Instead, Christiana couldn't stop focusing on the dress Sarah tugged around her middle. Christiana had never shown so much skin while still being dressed. The slit up the side would reveal her right leg from ankle to hip when she walked. The tight boning at her ribs threatened to squeeze her small breasts up and out. She yanked the draping at the top up in a vain attempt to cover her breasts. Sarah reached around and pulled the fabric back down. "It's meant to showcase your décolletage."

"I'll fall out."

"You won't. But we want a man to think you might."

Christiana blinked at Sarah's deadpan face in the mirror.

"You do want him to notice, right?" she asked Christiana's reflection.

Always.

Sarah fastened silver sandals on Christiana's feet, which immediately began to sting from the thin straps.

When Christiana stepped from behind the accordion screen, Jonathan crossed his arms and leaned back into the mirror. "I can take it from here, Sarah."

"Of course. Let me know your selections, and I'll have them sent over." Before Christiana could say thank you, Sarah slipped through a mirrored panel in the wall.

Christiana walked toward Jonathan. The fabric cascaded

down her legs from the weight of the crystals, yet they were light enough to allow the skirt to swish slightly as she walked. He took her hand and led her in a large arcing circle around the room. "I look forward to dancing with you in this gown, Christiana."

She sashayed back and forth, letting the fabric tease her legs. The muscles in her calves strained from the effort to hold her balance in those heels. She leaned toward him, inviting a kiss. Jonathan didn't return her gesture. Instead, he walked to the garment rack and took a small pouch from a gold hanger.

"Now I'm going to dress you." He unzipped the red bag and brought out a black lace bra, panties and garter belt. Laying them down on the bench, he said. "Come here."

Christiana walked to him, and he turned her to unzip the dress slowly.

"But, your sister—"

"Won't interrupt us."

The two sides of the dress fell open, and his warm lips caressed her shoulder. He slipped the silky fabric over her hips and let the dress fall to the floor. Christiana started to bend over to pick it up but was stopped by an arm circling her waist.

"Leave it. It's hardly my favorite."

"Which one was?"

"What you're about to put on."

He unsnapped the strapless bra, and it hit the floor. He whisked her panties to her ankles, and she stepped out of them.

"Of course, this is one of my favorite looks, as well." He palmed her breasts with his hand and tweaked her nipples. Shivers cascaded through her. She ground her hips back into his erection.

Jonathan swept her hair to one side and continued to kiss

her neck, thumb her nipples and arched his stiff cock into her crevice. It felt strange being this tall alongside his solid frame.

"Jonathan?"

"You mean *sir*."

The thought she'd only agreed to his overly formal address while in Charlottesville was overwritten by the contact of his lips on her shoulder.

He released her body and spun her around.

"Not yet." He sat back down and crossed his arms. "Put them on." It was not a request.

She eased off the silver sandals and picked up the night-black lace panties. She slipped them up her legs, the back leaving at least half of her cheeks exposed. Cool air skated through as it barely covered her most intimate parts. The mounds of her breasts threatened to spill over the bra's scalloped edge. The garter belt's straps tickled her skin.

"Now the stockings." Jonathan held up two gossamer wisps.

After slipping the diaphanous silk over each leg, she struggled with securing the tops of the stocking to the rubber clips. Jonathan stood in front of her and stilled her hands. "Let me." He expertly attached them in front and back, lingering sensuously over the adjustment.

He knelt and positioned the Louboutin's before her feet. Christiana held on to his shoulders as she slipped into them.

"Walk over to the garment rack, then back to me. I want to see you move."

Christiana moved slowly, still unsure of her balance in the four-inch high heels. She managed to make it to the rack of clothes with a slight sashay.

Jonathan's eyes held her gaze, steadying her walking. The heels boosted her confidence. When she reached him, his arms circled around her waist. He turned her, so she faced her image in the mirror. She almost didn't recognize herself. The black contrasted sharply with her pale skin though her face was flushed. The lace rubbed roughly across her nipples, only feeding the simmering fire he had yet to cool since the morning's "servicing" session.

Jonathan's broad chest pushed into her back, causing her to pitch forward.

"Hold on to the bench. Spread your legs wide," he said

She gripped the smooth wood, her face so close to the mirror her breath fogged the surface. She spread her legs wider and leaned her ass into his crotch.

"Good girl." He dipped his fingers between her thighs.

Christiana's skin tingled at his touch through the diaphanous fabric.

He smacked a cheek.

She huffed out a burst of air at the impact.

"Fuck, your ass is magnificent." A rush of fluid between her legs betrayed her anxiety over the possibility of his impending claim of ownership *there*.

Jonathan brought his hand down on her bared flesh several more times, each time propelling air from her lungs in small grunts. She pushed her behind toward his punishing hand and the swollen cock held imprisoned in his faded jeans. Her need arose so high, it nearly swamped her consciousness. She craved his hands on her in any way.

"Sir?" she panted.

"Yes, lovely."

"Please." She danced her ass backward more, wanting contact with his steely erection, held captive in his pants.

"Hmm, greedy." He slapped her haunch, and a zing of heat spread across her cheek.

A zipper sounded. Fabric scraped. His thick, rigid shaft nestled in the soaked fabric that barred his entry to her core. She spread her legs even more.

Jonathan gathered her hair in a hand and pulled her head back. "Shall I take you right here?

"Yes, please, sir. Fuck me." Words she'd never thought possible to say came out as easily as if she'd asked him what he'd like off The Oak Room menu. She didn't care if his sister walked in. She wanted him to take her.

Christiana gripped the edge of the bench harder when he jerked the sheer panties, stretching them over her legs until they ripped. She cried out as he hilted himself into her.

He dug his fingers into her hips and pulled her backward, pumping her flesh over his cock until his balls swung upward to slap her clit. Her breaths puffed out between each stab. A groan escaped from her lips when Jonathan's mouth bit while he massaged her insides with his cock in tight, short stokes.

"Fuck, you're sweet, Christiana."

Her clit ached, desperate for relief. Before her orgasm could tip over, Jonathan shuddered and thrust into her deeper than she thought possible, nearly sending her into the mirror. He breathed heavily into her hair for a minute and then lifted his weight off her back. He pulled his slick cock from between her legs.

Christiana straightened. A face print fogged the mirror, lip gloss smeared in one long swipe.

Jonathan pivoted her into a hug. His chin rested on her shoulder.

"Hmm, I see we have our own private Rorschach test on the mirror. I wonder what the good ladies of Washington would see in your imprint. I know I'll always see your face, slack with lust, reminding me how you take my cock deep."

Christiana thought it only read one thing. *Please, let me come.*

She tried to remember her earlier reward for patience. It suddenly seemed overrated.

20

When Christiana walked out of The Oak on Tuesday evening, Avery was outside leaning on a black Crown Victoria, giggling over something one of the rapt valet attendants had just said.

"Finally!" Avery said when she saw Christiana. "Jacob here has been keeping me company." Jacob flushed bright red. *More like letting you park in the valet area.*

Going out with Avery on her one night off that week wasn't her ideal scenario. But it might help abate the constant texts and voice mail messages questioning where Christiana had been. Christiana only hoped no one recognized her at Ireland's Four Provinces after her father's last visit to the bar. But Avery couldn't be swayed to go anywhere else. "Not when Chase's brother works the door, girl. Camden has always wanted me. We'll get free drinks!"

Why Avery needed free anything was beyond understanding.

"Well, I'm ready, let's go," Christiana said. She'd taken a cab to work, glad to avoid the thirty-five dollar parking fee for the day, knowing Avery would drive her home later.

"What's with your dad's Crown Vic? I thought you'd never be caught dead in it."

"It won't matter where we park. Federal judge perks." Avery grinned. "Here, take my purse and get out my perfume. Spritz yourself. I'm getting you a date this summer if it's the last thing I do, and you won't be attracting any men smelling like crab cakes."

Christiana spritzed scent over her hair. She didn't want to smell like Avery, but she knew her friend had a point.

Avery checked her lipstick in the visor mirror. "That Jacob guy is cute. Why don't you date him?"

"You've got to be kidding me."

"No, really. He was regaling me with a list of all the secret rooms in The Oak. There's like a million security cameras up or something."

"Washington gossip. Everyone likes to think they're in a clandestine CIA operation."

"He said some wild things go on there. You'd think you'd notice. You're there enough."

"I'm more of a 'don't ask, don't tell' kind of girl."

"Yeah, well, not everyone is so careful of their privacy as you. I'm just sayin'."

Avery sped up Connecticut Avenue, long since emptied of commuters heading north to their Maryland suburban homes and eased the huge sedan into a handicapped space just up the street from Ireland's Four Provinces. After all, what's a few parking tickets to someone with an endless parental expense account and federal judge license plates?

Avery marched past the long queue of patrons waiting to be allowed inside, ignoring the snide comments of guys waiting in line. Chase's brother, Camden, stood at the front door and opened it wide when he saw them. "Ladies." He threw Christiana a broad smile.

The bar teemed with tipsy patrons, jostling each other at

the long wooden bar. Christiana barely avoided getting beer spilled on her as Camden led her and Avery to a tall table on the side.

"Don't overdo it, girls," he said and slapped the table before turning away to return to his doorman duties.

"So protective," Avery mimicked. "Jesus, we're college students. If anyone's got a tolerance, it's us."

"You've gotten funnier since last year."

"So glad I amuse you. You've gotten more serious. You certainly work more."

The three-man Irish band struck up a lilting ballad in the corner. Avery bounced in her seat in time with the music. You'd think she hadn't been out in months.

"Good lord, do I need to serve myself?" she shouted. She jumped off her stool and headed to the bar.

"Hey, Chris, how ya been?" Christiana startled at Camden's voice behind her. He had to shout to be heard over the music.

"I'm fine." She was surprised Camden knew her name.

"Hey, listen, while Avery's occupied, I was hoping you could help me with something." He slid onto Avery's abandoned stool. "Can you talk to Avery about Chase? I mean, she's gotta stop calling him."

Christiana laughed. "You've got it backward. Chase can't stop calling her."

"I don't know what she's told you but when Chase breaks up with someone, he makes a clean break. Listen, he didn't want to hurt her last summer. But she's got to stop trying to reconcile. It's making him feel guilty. Just talk to her. Ya' know, as a friend."

He slapped the table and walked away. Camden had to have it all wrong. Avery Churchill would never chase a guy. Well, maybe one, and he was off-limits.

Avery balanced three beers in a triangle between her two

hands.

"That's a lot of beer, Avery. How'd they give it to you?"

"I have my ways. Besides, we have to make up for lost time. We haven't been out in ages."

Avery lifted a frothy mug to her lips and took a big gulp before setting the mug down with a dramatic thunk. "We need to catch up, girlfriend. So, first, remind me why I chose California 'cause the rumors of gorgeous blond lifeguards and actors were highly exaggerated. All anyone cares about at Stanford is saving the planet or launching a company sure to destroy it. We should go to Charlottesville one weekend, and I can see if I want to transfer. Wouldn't us two trolling the Virginia frat parties be a hoot?"

Christiana's heart dropped to the sticky bar floor.

"I don't think you'd like Charlottesville. Too small-town for you." Christiana took a small sip of the cold draught. "Hey listen, Camden came over and—"

"Don't tell me, he asked for my number, didn't he? He always did eye me like a piece of candy. Well, we need to toast. To you finally getting laid regularly."

Christiana nearly spit out her beer.

"You've been holding out on me. You said that guy Jeff at school wasn't exactly Don Juan. He get better or something?"

"I am not seeing Jeff." Christiana's forced laughter did nothing to cool the heat rising in her face.

"Bullshit."

"Swear to God, Avery. The rumors of hot preppy guys at UVA were exaggerated too."

"Well, who is he? Wait. He's married, isn't he? You're doing a *married* guy." Avery's eyes grew twice their size.

Christiana laughed for real. "No. *way.*"

"Okay, play it that way. You've got someone. I can tell. I'll get the truth out of you yet." Avery sipped her beer and scanned the crowd. "Jesus, where are all the men?"

Christiana took a large swallow of beer, hoping it would ease the tangle of guilt. She wondered if she'd ever be able to unravel truth from white lies and outright falsehoods after the last few weeks she'd had.

Avery droned on about the guys she'd met at school and the girls who threw jealous looks her way at every college football and soccer game. Christiana listened and sipped a second beer; Avery was already on her fourth. Or was it her fifth? Christiana's focus had begun to waver by the time Avery switched to her plans to the fashion show. She hadn't built her immunity to alcohol like Avery. But then, she'd never figured out where Avery got her suspiciously high tolerance, and Avery had never explained.

"So, what do you think of my idea?" Avery's lips curled into a smile. "Using real women as models? I mean, you're looking good these days. I guess sex becomes you." Avery leaned into Christiana's shoulder in a move of solidarity.

Christiana tried not to recoil.

Avery's face registered disappointment. Christiana clearly hadn't hidden her revulsion from her friend. "You used to love my ideas."

A vibration and a chirping sound came from Christiana's purse. Crap, how could she answer a call from Jonathan here? Relief flooded her to the core at the word "Dad" blinking across the screen.

Christiana slipped from her stool and answered. "Dad, where are you?"

"Hey, Chrissy, checking in. Sounds loud. Where are you?"

Christiana jogged to the end of the bar in a vain attempt at escaping the loud fiddle music.

"Oh, nowhere special. Where are you?" she asked.

"Tennessee. So, I'll be home next Tuesday. Got a special invitation to the club's annual fundraiser from Brond's office. Next Thursday. They suggested you come as my date."

"Oh?" Another lie, another thin string of deceit, wound around the knotted ball.

"Yep. Gonna be big."

She laughed. "See you then, Dad." She killed the call.. With Jonathan at the fundraiser, maybe it'd be different this year.

She headed back to a swaying Avery who seemed enthralled by the music.

"Hey, I'm headed to the ladies' room," Christiana called over the loud singing. "Watch my purse?"

Christiana stood in line with three other girls in the cramped hallway, stale beer and urine scents surrounding them. Christiana rethought her decision to pee. Well, she couldn't hold it any longer. She wondered how Avery managed to do so after so many beers.

Why did everything with her friend seem so awkward these days? *Because you're a lying, disloyal, and quite frankly, increasingly slutty friend*, a part of her accused. Wow, alcohol and guilt definitely didn't mix.

She finally was able to slip into the dirty one-toilet bathroom and relieve herself. Only none of the guilt drained away with the swirl of the flush. Time to face the music, literally.

The Irish music hit her as soon as she rounded the corner. She nearly stopped short as she watched Avery reach into Christiana's purse and pull out her phone. Had it rung?

Avery's eyes darted to Christiana, and she lifted her shoulders in question. But then she put the phone to her ear.

Christian nearly knocked over a waitress carrying a heavy tray in her attempt to get back to Avery.

"Hello? Christiana here," Avery said sweetly into the phone. "What do you mean where am I? Where are you?" Her face darkened.

"Give it back to me!" Christiana yelled. Avery's head

snapped backward as if slapped. Christiana had never raised her voice before. Then realization spread across Avery's face. *Of course.* Jonathan's voice was unmistakable. Avery slowly set the phone down on the table. Her eyes bored holes into Christiana's face.

"What ... the ... hell ... have you been up to?"

Here it comes. Over the cliff, burning.

"Nothing." Christiana grabbed the phone, her purse and spun toward the front door. The iPhone vibrated in her hand as she reached the exit.

"Where are you?" Jonathan's voice matched Avery's fury.

"Ireland's Four Provinces. Um, across from the Zoo."

"I'll be right there." The line went dead. Her insides did the same.

Christiana pushed open the door and lurched toward the street sign pole, using it to balance herself. Avery stood in front of her in seconds.

She had never seen Avery so angry, and that was saying something. "Why is Congressman Brond calling you? You interning for him, and you didn't tell me?"

"No. I'm not his new intern, Avery."

"Then what? Do *not* tell me you're going out with him."

"Not exactly."

Avery's chest rose and fell in angry pants. "Well, what then, *exactly*?"

"It's nothing." *It's everything.*

"So this is why you've been avoiding me all summer."

"Avery, it's not like that."

She crossed her arms. "He's using you. That's what he does, ya know. I hear 'short term' is his specialty." Her words hit Christiana square in the chest.

"You don't know what you're talking about," Christiana spat.

"I thought you were the last honest person in D.C. Guess

you showed me."

"You mean like how you've been honest with me? Camden told me how you can't stop calling Chase."

"Camden will say anything to get me. He's wanted me for years." Her voice dripped nonchalance.

"Yes, I guess everyone wants you, Avery. And only you."

"Not everyone, apparently. So tell me. Congressman Jonathan Brond cares for you? Wants to *date* you? Only for the summer, of course. Probably purely out of compassion because of your—"

Avery's words choked off at the sight of Jonathan's convertible swinging in a neat U-turn in the middle of the street, cutting off some annoyed drivers who started to honk. They abruptly stopped. The drivers either recognized him, or they were stunned by his looks. Confidence and composure flitted across Avery's face, and she straightened. Jonathan stepped from his car in a flash.

"I'll take it from here, Avery," he said as he took Christiana's arm.

Avery smirked her cat smile. "Hello, Congressman."

"When your father said to look after you in his absence, this was not the behavior I expected, Miss Snow." Jonathan's voice encased her body.

Christiana understood she was to remain silent. He spoke words he needed Avery to hear. After all, Christiana had learned to anticipate what he wanted all the time now, hadn't she?

"I'm getting you home," he said to Christiana.

Avery grabbed Christiana's other elbow like she was trying to steady a drunk. "Oh, don't worry about me, Congressman. I'm the responsible one here."

"Need cab fare?"

"She has a car," Christiana slurred.

Christiana didn't know how they'd gotten back into his

convertible so fast, she in the passenger seat and he behind the wheel. All she knew was they were heading down Connecticut before she had a chance to look back.

Jonathan was furious. Christiana's hair whipped into her face. Why the top down now?

"You need air." Jonathan answered her unspoken question.

"I'm okay. I didn't have that much."

"The way your head is swaying, I'd say you've had more than much." Jonathan slapped his steering wheel. "Are you going to make me go 24/7 on you, Christiana?"

She had no idea what he was talking about. She also understood he wasn't really asking her.

"Why do you hang out with that girl?"

"My Dad likes her." The honesty of her answer stunned her. She guessed alcohol was good for one thing.

"You don't feel she's using you?" The bitter tone in his voice cleared the fog in her brain as much as his words.

He was worried she was being used by Avery? The man who wanted her as a sexual concubine? The irony of her situation forced a giggle from her lips. He shot her a look, eyes narrowed.

"That's what Avery said about you," she said.

"She would." Jonathan stopped at a red light and turned his face to hers. "There is a vast difference between being used and being useful, Christiana."

Useful? She could be *useful* to Jonathan Brond? The new thought rattled inside her brain. She continued to turn the word around and around in her head until its meaning slipped from her grasp—and a migraine threatened her fogged head.

"I'm taking you home." His voice, quiet and cold, spoke of defeat.

God, she'd fucked up.

21

Jonathan slammed his fist on the desk. "Find out who broke into my house and why. Today." Upon returning home late last night, a police car had parked halfway up the walkway, as if they'd been in a hurry. An intruder had tripped his alarm system. They found a back window jimmied open and a file drawer in disarray. The one file he'd been too careless to put in a safe had been taken. Jesus, he'd never imagined he'd be so reckless about his greatest secret.

The muscle in Mark's jaw twitched once. "The cops didn't find any fingerprints. But I'd guess the person following you is tied to this."

"Then you better find out who's following me." Jonathan tried to sound calm.

"It appears to be a woman."

"What? It couldn't be—"

"No, she hasn't left the Jefferson in three days."

Jonathan's jaw clenched. "You didn't tell me? Tell Shane to cancel my meetings this morning until after lunch."

"It's not safe for you to be seen—"

"Concentrate on finding who's following me—and who

broke into my home. I have to check on someone this morning."

Mark began to speak but then snapped his lips closed when Shane stepped into the room.

"Congressman, we may have a situation."

"Not now, Shane."

"Sir, this can't wait."

"Nothing ever can, can it?" He didn't mean to sound so bitter.

Shane placed the Washington Post's Thursday weekend section onto his desk.

"The paparazzi took this the other night. It boasts how Irish bars are now the popular place to go. It says that even members of Congress attend. Single ones, especially."

Fuck. The front-page picture showed an angry Jonathan leading a young-looking blond into his car. The angle captured Avery Churchill in the background. She looked ready to crawl in right behind the girl in the photograph, who, though faceless in the paparazzo's shot, could only be Christiana. Hell, Avery would've straddled the hood of his two-seater and ridden to his house that way if he'd allowed it.

A sidebar picture showed him squiring Yvette DeCord out of The Oak. To think the Post used to be a reputable paper. Now they were one step up from *Hello!* Magazine.

"I promised Peter Snow I'd look after her. She needed a ride." He didn't have to look at Shane's face to hear how inept his words sounded.

"Thought Snow was on the arm's-length list."

"Listen, I'll deal with it later. Right now, I have another situation that's more urgent. Cook up your usual crisis communications plan. We'll talk this afternoon. And close the door behind you. Please." At least his voice grew calmer with each word, unlike his insides, which wanted to throttle a certain brunette.

Mark resumed his stance after Shane shut the door behind him. "Sir, if I may—"

"No, I'll drive myself. Meet me at The Oak Room for lunch in an hour."

Jonathan jogged down the steps under the harsh sunlight to his car. Over the last three days, the mysterious car had been behind him, everywhere: to and from his townhouse, meetings, and events. He knew the prowler would follow him to Charlottesville next. If the stalker breached his Alexandria home, an unrecoverable scandal loomed.

Christiana's world was about to change, significantly. He had to calm the storm about to break. Years of guarding his privacy had honed his crisis planning abilities to an art form. His mind spun a plan.

First, be honest. He'd taken an awful chance picking Christiana up at the bar the other night. He'd taken too many chances, everywhere.

Second, identify where he went wrong, where he lost control. His explanation to Avery of why he showed up in Christiana's life seemed plausible in the moment. For all he knew, though, Avery had hired the photographer and ensured the picture was published. She'd proven she hadn't inherited the Churchill's legendary discretion.

Several photographers were camped out front of The Oak Room when he pulled up. *Damn media.* They might have figured out Christiana Snow's identity and discovered where she worked. If he didn't get upstairs fast, there was no telling how he'd react to seeing Christiana, and the photographers mustn't catch his honest feelings about the woman.

Third, change the story. His inner fixer switched tactics. He knew what to do.

After handing his keys to the valet, he forced himself to

saunter through the hotel entrance and avoid the restaurant. Yvette didn't answer when he knocked on the suite door. Jonathan took out his master keycard and opened the door himself. A rancid smell stopped him in his tracks two steps in.

A long white gown draped over a chair in the entrance, several pairs of heels lay strewn about the hall. A trail of clothes littered the floor all the way into the main room. A room service tray sat on the antique desk in the corner. A half-eaten shrimp salad lay in one white porcelain bowl. A glob of dried, black crystals lay smeared on an abandoned piece of bread. *Caviar.* No wonder the smell. *Where the hell has hotel management been?*

"Yvette? Where are you, sweetheart?"

A rustle of bed sheets greeted him as he rounded the corner into the bedroom. A murmur broke from under the covers. Jonathan moved to the bed and gently lifted the sheet from a shaking body underneath.

"Yvette. Did Carson leave you like this?"

"Stop!" Her crying intensified.

He would kill Carson Drake. He would then kill himself for telling the man Yvette needed a strong hand.

"Shh, pet." Jonathan took off his jacket and loosened his tie, staring down at Yvette who shook in a half-dream, half-waking state. He threw both items of clothing to the floor and kicked off his shoes. He laid down, encircling Yvette's quaking body in his arms in an instant.

"I'm here. I'm here." Jonathan rocked her back and forth. "It's me."

"Jonathan?"

"Yes, pet."

She wrested away and turned to face him. Long trails of mascara streaked her cheeks, and she blinked, as if trying to focus.

"Yvette. Remember me."

"Yes. Yes, sir."

"No. It's me. Jonathan."

She let out a sigh and kissed him hard on the lips. He opened his mouth to her searching tongue and tasted the fear. He ran his fingers through her hair as she moved her mouth over his as if to force herself back to reality, like trying to wake from a bad dream.

He finally pushed her face away with his hands. "Look at me."

She blinked and grasped his chest, clawing her fingernails into him. How long had she been left alone?

"You came," she said. "I-I tried calling. I think."

"I'm sorry I didn't come sooner."

Her eyes darted over his face and down his body, as if she had trouble focusing. He had to ground her, quickly. Her nightstand was littered with half-filled prescription bottles. A quick check revealed nothing too strong—mild sleeping pills, an antibiotic, vitamins.

Jonathan held her for thirty minutes, her breath warming his chest until they both glistened with perspiration. When she finally relinquished her hold on his arm, banding her tightly to his body, he pulled her up to sitting. He leaned against the headboard and gestured for her to settle between his arms.

"What happened, Yvette?"

"I don't know. Carson was here, and then . . . he wasn't."

"He shouldn't have left you so ungrounded."

"He didn't. I needed more. He-he stopped, wouldn't go any further. I fell asleep. I think." She sniffled. "The papers arrived two days ago."

So Arniss finally did it. Well, she would be better off as a divorcee than shackled to that fucker.

"Are you staying here permanently now?"

She rubbed a nod into his chest.

"I do hope you're sending him the bill," he said.

"And ordering plenty of expensive room service on top of it." She laughed. Good, she'd emerged from her post-scene haze.

"I can smell it."

She laughed.

"Come on. We're getting you out of here. I'm getting you a proper meal." He would make sure she showered, dressed and joined him for lunch downstairs. He wasn't about to leave Yvette alone in this suite. The photographers would notice, of course, helping step three of his crisis plan: deflect them by appearing with another woman in Christiana's presence. Christiana would have to understand.

Brian threw Christiana a disdainful glance as she huddled in the corner of the kitchen, straining to hear her father's words.

"Chrissy, what is this about Congressman Brond picking you up at a bar?"

"Dad, I'm at work. Can I call you later?" Henrick stood nearby, and the way he cocked his head told her he'd been listening.

"No. I got a call from my office. What were you doing in a bar?"

Well, that's calling the kettle blackened and fried.

"Rumor has it Brond's been squiring women all over town," he said. "Didn't know my daughter might be one of them."

"It's not like that."

"He's too old for you."

"What makes you think I'm not his new intern?"

"Are you?"

"No. He knows you're on the road, and he's . . . ."

Her father laughed. "Don't tell me. Mentoring you."

"Yes, that's it." It wasn't a lie.

"You hate politics."

"He knows lots of other things, too."

"Be careful, Chrissy. He's got quite the reputation. You're a little—"

"What?"

"Gullible."

"Gee, thanks for the vote of confidence, Dad."

"I'm worried about you." He had to be sober. Well, it was only noon. There was time yet.

"Gotta go, Dad." She killed the call and ignored the barrage of missed notifications from Avery, though she knew she'd have to confront her friend—find out if they were still friends—sooner or later. If Christiana continued to ignore her, she might show up at The Oak.

"You've been rather distracted lately," Henrick said behind her. He handed her a plate loaded with a sizzling rib-eye steak and loaded baked potato. "Table seven." Before letting go of the plate edge, he added, "Be sure he's worth it."

Jesus, where'd everyone's sudden interest in her personal life stem from? Wasn't privacy nine-tenths of the law? Oh, wait, that was possession. Well, with Jonathan it felt the same, even though his recent texts had been short and noncommittal. She prayed she'd misread the good-bye in Jonathan's eyes as he pulled his arms away after tucking her into bed after the bar incident. At least she's managed to hold back the first tear until the closing click of the front door.

Christiana pushed the kitchen door open. The low roar of a full house helped dam the unshed tears. It was time to go to work, and she'd hold back her weeping if it killed her.

~

A young redheaded girl led Jonathan and Yvette to a table in the back where Mark sat already, waiting for them. Mark rose as they approached. Jonathan noted the surprise half-hidden behind Mark's face.

"Mark, you remember Yvette DeCord?"

Mark took Yvette's outstretched hand.

"Hello, Mark. Good to see you."

Yvette set her pert butt, covered in an ivory pencil skirt, down onto the plush chair Jonathan held for her. She did a good job of hiding the wince when the welts on her ass contacted the chair seat, memoirs of her last session with Carson. Jonathan vowed to find out the rest of the story from the other Dom. Yvette was many things: bratty, vain, needy. But Jonathan had never known Carson to leave a submissive in a bad state. Something wasn't right.

He wished he'd had a moment with his current sub-in-training, so she'd understand why he was handling things this way. The way Christiana's blue eyes widened upon seeing them showed him he didn't have that kind of time. Before Jonathan could rise from his chair and make an excuse to Mark and Yvette, Christiana had turned on her heel and headed downstairs.

"You'll want to go after her, Jonathan." Yvette never raised her eyes from her menu.

"Sir—" Jonathan silenced Mark with a raised hand.

"Mark, be sure Yvette has what she needs." He laid a chaste kiss on her cheek.

Several familiar sets of eyes from nearby tables caught his movement, and he knew the word would spread. Later he'd ensure a photo was taken of the three of them in front of The Oak. That should about wrap things up in the Christiana rumor mill.

His mind sorted the many things he'd say to Christiana when he caught up to the wounded girl. She'd be inside the ladies' room at this point. No matter, he'd have to risk shocking the ladies by barreling inside anyway.

When he entered, Christiana rested her head on the lagoon-blue tiled wall at the far end of the elegant room. Her eyes were closed in deep thought, and she rolled her head back and forth as if she was trying to massage out a kink in the back of her head.

"Do you have a headache, lovely?"

Her eyes snapped open. "You're standing in the ladies' room."

"I know."

She pushed herself off the wall and walked to the counter, laying hands on either side of a white marble sink. "You lied to me," she said to the basin.

Jonathan appreciated many things about Christiana. Her honesty and direct words were welcomed when she chose to speak, that is, though it pained him to hear her perspective now. He didn't want Christiana to accept anything that wasn't true.

"No, I didn't. Yvette and I are friends, and she's in trouble. I'm helping her through something right now."

Christiana straightened and faced him. Her stony face gave little away, but he knew hurt when he encountered it. Christiana was more disciplined than any nineteen-year-old he'd met. But he could tell holding back what she really wanted to say cost deeply. "I'm being punished for the other night," was her only response.

"No, you're not, though you should be. You're underage. You were in a bar." He ran his hand over his chin, acutely aware of how hypocritical his words sounded. Shit, he'd given her alcohol in measured doses.

Jonathan captured her chin. She tried to wrest her face from his grip, but he held a little tighter.

"I am not sleeping with Yvette DeCord. Not now. She needs my help. Mark is going to get her fed and then make sure she's safely back upstairs in her suite. I'm here to see you."

"I don't believe you. You're covering your tracks. I saw the picture."

Of course she had. Avery probably sent it.

"Do you honestly think if I were still seeing Yvette DeCord, I'd bring her to a restaurant where you work?"

"I don't know. Maybe you're a sadist."

A smile quirked up his lips. He grabbed her arm before she could step around him. "You've been researching. What did I tell you about that?"

"Let go of me, Jonathan. I swear—"

"Or what?" His clipped words snapped her eyes back to his face.

He softened his voice at the sight of worry lines growing deeper in her forehead. "Don't test me, my beautiful girl."

"Avery was right."

Her flippancy filled him with apprehension. Only a fledgling, green submissive would toy with her lion this way. He suppressed the notion that perhaps she was too young for what he'd let loose. No, he wouldn't let this go unchecked. Now that Pandora's box had been opened, he'd see it through. Jonathan measured his next words carefully. "If you mean what I think you did . . . ." he whispered into her ear.

She looked up at him. "Avery said you took pity—"

Jonathan spun her, so she faced the mirror. She tried to push away, but he pinned both arms to her sides in a bear hug.

"We have a problem," he said into her reflection.

"I don't have any problems."

"Oh, lovely, you have many. Right now I am only concerned about the one at hand."

"And what's that? Being your charity case of the week?"

"That you don't trust me."

"You don't earn trust by appearing with ex-girlfriends—"

Jonathan's instincts kicked in with a vengeance. He gave her a resounding whack on her butt. The black skirt muffled the slap, but the gasp that erupted from her startled face showed she'd felt it loud and clear. She stilled.

Jonathan steered her out the door past two startled older women, hands extended to push the bathroom door open. He only hoped their eyesight was as bad as their facelifts.

"Please, Jonathan. You'll get me fired."

"No, I won't. It's past the lunch rush hour."

Christiana didn't have a manipulative bone in her body. She responded moment by moment to whatever he said. She wasn't trying to win or make him angry. She was lost. Of course, she'd think he flaunted Yvette. Or perhaps Yvette flaunted him. Had Yvette planned the encounter? She knew Christiana worked at The Oak. He didn't know how she would've found out about his relationship with Christiana.

No matter. He wouldn't have Christiana questioning his fidelity—or anything else.

22

Jonathan ushered her across the hall into the Cabinet Room, where he had spent many late nights pretending to enjoy the company of seasoned members of Congress over whisky and cigars. This afternoon it was empty. It presented a perfect space for what he needed to do.

It'd be risky as hell, but she needed him. A submissive cannot wonder about her Dominant's loyalty or dedication to their arrangement—not *ever*. If she did, she'd never fully submit to him and always fear her safety. He wouldn't—couldn't—let her worry.

The door closed with a soft thunk behind them, and he clicked the lock. Enough light seeped through the smoked glass to show the outline of Christiana's surprised face. Her eyes also held a hunger. She needed him to prove his commitment. He would—in only the way a Dominant must.

She stood unmoving.

"Hold out your hands."

She slowly raised her palms, inches from his waist.

"Keep them there." He slid the short end of his tie from its silk knot, wrapped the silk around her wrists and brought

ELIZABETH SAFLEUR

them up to his chest. He pushed a finger between her wrist and the fabric to make sure the bond wasn't too tight.

Whispers of breath came from her parted lips. Her deep indigo eyes shone in the muted light, the soft planes of her face so perfect she could've been mistaken for an ancient Madonna.

"Now you're being disciplined," he said. "Not for using a fake ID to get into a bar but for discounting your worth to me."

She parted her lips to respond, but he pressed his mouth to hers to silence her. When he pulled back, her eyes flooded with acquiescence.

"And for believing the manipulations of a false friend," he added.

He led her to the long dining table, farthest from the door. Spinning her to face the heavy oak surface, he lowered her upper body to its surface. Her arms automatically stretched, above her head, and her cheek rested on the wood, presenting an angelic profile.

"Tell me what I should do with someone who doesn't trust me, Christiana."

Her forehead wrinkled as she searched her mind.

"And don't tell me to earn it," he added.

"No, I wouldn't—"

"You already did tell me, lovely." He placed his hand on the small of her back to remind her of his control. He pulled the elastic binding of her ponytail free. She moaned as he ran his fingers through her unbound locks.

"What happens when you don't believe me or trust me?"

A desperate sigh escaped her lips, and a single tear running down her cheek shimmered in the subdued light. She rubbed her cheek against the wood in a nod. A single word tumbled from her mouth. She barely whispered it, but he'd heard.

"Sir."

"I should remind you. Don't you think?"

His cock grew thick, as thick as the emotion in his throat. He tamped it down. This was no time for uncontrolled sentiment. She needed something more valuable—his full commitment.

Jonathan captured the stray tear with a kiss. "You didn't answer me."

"Yes, I—you should remind me." She choked back her fear. *Always in control. Always in need.*

"You will not indulge in mistrust. Your imagination tells you lies about me. If I have to paddle your ass every day until it rivals the sun to remind you that you are mine—that you are precious to me—I will."

He reached around under her waist, lifted her skirt. She pushed her ass back into his crotch, now bulging with the need to be inside her. Her pale skin glowed against the black lace panties in the murky light. His heart swelled with pride that she'd worn the lingerie he had gifted her.

He ran his fingers over her warm butt cheeks. "You trust too many of the wrong people, and they make you doubt yourself. I will not permit it."

He lightly pinched her flesh. She squirmed.

"So much beauty, so much worry." He knelt down and kissed her silky butt cheek.

Jonathan ran a finger up under the scalloped edge of the panties, then hooked it over the elastic and drew it downward. They slipped off easily over her snow-white ass.

He stood.

"Sir, please." Christiana's fingers entwined with one another and clenched.

He unfastened his belt and slowly drew it from his waist, knowing full well the effect the sound of the slither of leather through fabric had.

"Please, please." Her pleading held an urgency. She wanted to be corrected. Jesus, he'd never met anyone who wanted to trust as badly as Christiana. No wonder she was such an easy target for someone like Avery Churchill.

He traced his belt up her butt crack. "You will count each stroke with your fingers."

He held the buckle securely to make sure it was covered. Then, without warning or hesitation, he cracked the leather across her ass. She cried out, but she unclenched her middle finger. He chuckled. So he hadn't quashed all her defiance. He was proud of his little submissive. Still he said, "For that little bit of nonsense, I'll add an extra stroke."

By the time he reached five plus the additional smack for her impudence, her chest rose and fell on the hard wood surface. He slid a finger up her pussy, now slick with juices. Jesus, she loved being handled.

She'd be so easy to fuck here, only feet from the doors creaking open and clicking shut just across the wall from them. People going about their own business, not realizing the power play being enacted feet from their business dealings and small talk.

Fuck the risk.

Within two weeks, Christiana had risen to the top of his priority list. He would do anything to ensure their connection remained intact.

Jonathan freed his considerable hard-on from his pants. His knees dug into the back of hers as he crouched to nestle his erection between her moist lower lips, slipping inside her. He grunted as his low belly connected with the angry, red stripes across her butt, pushing his length slowly through her slick, petaled opening.

Christiana pushed her behind impatiently backwards.

He grabbed a handful of her hair and lifted her head off the table. She relaxed her grinding and laid herself down on the wood. God, she was good, responding exactly as he wanted. He pulled out, letting his cock, now slick with her personal liquor, hang heavy. He ran a finger up her inner folds and then brought the finger to his nose, inhaling her sweet but strangely sophisticated scent. He let his fingers dip into her nectar.

"What do you use, here? Your scent . . . ."

"Baby powder, lavender scented. I run around a lot." She breathed the words, still overtaken by arousal. Her practical assessment of something so sensual broke something in his heart. Her honesty slayed him. She was no brat. She told him exactly what went on in her head, moment by moment. He had asked her to open to him, and she complied. He kneeled behind her and told his cock to stand down.

"You are so beautiful, Christiana." She struggled as he sent his breath over her heated slit.

Without warning, he dipped his tongue deep between her swollen nether lips, searching for her opening. She gasped at the invasion but didn't pull away. He stilled her convulsing hips with his hands as he circled and stabbed with his tongue. He trailed up her labia taking in her unique flavor until he reached her tight back hole.

Christiana moaned excitement as he rimmed the floret. His fingers worked her lower lips, now flooded with response. She would come in seconds if he didn't stop.

Jonathan released his mouth and rose. His cock jutted forward like a heat-seeking missile, and Christiana offered an irresistibly hot target.

"I only want to bring you immense pleasure, Christiana," he said, as he oiled her anal opening with her own lubrication. She didn't hide the distress in her voice.

He let the casual name slide. Her vulnerability in this position demanded a little leniency.

"Many emotions come up from this area. Ride it out." He

rubbed her puckered hole in circles and then pressed his finger past her muscle. His cock responded as she groaned from the invasion.

"Relax. Breathe deep." He rubbed her lower back with his other hand.

A soft coo released from her chest.

"Good girl." He sent kisses up her spine as he slowly pushed his finger in to the first knuckle. "There are so many things I think you'll enjoy."

She whimpered as he withdrew his finger.

"I can't wait until that sweet ass is mine. For now I'm only preparing you for the day you want me. And only when you beg me for it, will I take you there."

He grabbed her hip and arrowed his aching hard-on into her pussy. She accepted his invasion with no hesitation. He fought the urge to impale her with battering strokes. Instead, he pulled back and left only his cockhead inside her hot cunt.

"You think it's important to earn things, so you'll earn this climax. I'm going to stay still and you'll move."

Her soft choking sounds showed she fought for composure. Christiana pushed backwards to recapture his cock. He circled his arms under her rib cage and lifted her up a few inches from the table. She flattened her bound hands down onto the surface, so she could push and pull, forward and backward, stroking his length. His eyes rested on her pale rear moving in front of his groin. As she pulled forward, his cock glistened from her juices in the low light. She dragged herself over him.

"That's it, lovely. Show me how much you need me."

Her whimpers were louder now. She was so close.

"Sir, may I?"

"Do you trust me?"

"I-I do."

"You won't ever question my judgment?"

"No, oh, please." She panted heavily.

"Then show me how much you mean it. Come hard."

She let out a wail as she shuddered underneath him. He dug his fingers into her hips. He wanted her marked with a reminder of his lesson, his *loyalty*. He released and flooded her convulsing channel. She collapsed forward as if praying to the table.

He grabbed several paper napkins from the bar, cleaning himself and stowing his still spent cock. After washing his hands in the small bar sink, he wiped between Christiana's legs and pulled her panties back up.

"You may rise, Christiana."

He released her hands from his tie. Of course, Mark and Yvette would know immediately what had happened as soon as he returned to them with his tie now crumpled beyond repair.

Jonathan moved a stray hair from Christiana's damp forehead and cupped her chin once more. He studied her eyes. She wasn't too steady on her feet, still flying from her orgasm and processing all that had happened in the last few minutes.

"Come here." He sat in one of the large chairs by the door and pulled her to his lap. She laid her head on his chest. For several long minutes, he nuzzled her hair and stroked her arms. When he felt her heartbeat slow to normal, he eased his hold.

"You are mine, Christiana. Never forget that. Now, I'm going upstairs. You'll take a few minutes to pull yourself together. Then you'll come take our lunch orders. After bringing us our food, you'll check on us every ten minutes. When we're through, I'll walk out the door with them. In fact, you'll hold the door open for us. The photographers out front will capture a picture of me escorting Yvette, a woman who heads the largest charitable fundraising committee in the country, out of one of the nicest restaurants in D.C. If we're lucky, the photo will appear in Sunday's style section, given Yvette's impending divorce. This will make sure they leave you alone."

Her chin quivered slightly. He knew which part of his speech she didn't like; he didn't like the thought of Christiana being forgotten any more than she did. She'd be etched into his past as the most beautiful and poignant memory he'd ever had the privilege of earning. If he wanted more opportunities with her, he needed to protect her from Washington's most notorious wolves—the press.

"This will make it easier for us to go away this weekend, back to Charlottesville." He pressed his lips to her mouth, and she leaned into him heavily.

"Yes, sir," she said quietly when he released the kiss.

"Are you able to go back to work now?" He needed to know she wouldn't drop the first tray of food she was handed on Yvette's head—by accident, of course.

"I'm fine. Good." She smiled.

"Back to work with you then, lovely." He reluctantly released his embrace.

23

Christiana paused at the entrance of *Covil Sereia*, allowing the clean, sultry bouquet of honeysuckle and orange wipe away the tension from the last few strange days.

After Jonathan's "correction" in the Cabinet Room, Christiana had served him, his aide and the beautiful, poised, *perfect* Yvette DeCord, as directed. Soft laughter had erupted from their table several times that afternoon, and Christiana strained to hear what in Mrs. DeCord's banter had them so amused. Yvette's polite words to Christiana only made her want to drop a plate of raw oysters over the beauty queen's flawlessly coiffed head.

The afternoon had played out as Jonathan predicted, even down to the photographers rushing them at the door that Christiana held open. Too bad Jonathan couldn't forecast and orchestrate the rest of her life.

Reality returned with a vengeance. She'd met with her dad's accountant, gotten the dishwasher fixed, and had the oil changed in her car, mundane tasks that suddenly seemed illusory. She'd avoided Avery, but her constant messages only added to the surreal nature her life had taken on.

Over the week, Avery's messages became increasingly sweet. Only after Christiana finally talked to her live did the reason become clear. Avery's light tone couldn't camouflage her intentions. "We should double date or something. Wouldn't that be great?"

Over my dead body. Most people underestimated Avery's intelligence. Christiana never had. Only after Christiana swore she wasn't dating Jonathan, that their relationships resembled mentor-mentee, did Avery stop her inquisition. But even that half-truth didn't prevent her from grilling Christiana about her weekend, and Christiana finally admitted to having out-of-town plans.

"My Dad, well . . . ."

"You're going to go meet him? Be careful." Avery's honest concern had only thickened the guilt stewing in her belly. Christiana *should* have caught a plane to meet her father. His messages had grown less coherent as Avery's attitude became more saccharine. A good daughter would have headed to whatever Holiday Inn in Tennessee he'd passed out in and chucked the mini-bar through the window.

"Come back to me." Jonathan's voice stopped her black thoughts. He set her bag down inside the door and stood straight and strong before the entranceway's Buddha.

"I'm here." Christiana stepped into his open arms. She inhaled his pure male scent. *This* is where she wanted to be. She just hoped she hadn't fucked it up with her jealousy.

He nuzzled the top of her head. "Go into the bathroom, strip off all your clothes, and slip into the tub. Wait for me there."

Warm steam enveloped her body two steps into the blue, glass-tiled tub room off the master bathroom. The surface of the water in the sunken tub glistened with milky bubbles in the soft candlelight flickering from a dozen candles. A tall bamboo ladder propped against the wall was hung with white fluffy towels. She knew they'd be warm without having to touch them.

Blanca must have been here only moments before they arrived, to prepare the bath. Christiana marveled at how Jonathan directed the dozens of people who must float around him and his life, making things happen as if by magic. She wondered if a few of them might have gone to Tennessee to check on a certain reporter.

Christiana undressed and laid her clothes on a chair in the corner. She smiled at a hair tie that sat on the counter, another detail he'd probably dictated to the unseen Blanca.

After securing her hair, now curling in the humidity, she sank her body into the warmth. Fizzy, paper-thin jets of water rose from the bottom of the tub, massaging her limbs. She rested her head on the terry pillow affixed to the back edge and opened her legs, letting a single angel-hair stream of water shoot up to tickle her inner folds. She focused on the tiny water fingers playing with her skin, teasing her calves, the backs of her knees, and areas she hoped Jonathan might attend to later. She adjusted her behind so another stream ran up her cleft. *So good.* One by one, her worries flitted away on a thousand playful bubbles.

Jonathan's leg brushed hers under the water. She hadn't even heard him enter the room.

"Lean forward," he said and eased himself behind her. His strong hands enclosed her shoulders, pulling her back to connect with his muscled chest, her ass firmly nestled against her favorite part of the sensual man. He wasn't aroused, but his considerable size trailed up past her crevice.

Jonathan's arms encircled her ribs, and she absorbed his strength. They relaxed in the water for several minutes, not speaking. His fingers ran up and down her arms. Soon her chest rose and fell in rhythm with his breath. He nuzzled her neck and, despite the hot water, a tremble ran through her middle.

"I'm sorry." Where did that come from? Their conversation in the car down to Charlottesville had been light, even fun. The water must have coaxed the unsaid and unfinished up and out into broad daylight.

"For what?" he asked.

She wasn't sure she could articulate her feelings. Maybe Jonathan could think on his feet, but she found her mind only caught up days after the events. Somehow words tumbled from her lips anyway.

"For everything. For getting drunk, for getting your picture in the paper, for not answering my phone so now Avery knows, for you having to correct—"

"Shhh, lovely. Forget that." His voice rumbled deep in his chest, vibrating through her back straight to her heart.

"For not trusting you before," she whispered.

His index fingers teased her nipples. The peaks awakened under his touch, hardening and tingling. His wet mouth latched onto her shoulder, and she sunk into relief over his silent proclamation. His tolerance of her obvious immaturity made her want to weep.

Before her mind could sift through more of her mistakes, Jonathan hooked his legs over her calves and pulled them open. All thought dissolved. Her legs relaxed from the magical water-angel fingers teasing her crevices. He seemed to know exactly where to place her, so she'd feel the most sensation, enough to stimulate but subtle enough to keep her on edge, a climax promised but kept in the distance.

"All's forgiven." His lips pulled into a smile on her shoulder. "But know you will beg to serve me before the sun sets tonight." The energy shifted in his hands, now kneading her flesh urgently.

"Christiana, this weekend you'll give me everything.

We're going to crush that worry you seem to carry around your neck like your pearls."

Jonathan grasped her wrists in one hand and trailed the fingers of the other down her stomach until they found her mound. He held her splayed open with his stronger legs, refusing to let her twitching legs close an inch in defense.

"Even in this water, I can feel how wet you are. A woman's lubrication isn't easily washed away, just as our deepest fantasies can't be rationalized away." He dipped his fingers inside to prove his point.

He released her wrists. "Put your hands behind my neck and keep them there. I'm going to wash you." His hot breath heated the side of her neck. "I am going to push you toward an abyss. You'll be afraid. You'll set aside your fear. Let go. You know I'll be there to catch you every time. I'll make sure you don't go over the edge too hard or too fast."

Her heartbeat rose under his sensual threat. She closed her eyes and focused on its heavy pounding.

"You're tensing," he said.

"I'm—I'm sorry."

"For today, you won't say 'I'm sorry.'" Water sloshed as he slowly rubbed a washcloth over her breasts. "You'll let go of any responsibility. I'm here to take care of everything."

"Yes, sir."

Jonathan ran the soft cloth down her belly and around her hips. He held on to her rib cage, rolling her nipple between his fingers, gently, slowly, but never stopping.

"I love your curves, Christiana. The way your waist dips in and then slopes out to that glorious ass." His cloth-covered fingers dipped between her legs and curved in between her butt cheeks. Out of reflex, her legs jerked anew, trying to close. He held them open.

"You won't bring them together unless I say so." The cloth

rubbed gently over her most forbidden area. Her legs quivered at the invasion.

"You liked when I touched you there, didn't you, angel?"

She knew better than to lie even if the thought of anything happening *there* scared her out of her mind. "Yes."

"Today, I'll take my time, linger over what is mine to take. I'll touch you, lick you, penetrate you, slow and easy."

He drew the cloth upward and swirled it inside her inner creases, sending a finger up one side and down the other of her petals. Washing her. Preparing her.

"I'm taking away your choices. I'll decide everything. You'll scream, thrash and beg me to take you. You want this now. You've always wanted this."

Adrenaline spiked as she focused on the way he swirled the cloth over her clit. A small moan escaped her throat.

"I'm glad you agree," he said. His legs released hers, but she kept them on either side of the tub. Jonathan pulled her arms free of their grasp on his neck—she hadn't realized until that moment she'd dug her fingernails into his flesh.

Water streamed down his torso as he stood, reaching for a towel. "Good girl. You may get out now."

She hadn't moved. She had kept her legs open as directed. But now she stepped out.

Jonathan slowly ran the warm, downy towel over each of her limbs. His intent devotion to each part of her quieted the unrest inside and allowed desire to rise.

He pulled a stray strand of hair from her cheek. "I'm going to give you a safeword, for the weekend. It's 'Washington.'"

He stared down at her in that way he had, as if giving her time to catch up. She both loved and hated that he had to do it. She knew what a safeword entailed, but hadn't thought she'd ever need to utter one with Jonathan. His ability to perceive her needs, her discomforts or fears—even before she could comprehend them—had seemed enough. Yet if last weekend was any measure of his capabilities, anything could be in store.

As if reading her mind—or at least her quivering body—he gave her no more time to consider what was next. In seconds, he'd scooped her up, stripped off the towel, and gently laid her on the bed. Red lights from tiny recesses drenched the room in an eerie glow. An erotic chill danced over her skin.

"Get on all fours. Forehead on your hands. Bottom up." She heard Jonathan open a drawer. Clinks and muffled scrapes of objects from the drawer piqued her curiosity. She quelled the urge to peek. What else had he pulled from his cache of delicious torture?

Jonathan's jean-clad legs kneeled between her open thighs. The contact helped her manage the fear mixed with excitement.

A musky scent rose up as his hands slid down her buttocks, oiling them with a warm emollient. He worked his fingers between her cheeks and breached her anal ring, sliding past the resisting muscle with no warning. She gasped at his immediacy.

He moved his finger in and out a millimeter. "This is a special oil with benzocaine to help you relax more,"

"But you said—"

"And I meant it."

Oh, God, did he really think she'd beg for that?

He reached around her waist with his other hand and circled her nerve center with clever, knowing fingers. The two sensations together sent a gush of pleasure up her back and down her spine. She would have never anticipated the dirty thoughts his invasion created. His finger slipped out, and she moaned from the release.

Okay, maybe the idea wasn't off the table completely.

"Tell me what your safeword is, Christiana."

"Washington."

"If you say that word, everything stops. Do you understand?'

"Yes."

When the whirring started, Christiana's heart set off racing. Now that she knew what such sounds led to, a new level of foreboding, both thrilling and frightening, fueled her nerves.

Four long swaths of midnight blue cascaded from the ceiling. For a second, she was sure she'd suffocate with so much fabric surrounding her.

"Sit up," he said.

More electrical sounds. He eased a tight leather mask over her head. Her sight gone, her hearing muffled, she calmed herself with deep breaths. He pulled the offending mask down to the bridge of her nose. The image of Catwoman came to mind, and she might have giggled at her thought if a crushing alarm hadn't threatened to take over.

"Jonathan?" She couldn't help herself.

She wished she had. She yelped at the unexpected impact of his hand to the side of her ass. She knew her direct question in such an informal address had earned her the resounding swat.

"Permission." His tone, quiet.

"Sir, may I ask you a question?"

"You may."

"Can I see you? Please?" She needed him to say yes.

"Not yet." He fastened a thick heavy cuff to each wrist and ankle, inserting fingers in between cuff and skin, pulling to check their fit. He raised her hands so high she rose up to her knees. The click of a metal clip sent another jolt of nerves through her middle. Her arms and legs shook as she realized she hung from the steel girders overhead by some devious contraption.

His breath ran hot over her breasts, as he leaned in close to deftly wrap a swath of fabric around one knee and up her thigh. "In case you have trouble keeping your legs open, I'm going to give you a little help."

One knee pulled out, and the slip of fabric being draped around something else filled the quiet space. Jonathan treated her other leg similarly, the silk teasing her inner thigh under his careful wrapping. Moisture leaked down her legs in response to the erotic constriction of fabric encasing her limbs and the stretching in her groin. Another pull and her knees splayed out wide. He must have secured the ends to the bedposts.

Jonathan pinched her nipples, and then his tongue swirled around the tips until they were raw. She heard a low, muffled snap. Sharp pain shot through her breast, and she cried out. She pitched backward as much as she could.

"I have many presents for you today. That one's a nipple clamp." Another yelp erupted from her throat as he attached another to her other tip. A thin metal chain touched her belly. He tugged on it, her nipples pulling with the unexpected jar. She wriggled.

"So beautiful," he said, tracing his fingertips along her jawline, down her neck to rest on her shoulders. "Anything hurting too much?"

"No, sir."

The bed dipped, and a rush of cooler air replaced Jonathan's body heat.

"Good. I'm going to take a moment to admire your beautiful body, bound and hung for my pleasure."

Jonathan's seductive touches and soft kisses had always accompanied firm, demanding hands and cock. But something in his voice revealed a new, brutal intent.

Christiana balanced on her knees and calves and . . . waited. In the silence, splayed out for Jonathan's wishes, a new insight formed. Today, Jonathan would demand her complete submission. He'd indelibly stamp his dominance on her heart and body. She wanted it, *craved* it.

24

Christiana hung in space, unanchored and disoriented. The thin chain dangled oddly heavily on her stomach. Her nipples, clit and backside all competed for attention. Her awareness fought for a tranquil place to settle—and lost. Long minutes passed with no sound, no touch and no warmth from Jonathan's body to keep her company in uncertainty.

She startled when his hand touched her behind. More warm oil was rubbed over her butt cheeks, his fingers skating her crack. Then he pushed a finger into her tight back hole. He curled his finger, earning a contented purr. She pushed her ass back to meet his probing finger, which earned her another slap on the fleshiest part of her ass. Her skin flushed with blood when he chuckled, withdrawing. A flash of almost-unrestrained desire to capture his cock into her rear shook her to the core.

Wet clicking sounds joined his whisper. "You should like this present then."

He spread her cheeks with his hands, inserted something small and round with a gentle push. "The first of many gifts."

ELIZABETH SAFLEUR

She groaned loudly as he inserted the second, third and fourth bead.

"What-?"

"You seem to like pearls, so consider these pearls of pleasure."

Her sounds grew more desperate as each one was pushed up her awakened backside. Something like a cord dangled alongside one inner thigh, which he gently tugged. A shameless growl released from the back of her throat as the beads shifted.

Jonathan reclaimed her breasts in each hand. His cock probed between her folds.

"Feel them inside you, Christiana. Feel me." Jonathan rubbed his length through her puffy inner lips and her thick wetness. He smelled so good, familiar warm skin and fully aroused male.

One more stroke, and she'd peak.

He played with the chain connected to the nipple clamps, and she yelped.

"You will not come until I say."

"No, sir. I won't, sir."

"I have a second present to make sure you do not."

Something small and rubbery ran smoothly across her pussy. Back and forth, he trailed the edge until it glided from contact with her womanly fluid.

Without warning, Jonathan smacked her ass with the small, moistened paddle, the slapping sound loud against her oiled cheek, not hard, but she'd been taken by surprise. He brought the small square down on her behind, the beads shifting as she clenched.

"Such lovely marks, *my* marks, on your ass, Christiana." Jonathan ran the paddle up her inner thigh. When he tapped her exposed pussy, her legs lurched in her bindings.

He tutted.

Jonathan lightly smacked her three more times, producing a longer cry more from anger than pain. "Ow, ah, nooo."

His answer was another sharp slap of the paddle.

She cried out an obscenity when he slapped her clit a fifth time with the flat rubber object.

"Such strong language from such a little girl," he said. More stinging blows to her oiled bottom sent her keening forward. Jonathan reached around to hold her up by one breast, the nipple clamp biting into her flesh.

Tiny stings erupted over her behind as the devil worked each inch of her exposed skin with the evil paddle. He stayed away from her pussy, but the beads moved, taunting and reminding her he'd just begun, that he had other ideas she'd be helpless to contradict.

Christiana had wanted to give herself totally to Jonathan. To be *taken*. Now that he'd accepted her offering, molding and shaping her obedience in new, strange ways, her psyche protested.

He smacked her with another instrument, wider and thicker, like solid wood.

"Fuck!" The word exploded from her mouth.

He pried her mouth open and inserted a short, thick dildo. "You'll suck on this like it's my cock. It'll give you something to do with that uncontrolled mouth. I can still hear your safeword around it."

Christiana was actually relieved to have one less thing to think about controlling. Her legs shook as if she'd been shocked with electrical current.

Did he pay attention? He stopped to knead her shoulders. Okay. Jonathan hadn't abandoned all safety. The respite didn't last.

More smacks with the wooden hand came fast and hard. She stopped counting after six.

He would show no mercy unless she cried out the one word that would stop him. She didn't want him to stop. Yet she wasn't sure she could go where he was taking her, this heaven-hell combination with a promise of something unspoken.

Metallic scraping overhead mixed with her labored breathing.. Leather and flower scents wafted under her nose. The tension on the tether loosened. Jonathan's arms circled her ribs and he lowered her forward to rest her forearms on the bed. The chain clinked on fabric under her, but the clamps brushed the coverlet, sending new pointed sensation to her captured nipples.

Jonathan nestled his hard-on between her slick folds and slowly dragged through her cream. When he tugged slightly on the string dangling down the back of her thigh, she let out a muffled whine.

"Keep your hands overhead." She stretched out her arms as far as she could, until she touched the edge of the bed. She hung on to the end of the mattress to help anchor her senses to something, anything, outside her own body.

Jonathan pulled her hips backward. She lost her grip on the mattress and whimpered slightly. Her disorientation returned with a vengeance. She concentrated on his hands gripping her legs, as if checking the silks' hold. She would have assured him they held fast if she could've spoken.

Her ass stung, but the delicious provocation from the beads lodged firmly in her behind trumped the pain. She lay face first on his bed, butt in the air. Rage sparked at the edge of her consciousness. Something dark and dangerous unfurled inside and mixed with the unnatural lust Jonathan had raised. She clamped down on the dildo, hoping she left teeth marks, as a darkened beast rose up inside.

Fingers probed her most intimate parts, and then

Jonathan's broad cockhead teased her opening. He pushed inside, a declaration of ownership and power.

Something sinister, something unwanted, erupted in response. She sucked and wailed behind the gag as he slammed into her, fulfilling his own needs.

She suddenly didn't want to be this person, this subservient, never-in-control, mass of craving, being flayed, worked and punished. Christiana thought she knew who she was, and it was not this unnatural creature who allowed herself to be splayed open, taken, and touched in places she hadn't dared.

The struggle inside split into two camps. One set of reasons told her to scream her safeword at the top of her lungs, as much as she could with the gag. The other side told her to let go, have faith that surrendering her entire being to Jonathan was right, that he was taking her somewhere.

Washington.

Say it.

No, don't speak.

The parachute fabric heated as he pushed her forward. They'll burn your skin, he'd said. Was he paying attention? Jonathan pulled her backward, momentarily loosening the fabric, as if he'd read her mind. The gentle caress along her inner thigh pitched her over to one side of her internal civil war. Christiana wanted to prove to him, to herself, she was worthy of his attention, his *choice* of her. She'd endure.

Jonathan dug his fingers into her hips as he savagely pounded into her.

"Come for me," he growled.

Pop. Her back channel muscles pulsed as he pulled out one of the beads. She squealed behind the wicked rubber dildo as *pop, pop, pop,* a long string of anal throbs sent her to the top of a precipice. He was going to tear her apart.

"Come." His strained voice growled with authority. His cock pounded inside her, another order to obey.

Christiana tipped over the edge, shattering into a million pieces that shot up through her like a fountain. Saliva ran down her chin as she screamed. She lost all sense of her body, its form, sure that it had exploded. Shards of her climax continued to course through her limbs for more minutes—even after she fought for breath.

Christiana realized that now she experienced the *real* Jonathan Brond. He had held back before.

Jonathan marveled at Christiana's beauty. Her pale skin was stark against the blue fabric that had held her legs open for his wishes. Her cheeks flushed a deep rosy color, and her inner thighs glistened with her ecstatic flood. He fought the urge to lap at their trails. He could have watched her for hours, spasming in the parachute silks holding her captive.

Jonathan kissed her shoulder and slipped the gag from between her lips. He wiped the saliva from around her mouth.

"Now, baby, deep breath." He pinched the clamps free from her nipples.

She cried out as the blood rushed to her tortured buds. He held her in a bear hug until her whimpers subsided.

He untied the ends of the silks from the bedposts. She splayed onto her stomach, unable to hold herself on her knees any longer. As he slowly unwound the sodden fabric from her legs, he checked her skin for burn marks. No bruises or signs of distress. He'd been lucky with his ruthless taking. He'd been so enchanted by the gorgeous creature in the center of his bed he'd not paid enough attention to her comfort.

This last session, as short as it was for him, tested her limits. Something had cracked inside Christiana. He hadn't expected her profound reaction, her cries uncontained and feral behind the dildo gag. Of course, even introductory anal play brought much to the surface, as the back door proved to be a true center of emotion.

Jonathan rubbed his hand across the little harlequin squares across her butt left by the rubber riding crop and wooden paddle.

"Oh, lovely, our skin glows in this light," he said.

Christiana breathed hard, yet she remained pliable and soft under his hands.

Jonathan sent the two long bunches of fabric back up to the ceiling to be dealt with later.

He had to keep her going, push through the crack that had surfaced.

Jonathan touched her back. He ran his hand to clasp the back of her neck with his message. *I'm here, with you, caring for you, but make no mistake who's in control.* The connection ensured she wouldn't spiral downward. The first thing he'd learned about Christiana was how important touch was in her world—the touch of someone who wouldn't let her down.

He ran his fingers up her greased legs. She let out a dainty gasp. Her authentic reactions to a single touch were unrivaled. Jonathan's history held dozens of lovers, all who proclaimed their admiration of his skills, his attention. Yet even his more-than-healthy ego stood in awe of Christiana's surrender. He vowed to take her far today—as far as *she* needed—as far as he'd ever dared. She needed to be taken to the edge, pushed to give in, let go, and shown she wouldn't die if she trusted someone else. She'd never understand her own power otherwise, when to give and when to withhold.

Jonathan had slowed down, but Christiana knew it wouldn't last; he maintained a rapacious hold on her thighs. She searched the silence for what he wanted.

No words came.

He spread her cheeks. His adroit tongue traced her rim, involuntary sounds erupting from her throat at the sensation until she felt herself softening, opening, wanting him *there*. Her pussy joined the call, slight contractions beginning at the marvel of the ecstasy his mouth could produce from her backside, an area she'd never entertained as pleasurable.

A soft, disappointed murmur left her throat when he stopped. The sounds she was helpless to stop still touched a place of shame deep within her, as if to say *try to regain your dignity, at least a little.*

He pulled her up, so she rested on her knees, her behind high in the air, her covered cheek resting on the bed covers. The snap of a bottle top sent stabs of lustful apprehension to her licentious pussy. Something cool and unyielding slipped inside her rear, sending a strange new pressure to her backside. "This butt plug will train you to open up."

Fingers dipped under her pelvis, and he played his special tempo on her clit. An unfeminine moan escaped from deep within her chest as the dual sensations of his teasing fingers and the intruder in her ass intensified. She knew the rhythm well. She had cursed herself many times for not being able to conjure it up herself on the nights when separated from his talented hands.

"You're doing so well, baby. Let it out." Beard stubble scratched her back, and a new layer of herself split.

His scent, strength and presence replaced any sense of herself. Against such a man, Christiana felt small and delicate. His large hand grasped her upper leg, as if to make the point. Never before had she felt so female, and Jonathan so male.

Fingers worked her sensitive jewel, and a flaming twinge ran up her middle as his crotch pushed the anal plug. Sensation overcame any sense of her body's borders.

"Relax." He drew out the word in his deep, rich voice.

With one thrust, he seated his cock inside her pussy, taking renewed custody. Her flaming ass pressed into the silky hair surrounding his shaft. She cried out from the indescribable heaviness; he and the plug took up too much space within her. Instinct screamed for her to pull back, but with nothing to grip but a silk sheet, she couldn't.

Jonathan withdrew only to ream her insides with his cock several more times. He steadied her hips to keep her from rocking her away.

She whimpered, and his thumb circled over her swollen charm in response. Her anal muscles relaxed a little, and soon her honey flowed down her inner legs. Stains of her arousal must mar the bedsheets, but her desire batted away that concern. Nothing but his hands on her, his cock inside, mattered.

His taunting hand slid away, trailing her feminine ambrosia. He grasped both hips, and his leg hair tickled the backs of her legs as his cock dragged, too leisurely, through her too-tight pussy.

"You're mine, aren't you?" he gritted out.

Instinctively, Christiana knew his eyes caressed her body as they had many times, full of anticipation and demand. "Yes. Yours!"

God, she craved him to split her in two with his ramming cock, even with the indescribable fullness. Her leg muscles ached with a desperate need to spread wide. If he'd asked her to count these strokes, she'd start at one hundred by now.

She'd have gladly started over from one if he'd keep moving in and out of her heat.

She fought the urge to rip the mask off her head. *Let me see you.*

Feel me, his body demanded instead.

She clenched her ass around the plug. He growled satisfaction in reaction. She writhed as his strokes shallowed, shortened. Unintelligible sounds that would have colored her skin crimson weeks ago now flew from her throat as she tried to inch her pussy closer to capture his fullness.

A slap on her ass told her he had other plans. More short pulses teased her throbbing pussy until her cries were only interrupted by her need to take in air.

He lunged forward, his root connecting with the plug. Her climax came hard and fast, her body shuddering so harshly she was sure she'd have burns on her knees. Not even the smacks on her ass by Jonathan stopped the involuntary clenching of her inner muscles.

"Bad girl." His voice was gentle. Christiana knew it displayed Jonathan's self-discipline, not his forgiveness for her coming without permission once. Impossible to stop, yet most definitely punishment material, and worth it. She couldn't wait.

Christiana kept her hands in prayer position against her chest. She writhed on the silky bedcover in the knowledge that inches away was a man who prepared to take more pleasure from every inch of her exposed skin and who would wring out orgasm after orgasm from her. She lay helpless to stop him.

More dualities threatened to break apart inside. One side wanted this man to crack her open, take his pleasure between her legs, rudely and without shame. The other shouted to snap her thighs closed, that whatever he was doing was *too much*. The truth settled the matter. Christiana wanted to *belong* to Jonathan.

He urged her to roll onto her back. He pushed her knees up to her chest, and soft cotton ropes wound around her ankles up around her calves to her knees, spreading open her legs to expose her private parts once. He tethered her hands to yet another rope on the bed.

Where did all the goddamn straps come from? Her pussy wept as she pulled and tested her arm fastenings.

"Still, Christiana."

Jonathan pulled on the anal plug. The unearthly sensation of its slow glide banished any hope of remaining silent or unmoving. She'd felt every millimeter of its length drag through her muscle.

Any last thoughts about her good-girl self-image, of the young woman who did the right thing, kept quiet, and obeyed the rules, burst like a balloon.

I want this. "Sir!?" she cried.

"A question, Christiana?"

"No questions. What do you need?" Okay, it was a question.

A heartbeat of silence followed. Did she ask the wrong thing?

Instead, a well-lubricated dildo entered her inflamed pussy, a slim pressure filled her anus. More buckling of a strap followed the double penetration. A subtle vibration began. She panted at the low humming running through her sore areas. She knew she would only teeter on the torturous precipice of completion within moments.

"Oh, God, p-please," she rasped, her voice hoarse from screams.

"Open up." He straddled her waist. The swollen, weeping cockhead teased her lips. She took it deep enough to touch her gag reflex, resolved to make him come hard and soon, show him she could service him to the fullest.

She sucked, swirled, and licked like a greedy child with a treat. He held himself back, only allowing her access to half his length. She gurgled against his steely cock, begging for all of him. She tried to lift her head more to take him fully, but he held her head fast by her hair, the pull on her scalp adding to the delicious torment of needing more.

Her hips arched up in reflex. But her bound limbs ensured she could only squirm like a trapped animal under the tent of his legs. His hand tightened in her hair. The vibrations in her ass and pussy dialed down, the threat of the promised convulsions retreated. The mischievous device lodged firmly in her orifices teased and taunted at a conclusion that Jonathan wouldn't permit.

Unintelligible sounds erupted from her throat.

"Yes, I'll let you service me. Suck me hard, Christiana, and I'll let you come—later."

He eased out so she could take a much needed breath and then pushed in, holding himself there for a few seconds. He set the pace. Each time he pulled out, she took a lungful of air, letting it out as he pushed back in and down her throat. He was slow and deliberate until tears ran down her cheeks, leaking from under the leather. He held out for a long, long time though she heard his rasp from deep inside his own throat each time he pushed in.

A small groan escaped when the now-familiar pulse of the vein on the underside of his manhood promised his release. The first spurt into her throat nearly gagged her, but he mercifully pulled back to allow her to swallow. As she milked his cock to completion, she knew the small favor wouldn't last. The vibration between her legs stopped, and his hand found her swollen clit. She let out a complaint when he pinched.

"Very good. Now let's see what else I have for you, my beautiful, lovely pet."

Christiana lost track of time, suspended in a place where Jonathan's body and her own connected, making their own corner of the universe. Whatever he offered, she took. Whatever he asked, she did. Whatever he did, she sunk into like quicksand. Jonathan moved her around the bed like a precious rag doll. Limbs placed. Mouth taken. Pussy filled. Legs open—always, always open.

At some point, he removed the mask. His emerald eyes bathed her face with warmth, control, *approval*. He wrung out new orgasms from her body, always on command. And when she thought she couldn't give any more, he resurrected even more from deep inside her womb. Jonathan never released her eyes, and she felt his ultimate reward into her core.

25

Christiana relaxed on a deck chair and looked out at the trees. Jonathan had needed to make some phone calls in his office. His forehead wrinkled when his phone kept ringing over breakfast. He hadn't needed to tell her he required some privacy. She needed time as well.

She drifted into a mesmerized haze, lulled by the soft rustle of leaves. The trees moved in the slight breeze, unadorned by the usual gangs of blue jays and warblers. The hot morning sun must have sent the birds to cooler resting places.

She was tired, but couldn't sleep anymore. Her legs trembled every few minutes as if recovering from a triathlon. Well, last night had been a marathon.

Sometime in the night, she'd descended from orbit: soft caresses accompanied by Jonathan's reassurances helped her spiral downward into her body—sore, worn out, and euphoric.

Jonathan made her sip an Emer-Gen-C drink in between spoonfuls of a thick, creamy soup. Was it potato or cauliflower? She was in such a daze she couldn't tell. He'd left her in the bed, sheets snuggled up to her chin, with orders to sleep as long as she wanted. She didn't want to close her eyes. She never wanted to close her eyes.

Jonathan was right. If she'd trusted him, he would show her everything she didn't know she wanted. For the first time, Christiana understood the difference between acquiescing and trusting someone else's judgment. Last night, he hadn't used her body as much as *serviced* a need that had lain dormant, pulling out something primal that he then worshipped.

Christiana rose and walked back into the house. An abrupt need to be next to Jonathan surfaced as if a hypnotic suggestion had been awakened.

The sound of his voice grew louder as she moved across the house. His laughter spilled out into the hallway, beckoning her to quicken her pace. She loved him happy.

But the laugh morphed into a snicker. "No, I'm not really looking forward to it, Sarah. He only cares about my re-election. I look forward to seeing *you*, of course."

His re-election? And, he's seeing Sarah? *But, I'm here.* A little petulant girl arose at the thought of Jonathan being cheered by anyone but her. *Don't be a baby, Chris. Jesus.*

Christiana stepped into the doorway and leaned against the frame. She pushed her hip out, knowing the effect she had on him—now. By the way his eyelids hooded, Jonathan appreciated her stance. He winked.

"Yes, I know," Jonathan said into the phone. "Good intentions and all that." He put his hand over the mouthpiece and mouthed, "Five minutes. Go start a bath for us. I'm not done with you."

She tossed her hair over her shoulder before heading to his bathroom. So, *Sarah* had Jonathan's attention for five minutes. She'd figure out how to reclaim him.

∼

"You do know the antidote to your father's wrath?" Sarah asked.

"Marry Marla Clampton?" Jonathan chuckled.

"There you go, Jay. You knew the answer the whole time." She laughed softly. "It's a few more months. Get through the election before you return to the beautiful girl. She's beautiful, but—"

"I have no idea who you're talking about." He picked a piece of lint off his cotton pants.

"Jay, this is me you're talking to. I don't think taking risks is in your best interest right now."

"Risks? This is me you're talking to, Sarah."

"True. Forget what I say. Show up by five on Thursday and escort me to the big fundraiser so we both can get Brond Senior off our backs."

"Still trying to fix you up with eligible men?"

"The old man never gives up. But, then neither does my mother."

"You don't have to tell me. See you then, Sarah."

After he hung up, he stared out at birdless trees. They probably hid from the heat too. Such simple lives they lived. *Short, but simple.*

Sarah was right. He had neglected his duties. He had staff, constituents, business partners, all counting on him. Just because his father tried to run his life was no reason to forget his responsibilities. He'd agreed to run for office. He had no one to blame but himself for joining the family business of politics.

Of course, he had not foreseen a certain nineteen-year-old. He had planned to care for no one—until the right time. Timing was everything in Washington.

Too bad he'd met the perfect woman during an imperfect time.

Last night, Christiana had wrestled with her demons and won. He witnessed her stunning fortitude in letting go. She'd taken everything he'd dished out and reveled in his command. If he'd only met her five years from now. He'd have married, cherished and protected her every second of her precious life, not to mention fucked the living daylights out of her every available moment.

You're an animal, Brond. You'll let her go—for her sake, remember?

If only he could figure out a way to keep her with him beyond the summer or at least squirreled away until a better time. Why couldn't he pack her off to school, and then spend long weekends at *Covil Sereia*, feasting on her submission?

His ten-year master plan smacked him upside the head. *No ties, no complications.* His family and position didn't have room for—for what? Someone so pure the dirt clinging to him, to his family would show?

A dozen men could fill his place. She'd want someone tall, confident, imposing with a touch of gentility. He could find such a man.

No. He couldn't stand the thought of another man touching Christiana. Not ever. He just didn't know how to make Christiana a permanent part of his life. Too bad he wasn't religious. *Because I need a miracle.*

When Jonathan entered his bathroom, Christiana crouched before the tub, testing the water temperature. She smiled up at him when he entered. Seeing her on her knees, he couldn't get his clothes off fast enough. Christiana only added to his urgency by slipping off her skimpy tank dress to reveal nothing but temptation.

"Fuck, Christiana."

"You're such a romantic."

"In the tub, now."

She slipped into the rising water and twisted her hair up with an elastic. He stepped into the tub and pulled her to straddle his hips.

"Can I ask you a question?" she asked.

"Always."

She puffed out a half-laugh. "How do you get away with all of this?" She rubbed one eye, like a small child might. "I mean, this dual life?"

"With great difficulty. Fortunately, given sufficient justification, people will believe anything. What they can't stand is mystery. The more open you are, the better. Like the other day at The Oak. All they need is one plausible story."

"Well, you're pretty mysterious. Doesn't anyone wonder how you spend your weekends? If I was one of your voters, I'd want to know where you were all the time." She traced his forearm.

"No one cares where I am, only that I'm doing something they approve of."

"Would they approve of us?"

"Not at all." He smiled into her eyes.

A flicker of pain crossed her face. He hugged her closer to his chest. Of course, she wasn't suitable. Only a twenty-five-year-old socialite, ripe in her childbearing years and from a good family, would be suitable. He'd die of boredom in the first six months.

Jonathan searched for something to say to soothe the wound his words created but couldn't find anything that wouldn't also promise something he wasn't sure he could deliver.

"I'm proud to be with you, Christiana. I just want people to think there's nothing to discover. I let people know you're the daughter of a reporter I talk with, who might need a little mentoring. None of it's false, and it gives people a reason for you being in my company. This way, they won't make one up."

Her shoulders trembled. *Tears.*

He scooted her up higher on to him, so her face nestled deeper in his neck. "You're crying."

"We can never be seen together. I guess I understand that . . . but somehow I wish things could be different." Her voice cracked. After last night, she'd float in a delicate state for a while.

"We have a special connection, Christiana. We always will." She'd wrung more truth from him.

Jonathan tightened his hold and rocked Christiana slowly. Her breathing deepened. She'd drifted to sleep, still exhausted from their encounter.

In the stillness, the idea of Christiana finding someone else rose. Perhaps he'd been insensitive to give her a taste of the powerful connection between a Dom and his sub. She'd now crave it moving forward. Hell, she'd be lost without it. Now she knew what to look for and what to expect. He could find someone for her—he'd done it countless times when submissives grew too close—a man who would be firm but gentle, with an all-consuming passion to care for and protect her, and treasure the gift of her submission.

Sooner or later, he always arrived at this place, an unpalatable choice—a meaningful relationship or his political career. It's why he'd rarely uttered those three little words all women seemed to live for. A shudder ran through him as he articulated what he'd always known but never admitted: he didn't know how to reconcile his career with his love.

What if he tried to have both? Go beyond the summer and incorporate Christiana into his life somehow. Would she even want that? *Who'd want a life of fundraisers and political rallies?*

She deserved better.

Another thought fought itself forward, unsettling him more. Yes, *he* could be replaced in *her* life, but he'd never find anyone to replace Christiana in *his*.

An oppressive silence descended with his newfound realizations. He concentrated on Christiana's soft breath moving over his neck, like a meditation. He caressed her hair and trailed his fingertips down her neck to her shoulder. He cherished every curve, every gentle rise and fall of her chest and sought to memorize her unique scent. *Irreplaceable.*

26

Christiana clutched her father's arm and tugged the gossamer gown's bodice one more time before stepping inside the ballroom door. Sarah had said to keep it down so her breasts threatened to spill. She hoped that remained only a threat.

She'd let her father believe Avery lent her the dress. No reason to burst his bubble with the news that their friendship stood on a rocky cliff.

Her father, clad in his old black tuxedo, had slicked his hair back and smelled of Old Spice. Christiana glimpsed what must have captured her mother's interest when he circled in front of her in their living room.

"Still fits," he beamed.

"The ladies don't stand a chance, Dad."

As promised, Jonathan had sent her dress and two large embossed cards providing entry to the Club's annual Fourth of July fundraiser for the American Mental Health Research Center. All year, the club's philanthropy committee planned for the event, which included a dinner, fashion show and then cocktail party on the outside terrace to watch fireworks explode over the bay. It was the "grandest event in all of Washington," according to Coco Churchill. But Coco declared all affairs grand. She would know, having been bred from birth to chair philanthropic committees, host parties, and help her husband up his career ladder with her own socialite family's connections.

Christiana had never been officially invited to this event before, only brought in by Avery to help dress the runway models.

"You look beautiful, Christiana." Her father gave her wrist a squeeze in the ballroom doorway.

She prayed her father was right. Over the weekend, she'd given Jonathan all she had. Then he said there was nothing to discover regarding their relationship. Well, she'd be sure he'd discover something tonight—her candidacy for a more permanent relationship.

Jonathan had dropped her off Sunday night, leaving her weak-kneed and wet from a long passionate kiss. Then few words came during the week. His note accompanying the dress on Wednesday was short and polite. Stingingly so. His texts were no better. She'd let her fingers hover over her phone every night to demand his sudden emotional retreat. Something told her to wait. She'd already displayed enough immaturity.

But tonight? Well, she wasn't waiting anymore.

Between Sunday and today, she had put all her mental energy into ways to get Jonathan to agree to keep seeing her after August. They could see each other on weekends. She practiced her speech to him in front of her mirror. She couldn't let her face give away the desperation festering behind it. She had a feeling he didn't respond to that particular emotion.

"You look so much like your mother tonight, Christiana," her Dad said. "She'd be so proud of you."

Words stuck in Christiana's throat. Her father hadn't mentioned her mother in years.

Her father jutted his elbow out in invitation for her hold. "Ready?"

"Thanks, Dad." She bumped him with her hip, trying to lighten the mood. She needed to focus on her future tonight and didn't need her past creeping up to bite her in the ass. Only Jonathan was allowed to do such things.

They stepped into the sea of Washington's elite.

Red, white and blue bunting hung over a dozen bars, interspersed through the tables, where tuxedo-clad servers doled out glasses of champagne and tumblers of scotch. Waiters, balancing trays of canapés, wove through small groups of men in black tie and women in long dresses— Christiana could see shrimp toast and caviar points and smoked salmon adorning dollops of cream cheese on bagel rounds. White linen-draped tables laden heavily with steaming chafing dishes promised fragrant fish in béchamel sauce and succulent roasted chicken.

A woman in a long red gown swished by Christiana, nearly knocking her off her feet with the stiff taffeta skirt. Christiana recognized her as a newscaster from the evening news. Okay, maybe Coco was right about "anyone who's anyone" attending tonight.

Jonathan had said he might not be able to talk with her much at the event, given its size. She believed him. The large crowd tested the size of the ballroom and probably the fire code. She wondered how she'd find Jonathan in such a horde. She craved seeing him in black tie.

"You look so grown-up, I think it's time for a little champagne," her father said.

"Oh, no, Dad, I'm fine. Really." She couldn't afford to be anything but steady on her feet.

Her father headed to one of the bars in the room, leaving

Christiana to stand alone. Before she could scoot to the side, a hand touched her shoulder. She turned and faced Avery, nearly blinded by the diamonds cascading down in an intricate pattern over her friend's décolletage laid bare in her strapless ivory gown.

Avery's eyes trailed up and down Christiana's body. "Wow, where'd you get the Herrera?"

"The what?"

Avery let out an incredulous huff. "The *dress*?" She raised her eyebrows.

"Oh, it's on loan. How is everything going backstage?"

"Frantic. I need your help. Jessica Sterling is in the bathroom puking her guts out."

"You need me to hold her hair?" *Not in this dress. No way.*

"No, you've got to take her place."

"Doing what?"

"Modeling."

"No way." Christiana turned away from Avery's stricken face to search for her father.

Avery grasped her arm. "*Please.* My mother finally let me handle something this big. It has to go well!"

Christiana had rarely heard Avery beg. "I'm not a model, Avery. I can't—"

Avery tugged her toward a side door. "I have just the thing for you."

"Forget it. I am *not* getting on that runway." Christiana wrenched her arm free.

Avery spun to face her. "Listen, I haven't asked much of you. How could I? You're always disappearing. But I really, really need you to do this for me." Her lips curled into a smile. "You're gonna love it. It'll make any man notice," she hissed into her ear. "Who wouldn't want that?"

Well, attracting men was Avery's specialty. Perhaps it could present a perfect opportunity to show Jonathan her adult side—this time with clothes *on*, rather than off. How bad could it be?

Christiana sighed. "Okay."

She failed to signal her father she was headed backstage. He stood engrossed in a conversation, already with a drink in hand. He wouldn't miss her anyway.

Before they stepped into the hall, Christiana caught a glimpse of a familiar, blond head. He entered the ballroom from an entranceway at the end of the hall talking to two gentlemen. Jonathan laughed and slapped the back of a man's shoulder, earning him a broad smile. Her heart swelled at the sight of his broad shoulders clad in a finely cut black jacket. The memory of a summer wool and linen scent enveloping her on a dance floor arose.

Avery's grip brought her back to full reality. "Wait 'til you see the dress!"

They entered a small meeting room turned dressing room. Several older women tittered in the corner over a woman in a white dress who couldn't seem to get her zipper up, while another woman stepped into a cascade of bright red sequins.

Jessica rushed up to Christiana. "Wow, Chris, you look good."

"Yeah, can you believe a Herrera?" Avery answered.

"Well, look what we have for you. It's so hot!" Jessica held up a mass of midnight blue ropes. "It's a crocheted dress. All the rage."

Christiana raised her eyebrows and turned to Avery to protest. "No way. I am *not* wearing that."

Avery sighed. "Chris, be a team player here. Come on. Try it. Trust me." Avery snuck her hands underneath Christiana's arm to fiddle with her side zipper.

Avery knew fashion, so it wouldn't be ugly. Christiana just wished there was more of it.

"What do I wear underneath?" Christiana asked.

"That's the best part," Jessica squealed. She lifted up a red, lacy strapless bra, embedded with crystals. "It'll peek through, like fireworks in the night sky."

Christiana reluctantly took the crocheted material, bra and thong.

"You are going to have every man wanting you," Jessica sang.

Christiana stepped out of the puddle of blue fabric at her feet and slipped behind a tri-fold screen. She peeled off the lingerie Jonathan had sent over and replaced it with the gaudy thong and bra. At least they were the right size, if you could call the thong barely covering her mound a "fit." Sarah was right about one thing. Red was not her color.

She slipped the crocheted fabric over her head and pulled it down to cover her ass. The fabric, stretched, reached mid-thigh. Whether it would stay there when she walked was another matter.

Christiana stepped out from behind the screen. Avery and Jessica gave each other a look.

"Oh my God, it's perfect," Jessica said.

Avery smiled. "It'll be the highlight of the show, Chris."

"Oh, come on. You can see everything. I can't."

Avery spun her around to face the mirror. "Yes, you can. It's just enough. All eyes will be on you."

"Avery—"

"Woman up, Christiana. *Jesus.* But, hey, if you're not brave enough to wear this, I can put you in some boring white gown that will make you look like everyone else. Fine by me, but don't come boohooing to me when you find out you've blown a chance to wear something *this hot.*" She ran her hands over Christiana's hips to emphasize her point.

"Where's your mom? She should see this, first, don't you think?" Coco Churchill had been the event's committee chair for a decade and was usually running around the dressing room in her tall heels, barking orders in her high-pitched voice.

"Coco couldn't be bothered with the models this year. She let me decide everything. I think I might go into this, as a profession." Avery leaned into Christiana's ear. "I am *really* good at this. Trust me."

Sarah had said the same thing during Jonathan's dress-up day. Well, Avery had nailed one thing. No one would *not* notice her in this outfit. She only hoped the one man tonight she needed to captivate, would.

Christiana studied herself in the mirror. How bad could it be? So far everything new she'd tried this summer had worked out—sort of.

Jessica peered over her shoulder. "Those are real Swarovski crystals on the lingerie. They'll twinkle in the light when you move."

"You-know-who is out there, ya know," Avery whispered.

Coco walked up to them. "Ladies, ladies, please move faster." She turned to Christiana. "Why, Miss Snow, well, no time. Avery, I need you backstage, *now*."

Loud hip-hop music erupted from the ballroom. Laughter and clapping ensued. The show had begun.

A line of twittering women lined up along the back wall to exit the dressing room for the catwalk. Jessica positioned Christiana between a woman in a long, red sequin sheath and another in a frothy white dress with layers of pearl-beaded tulle and lace. "You're second to last. The fireworks are always at the end of an evening, right?"

The woman behind her leaned toward Christiana's ear. "Unless there's a wedding dress involved. That's always the last look in a collection, the show stopper." She gave Christiana a warm smile.

Christiana took a deep breath and followed the other women out the door to the backstage.

∾

Jonathan had given Mark strict instructions to get Peter Snow home that evening. After watching the man down his fifth glass of cabernet, no way would Peter go home with Christiana alone even if taxicabs lined the club entranceway for such a situation. He might stop at a bar on the way home. No, let Mark drive Peter home in his limousine. Jonathan would get Christiana home in his own car, also nestled safely in the parking lot downstairs in case he needed to make a break from the paparazzi. Photographers always followed the limos.

Or maybe Jonathan wouldn't take Christiana home at all. He'd take her to his own bed. He'd been separated from her for three days, and already he'd crushed his resolve to stay away until Saturday.

His fingers had hovered over his phone every few minutes, tempted to call Christiana and demand she meet him somewhere, anywhere. He stopped himself each time.

Christiana must be backstage. He hadn't seen her all night. Last weekend she'd shared that Avery roped her into helping in the dressing room the last three years. No wonder he'd never run into Christiana before. He was certain Avery ensured her friend sat hidden backstage most of the time.

Completely inappropriate music thumped from the speakers. He had to admit the crowd seemed to enjoy the change in pace though. Chamber music and Washington Opera singers belting out arias accompanying young models gliding down the runway had grown stale.

Jonathan ran his fork through the remains of his tiramisu and half-heartedly listened to Sarah entertain Congressman

Pickard on her right. She read Jonathan well. She could tell he was in no mood to be lobbied by a colleague seeking support.

"You're distracted," Sarah said into her glass of wine.

"A little tired. It's a busy time."

"You're not going to tell me it's an election year, are you? That's kind of like talking about the weather around here."

Jonathan smiled at her bull's eye.

"Or perhaps you're thinking of someone?" Bull's-eye a second time.

A large hand enclosed Jonathan's shoulder.

"Son, Sarah." His father's unmistakable voice sent Jonathan's last good-mood molecule to the floor. Brond Senior leaned down and kissed Sarah's cheek. Jonathan rose out of courtesy and extended his hand, which his father took roughly.

"Your mother and I are seated with the Blanchards. Jesus, what a mess. But loyalty is loyalty, right?"

Loyalty. As if his father understood the meaning of the word.

His father turned to Sarah. "Your mother has someone you should meet."

"I'll bet." Sarah threw Jonathan a knowing look. Claire wouldn't rest until her daughter married and grew round as a basketball with some business mogul's child.

His father's practiced smile fell into a facial expression of practiced concern. "Jonathan, we need to talk. *Soon.*"

"About?"

"Want you to set me straight on a few rumors."

"I thought you took little stock in gossip, Father. Besides, as you can see, I'm here with Sarah, doing my duty." Jonathan sent his hand to his heart in mock sincerity.

"Which is doing neither of you any good. Claire's cousin over there's been asking about you." He threw his chin to his table where a woman sporting a Washington-approved blond bob smiled back at Jonathan's quick glance.

"Spending a little time with Marla Clampton would be good for everyone, all around. Get your reputation back on track." He leaned in closer. "Marla would be good for you. She knows her worth." He emphasized the last words as if imparting some secret of the universe, as if his own past with women provided the model for relationship advice.

His father squeezed his shoulder and then turned his face to the other people sitting at the table. "Well, I came over to say hello to my favorite son. I see the show's starting. Must get back." He leaned into Jonathan's ear, "Jay, come pay your respects to Blanchard. He understands mistakes, and if you don't listen to your father, well, he may have some advice for your *situation.*"

My situation?

Christiana snuck a peek from a side curtain and found Jonathan sitting at a table banking the runway. Sarah sat next to him.

Stiff taffeta fabric brushed the back of Christiana's ankles. When she turned, Avery stood smoothing down the front of the ivory, bejeweled wedding dress.

"You changed your mind," Christiana said.

"My mom thought I should be the last one down. Ya' know, a last hurrah as a model and all."

Christiana had to give Coco credit. She left no chance untaken to show off her daughter as a potential wife available for purchase.

Avery smiled. "Don't look at me like that. No one's going to pay any attention to me after they see you in your glory."

Christiana pulled the netting over her hips, feeling the

stretch of the crochet slip down and then recoil. Well, there was no turning back now.

"Jonathan Brond will certainly see a new side to you," Avery said.

Christiana returned her attention to the runway. Her turn was coming up, and she didn't have time to respond to Avery's words.

Avery leaned over her shoulder. "Whatever you do, don't trip." Christiana kept her eyes forward. She had no intention of stumbling, even if the dress rode up her entire ass.

Jonathan turned his eyes to the stage as a woman in a red gown stepped onto the stage. He found the overabundance of red in the room irritating, like rivers of blood moving through the ballroom and clotting at each table. A woman in a fluttering white lace dress walked down the aisle next. It calmed him a bit. Jesus, his nerves must be on edge if fashion had an impact.

He fiddled with the stem of his wine glass, still full, wondering what his father meant by *his situation*. His father and he were nothing alike, especially when it came to women. Jonathan's life may have been filled with short-term relationships, but he ensured every one of his past lovers could count on him as a friend, forever. He also ensured their reputations—and his—remained intact. His father, however . . .

Sarah touched his arm in silent commiseration. He must be telegraphing his misery.

"You like that one?" he asked. Fashion was as good a topic as any to keep things light.

"Are you offering to buy it for me?"

"If you'd like."

"No. I prefer something bolder."

He smiled. "I know."

The music changed to a sultry hip-hop beat. A female voice started half-rapping, half-singing. The song title, "No Panties Coming Off" by Trina, slipped into his mind, as Christiana stepped to the end of the runway.

Holy fuck.

Christiana paused at the end of the runway for several seconds, like she had seen Avery do so many years when she modeled. Avery called it "presenting," letting the audience really admire what you're wearing before you start to move. She said it helped them catch up to what they were seeing. Christiana put her hand on her hip and caught a flash of crystal on her breast in her peripheral vision.

She kept her head high as she stepped forward.

The slick runway surface slowed her pace. Her hips were swung out by the leisurely stroll, but she wouldn't fall down. She set a hand on her hip and pulled her shoulder blades down her back. Jessica had said the bra would resemble Fourth of July fireworks, so no use hunching over to hide their sparkle.

As she reached the center of the runway, a guy's wolf whistle broke through the loud driving music. Then, as if a dam broke, more catcalls from men erupted. She slowly pivoted at the end of the runway. A loud "Yeah" from the back almost made her stumble.

Now facing away from most of the crowd, she could glance around more. She darted her eyes down to Jonathan's table and caught his glacial expression. His eyes looked past her, as if concentrating on a speck on the wall.

She'd made a mistake.

Avery stood in her wedding gown at the end of the runway, a sweet smile plastered across her face. The contrast between the two of them struck Christiana in the chest. She cursed herself for being so inside her own head, she hadn't noticed. She presented the slut. Avery would glide down the runway as the Madonna, the perfect woman for any eligible man seeking the perfect Washington wife. The kind of woman Jonathan would marry.

The wolf calls quieted as Avery descended toward Christiana. The music changed. Moonlight Sonata. It was the perfect backdrop to Avery's modern take on class and style.

Christiana brushed past her. "Don't trip, Avery." It was a wimpy warning shot. But Christiana couldn't muster more at the moment, knowing Jonathan bored holes in her back.

"I never do," Avery whispered in return.

No, she never faltered. Christiana's father said she could learn from Avery, told her to watch how she navigated her world with such ease and grace. Avery's real talent lay in setting the stage before taking it over.

"Okay, Jay, lay down your sword. She looked fantastic." Sarah leaned back in her chair. She had assessed the situation clearly, unlike Jonathan's pride, which blinded him to the most basic understanding.

"Did I say anything?"

"Yes, with every atom in your body." She took another sip of wine. "Go see her. I'll get myself home. By the look on your face, she's going to need to hear you're not mad."

"I'm not mad."

"No, you're enraged that your love was appreciated by many male eyes."

"She is not—"

"Have you told your heart this?"

Jonathan rose, and Sarah grasped his wrist. "Remember she's young, Jonathan. She's trying to get your attention in the only way she knows how."

"She's smarter than that."

"She's desperate like that. Remember, you have a way of making women do things."

Christiana threw off her four-inch heels as soon as she stepped behind the stage curtain. She had to get back into her blue gown as quickly as possible. She'd try and play this nonchalant. Perhaps sashay over to Jonathan's table and say hello. Sarah's fashion background would be a good way to start a conversation, check in to see how Sarah felt about the show.

Then she'd ask Jonathan to take her home. Her father wouldn't mind. He'd be the last one to leave with the political bigwigs laid out like a smorgasbord. In the car, she'd convince Jonathan that her dress was a silly mistake and "no big deal." That should work, right?

As she turned the corner, Jonathan's chest stopped her advance. Words froze in her throat. She wished she'd conjured up a plan B because plan A wasn't going to work. No way would he think what happened was "no big deal."

He slipped off his jacket and pulled it around her shoulders, more gently than she expected. His grasp on her arm, however, matched the anger threatening to spill from his eyes like lava from Mt. Vesuvius.

"My dress. It's in the other room," she choked out as he led her down the hallway.

He didn't answer, just continued to pull her through the crowd. Necks careened at their march. The jacket fell below her ass. From behind, her bare legs and bare feet made her look naked under his jacket—worse than the flimsy pieces of fibers she wore.

As they neared the entrance, Mark pushed himself off the railing and handed Jonathan a set of keys. "Last spot on the left."

Jonathan turned to Christiana. "Put your shoes on."

He steadied her long enough for her to slip on the torturous stiletto sandals before leading her through the parking lot. Distant traffic noise and the tree frogs singing their songs were the only accompaniments to their walk. Twilight had fallen.

27

Jonathan pulled off the George Washington Parkway and into the Washington Sailing Club's parking lot. It had taken him only twenty minutes in spite of the slow Fourth of July traffic due to lanes closed for parades and tourists who didn't understand the web of one-way streets. The weather service had called for a storm to skirt the Potomac River and head out to the Chesapeake Bay. A sprinkling of rain and some choppy water would not cause any trouble for sailing—or his plans.

"I said I'd show you my boat." Jonathan pulled into his reserved spot in the nearly full parking lot.

"You did?" Christiana sank further into his jacket and her indecent outfit if he could even call it an outfit.

"At our first dinner. The night you said you were interested in spending time with me."

"Y-yes. I think I remember."

He turned off the ignition and turned his eyes to her ashen face. Jonathan absorbed her apprehension. "Let me remind you then. It's a beautiful evening for sailing, for seeing the fireworks." He regarded the grey-blue water tossing the boats, tied to the dozen long docks that lined the small marina. Most sailors had already cast off into the choppy water.

"I don't like the water very much." Her voice was small, uncertain.

"But you were so brave tonight, Christiana. Let's see how far your courage extends."

"Jonathan, please." A cry caught in her throat. "You've been so distant since the weekend. I wanted—" Tears spilled down her cheeks.

"I know what you wanted." When he came around the back of the car, she was already out and jogging around the side. She slammed into his chest and wrapped her arms around his neck.

"Please. Don't be mad at me. I was trying—"

"I know." He pulled her arms down to her sides.

Jonathan held her face with his eyes. He knew exactly why she strutted in fuck-me stilettos and a see-through dress. It wasn't his fault, but he was responsible. He'd failed at his most important task—to help her feel her power. "Come with me."

She stepped backward. "I can't. I'm deathly afraid of deep water, especially in the dark. I don't want to get on your boat."

"I will always take care of you."

"I-I know, but I'm still scared."

"The best way to overcome your biggest fears is to face them."

She grasped her bottom lip with her teeth, debate filling her eyes.

"Do you trust me enough to keep you safe?"

She nodded.

Christiana hugged her chest as she followed him down the narrow concrete path to the dock. One hand steadied

Christiana on her heels on the swaying dock, while the other punched in a code on the iron-scrolled gate. It snapped open. Jonathan gestured for her to follow, and she obeyed. Her footsteps echoed behind Jonathan as he walked to his white schooner, rocking lazily in the water.

"It looks like there's not much wind." Her voice shook a little.

"We'll motor out then." He uncoiled the rope from its iron pike and threw it to the boat deck. Christiana startled when it thudded on the white cedar planking.

"Slip off your shoes; then take my hand." His eyes narrowed when she hesitated. "Christiana. I won't let anything bad happen to you."

"I know." She placed her small hand in his and sent him a weak smile.

She didn't know. Christiana Snow didn't have faith in anyone. Her life had given her good cause for growing up suspicious, but she had no excuse for laying her trust in the wrong hands anymore. His whole body shuddered with his failure. While they were together, she laid down her defenses with him many times. Yet once they were apart, almost anything would send her hurtling back into doubt. If he was seen with another woman, which he often was, or Avery Churchill made one of her covert hostile remarks, Christiana would jump feet-first back into the abyss of uncertainty.

Another single truth gnawed at Jonathan's ego. He'd cracked her open, taken her to the edge, but then left her without completing the job by rebuilding her self-confidence. He'd under-estimated her need. Well, tonight he'd make sure her strength was restored or they wouldn't re-dock.

The boat bobbed upward and caught her foot.

"I'm going to check the lines. Under that bench is a life

preserver for you. Pick the yellow one. It's Sarah's and should fit."

After fitting the lifejacket over her head, Christiana clutched the bench. Her sandals lay at her feet. Jonathan picked up his abandoned tuxedo jacket and placed it over her legs.

He hoisted the staysail, and it snapped in the light wind.

Christiana sat silently as Jonathan steered the boat deeper onto the Potomac through the dozens of sloops, cutters and speedboats that had taken anchor for the fireworks display. He navigated to the outskirts of the crowded anchorage. While he needed her to see the other sailors surrounding them, they also needed privacy.

He dropped anchor while scanning the nearby boats. He should drop the second anchor given the wind conditions. No, he wouldn't. Let the boat swing. It would add to the exercise for them both.

Once the boat was secure, he kneeled before Christiana.

"Those crystals must be uncomfortable." He lifted both of her ankles to his shoulders, tipping her back on her elbows. He slid his hands up her legs to her hips and hooked his fingers through the thin strips of fabric of the red sparkled panties.

"People are looking," she gasped, but lifted her hips.

"No, they aren't." He pulled down and tossed the thong over the side of the boat.

"Jonathan! That's not mine. I have to return—"

"No, you don't. Sarah likely bought it. Besides, it's not your color."

She smiled, visibly relaxed at his light remark. "It doesn't seem her style, but then I only met her the one time. You never talk about your step-sister, Jonathan."

"I will tonight." He smiled.

～

Jonathan wasn't mad. He acted . . . disappointed. She could fix that. She'd explain what happened if she could find the right words. Before she could speak, he claimed her mouth. His tongue reached inside, as if demanding an answer she couldn't voice.

He grabbed his jacket from her knees and pulled her toward the center of the deck. "Up," he directed.

Christiana scrambled up onto the hull. "Is this the best view?" She teetered from the boat's incessant rocking.

"Almost. Hold on to the masthead." She stood, clinging to him, unable to gain her footing even though the pole behind her helped a little.

She grasped the T-bar near her waist. He reached around to her back and through the dress, unhooked the bra and pulled it out through her neckline.

"Jonathan!"

He brought a finger to her lips. "Hush."

Christiana kept her eyes on him, even when he tossed the bra down to the deck.

"I'm going to tell you a story—about Sarah." Jonathan ran fingertips down her face. The pitching of the boat seemed to increase as Jonathan released his touch and stepped behind her back.

Christiana clutched the bar and tried to forget she was in the middle of the bay, in deep water, on a boat that rose and fell, swayed and bobbed—and that she now stood wearing nothing but a see-though dress.

A soft cottony cord wound around her wrist. *Where did he get rope?*

"Is that too tight? Move your fingers," he said.

She opened and closed her fist, then re-grasped the bar.

He soothed her arms with his fingers. "When I was

twelve, my father married Sarah's mother. I'll never forget the day we met, my father's chest stuck out, so proud, pushing Claire in front of me like, 'Here's your new mom, Son.' Such bullshit."

"Ow."

Jonathan had wrapped a length of rope around her wrist too tightly. He loosened it and ran his thumb over her wrist line, sending a shudder down her spine.

"Better?"

She nodded.

"But then, Sarah stepped from behind Claire. Sarah may have been fourteen, but she was practically a grown woman at that point. Full developed in both body and mind. She knew who she was. It was intoxicating, watching her walk into a room at that young age and have all eyes turn to her. Not to ogle a beautiful young girl, but rather to regard her with respect and admiration. Every fiber of her being demanded it.

"Sarah took a liking to me. Let me follow her around like a puppy dog." Jonathan helped her release her other hand from its grip on the cool metal. More rope wound around her wrist. "We went hiking and sailing together back in Newport. Went to a lot of society events. Sarah liked dressing me up." He laughed.

She sent her mind back to his voice to distract her from the fact her wrists and forearms were now lashed to the bar —and that his past rose up in his memory with such fondness.

"The summer before she left for Vassar, we went sailing— a lot. Fourth of July we decided to head out to sea instead of suffer through another one of Claire's barbeques. Sarah wore the skimpiest bikini known to womankind. She did it on purpose, of course. My incessant hard-on let her know she'd won that game." Jonathan faced Christiana, eyes dropped to her waist. "I thought she'd laugh her head off. Instead, she tied me to the mast and deep-throated my cock until I came . . . twice."

Christiana was sure she stopped breathing. "But she's your sister."

"Stepsister. No genetic relationship. We didn't spend our childhoods together." He paused. "I was her submissive for six weeks that summer. Man, she worked me over. Hard." He shook his head, clearly bemused, as if remembering a fond, family Christmas day.

"She's—"

"A female Dominant."

"But you're a Dominant."

"I am now. That summer she showed me what I was and was not." Jonathan cupped her chin. "That's why I know what you're going through. Why I know how to do this."

He stepped back, and the wind he had blocked blew her hair backward.

Christiana's feet splayed out in a vain attempt to steady her footing. Cool breezes ran through the crochet over her skin. If he stepped back anymore, all the other people on boats would see her secured to the mast, bare-assed.

"People will—"

"Think you're merely holding on, enjoying the view. People see what they want, remember?"

"Jonathan, please." She dropped her head, her face heating.

"When you give yourself over as completely as I did to Sarah, it changes you," he said. "Gives you a confidence that is unshakeable. That's what you need. So when someone like Avery Churchill comes your way, you'll know to walk away."

Jonathan brought both hands to the crocheted V in the front of her dress and pulled. She cried out at the ripping sounds more than the act itself. He let the shredded dress fall, unraveled, to her feet. Water slapped the side of the boat, and the wind in the rigging sent a burst of wind that chilled Christiana's bare skin. Jonathan leaned down to pick up his tuxedo jacket and hooked the enveloping suit coat over her shoulders, tied the jacket arms around her back. It stayed on, but it barely covered what needed to be covered.

"You're scaring me." Shit, she was nearly naked, secured to a mast in the middle of the bay with probably hundreds of people watching. How could she not be frantic?

He ran his hands down either side of her face. "A little fear isn't bad. But know this. Getting hurt is an impossibility when I am here. I'm going to give you what you're afraid to ask for. Push you beyond more limits, Christiana. And you will submit to me, fall so deeply into trust you'll understand from that moment forward what it really means and not just to earn an orgasm."

"I know—"

"You only think you know. Avery Churchill convinced you to walk down that runway, didn't she? Played on your greatest fears? Told you you'd only be brave if you do what she says?"

Christiana muffled a sob. "Yes."

"Why did you trust her?"

"She's my friend."

"Are you sure about that? She knows how to take care of herself. I wish I could say the same for you."

"I don't like the water. Jonathan, please . . . ."

"I know, lovely." Jonathan traced a finger down the side of her forehead. "Now, tell me how you got that scar."

A cry erupted from her chest as the first firework burst overhead, a brilliant red and white chrysanthemum. *No. I can't.*

28

Jonathan yanked his tie free and threw it to the deck. He loosened the jacket covering Christiana so his hands could slip underneath. His whispered reassurances were barely audible over the fireworks crackling across the sky. He palmed her breasts until her cries stopped, and she pushed into his kneading hands.

"Christiana, tell me about it." He dipped his tongue to her neck, tasted the fear, while his fingertips played her nipples lightly.

Even though lashed to the pole, she shook with panic. Far from the water churning around them, he knew her greatest fear was he'd give up and not crash through that final barrier of hers. The fire he'd seen behind her eyes that first day at the country club when they collided wasn't spirit alone. It was hunger—not just the pining of a young girl, desiring love and romance, but something much deeper.

Bursts of colored light scattered their reflections across the deck, painting Christiana in flashes of color as she thrashed in her bindings.

"You say you know you are safe with me, but you don't act like you feel safe now."

"I'm tied to a masthead in the middle of the Potomac. Of course I don't feel safe!" Christiana struggled against the ropes like a wild animal. "Untie me. Let me go! I can't do this!" Her voice grew more fraught with each word.

"After you tell me what happened." His heart wrenched when another sob broke from her chest.

"There's nothing to tell."

"You trust Avery Churchill enough to let her get away with that dress stunt, and you don't trust me enough to say how you got hurt?"

"It wasn't a stunt. I—I . . . wanted you to see me."

"I do see you, Christiana."

"You don't want people to know about us. You are willing to be seen with all those other women, but never with me. *Never* with me!" She choked on a sob. "I'm supposed to be invisible."

"If I could, I'd parade you on my arm down the middle of the White House lawn." Jonathan circled to her front, lifted her chin and captured her mouth. When he released her lips, he ran a fingertip over her scar. "Now, what happened?"

"I-I fell when I was seven, okay? It was nothing." Her voice's high pitch made clear that what had happened was *everything*. It *owned* her.

"Were you alone?"

"No. I-I don't know. Why does it matter?"

"Everything that's ever happened to you matters to me, Christiana." Jonathan laid his hand on Christiana's shoulder and kept it there as he walked to her back, banding his arms around the masthead and her quaking body.

"Now, you fell when you were seven . . . ." Jonathan nibbled her neck.

"My mom shouldn't have been alone with me," she spat.

"We were feeding ducks in a park. Dad went to get us ice cream, I think. I don't remember."

"And?"

"That's when she took me . . . in a boat. I fell out. Hit my head."

"Tell me what you're leaving out."

"I almost drowned."

A fire built inside Jonathan's belly. He'd known about her mother's mental illness. But this? He held on to her tighter.

"Dad shouldn't have left me alone with her. Mom wasn't reliable."

"Who saved you?"

"A man. Just some man. A stranger."

"No wonder you don't trust people," he said into her hair.

"I trust you." She brushed her cheek against his face as her head lolled backward onto his shoulder.

He wanted to erase the anguish from her beautiful face. He wanted her to have confidence in him, more than any woman he'd ever encountered. He wanted all of Christiana Snow.

The boat rocked suddenly. She cried out and not even the darkness between rockets could mask the distress on her face, illuminated in the bursts of color from overhead. She banged her head backward into the mast. "Don't let me fall overboard!"

He circled to her front and grasped her face in his hands. "Never." Jonathan claimed her mouth in a kiss, and she softened. He released her mouth and pressed more soft kisses along her hairline, finally resting his lips on her scar. She crumpled forward. If the ropes—and Jonathan—hadn't supported her, she'd have collapsed to the deck.

"The boat was supposed to be fun. She said it would be an adventure. Mom said I was her mermaid and that Dad was a merman and I had to go find him. I was afraid of the water. It was so black. I didn't want to go. She hit me over the head with the oar to make sure I did."

Her words were barely audible over a dozen red, white and blue bursts of sparks in the night sky. The air had grown thick with acrid cordite smoke from the fireworks.

Tears streaked her face. "I don't come from the perfect family, like you. Mom couldn't handle raising a kid, so she checked out. Dad liked his bottle more than me. Even you don't want to be seen with me. Don't you get it, Jonathan? I'm invisible."

And there it was. Finally, the truth of Christiana Snow revealed itself in the middle of the Potomac River. She didn't feel used. Christiana grew up believing she was unwanted. She felt erased.

Yes, he had gone too far. "Oh, baby."

Jonathan realized in that moment what his father meant about Marla Campbell. *She knows her worth.* It wasn't the strong women who were hard to handle. It was the ones who believed they were not enough, *unwanted,* who'd test a man's mettle with every self-defeating thought and action. Like Christiana Snow. Worse than feeling unwelcome, she didn't know how to be loved. Jonathan had promised himself he'd be the man she needed. Her eyes spoke the truth of his failure in that one simple task.

Every person who declared her important had betrayed her. She'd been caretaker to her father, handmaiden to Avery, and now lover to the most selfish man he'd ever known—himself. He'd hidden her away from others, so his precious career remained intact. He'd awakened her hidden sexual needs and when she was the most vulnerable, he'd left her alone, floundering. *Like father, like son.*

He hated himself.

∿

Christiana didn't let go of the bar even when Jonathan yanked the long tail end of the lead, releasing one of her arms. She slumped forward slightly, onto his chest, as he freed the other arm.

Oh, she was tired. He'd pulled out her last grain of despair. Until tonight, Christiana didn't indulge in the memories of that fateful July Fourth eleven years ago. The taste of strawberry ice cream at the kitchen table, her fingers playing with the white bandage over her forehead—*a pirate's mark of having an adventure,* her father had said.

"I never saw her after that day." Christiana couldn't focus her eyes on anything but the dark grey water, sparks of silver dancing over its surface form the city lights. "My dad said she'd return when the bounty's been paid."

"The bounty?"

"The pirates. Dad said she'd been captured. I guess that's what you tell a seven-year-old instead of her running her car off the road during a manic phase."

Christiana raised her eyes to Jonathan's face, now colored in such sorrow—pity—her heart cracked. He set Christiana upright and placed his mouth on hers. His tongue reached in and took possession of her wariness. Instead of dueling with his probing, she followed his lead, letting him set the pace. He released her mouth, and the last remnants of hope inside her sank to the bottom of the river in an instant. Unlike all the other times he had kissed her, there was no demand, no passion. It was a kiss of comfort, consolation—and good-bye, like a final brand of completion. He had demanded her confession, and she had given it to him. Her purpose—to provide him an opportunity to be a white knight—had been fulfilled. Inside the jacket, Christiana pressed her fists against her sternum as if keeping her heart inside her chest.

"Take me home," she said. *Before my soul drops onto the deck next.* He unhooked the jacket arms and slipped it around her back. She sunk her arms into the sleeves, grateful for the extra coverage. He lifted her chin back up with both palms.

"No."

"You've heard my pathetic secret; now take me home. I don't want your handouts or your pity. I don't need your help. I can take care of myself. I've had a lot of practice."

"We've just begun, Christiana."

"You've done enough."

"I've not done nearly enough."

"I am not your charity case of the week!" She wasn't sure where she got the energy to scream. Jonathan's green eyes darkened so quickly Christiana sucked in her breath. She would've jumped backward, but Jonathan moved too fast. He growled like a wild animal and pulled her toward the edge of what?

"We . . . are not . . . done. I won't let you wallow in self-pity." Jonathan jumped down to the lower walkway and yanked her down, so she fell into his arms. "You will not accept you're worthless."

"Stop it! No!" Christiana pushed his shoulders and kicked her legs.

Christiana cried out as her leg scratched the narrow passageway walls leading to the cabin below. Jonathan pinned her to a thin mattress in the back of the hull.

"Don't move." Feral and predatory, Jonathan's eyes restrained her against the small bed.

Christiana lay back on her elbows and watched him undress slowly in the shadows of other boats' lights and moonlight streaming through the small, open porthole. Her eyes darted around the small space. By the look in his eye, he'd tie her to the bed with his clothes to avoid her getting away. But where would she go anyway? Swim back to shore in the dark?

He yanked the jacket down both her arms until they were

held to her side. He kneed her legs open and slammed himself inside her. To her mortification, she was ready for him. Her treacherous body was yet another betrayal. It was always ready for him.

Yet, her topside confession had left her feeling vulnerable, but, strangely, not weak. Jonathan had forced her to confront dangerous feelings. Now she only desired to escape *him*. She'd walk off this boat with her last scraps of dignity if it killed her. Christiana snarled, leaving what little poise or femininity she had behind. She sank her teeth into his shoulder.

Jonathan didn't seem to notice, instead opening her insides with his thick cock. Fluid ran down her ass as he hitched one of her legs over his shoulder and seated himself more deeply inside. Her fury did nothing to abate the arousal his possession raised.

She wrenched her body back and forth underneath his hold. She dug nails into his hips, the only thing she could reach with her arms trapped to her sides. He sent a hand down to rub her clit while he continued to stretch her open too fast and too hard. Wet, sucking sounds filled the cabin as her heat rose under his claiming her body.

Jonathan lifted her hips up. She freed her hands from their fabric prison and shoved against his belly. He grabbed both wrists in one of his larger hands and pushed them above her head. Her fingertips brushed the hull wall while he continued to lunge forward.

"I can't . . . *can't*." She had trouble catching her breath with Jonathan's large body crushing her into the firm surface. Hysteria threatened to overcome her anger, but she refused to fall apart. She'd just needed to pull herself together and deal . . . like she always did.

"Yes. You can. Give yourself to me." He pitched forward

into her and that familiar heated tornado began to lift off inside. "Don't be afraid."

"I won't survive you," she cried to the hull's ceiling.

"I won't let anything bad happen to you. Let go."

"Dammit, Jonathan. You want me to-to . . . service you!"

He stilled his assault though his eyes held fire. He slapped her ass, hard. "You are everything. I would do *anything* for you." He released her wrists.

"No, you won't."

"Yes, I will. Just tell me." He cupped her face.

Her pants filled the small cabin. "Anything."

"Yes."

He couldn't mean such a thing. No one did anything, however small, without an agenda. *I can't trust him. He'll abandon me. I'll drown.* Unfortunately, her heart never was very logical.

"Then, please, don't leave me alone. Don't hide me." Her face crumpled as she fought back the tears.

"I won't." Understanding crossed his face. "You're not alone. I see you. I'm *with* you."

Something inside broke free, completely and irrevocably. All her anger and frustration rushed out. She clutched his torso and pushed her face into his chest. Sobs racked her whole body, and Jonathan engulfed her with his arms, his cock still firmly seated inside her tender tissues.

After she didn't have another tear left, Jonathan released her body and leaned back, gripping her hips. He dragged in and out through her slippery heat. Christiana hitched her leg around his waist, digging her heel into the small of his back and held his gaze. She clenched her insides, urging him forward. He continued his slow rocking into her, his eyes never leaving her face.

"Mine," he whispered.

A warm sense of well-being for being cared for, overwhelmed her emotions by the simple word. *Mine.* Self-preservation told her to threaten to leave after being cracked open. But she wouldn't deny the truth. He claimed her body weeks ago, her heart shortly after, and—if he wanted—her soul lay splayed open for his taking.

All the things Jonathan had done to lure her into his world unfurled like banners in her mind. Jonathan holding her, whispering assurances and caressing her hair, her face and her body when she grew fearful. Opening the door, pressing his hand to the small of her back. Calling her at night to ask about her day. Programming her phone so that his number was the first on her speed-dial. Letting her know he should be the first person she should call, always.

It was all there. *He* was there even when he wasn't.

"Yes," she breathed.

Jonathan drove in and out faster, the sweetness building. The need to have him spear her all the way to her heart made her hips twitch under his prodding.

"Jonathan." She clasped his hand resting on her butt cheek. "I want you." She pushed his hand underneath her more.

Jonathan's eyes deepened. He slipped his finger between her cheeks to find her more intimate place.

She nodded. "I want you everywhere. I'm begging you."

He grabbed her ankles and brought her legs down. She flipped to her belly and rose on her knees, sending her ass back toward Jonathan's crotch. He laid one hand on her lower back and laid a kiss on her shoulder.

The fireworks show had ended. The silence allowed the slapping sounds of waves against the boat to join them in the cabin. She heard the snick of a drawer opening and the scratch of items moving.

Both of Jonathan's hands rubbed up her back, his thumbs

running alongside her spine. She moaned out tension as he kneaded her shoulders.

His chest and mouth came down on her skin, and he ran his slick, hard erection back and forth between her labia folds.

She laid her forehead on her hands, rocking herself to match his motions. She stood on a precipice, aching to tip over but wanting to balance on the edge longer, delay the spike she knew Jonathan could deliver.

Jonathan oiled her ass, lightly kneading and massaging her cheeks. He slipped a finger up her crack and touched her back opening, massaging but not entering.

She moaned.

Hands spread her ass cheeks wide.

She panted at the indescribable feeling of his tongue rimming her puckered hole, hot breath heating up the oil to tingle and taunt her awakened nerve center. She sucked on a knuckle to stall the cries from her throat. He inserted a thick finger and returned his other hand to her clit. He eased his finger deeper inside, and she swayed against the invasion.

"That's it, lovely."

A burning pinch in her anal passage told her he inserted a second finger. A spear of pleasure-pain ran through her. She moaned loudly, unearthing a raw primal urge to have him take her there.

The two fingers in her rear slipped out, and he released her pussy. Slick, wet sucking sounds behind her told her he was slicking himself with lube. She pushed her ass back toward him, wanting. *Now.*

His cockhead found her opening. "Relax, lovely." She cried out from the burn of his assault, but he held her around her waist with one arm, his other hand circling around to find her clit. He didn't move in any further. Instead, he worked her cunt with his fingers until she drenched his hand with liquid need. He pushed forward another inch and dragged himself backward.

"Oh, Christiana." His voice, thick with emotion, cracked any remnants of fear inside. "I've wanted this . . . you . . . ."

More oil drizzled down her ass and dropped to the sheets underneath. He thrust forward, and the soft hair encircling his root met her cheeks. Being filled with Jonathan pushed up the last bits of emotion to the surface. She didn't try to stop the tears.

"Oh, baby, am I hurting you?"

"No, please. Please don't stop. Don't ever stop." She didn't want a single part of her untouched by Jonathan. She needed him to go deeper, take over, even if it meant she didn't survive.

She rocked against his arrowing through her most private fire. "Harder." She didn't want careful. She wanted sore muscles and bruises in the morning from his lunges inside.

His balls banged her butt. He tapped her clit with fingers as he pierced her. The build inched its way to a higher point than she'd felt before. Was it the raw, animalistic coupling or the fact she'd finally let go of . . . let go of what? *Time.* Time didn't exist, just his cock buried deep, his muscles holding her in position.

Jonathan's mouth fell to her shoulder as he grunted. His thrusts became more determined, laid a stronger claim to whatever was inside he tried to reach.

"Oh, Jesus, Christiana."

She turned her head to catch his face in her peripheral vision. Jonathan's virility always stunned her, but the sight of the cording on his neck, the strain in his face, as he pushed into her, shot up her spine, small ripples running up her inner thighs.

"Can I–I need to—" she began. His hand held the back of her neck, holding her down. His command of their coupling only sent more energy to her core. He slowed his pace. His fingers curled around her throat, and a long groan broke free from both of them. His silken strokes, in and out, back and forth, taunted her thwarted orgasm that lay under the surface.

"Shall I let you come, Christiana?"

She wanted to scream *yes, please, please let me come.* "If you wish, sir," she said instead.

"Then come for me."

She spiraled out of control from his first word. Spasms made her back arch and her legs give out. Jonathan worked his oiled fingers, rocketing her higher. Her shrieks bounced off the hull walls.

Jonathan's own spasms filled her back channel. Finally spent, Jonathan pulled out and released her neck, collapsing beside her quivering body. He pulled her closer and nuzzled her hair in the protective C-curve of his embrace. She inhaled his unique male scent and tuned into the gentle rocking of the boat until she caught its rhythm. Her heartbeat slowed, matched the movements of the water. Her breathing evened. Then the tight coil in her belly released. She hung suspended, like gravity had shifted.

As if sensing she might float to the hull ceiling, Jonathan pulled her closer. An overwhelming sense of wholeness overcame her consciousness and sleep soon threatened. But before slipping into the familiar darkness, she tried to put words to the comfort bathing her. Only when one word surfaced did she finally let go. *Unbroken.*

29

Avery had to know Christiana wouldn't answer her calls or texts. That was probably why she'd driven over to Christiana's house and now stood on her front step. Hot summer air poured in from the open doorway.

"Hey, I came over to apologize." Avery hitched her Chanel handbag strap over her shoulder.

Christiana didn't have time for a scene. She had an hour to get to work for the late afternoon shift.

Besides, Christiana knew Avery had only come over to find out where she'd gone with Jonathan. At least a hundred people saw her march through the lobby last night in Congressman Brond's tuxedo jacket, barefoot, bare-legged— and thanks to Avery—practically bare-assed.

"I didn't think people would react to that outfit like they did," Avery said.

"Yes, you did."

Avery's head snapped back, but she recovered almost instantly. "Well, I didn't plan—"

"I think it went exactly how you planned, except for one small detail."

"Oh, you mean that Congressman Brond took you home?"

"He did more than take me home." Jesus, she shouldn't have said that. But then she smiled, remembering Jonathan's long goodbye kiss this morning in his car. They both had work to handle before tomorrow's jaunt back to Charlottesville—a place Avery Churchill would never see.

Avery's lips curled into a sinister smile. "Brond's a womanizer. He'd know an easy lay when he saw one."

Christiana tried to slam the door, but Avery caught it with her open palm. "I'm sorry, I'm sorry," she said. "I didn't mean that. Hey, are you going to let me in or what? I want to make it up to you."

"No."

"I have something you're going to want to see. It's about him."

"What do you mean?"

"I found something. Jesus, let me in." Avery pushed her way past Christiana. Christiana closed the door and turned to face her. Avery looked tired, but hadn't neglected her make-up and hair "Well, what?" Christiana asked.

Avery sighed and headed to the living room. She set her bag down on the couch. "Come here. Sit with me. I'm worried about you."

"Why? I'm great."

"You alone? Where's your dad."

"The road. He left this morning." Before he'd left, he had asked if she had "fun at Avery's slumber party"—obviously the story Mark had planted last night when she'd disappeared. It would stay a story because the devil himself couldn't get Christiana to set foot into the Churchill mansion.

Avery sat down and patted the seat next to her. "Believe me, you'll want to be sitting for this."

Christiana wished she had sat when Avery held up her phone and showed her an image of Jonathan with Yvette DeCord.

"They're a little blurry 'cause of the iPhone, but you can see enough," Avery tapped her phone to show several more. Jonathan and Yvette at The Oak.

Christiana couldn't believe Avery would sink to spying. But why was she surprised? "So? They're friends."

"Yeah, right. You work at The Oak. You know what goes on there."

Christiana certainly did. "How long have you had these?"

"A few days. I go by The Oak every once in a while to see if you're there. Are you with him? I never see you anymore."

Avery looked honestly sad. Christiana guessed even a vain bitch is human underneath.

Christiana also knew the time for lying had passed. "Sometimes."

"Yeah, well, this one?" She flipped her finger across her screen and then held up a picture of Yvette inside Jonathan's SUV, laughing. "It was taken about three hours ago." Christiana's heart dropped. "Listen, I know you went home with him last night and lots of other times. But he's using you. I'm certain of it."

"It's not like that."

"Chris. Listen to me. What kind of future does a thirty-year-old member of Congress—who people say is headed to the White House by the way—have with a college student?"

Last night, Jonathan had irretrievably cracked the hold Avery had on Christiana's self-confidence. Avery would do anything she could to secure the future she felt she deserved. Yet Christiana knew the truth when it landed. Too bad Jonathan didn't tell her how to handle the one detail she'd ignored. Jonathan's prospects looked nothing like Christiana's future of textbooks, internships and buying her first interview suit.

Avery pulled several large photographs from her bag.

"He's also a pervert. I mean look at these." A woman lay face down strapped onto a suspended bench over a bed. Dark blood-red suede peeked out from her legs being splayed open by black parachute fabric. *The sex cradle.*

Christiana couldn't deny it looked like Jonathan's hand on the back of the dark-haired woman.

"Where did you get those?" Christiana choked back the lump in her throat, which threatened to break free when Avery laid her hand on her shoulder as she sunk to the couch.

"I have my ways. And, really, does it matter? Hey, you look pale. Haven't you ever seen porn before?"

Porn.

Avery's hand on her neck pushed her down to the couch and her face between her knees. "Just breathe."

Through flecks of light coloring her vision, Christiana stared at the picture of Jonathan's strong, tanned hand. It held the woman down. She recognized the cuff of his charcoal gray suit that smelled like expensive linen and leather. He wore it the night he proposed their "exclusive" relationship at the Lodge, where he gave her champagne, held out her chair, and rubbed his thumb over her wrist, calming her, caressing her, letting her know she was in good hands.

She was an idiot. Of course he'd had other women. But this summer? When he said "exclusive," perhaps he meant exclusive to *him. No, it's another of Avery's manipulations.*

Christiana shrugged Avery's hand off.

She looked stunned. "You're not going to go mental on me, are you?"

Christiana could feel Avery's eyes on her back.

"I'm fine." Christiana pulled herself back to sitting and pushed the hair from her face.

"Well, good, cuz I wouldn't want you to fall apart like your mom."

Christiana snapped her head to look at Avery, who appeared unfazed. "What do you mean?"

"I mean, your mom had troubles, right? Ended up in a mental institution? I'm really sorry about that too. I mean, my parental units are annoying as shit, but they didn't abandon me."

"I know all about that." *Sort of.*

"Well, my mom said something this morning. I mean, after she yelled at me for putting you in that dress. Hey, I really am sorry—"

"What did your mom say?"

"Well, she said your mom would've worn that dress in a heartbeat for attention. That she loved turning men's heads. And, apparently, your dad didn't give her enough of it. That's why she killed herself." Avery's face remained stony.

"She died in a car accident." Her father finally told her years later what had happened during one of his sloshed rants.

Christiana recoiled when Avery touched her shoulder. "I don't see how our mothers would have ever met. It's not like we travel in the same circles." Christiana rose. "I have to get ready for work."

Christiana couldn't listen to Avery's lies anymore. She would call Jonathan. He would remind her not to listen to a word that came out of Avery's twisted mouth. So what if other women filled his past. He said they were exclusive, and she chose to believe that exclusivity went both ways.

"Look, I really was trying to help. People have lied to you." Avery began to gather her photos of woman restrained on the bench.

"No, leave them."

"I'll take them, get them out of your way," Avery said.

"You're afraid I'll show Jonathan. Tell him you were trying to turn me against him."

"It's Jonathan now, huh? Suit yourself. But you should walk away, Chris. Move on."

"That is exactly what I am going to do. Goodbye, Avery. Good luck with your life."

Avery raised her chin. "Remember, I taught you everything you know. And then you went and stole him from me."

Christiana snorted out a laugh. "That fantasy is over, Avery."

"So is yours. This isn't over. Not by a long shot." Avery's face reddened, and she turned on her heel.

Christiana called The Oak and let them know she wouldn't make it in. She didn't care if Brian fired her butt. She needed to see Jonathan. She'd be damned if she let Avery Churchill's seeds of distrust grow this time.

Of course, Jonathan had other women before her. Thirty-six pages of Google findings had told that story. So why did it bother her so much, especially after last night?

Regardless of his bachelor past, she had to find out the truth behind those sex cradle pictures. No photographs, he had said. He'd promised.

The heavens opened up, and Jonathan barely made it inside before the torrential downpour soaked through his suit. He had a spare in his office, but he was late to his meeting with the re-election committee and didn't have time to dally. He'd spent his morning setting Yvette's attorney straight, leaving little enough time to grab an apple for lunch on the way back to his office.

Another missed call from Christiana blinked on his phone. Submissives often crashed the night after intense scenes. After last night, Christiana likely had fallen into a black hole. He would have stayed with her if it weren't for being summoned by his committee head for the second time this week. He should have Mark go pick Christiana up, take her somewhere to be watched. He noticed how her shoulders relaxed in Mark's presence, subconsciously recognizing a fellow Dominant.

Jonathan hit her speed dial number and then killed the call before the first ring. Shane had jogged up to him with his usual panicked face.

"Sir, you're going to want to take this call." Shane held up his cell phone. "It's Clampton. Said he couldn't get hold of you on your other lines."

"Senator?" Jonathan said as he walked toward his own office. Shane trailed behind. His assistant panicked without his iPhone.

"Congressman, you're a hard man to find."

"Well, re-election and all that." Jonathan slipped into his office with a nod to Shane to close the door.

"Yes, yes. Well, I hope you can spare a few minutes for me today."

"Of course, Senator. If you're in your office, I'll be right over."

"Grab an umbrella. I hear it's quite the storm out there." *If you only knew.*

He tapped a quick text to Christiana. *"I see you, and see you soon."* Seeing Christiana was the only thing he wanted to do at that moment. But there was no time. She would have to wait. *Fuck, fuck, fuck.*

~

Christiana paced, fingering her phone. His text made her feel a little better, but Jonathan didn't answer her repeated calls. She ran through her conversation with Avery a dozen more times. She examined the eight by ten glossy of the sex cradle a hundred more times.

The CIA should hire Avery. Christiana shuddered at the thought of Avery unraveling the toughest Al Qaeda spy. Well, Christiana wasn't going to come unglued. But no matter how many times she told herself that Avery's lies were to get even for Jonathan, her eyes still pricked with tears. *Killed herself.* It had to be another one of Avery's attempts to overthrow Christiana's confidence.

Shaky legs carried her to her father's room. Christiana steeled herself in the doorway to his messy bedroom. If she didn't do this now, she'd lose her courage. In the back of his closet sat a fireproof safe. Damn, she didn't know the code. Christiana pushed some random numbers. Her parents' wedding anniversary, his birthday, and then her birthday. It opened.

Stale air hit her nose, but then passed quickly. Two folded stacks of paper bound by brittle rubber bands lay on top of several manila folders. One long oblong box and a smaller square one sat on top of them. She found life insurance papers, a will and several more legal-looking documents. She unbound the second stack and nearly dropped the first piece of paper she unfolded. Large block letters on the top read *Death Certificate. Alexandra Vidar Snow.*

She squeezed her eyes shut and a tear escaped down her cheek. Hadn't she cried enough this summer? Christiana slapped the offending drip away.

Cause of death: Suicide.

Christiana leaned her body back into the hanging clothes at her back. Metal hangers clanged above as clouds of Old

Spice and pipe smoke took her over. She released the paper holding the truth of her mother's death. Her mother *had* killed herself. And she had to hear the truth of her mother's death first from Avery Churchill.

30

The majority leader swiveled back and forth in his over-stuffed leather chair, laughing into the phone. He gestured for Jonathan to sit. Jonathan took the seat angled away from the door. Clampton rarely shut it in some sense of feigned transparency.

"Well, Congressman," the burly man said as he laid the phone back in its cradle. "It seems we're looking at a good election year. Poll numbers show we'll pick up a few seats in the House this go around."

"Good news."

"Yes, yes, it is." Clampton leaned back and appraised Jonathan. "We're both busy, and it's a holiday weekend. So I'll get straight to the point about why I wanted to talk to you."

"Wouldn't have it any other way."

"You've been a little absent lately."

"I'm here now."

"Yes, I guess what I'm trying to say is, your priorities regarding some extracurricular activities have put some stress and strain—"

"Excuse me, Senator. But to what are you referring, specifically?"

"I'm talking about a certain young lady."

"Oh? I'm a single man, Senator. It's no secret I date."

"She pulled me aside at the club event last night. You know her. Avery Churchill."

"Yes, through her family. Both of our families have supported that event for years."

"She told me of another young woman who caused quite a splash on the runway. I missed it, as I had to leave before the show. Promised to take the grandkids out on my boat to see the fireworks. She then pointed to you and said—her exact words—*one of your most promising young congressmen could use some mentoring in that department instead of going out with that teenager over there.* She pointed to another lovely young woman, a blond, and no teenager in my book. But my eyes are failing me."

"I'm surprised. Listening to the gossip of a girl with puppy love, the woman she refers to might be the daughter of a reporter who's frequently out of town. I gave her a ride home one evening and that was that."

"Oh, I didn't pay it any mind at the time, until I thought I saw you with her in the middle of the Potomac. But . . . my eyes." He shrugged.

"Yes, I was out with some friends. Lots of blonds in this town."

"This morning, Judge Churchill confirmed your love of the, shall we say, *younger* ladies."

"Excuse me?"

"More like a side comment on the golf course about your 'tastes.'"

"Well, I'll have to think long and hard before killing the Honorable Judge on the racquetball court. As I said, nothing more than idle gossip, people reading something which wasn't there into an encounter."

"Good, just wanted to hear it from the horse's mouth. The party can't afford to lose any more seats." He rose and extended his hand, which Jonathan took readily. "Let's never forget that we're magnets for gossip, and sex scandals lose elections. It's good to get it all out in the open, squash it amongst ourselves, don't you think?"

Christiana wanted to drift aimlessly into nothing for a few minutes. Instead, pictures drifted up, like old photographs left in the sunlight too long until the images faded into sheer ghosts floating on small, curled up squares. Her father—hell, everyone—thought she was too fragile to hear the full truth about her life. *A charity case.*

No, she wouldn't let them.

She lay on her side and pressed the phone closer to her ear. She silently begged Jonathan to pick up. He didn't, and the line went dead, just like her heart.

She smashed her phone against the metal frame of the safe. The crackling sound oddly comforting. She threw the phone down to hear the crash once more. When shards of glass loosened from the phone screen, a sliver of victory sliced through her haze. She was done being afraid. She wanted to smash something else. Windows, dishes, anything she could get her hands on. Her hands curled around the paper holding the truth of her mother, fists waiting for a target.

Jonathan wished he could give Avery Churchill that spanking she deserved if he could be sure it would do the trick. She'd probably have him locked up for assault for ignoring her advances.

He looked down at his phone as he entered his office. Four more calls, but no messages. There was a God.

"Sir," Shane sidled up to him. Jesus, the man emerged from the walls.

"We've been getting calls."

"It's a holiday weekend." Jonathan threw himself into his chair.

"The Dardens thought you'd make their annual Fourth of July picnic. Mrs. Darden in particular was rather upset."

"How upset?"

"Um, 'pulling support' upset."

Jesus, he couldn't be in Rhode Island and Washington at the same time.

"Get her on the phone. I'll calm her down," Jonathan said.

"Well, she had some pretty insulting things to say. Something about women." Shane held up his hand in a mock shield. "Her words, not mine."

He itched to call Christiana, but at this point he wondered if his phone's security had failed and was bugged. Did he even care? She was the one person who couldn't give a shit about his title and re-election.

The taxicab driver asked Christiana three times if she was alright. She nodded. He dropped her off at the Capitol Visitor Center. They would know which building housed Jonathan's office—a place she hadn't thought to look up before. *Such a fail.*

Her legs limped forward, filled with lead. After ten steps

she couldn't go any farther. She dropped to a concrete bench to rest. Raindrops splashed the empty walkway. Christiana raised her face to let the cool rain mix with the angry tears that wouldn't stop. It only maddened her more.

They'd never let her inside the building looking like the incensed woman she'd likely resembled, now dripping wet. Besides Jonathan could be anywhere. *Maybe Avery was right. He could be with Yvette doing the things he did with me, promised were only for me. But only for the summer, Chris.*

Wet and heavy footfalls caused her to open her eyes. She startled at the body looming over her. The man's hair was plastered to his forehead, revealing a receding hairline. He seemed so different, but not.

"Mark?"

"Miss Snow, let me help you up."

Christiana's knees buckled when Mark hoisted her up. He lifted her into his arms as if she weighed nothing.

Christiana laid her head against his warm shoulder. His build was heavier than Jonathan's, and a cry welled up from her rib cage. *It should be Jonathan holding me.*

Mark laid her on a car seat in the back. Rainwater sluiced off her legs onto the leather. She hoped it left a stain. Mark jogged around to the driver's side and raised his fist at a honking car. He settled into his seat, and the car lurched forward. He spoke into his phone. Christiana couldn't focus on his voice well, as he spoke low and the rain pounded the roof of the car. She could only pick out random words.

"Yes, sir. Not too well, sir . . . of course . . . I'll be right there."

"Where are you taking me?" she asked once he killed the call.

"To where you belong," His voice was kind, but he didn't look into his rearview mirror when he spoke. Christiana didn't know where she belonged. She laid her cheek against the backseat, wishing she'd fall asleep, into the abyss, anywhere but awake. Otherwise she might punch someone.

Jonathan got to the backseat door before Mark could unfasten his own seat belt. Mark was right. Christiana looked like hell. Her soaked T-shirt and jean shorts stuck to her skin, and her bare legs were slick with water. He laid her on the couch in his front room and brushed wet hair off her forehead. "Christiana. What were you doing?"

"Singing in the rain." She pushed herself up and raised her eyes to Mark. "Thanks, Mark. Sorry to be such trouble."

"No trouble at all, Miss Snow. Sir, you'll let me know if you need anything else." Mark gave Christiana a soft squint before turning on his heel.

Jonathan threw off his jacket and grabbed a fluffy towel from the powder room under the staircase, wrapping her in the plush, dry bath sheet.

He sat down and cradled her close. "I shouldn't have left you today. Not after last night."

"I got some bad news today, that's all." Her words came out tight, focused.

"Tell me about it. You can tell me anything, remember."

She pursed her lips and lifted her shoulders.

He understood the gesture. Frustration poured from her body.

"Okay, I'll name some things, and you nod. Does this have anything to do with last night?"

She nestled into his chest, a clear signal the night's memories weren't the issue.

"About work?"

She shook her head.

"Avery?"

An angry cry escaped from her lips. *Bingo.*

"Would you like me to have her assassinated?"

"Yes." Her teeth bit into his pec through his thin shirt.

That makes two of us.

She pulled her hand away and fisted his shirt. "I have something worse in mind. We'll make her wear a pink, taffeta bridesmaid dress for the rest of her life." She exhaled irately. "She brought me pictures. Of you. At *Covil Sereia.*"

"She couldn't have."

"I recognized the suspension thing."

Jonathan released his grip on Christiana and stood. "Son of a bitch. She broke into my house." So Avery Churchill stole the missing photographs. His brain clicked into gear. Avery's stupidity for leaving them with Christiana could finally shake him free of her unwanted advances. A well-timed negotiation might keep her from gaining a criminal record for theft and avoid a scandal from the pictures being shown.

"Where are the pictures now?" he asked.

"Under my mattress."

He chuckled at her sense of protectiveness. "Good girl. They weren't of me, lovely."

"But—"

"Christiana. They were of a friend."

"I saw your hand—"

He sat back down. "*Carson's* hand. He took the pictures, so I could see how he had built his system in his home. He has less to lose than I, though not by much. I would never photograph anything we did together or anyone else for that matter. Now, what else? You haven't told me everything, have you?" Some people wore their hearts on their sleeves; Christiana wore her secrets.

Her eyes softened. "My mother. I found out something."

Jonathan pressed a kiss into her forehead. "You found out

how she died."

"Does everyone know? Am I the only one completely in the dark?" Her shouting was a good sign, a release of energy she needed to unload.

"No, lovely. I know that she must have suffered greatly, and while trying to get care, she decided it was too much."

"But how could she? And my dad didn't tell me. And you didn't either!"

"I didn't know until recently."

Christiana didn't need to know of Mark's investigation, and how Jonathan asked him to keep digging, keep going, until he uncovered all details about her troubled past. He knew a reporter would know how to bury facts as well as uncover them. Peter Snow had done an admirable job in keeping his wife's death under wraps though a second set of initials on Alexandra Snow's admittance papers to the mental institution piqued his suspicions.

"Your father was probably trying to spare you. You were only seven."

"I'm not seven anymore."

"I know, lovely."

Jonathan rocked her back and forth and listened to the rain pound the glass on his bay window. When he thought her breathing had calmed, Jonathan spoke words he hadn't in years. "My mother spent time in a mental institution, thanks to my father's misguided sense of dealing with depression."

Christiana pulled back and peered up at him. "I'm so sorry, Jonathan. Here I am blubbering on and on. Is she . . . did she . . . ."

"She got out and spent her remaining days in her room with curtains drawn. My father divorced her, remarried. She died of a broken heart. I was eleven."

The dam he'd built to restrain these memories hadn't been in danger of cracking in years. But Christiana's anguished face probed the softest places of his heart. Was this how his mother felt when his father announced his intentions to divorce? Or when he delivered his final betrayal, renouncing her very existence?

Jonathan recalled pressing his ear to his mother's bedroom door, her sobs washing over him, his father's rumbling voice. Doors slammed. Water rushed through pipes. Long still nights broken only by his own breathing as he listened, hard, for any signs of life from his mother's room. She'd threatened to swallow the contents of every pill bottle in her medicine cabinet. She never did. She did worse. She withered. Faded away. Left him while still alive.

A single tear ran down Christiana's cheek. "I don't want to die of a broken heart. Don't leave me. Don't make this just for the summer. P-please, please, please."

Her words cut.

Jonathan placed his lips over her small mouth. She lost herself to the gesture as if obeying his actions was the easiest thing she'd ever done. He deepened his kiss, playing with her tongue. She whimpered into his mouth when he pulled her over her lap, settling her crotch over his rigid length just like the first night they spent together at *Covil Sereia*.

After carrying her up the stairs, Jonathan laid her on the nubby, white bedspread covering his king-sized bed. His room was plain—dark walnut furniture, Oriental rug, porcelain lamps. Sarah decorated it years ago. He'd spent so little time at his Alexandria home, it looked like a showroom floor. But Christiana sitting on the edge of the bed instantly warmed the place. He couldn't imagine being anywhere else, provided she never left.

Jonathan pulled his tie through from his shirt collar, while toeing off his shoes. A memory of the Cabinet Room cut deep into his heart when his belt zipped through his belt loops.

"When you look at me like that, it makes me want you more," he whispered.

"I like your *more*," she said into the vee of hair above his long, stiff cock that seemed to reach for her. He almost came on the spot when she licked her lips.

Jonathan reached for her jean's buttons, and soon her clothes joined his abandoned pants on the hardwood floor.

"I'll never get tired of having you, Christiana. Of needing you." He slipped his cock into her slick seam, and she accepted him fully.

"Then don't leave me," she breathed into his mouth.

Leave her. The idea beat at his insides, a mental movie playing over and over until every fiber of his being furiously fought back. Another man slipping between bedsheets to sidle up to her nude body. Another man making love to Christiana. Another man making her round with *his* children —beautiful, blond toddlers with large, blue eyes running around her exquisite legs.

Fuck, that last one hurt.

There were so many obstacles to keeping her permanently. Hell, it seemed impossible. His family counted on him, his constituents put their faith in him, and his father may have been right—he may not be good at anything else.

A public life wouldn't suit Christiana, and his life would always be public. He'd carry the mantle of once being a member of Congress for the rest of his life. The media, the watchdog groups, the civic organizations —they'd watch his every move so long as he lived.

So what? Figure it out. He couldn't imagine life without her. He had to keep her, even if his conscience told him doing so might be the most selfish thing he'd entertained to date.

Jonathan held her blue eyes with his own. "I'm not leaving you, Christiana. Never."

31

Jonathan jogged down the brick steps of his townhouse. The full moon illuminated the cobblestones on Old Town Alexandria's oldest street. A cooler weather front had settled over the region, making it a perfect night to walk.

He headed toward the waterfront restaurant where the Dardens waited for Jonathan to fall on his sword over his absence from their annual July Fourth picnic. Such outrage was par for the course. Large campaign donors required continuous grand, even grandiose, reassurances of their place on the totem pole of his affection. Well, no matter. Nothing could unseat his good mood. Not even groveling like the public servant he was at the feet of those whom he served.

At the corner of Union Street, he drank in the historic Federal architecture of the homes. An elderly couple crossed the street in front of him, while young people laughed and entered an art gallery. The broken streetlight allowed the moon's glow to cast impressive shadows under the large trees lining the small green space. It'd been too long since he'd taken in a lungful of air scented with magnolia blossoms.

He chuckled to himself over his blatant romanticism tonight. *Two hours.* Then he'd allow fantasy to take over between a certain woman's thighs. He didn't care who'd disapprove.

Christiana got off at ten tonight. He'd pick her up from The Oak after they both had completed their duties. Then they'd take all night to attend to one another and every night thereafter.

Jonathan cut across Union into the empty Founder's Park, pausing only to glance at a form leaning against a tree just inside the park entrance. A large hat concealed her face, but she seemed familiar. She mumbled a greeting, causing him to stop and turn toward her. She stepped out from under the outstretched tree limbs, lips curled into a snarl underneath the hat brim. She held out her hand.

Jonathan stumbled backwards. A steel arrow of pain pierced his left side, followed by a dull throb spreading across his shoulders and neck. As his eyesight faded to tiny pinpricks of light, the concrete sidewalk smacked the side of his head. He tried to grasp the sudden shift in gravity, but only felt small stones under his fingers.

Someone wrestled with his jacket, stopping his words. Just before the black space sucked the last bit of oxygen from his lungs, an apparition flickered before his fading vision. An angel peering up at him shyly from underneath her lashes. *Christiana?*

Christiana began to doubt the clock over the kitchen exit still worked. The minutes clicked by so slowly she felt she'd entered a time warp. When ten o'clock finally arrived, Christiana was sure she'd worked for eight days, not eight hours. After dropping off a tray of abandoned beer glasses and lipstick-stained wine glasses to Josh, Christiana sat in one of the booths and scrolled through the screen of her new iPhone. At some point she'd have to return her father's messages and deal with his lies about her mother and their past. But for now, she only wanted to talk to the man who colored the future she desired.

Jonathan had a dinner planned with a constituent who threatened to pull support, and he promised it would be over long before Christiana's shift ended. She fought the urge to call him. A blond-headed news announcer's face filled the screen and an eerie hush settled over the bar. Josh aimed the remote at the screen and the blond helmet-head's voice grew louder.

"Shit, wow, man," one of the drunks said.

"Shhh!" Josh's eyes darted toward Christiana.

Christiana stepped forward to the bar as the announcer's words cut through her rising heartbeat.

An attempt was made on the life of Congressman Jonathan Brond at approximately eight o'clock this evening in Old Town Alexandria. He was walking on Union Street, near his Alexandria residence, when the gunman opened fire. No other bystanders were harmed, but the congressman has been taken to Saint Joseph's for immediate surgery. As soon as we have more information, we will be sure to update you. Again, a member of Congress has been shot, his condition is unknown, no one else hurt, and we will have more details shortly.

In other news . . .

. . .

Christiana stepped back, glass crunching under her feet. She must have grasped a tray of champagne flutes, sending them to the floor.

Josh's voice barked in her ear. "Christiana, don't move." He crouched at her ankles, mopping up broken glass with a rag.

Christiana's cell phone vibrated in her hand.

"Christiana? It's Mark. Jonathan's been hurt."

She jogged to the emptiest part of the bar. "I just saw the news. Please tell me he's okay—alive."

"Yes, he's alive."

"Who would shoot him?"

"We don't know yet. Now listen." Mark's voice demanded attention. "The best way to help Jonathan right now is to go about your life. Act normal."

"W-what? No, I have to—"

"Stop." He hadn't shouted, but the chilling effect was the same. "Do not call attention to yourself with grief that may seem unnatural . . . anything that may lead anyone to deduce your relationship."

Christiana almost broke under his tone, so like Jonathan. "I'll try."

"If you care about Jonathan, you will do this."

"I will." The phone line went dead. Act normal? Was he kidding? Mark's words mixed with the news announcer's until she couldn't think anymore. She stared at her silenced phone. *Act normal. Do not call attention. Be invisible.*

Christiana stood and stepped up to the bar. "Give me a rag. I'll clean it up."

Josh handed her a moistened towel. "I'm surprised at you. You're normally so steady on your feet."

The undeserved chilling look she shot his way must have landed, as he turned away with a forced shrug. She felt mildly triumphant that at least something lay in her control.

For the rest of her shift, Christiana kept one eye on the television while taking the last few drink orders. She returned change. She deposited dirty dishes into the kitchen. She didn't hear a word anyone said.

Somehow she got home, unaware of the cab drive until her key clicked in the front door.

She crumpled to the floor, a sob bursting from her chest like a bomb. Mark had told her to act calm, cool, and detached, as if her world hadn't caved in. She couldn't do it. She couldn't.

But, you promised him, Chris. You must do this.

She stood and stumbled to the living room. The real waiting began.

Christiana spent the next two nights, all night, sleeping on the couch. CNN blinked its images over her body. Her ear attuned to the droning of the anchors, listening for any word about Jonathan being released.

During the day, somehow she obeyed Mark. She worked. She breathed. She lived. Her head threatened a migraine. Her insides churned with every step and every false word from her mouth. She now knew how she'd react if he hadn't agreed to stay together. She wouldn't have survived. Being apart, she knew what her life would look like without him —excruciating.

Avery didn't call. But then the Style channel didn't cover assassination attempts. Her father didn't call either. But then why would he? Her relationship with Jonathan had been a secret.

Then, finally, *finally*, Mark made good on his word. Two days and fourteen hours after Christiana heard about the assassination attempt on Jonathan, Mark stood in front of her at The Oak room kitchen door.

"Your supervisor would be delighted if you'd take a break," he said.

The tension in her stomach returned when Mark, ever the careful driver, refused to drive over the speed limit at any point on the way to the hospital. He pulled into an underground lot and circled the black sedan to the lowest level.

"Photographers are generally too lazy to leave the first floor," he explained. Christiana knew the time of day was no accident either. Three o'clock remained the final hour for reporters trying to make four p.m. deadlines.

They rode the elevator in stillness, except for Christiana's leg shaking impatiently. Mark glanced her way and pulled her closer in a brotherly shelter. When the elevator doors opened, he led her to a room halfway down a nondescript hallway. Men in dark suits stood guard at his doorway. They nodded at Mark as they approached.

Clicks and whooshing burped from machines surrounding Jonathan's pale, prostrate body. Dark circles blued under his eyes, and his cheeks hollowed his face. A small white bandage ran across his forehead. A white sling held his arm close to his shoulder, blood tainting the bandage. She forced herself to not throw herself on top of him.

She squinted in the harsh light. The antiseptic smell rose heavy under her nose. She touched his arm, and his eyes cracked open. His hand captured her fingers.

"Hey, lovely."

"Jonathan." She whispered his name as if any sound might harm him more.

She rose and set her hip on the mattress. It dipped, and he winced, but grasped her waist tightly when she tried to retreat.

"Does it hurt much?" she asked.

"Yes. But it will heal." His words slurred together.

"Oh, God . . . ." Her voice cracked, and she laid her head gently down on the pillow, breathing in a medicinal scent that filmed his body.

"Hey, no tears. I'm fine."

From the corner of her eye, Christiana noticed Mark faced the hallway like a sentinel.

"You scared me." Her voice wobbled.

"I've heard that a lot recently."

"I don't know what I'd do if anything happened to you."

"Nothing's going to happen to me. Or to you." He winced, as he tried to pull himself up more.

"Don't try to move." She pulled the pillow up behind him to brace his back. "Do they know who did it?"

"They have a number of leads. That's what I need to talk to you about."

"Anything."

"I need you to go back to your life—"

"Anything but that."

"Just until I can sort this out. The FBI is all over the place. Anyone who I've been seen with in the last few months will be considered a viable suspect. I can't let you get caught up—"

"I can lay low. Sneaking in here and there. When do you go home? I could go there and wait for you."

"No, lovely. You need to go on with your normal routine."

"But when will I see you?"

"It won't be long. I promise. Come here." He beckoned her down to his face. He pressed a kiss to her cheek. "Mark is going to take you home now. Then, when it's safe, I'll call you. Don't call me. The FBI has my phone. Mark erased it."

"But—"

"Be my good girl." Jonathan's eyes closed.

Christiana experienced Mark's full strength for the first time as he pulled her away from Jonathan's hold. "We walk now. Detectives are coming." Mark led her by the arm out the door and down the hall to a set of stairs.

As soon as the stairwell door clicked behind him, he took Christiana by both shoulders. His gaze pierced through the tears that had taken permanent residence in her eyes. He handed her a crisp square handkerchief, so old-fashioned it had to be new. "I'll make sure he calls you later."

"Thank you, Mark." Christiana wiped under her eyes.

"You're welcome. It's the least I can do to avoid being punched."

"Mind reader."

"All part of the job."

They descended the stairs in silence. When they got to the garage, Christiana's head had cleared. She promised herself she would see Jonathan soon, even if the CIA, NSA, FBI and the rest of the alphabet soup rained their security forces upon her. Most importantly, she'd master the art of simple verbal communication and tell Jonathan what she left out before leaving his room. *I love you.*

She turned to Mark. "I'll need your cell phone number, Mark. I won't be left waiting by the phone anymore."

Christiana wasn't sure, but she could have sworn he suppressed a smile.

Damn his father and his singular attention to Jonathan's career.

Sarah rose from the side of Jonathan's bed. "You know he means well, Jay."

His face winced as the stitches along his shoulder pulled.

"He's thinking about how to turn this—how did he put it?—this unfortunate occurrence into more voter support."

She smirked. "Well, the offer of body guards was kinda sweet."

"If it'll help keep Marla Clampton from visiting."

"Are you sure, Jonathan? It might take the heat off some of the other rumors."

"Not you, too."

"No. But Mother called. Senator Clampton's wife is her bridge partner, you know. Your father is suspicious. Jonathan, you have to be more careful with Christiana. If anything was ever validated—"

"Nothing's going to happen, Sarah. I've been careful." *No, you haven't.*

"I'll go talk to the nurses, find out when they're sending the papers up for your discharge. I'll also be sure to forget to tell Brond Senior. That way he won't rush over to your house with a draft crime bill for you to sign." Sarah kissed him on the forehead, and he softened. No one could calm him like Sarah—except for a certain, young submissive.

Mark cleared his throat in the doorway. "Sir, how are you feeling?"

"Like I've been shot." Mark didn't deserve the tone, but Jonathan's ire hadn't abated since the haze began to clear in the surgery recovery room. He waited for the fear to kick in, remind him someone tried to kill him. Instead pure, undiluted rage had filled his body. He'd barely contained his fury during Christiana's visit.

Jonathan pulled himself up with a grimace. Mark didn't move to help him, recognizing that would only underscore Jonathan's vulnerability.

"House?" Jonathan asked.

"Secured."

"Personal records?"

"Protected."

"Christiana?"

"Safe."

"Are you sure?" Jonathan rarely questioned Mark's abilities. Recognition of the anomaly showed on his friend's face. Yes, he was his friend. He'd proven it over the last few days. Jonathan now understood how your life could flash before your eyes when faced with death, and the most important people rise to the top.

"No one suspicious has been snooping around. Her house, The Oak, all seem normal."

"And the media haven't started sifting through my romantic liaisons to spice up their stories?"

"A little. But nothing leading you to Christiana yet. Your phone's been wiped, computers, all of it."

"What about Yvette. Still calling?"

"Every hour. Even offered to call on Arniss for you."

Jonathan grunted. "I must be in danger. Make sure she's okay, too."

Mark nodded. "I know who's been following you, sir. The car was registered to Judge Marcus Churchill. It made no sense for the stalker to be the Judge, however. So I investigated further."

"And?"

"Avery Churchill crashed her Fiat over four weeks ago."

"So, she was driving a car licensed to a federal judge."

"In all probability, yes."

"Well, that's not entirely bad news. She's had a crush on me all summer. Christiana can confirm that. And, fuck, she broke into my house. What's happening on that, by the way? No fingerprints found on the photos, nothing?"

"No, sir. And, I think it's more serious than that. I did a little more digging. Avery Churchill failed her first year at Stanford.

In addition to the failing grades, apparently some trouble involving the son of an Internet mogul arose. The boy's family got a restraining order on her. And there's something else. The bullet in your shoulder matches a gun registered to—"

"Judge Marcus Churchill."

"Not sure it's enough evidence to get a warrant, but it's a start."

"Call Judge Henderson. Get the gun. Prove it."

Mark left, ostensibly to give Jonathan time to absorb the new developments. Jonathan's mind roiled. If Avery Churchill sent a bullet his way, she'd probably reserved several more for the object of his affection. He told Mark to do whatever he needed to do to protect Christiana, including letting the precocious, *insane,* Avery feel a bullet herself, if necessary—warrant or not.

Jonathan listened to the machines click in time with a nurse's squeaky footsteps in the hallway. An assassination attempt was not part of his ten-year master plan, yet Christiana hadn't been either. He'd taken many risks with her, though every second seemed worth it. *This is why you've never gotten heavily involved.* His world proved too treacherous for love—for Christiana. He knew what he had to do. He couldn't sacrifice her life for his own selfish lust. That was his father's way.

Regardless, it was time for a new plan. He let his life blueprint crumble to the ground.

Slurring feminine words came over her phone. Christiana asked, "Who is this?"

"Oh, Christiana, dear."

"Mrs. Churchill?" Christiana hadn't expected Avery's

mother's coherent voice to follow the incoherent sounds she'd been trying to decipher.

"Yes, dear, I'm so sorry. But Avery isn't feeling well."

"Oh, I'm sorry." *I think.*

"I'll tell her you called."

"But Avery called—"

"Ta-ta, dear!" The phone line went dead. So, that's where Avery learned how to craft her own reality. Mrs. Churchill's ability to paint her world as she'd prefer to see it rivaled Matisse's.

Christiana's phone rang again. "Mark?"

"Who the hell's Mark?" her father's voice rang out. Shit, she should have checked the caller ID before answering.

"Hi Dad. I was expecting a call from work." Lying came so easily now, too easily. "But I'm glad you called."

"I'm on my way home." His gruff voice showed his irritation.

"Good," she said. "Cuz I need to—"

"We'll talk then. Make sure you have on more clothes than a macramé pot holder when I arrive."

Great. Her hope he hadn't recognized that girl on the runway had been futile.

"Dad—"

"Soon, Christiana." He sounded stone cold sober. It was official. The world had gone mad.

32

"Sit down, Congressman." The Judge motioned toward the two wing-back chairs in front of the blackened fireplace.

Jonathan stood. He'd been out of the hospital for a day, and already he'd been summoned to the shooter's home. Damned if he was going to stand in front of the man's desk like a kid sent to the schoolmaster. The meeting was timed, of course, so that Jonathan still reeled from blood loss and trauma. Judge Churchill handed him a tumbler of scotch from the bar cart.

"I'm a vodka man, myself."

"Suit yourself."

Jonathan walked to the fireplace. "Going to order me to stand down on filing charges?"

"Do you need to be ordered?"

"What do you think?"

"Getting a little hot under the collar, aren't we?"

"Getting shot will do that to you."

"Fair enough. But I'd rather . . . negotiate."

The Judge couldn't have any incriminating evidence that would stop him from ensuring Avery got what she deserved.

The few pictures Avery had stolen could be explained as research findings on the dangers of the Internet to minors, perhaps. After all Jonathan was the Internet piracy guru on Capitol Hill.

"We wouldn't be here if Avery wasn't left to run amok. She could have used some discipline."

"Giving me parenting advice? Yes, I understand you like discipline . . . among other things." The Judge sipped from his glass.

"Let's talk about your daughter, Judge, and her attempted murder charges."

The Judge's face didn't register Jonathan's words. He settled his ample posterior in one of the wing-back chairs. "My daughter took quite an interest in you."

"Interest not returned."

"Now that I know more, I'm quite glad it was not. I have no intention of my daughter ever getting near you."

"I'm quite relieved to hear it, given her aim."

"My daughter is many things, Congressman, but a murderer she's not." The Judge sipped his drink and appraised him. "Please, Congressman, sit, sit."

Jonathan settled into the chair opposite the Judge's practiced congenial smirk.

"You know as well as I do that Avery shot me." Jonathan coolly dangled his glass off the chair's arm.

"You'll never hear that from my mouth."

Deny the inevitable. She'd already been named a suspect after the Judge's gun was confiscated, thanks to Mark's tip to the police.

"God knows why Avery has a thing for you, even after what she discovered—" the Judge said into his glass. "She really should go into intelligence. I'm sure the National Ground Intelligence Center would appreciate her sleuthing abilities. Really, Jonathan, you sick fuck. With a nineteen-year old? Chris Snow, of all people, too."

"You leave Christiana out of it."

"The Snows always were a lot of trouble," the Judge said into his glass as he took another large swallow.

"The Snows?"

The Judge softened, as if a memory had brushed over him. He swirled the ice in his glass, his cold demeanor returning in force. "Let's get down to brass tacks, shall we? I won't see the party harmed from a scandal. Something tells me the majority leader wouldn't be pleased to learn about your sexual antics. Some of them with a girl barely of legal age—and her age is only the tip of the iceberg." He arched an eyebrow at Jonathan. "Let's say I'll avoid the Cabinet Room from now on."

Until that moment, it hadn't occurred to Jonathan The Oak Room had so much security. He wished he knew how Avery got ahold of the surveillance video—and why he hadn't already been blackmailed by some security guard attempting to make a name for himself.

Jonathan shrugged delicately. "Have you seen what's gracing the New York Times Best Seller list? I'll be every woman's fantasy lover. And your daughter? Just another pathetic, mentally unstable rich kid who didn't get the toy she wanted. The exposure in the press might push her right over the edge."

"You seem awfully sure of yourself, given your *situation*."

Jonathan's languid eyes held the Judge's with mocking challenge. "Bring it."

The Judge rattled his glass. "Fantasy lover to every woman, is it? But, you don't want *every* woman, do you, Congressman? Just one in particular."

A steel arrow of fury shot up Jonathan's spine.

The infernal Judge continued to swirl the ice in his glass.

"The minute my daughter is revealed in this unseemly affair, your precious Christiana will be too, along with your sick ways. Ways that might cause a woman to want to, let's say, defend herself?"

"My shoulders are broad enough to take the heat. Can your daughter?" Jonathan casually brought the vodka to his lips and sipped. "If she was mentally unstable before, I hesitate to imagine what being so exposed to the hyenas that pass for the media will do to her."

The Judge stood. "You have twenty-four hours to decide. After that I blow the roof off."

"It's a little early for clichés, don't you think?"

"Oh, Congressman. It's later than you know."

Christiana tamped down tears that threatened to rise. Brian's admonishment for missing so much work almost tipped her over the edge. Christiana wouldn't break her promise to herself to master her emotions even if the one person who could stop the spiraling inside remained out of her reach.

Jonathan hadn't called like Mark promised. She couldn't go to his office or home, given the likelihood of paparazzi. Jonathan had said he'd need to stay away for a few days until things cooled off, and she'd complied. It almost killed her.

"Christiana?" She turned to face Yvette DeCord.

"Mrs. DeCord." Christiana dipped her head and then blushed for acting so reverential.

"What may I do for you, Mrs. DeCord?" Brian stepped in between them.

Christiana noticed Brian's posture straightened in Yvette's presence as well.

"I was hoping you could spare Christiana for a few minutes, Brian. I need her help. Upstairs in my suite?"

The elegant woman led her away and leaned into Christiana's shoulder. "We have a mutually beneficial relationship that needs tending," she whispered.

Yvette turned to her as soon as Christiana stepped inside the suite door. "First, call me Yvette. It's high time we met officially."

Christiana returned her handshake. "Christiana."

Yvette smiled warmly. "Please, come inside, sit down."

She followed Yvette into the elegant sitting room and took a seat on the burgundy silk couch in front of the floor to ceiling stone fireplace. Yvette shook a champagne bottle free from a perspiring ice bucket on the side table. She lifted it to Christiana in question.

"No, I'm fine."

"I'm making it a project to empty The Oak's wine cellar. Compliments of my soon-to-be-ex." Yvette slowly poured herself a tall flute of sparkling bubbles. "Have you seen Jonathan?" Yvette lifted the glass to her lips.

"Mark took me to see him once. But Jonathan said I had to stay away."

"And you honored that."

"Of course." She lowered her eyes.

"Good girl."

Christiana's head shot up at the endearment she'd only heard from Jonathan. Yvette's warm smile soothed her anxiety. "Oh, yes, Christiana. I know how well you follow instructions. But I also know that just because you're a natural-born submissive doesn't mean you don't know how to fight."

"What? I mean, how do you know—?"

"I saw it in your eyes the first time you set down my room service order on that settee over there." Christiana swallowed surprise that Yvette had ever noticed her, let alone remembered her name.

Yvette lifted her glass and studied the bubbles. "The begging to be told what to do, to have that mantle lifted from your shoulders." She returned her eyes to Christiana's heated face. "It's nothing to be ashamed of, or giving over your power once in a while so you can breathe." Yvette placed her hand over Christiana's. "Just remember to take that power back when you need it. Like now. Christiana, you and I are more alike than you know. We both want men who'd make sure our lipstick wouldn't stand a chance against one single kiss.

"Don't look at me like that either," Yvette added. "I've just been around a little longer than you, that's all. Though I'm impressed you've come into yourself so quickly. It took me longer, and now . . . ." She trailed off and stared over the back of the sofa out to Pennsylvania Avenue. "Well, let's say I may be batting for the other team soon."

Christiana pulled her hand back instinctively.

Yvette returned her gaze and patted her on the hand once. "Not *that* team, dear. The Dominant one. Spend a little time with a submissive *male*."

"I know someone who could teach you how to do that."

"Sarah." Their unison answer had them giggling as if they were old girlfriends.

The doorbell chime broke into their laughter. "Speaking of the little Femme Domme. There she is now." Yvette rose and disappeared for a few minutes to return with Sarah. The click of their heels tapped a syncopated rhythm on the marble floor.

Sarah stopped at the edge of the couch. Concealer had creased in the bags under Sarah's eyes, and worry lined her mouth. "I just came from Jonathan."

Christiana stood up immediately. "How is he?"

"He's been better. Please, sit." Sarah sank to the couch,

pulling Christiana down with her. "He's home now, and he'll heal. He was lucky."

"I can go see him then." Christiana almost stood, but Sarah's arm stopped her rise.

"Do they know anything?" Yvette asked.

"I'm sure Mark knows who shot him, but he's not saying. Not until he clears things with Jonathan first. I have a feeling things are going to get messy." Sarah turned to Christiana. "How are you holding up?"

"I'm fine."

"Putting on a brave face is good, Christiana. But this is no time to not be honest."

Jesus, Sarah was like Jonathan. "When can I see him?" She could not squelch the pleading in her voice.

"Soon. But we asked you here because we need to know something."

"What?"

"I think somehow you're involved, Christiana. Not that you had anything to do with the shooting. But something's not right. He's thinking about ending things with you, immediately."

Christiana's throat hitched. "He-he can't."

Sarah covered her hand with hers. "I think it would be a mistake too. I haven't always been a fan of the risks he took to be with you. But quite frankly, when your name comes up, you'd think he was a lion protecting his pride. I've never seen Jay make a decision based on a woman. You're the first such woman, and the only reason he'd let you go is if you're in *real* danger."

Christiana's mouth fell open. Her eyes dropped to her lap.

"Yes, you are most definitely his sub," Sarah said.

Yvette sighed. "I told you."

"But there's more."

"You think he's in love."

Christiana's face shot up. "He told you that?"

"Yes, I think he loves you. No, he didn't say so," Sarah said.

"Are you sure, Sarah?" Yvette's question emerged as motherly, rather than catty.

"Positive. Sorry, Yvette."

"I saw it that day he took me to The Oak. Sorry about that, by the way." She sent Christiana a warm smile. "I know it distressed you. But that's when I knew too. He's in love with you."

A single tear escaped down Christiana's cheek. She swiped it away. "I hate to cry." She dropped her head. "So weak."

Yvette handed her a tissue. "Weak is not a word I'd use to describe you."

"Do you love him?" Sarah's voice was even and controlled.

A calm wave washed over Christiana, as if Jonathan's smooth voice had asked the question. "I'd do anything for him," she said.

"That's not the same thing." Sarah raised her hand and stopped a protest from Yvette.

"Yes. I love him." She tried to sound as resolute as she felt.

"Good. I believe you. So." Sarah slapped her lap and rose. "We need a battle plan. His father is doing something right for once and working his connections. But there's one thing he can't do. Figure out why Judge Churchill wanted to talk with Jonathan so badly. No way was Judge Churchill offering support. He hates our family."

"Why?" Christiana asked.

"He once ran against Jonathan's father. He's been trying to bury Jonathan's chances in office for years now."

Finally, a puzzle piece hovered over the giant mess. The tight band across Christiana's chest loosened an inch, not nearly enough to make her breathe easier but enough for the lump in her throat to drop.

"Judge Churchill has to be connected to Jonathan's assassination attempt in some way." Sarah examined Christiana's face. "Christiana, how close were you and Avery Churchill?"

"I don't know how to answer that anymore."

"Did you talk to Avery about Jonathan?"

"No. I never told her anything, but she found out by accident."

"My mother plays bridge with some of the loudest mouths in Washington. Apparently, Avery talked to her father about Jonathan dating a younger woman, so the Judge feels he has some blackmail material. I'd expect nothing less from the Dishonorable Churchill. He's not above kicking someone when they're down," Sarah spat.

It made sense. Avery had run to her father when Jonathan spurned her advances. The Judge had thrown down the gauntlet to ensure that the man whom his daughter imagined had scorned her advances did not go unpunished.

Sarah cleared her throat. "Then there are . . . pictures."

Yvette's eyes shot from examining champagne bubbles to Sarah's face. "Not of you," Sarah said.

"I know about those. Mark has them now. But they're not of him, right?" Christiana asked. "She just got them from his house?"

Sarah nodded coolly, eyebrows knit together in thought. "We have to assume Avery likely copied them."

Of course she did. Avery may be a bitch, but she wasn't stupid. Christiana sent her eyes back and forth between Sarah and Yvette, wishing she had some intelligence to add. These women had a treasure trove of experiences and wisdom to access. She had nothing to offer, except how to balance six dinner plates in two hands and which routes in the city had police set-ups for drunk drivers. Too bad all those years of jogging after Avery and her father at events didn't lead to greater connections she could tap into today.

Wait.

Christiana stood. "I can help." Sarah and Yvette's heads snapped up. "My dad revered the Churchills for years, pushed me to be friends with Avery. He might know what's going on—or at least find out more."

"Well, anything you can—" Yvette began.

"No," Sarah said. "Jonathan would want you out of this. I just wanted you to be informed that we're on it. But I won't have you tainted in this mess."

"But my dad—"

"Is a reporter who will sniff out a best-selling story before Twitter has a chance to blast it."

"He won't."

"How do you know?"

"He's my father. He's not about to drag his daughter through the mud. Not after what I have."

Yvette cocked her head. "Have what?"

Christiana steadied herself. "I mean, he won't. I'll guarantee it." She wasn't about to mention her mother and what she'd discovered. To save Jonathan, she wouldn't be above blackmailing someone else herself, even if it meant making her father feel guilty about all his secrets, *their* secrets.

"Are you sure?" Sarah asked.

"I've never been so sure in my life."

"I knew you had a spine." Yvette stood and wrapped her arm around Christiana's shoulder.

"Okay, then. Time to steel yourself, Christiana Snow. You're about to experience the real Washington." Sarah lifted herself from the couch.

Christiana flushed as Sarah spun on her heel and marched to the suite door. "I'll continue to press Mark. Let's talk tonight and piece together what we've learned." The snick of the suite door echoed across the marble floor.

"I work 'til closing."

"Don't worry," Yvette said with a seductive purr. "I'll handle Brian Bishop."

Yvette's word rang true. Brian didn't protest when Christiana simply gathered her things and headed to the parking garage.

In one afternoon, Christiana's understanding of power had shifted. She couldn't quite nail the definition yet. But somehow she knew she was about to encounter real influence.

33

Christiana drummed her sticky palms on her knees. Her butt had imprinted the couch with a large dip from rising and sitting over and over, impatiently, at every car sound out the front window. Her father's plane had landed ninety minutes ago. He should have been home by now.

Fragments of disparate information zipped through her brain, refusing to lock themselves into a pattern. Someone shot Jonathan. He then wanted to break things off with her because *she* was at risk, not him. Why? Judge Churchill hated Jonathan. Just because he lost an election to his father? He had to have something on Jonathan more than a handful of pictures stolen by his vain daughter. They couldn't be enough.

Her mind returned to the last puzzle piece that floated above all others. *Letters.* A stack of envelopes bound with a faded blue ribbon. After charging back to her father's safe, she couldn't believe the gold mine she'd unearthed. After reading every word of the dozen letters, she had more than a few choice words for her dad.

Her father's key clicked in the front door.

"Dad, where have you been? I've been trying you for ages." Her father dropped his bags inside the door, his face etched in surprise. Christiana normally didn't accost him at the door.

"It took a while to extricate myself, get back home. My damn office wants me on the Brond shooting right away."

"That's good. Because I need to know what you know."

"Whoa, slow down. Why?"

"Dad, there's no time. I need to talk to you about Jonathan. He's my boyfriend." His already-stricken faced paled. While she'd been fashioning a butt print in the couch, she'd decided shock value would be the best approach to getting him to focus. She was glad to see it worked.

"I have lots to tell you, Dad. Sit down. I need your help with something. But I'm going to go first. So you know what's at stake."

Christiana didn't know how to start, but once the words started, she found she couldn't stop. She had to give her father credit for listening to the whole truth of her relationship with Jonathan. How she had gone away many weekends and kept it secret from him and Avery. Naturally, she left out the sex—and the power dynamic. He blushed anyway.

He hadn't moved a muscle once she got him to the couch. "So, how disappointed are you?"

"I'm a little in shock, that's all. Right now all I can think of is that ten-year old, with her pigtails flying, sliding down the hallway in stocking feet."

"I'm not that little girl anymore."

"Clearly. But a congressman? And Jonathan Brond? With his reputation? I need a drink."

Christiana stopped his rise from the couch. "He's not like that."

"He's too old for you."

"My years of life experience make up for my age." She steeled her voice.

He slumped back against the couch as she'd thrown a weighted ball onto his chest. He took a deep breath. "Yes, they do. But, you know, it wasn't until the fashion show that I really saw how grown up you were. Which, by the way, young lady, we have not talked about yet. That dress?"

His fatherly turn stunned her. She hadn't heard that voice in years.

"What in God's name was that outfit? I nearly decked a guy to my right who wouldn't stop whistling. I spilled my wine all over his tux, I'll have you know."

"Jonathan wasn't pleased about that night, either."

"Good. His stock just went up with me. Because if he put you up to that—"

"No, Dad, it was Avery."

"No surprise there. The Churchills always did like moving their little chess pieces around."

"It's time they stopped. Which is why I want you to tell me about these." She picked up the stack of letters she'd tucked under a magazine.

"What were you doing in my safe?" her father asked.

"Looking for answers. Why didn't you tell me my mother killed herself, and why the hell was Marcus Churchill writing love letters to her?"

He grabbed the stack and threw them across the room to hit the TV. The ribbon loosened, sending them scattering in all directions.

Christiana sat in stunned silence for long moments.

Her father sighed, his face staring at the floor. "Jesus, you're so much like your mother, do you know that?"

"You're not going to tell me I'm mentally ill."

"No, that's where you differ." He raised his eyes to meet hers. "You're strong. So damned strong. But that's what I wanted for you. Why I wanted you to be friends with Avery. She seemed similar."

"We're nothing alike."

"I didn't want you to be *like* her, just more confident than you seemed to be, because I knew you had it in you."

"Jonathan brought it out."

Christiana studied her father's face, misery etched in lines she hadn't noticed. Crinkles ran deep across his forehead and gray hairs lined his temples. Now, with the past raised, he appeared older, more worn out than even a few days earlier. Her mother's death must have been an awful blow. Her mother didn't just leave *her*. She had left them both.

"Okay, I'll tell you." He stood and paused. "Man, your mom was gorgeous. How she ended up with me I'll never know."

"You undersell yourself, Dad."

"No, I don't. Which is why Marcus Churchill was able to do what he did."

Christiana held her breath.

He rubbed his chin. "We were at the Kennedy Center for an opera or some God-awful play. She tripped coming up the stairs. Her dress tore, and you'd think it was the end of the world. Hell, it looked to me like a larger slit than what was running up the side already. The Honorable Marcus—only he wasn't so honorable back then, being a clerk for some Supreme Court justice—stepped in and offered to help. He kept saying things, charming little nothings, the whole time. And there I was, trailing like some legislative aide waiting for the order to get some water."

He shook his head as if the night replayed in his head. "I didn't find the letters until much later. I don't think they had an affair, no evidence of it. But she kept the letters, maybe as a reminder of what she could have had." His voice cracked. "They were with her belongings at the hospital."

"So why encourage me to be friends with Avery?"

"You needed to be better prepared than your mother to deal with those types. I thought if you could learn from the source, you'd be stronger, more capable of handling those people."

"Dad. Now that you say that out loud, you do know that's crazy, right?"

"Well, now that I have to articulate it, I can see how it sounds."

"And you're the writer. Jeez. But, that can't be all of it. How'd she get into—"

"After she was diagnosed with manic depression, it got worse, like she'd been given permission to misbehave. There were days I'd be afraid to leave the house and leave you alone with her. I never knew what she'd do."

She remembered her mother being the most fun person ever. Except when she wasn't. They'd sled down hills on large dinner trays and went on sudden jaunts to get ice cream only to stop at Dunkin' Donuts on the way home. But then, her mom also spent long days in bed, bedroom curtains sealed against daylight. Her father made pancakes at night while her mother lay in the darkened room.

Christiana thought she was lucky to have such unorthodox parents, except none of the other kids were allowed over to play. She'd grown used to being alone. Then Avery singled her out. No wonder Christiana latched on to the little bitch so fast.

"You put her in an institution when she almost drowned me, didn't you?" Christiana almost darted off the couch at the choked cry that erupted from her father's throat. She'd never seen her father cry.

"I had to. None of the medication worked, and finally I just had to." Reddened eyes peered up at her. "I tried to get her out. But couldn't."

"What do you mean, couldn't?"

"The court had deemed her dangerous to a minor in the household and a danger to herself. I think that's how they put it. You see, she was accused of—."

"Almost drowning me." The words didn't scare her anymore. She'd learned to be scared of larger things, like losing Jonathan forever.

"While I worked the bureaucracy, she gave up."

"Killed herself."

"Yes, not easy to do in a lockdown situation. But she hoarded the medication she pretended to take."

"Not in a car accident."

"No."

She looked at the letters. "Dad, did you ever read these?"

"Not after the first one. I couldn't."

"But you kept them."

"As a reminder of what I had to do . . . to protect you."

Christiana would have cried at his statement if they hadn't been running out of time. Christiana knew if the tide didn't turn soon, Jonathan wouldn't go back on his decision. He'd stay locked in his congressional post and make damned sure she never got near him, all out of a sense of misguided protection when really *he* needed the protection more than anyone.

"Well, I read them. And I think Judge Churchill had everything to do with Mom's fate," she said. *And blackmailing Jonathan.* She'd keep that last thought to herself. No use giving her father a story that might not be true.

Christiana pulled out the two most important letters she'd found and handed them to her father. As his eyes skimmed over the pages, color returned to his face. By the time he finished the second letter, rage replaced the tears in his eyes. Good, he was now ready to help.

"Dad, what's the worst thing that can happen to a federal judge?"

He held out his hand to help her from the couch. "There's a Swedish proverb your mother loved. *Worry often gives a small thing a big shadow.* I think I understand it now."

Christiana called Mark as soon as she and her father cooked up their plan.

Mark had been stopping by her house and The Oak every day since Christiana visited Jonathan in the hospital. During each visit, his words had been the same, *Jonathan will call soon. I promise.* Seeing Mark during Jonathan's silence made her feel better somehow, like all hope wasn't lost if Mark remained in touch. Now she needed Mark to do more than just check on her well-being.

Because Jonathan didn't call. She felt his presence slipping, the unseen tether she'd felt before fraying. She felt adrift. She wouldn't let any more distance grow.

Mark answered on the first ring. In a gush of words, Christiana told Mark about Judge Churchill's involvement in her mother's death. As soon as she said it out loud, she realized how much she sounded like a third grader on a playground asking a friend to stop pushing another friend off the swing set because, well, it just wasn't nice. Before she could dig herself into a larger hole, Mark filled the silence.

"That could buy him some time," he said slowly.

A rush of relief wiped away her embarrassment. "Judge Churchill has something on Jonathan, doesn't he? I mean, could he have copies of the pictures?" She amazed herself by not blushing.

Mark didn't answer. She sighed into the phone after a full minute ticked by.

"Your letters likely wouldn't hold up in court," he said. "But it's worth trying to unnerve the Judge."

More silence. "Jonathan has an appointment tomorrow. I can't tell you with whom. But, if you guess—"

"Judge Churchill."

"Yes." He phrased it like a question.

"At his house."

"I can neither confirm nor deny that. But if you enter the GW parkway via the Spout Run exit at three p.m., you might notice a familiar SUV. If Jonathan notices, well, I can't very well outrun you. I'm sworn to obey the speed limit."

"Mark. I promise never to want to punch you again."

Christiana swore she felt a smile come through the phone.

Christiana fiddled with her pearls, pooled in her lap. She glanced over at her father who gripped the steering wheel. He looped a finger through a pearl strand and held her fingers still. She suddenly felt selfish for having been so cavalier with her mother's prized necklace over the years. His heart must have cracked a little more every time she sashayed by, the pearls' long strands clicking together, like a little girl playing dress up—only with a priceless set of opera-length sea pearls passed down from generation to generation.

They entered the GW parkway at precisely three o'clock. The Potomac glistened under the summer sun to her right, and Christiana watched the boats cut through the silver-blue water. A longing to stretch out in her bathing suit on the deck of Jonathan's sailboat warmed her more than the sunlight streaming across her lap.

Her father's voice broke her daydreaming. "Right on time." A black SUV had pulled in front of them.

"I wonder if Jonathan even notices we're behind him," Yvette said.

Sarah and Yvette sat in the back. They both seemed unaware of the boxes of papers at their feet and between them. Sarah used one as an armrest. Christiana hadn't expected the two women to tag along. But who was she to say no?

"Did Arniss find anything?" Sarah asked.

Christiana's eyes flew to Yvette's face. "Yes, dear, I asked for his help," Yvette said. "We may be getting divorced, but he's the best criminal attorney in town. He advised us to stay home, and let the law do its job. Coward."

"No matter. We still have Christiana's trump card," Sarah said. "And she should deliver the news. It'll have more punch. He won't expect it."

Her father released her hand and grasped the steering wheel tighter. "Fat chance. I'm not putting Chris in front of that bastard. I want to punch the asshole in the gut with what I know." Yvette sat forward and touched his shoulder. "Okay, but if he gets rough, I'm stepping in." Her father's shoulder relaxed, and his eyes re-focused on the road ahead.

Christiana had never seen anyone steer her father away from an agenda. She hoped Yvette's presence would have the same effect on the Judge and whatever scheme he'd designed.

34

Her Dad pulled in behind Jonathan's SUV in front of the Churchill mansion. They both stopped at the front entrance, blocking anyone from continuing down the circular limestone drive. A surge of pride filled Christiana at the alpha male move, even if they did it unconsciously.

Christiana stepped out of the car as Mark opened Jonathan's door. He stepped from the backseat. "What are you doing? Christiana, no. You are not going in there."

A wash of longing ran through Christiana when she saw his arm in a sling. His stride toward her was stopped by Sarah. She slipped in between them and laid her hand on his chest. He stilled.

Forget Avery. Christiana should've been studying Sarah and Yvette. She'd never experienced such subtle control.

"Are you all going to stand out there yacking all day, or are you coming inside?" Judge Churchill's voice boomed from the open front door atop the wide front stairs.

Peter strode forward and placed his foot on the bottom step. He turned to Jonathan. "We're all going in, Congressman."

Christiana followed her father, Jonathan, Mark, Yvette, and Sarah into the massive marble hallway to face the Judge, now encircled in his wife's arms. Coco fit well in the ornate circular entranceway. She stood like part of the artwork—beautiful, statuesque, and immutable.

"Well, we're here," the Judge said.

"What? No sit-down in the front parlor?" Jonathan asked.

"Say what you need to say, and then we'll all go our separate ways."

"Mrs. Churchill, is Avery here? Last time she called . . . I mean, is she okay?" Christiana asked.

"No," the Judge answered. Christiana wasn't sure which question the Judge had answered, but Coco's smile sent a silent *thank you for asking.*

The Judge's eyes grew colder. "So you've come to give me your answer, Congressman?"

"Yes. The answer is 'no.' No more deals, no more lies. We've had enough of those." Jonathan shot a look at Christiana. "I'm sorry for what you're about to hear, Christiana. And probably you, as well, Peter." He lifted his chin toward her father.

Jonathan stepped toward the Judge. "I'm not about to drop charges against Avery. I won't be bullied into justice not being served. I don't care what you do to me."

"What?" *Avery.* A hard, emotionless cloud descended, and Christiana's body filled with a cold, dark rage like plaster of paris.

The Judge's cocksure posture hardened. "Your proof is thin, Congressman."

"Judge, your daughter will rot in a jail cell surrounded by—"

"Enough of the theatrics. You have no idea what I'm capable of."

"You have no idea what I'm willing to do." A crimson stain spread up Jonathan's neck, and he widened his stance.

Coco's chest anxiously rose and fell. Christiana faced the mother of the woman who had shot her beloved. An unspoken understanding passed between them that the conversation wasn't headed in a downward spiral. They headed to war.

Her father hadn't been a good father. But she hadn't realized until that moment he was a stellar teacher. *Think forward.*

She concentrated on the sunlight streaming between the Churchills and her family—yes, Jonathan, Mark, and even Yvette and Sarah were now her family. Her battle plan shuffled and rearranged in seconds. Avery may have started this battle, but Christiana knew how to win the war.

Jonathan's voice, normally full of conviction and power, adopted a deadly edge. "Judge, Mrs. Churchill. Get ready—"

Christiana clutched his suit jacket. "No, Jonathan. I have something to say."

She almost smiled at the punishing look he gave her for speaking his least favorite word: no. A small tickle licked at her nether regions. She clamped down her lust that rose under his steely stance.

The Judge disregarded the fact Christiana spoke. "You can say all you want, Congressman. I'm blowing the lid off your practices."

Christiana straightened. "I don't think so, Judge."

"Oh, really? Perhaps your father would like to know what you and the *Congressman* do in the dark?"

"It wasn't always in the dark." The stunning quiet fed her resolve. She held the floor. She also knew it wouldn't last.

"It's none of my business," her father interjected into the stillness. The shocked look on Jonathan's face probably matched her own—and the Judge's. Leave it to her father to understand the power of not being attached to whether information was revealed or not. "Christiana is a grown woman who makes her own choices. She's of legal age."

"You won't feel the same when you hear what I have to say."

"Judge, you should listen to me first before you say another word. For your own sake." Christiana walked two steps forward. She lifted the strand of pearls hanging low on her nervous belly. "Do you recognize these? They were my mother's." The Judge's face registered she'd hit a nerve. Naturally, he recovered in seconds.

Coco's face dropped. "Marcus."

"Little girl, I'm wholly disinterested in whatever you have to say. I am sure you're an innocent in this unseemly affair. But, know this. If you continue, you'll be treated as the adult you pretend to be." The Judge put his hand over Coco's, which still rested on his wide chest.

"Judge, you'll listen to her. The question is, do you want to do it now, or hear it on national television tonight?" Peter's voice rang out as if addressing a press conference. Christiana saw for the first time his true gift—the ability to steer a conversation to the real story at hand.

The Judge turned to her father. "Get out of my house. I don't recall inviting a reporter. Besides, you know as much as I that fear makes people say the stupidest things."

"I'm not afraid of you. But you should be afraid of me. There's nothing like a young woman to go on national television, courtesy of my father's help of course, to explain how the Churchills wouldn't let her mother out of a mental institution. It's part of a new series on the mental health atrocities committed by the legal system." Christiana had made her voice low and even, pretending she spoke like Jonathan.

"A story no one would believe—or care about," the Judge said.

Christiana's father stepped forward. "Oh, they will when I publish the love letters you wrote her, including the one that threatened no man would have her but you, even if it meant —let me get the exact words right—locking her in an ivory tower and throwing away the key. Rather clichéd, but I can roll with it."

The Judge sniffed. "Not exactly hard evidence that I had anything to do with Alexandra's unfortunate demise."

Christiana watched her father's nostril's flare.

"Breathe," Mark whispered.

She obeyed.

"The fact your signature is all over her restraining papers is an added touch." Yvette's silky voice filled the space, and for a moment cooled the room. She placed a diamond-studded hand to her heart. "I don't know how you people get away with such things," she continued. "Let me see, and I quote, 'If the court or jury finds that the person is mentally ill and, because of that illness, is likely to injure himself or other persons if allowed to remain at liberty, the court may order his hospitalization for an indeterminate period, or order any other alternative course of treatment which the court believes will be in the best interests of the person or of the public.' End quote. Alexandra's depression didn't fall into that category, I'm afraid."

Yvette turned to Christiana. "Arniss talked in his sleep. It was the most interesting thing he did in our bed." She winked a long set of eyelashes.

Christiana clamped her lips shut, knowing her mother probably did fit the description so eloquently recited by Yvette. But, only three people knew the truth, and one of them had killed herself over it. Christiana bit her tongue. Raising her mother's reality now would only destroy more lives.

"So this is how it's going to go, Judge," Jonathan said. "You will leave Christiana, the Snows, Yvette, my family and anyone else I deem, now or in the future, alone. You will not talk about me to anyone regarding my personal life, ever. And as for you daughter, we will let the investigators discover what they will, and justice will be served as the district attorney states."

Coco turned her face, wrought with anxiety, toward her husband, as his cheeks turned a mottled shade of red.

"Wait! I have a counter offer," Christiana said. "Jonathan, I need you to do something for me."

For her whole life, Christiana had felt one step behind everyone else. For once, she felt ahead. There was only one way out of the scenario Avery caused. She'd have to do something no one else in the room seemed willing to do.

"What are you doing?" Jonathan asked.

The Judge snorted. "You're going to lose your seat."

"Stow it, Judge." Jonathan didn't take his eyes off her face.

Christiana ignored the Judge's imposing figure to her left, his neck muscles still bulging in anger. "I want you to tell the police to drop charges against Avery, I mean, tell them no matter who they find, you won't prosecute." She spoke loudly, just in case her voice didn't bounce enough off the marbled room.

"Christiana—"

"No, please. I know what it's like to be lost. To feel that kind of desperation inside, when you want something . . . someone so badly. When you're just hanging on."

His face rivaled the Judge's. "Avery Churchill grew up in one of the most privileged families in Washington. She had everything."

"And she still has nothing." The Judge stood in her peripheral vision, and she sensed his stance loosened. Perhaps he recognized Christiana as an ally to lobby for Avery's release. But Christiana's instincts screamed she had speared the truth, lifted it to his eyes, and he now wrestled with his part in the mess. The realization wouldn't last long. The urge to be right ran deep in someone who spent his life judging and doling out answers and punishments.

"Jonathan, the truth is, I would have stepped in front of that bullet for you if I could have. But I'm here now, and I want to make sure we have a future. Knowing Avery is in jail may feel good for a little while. But, I know you. In the end, you'll feel guilty that she didn't get what she really needed."

"And what's that?" Sarah finally spoke.

"Help." Christiana threw the word directly at Coco, who looked like she held back a sob. All motion and fidgeting in the room stopped, as if everyone waited for her to repeat the word. "I've been a terrible friend. I saw the signs. I didn't do anything. I was so wrapped up in you." She turned to face Jonathan on her last word. "Avery needs help. Neither of our mothers got what they needed and that meant we didn't either. Now this might be the chance."

"Pulling the mother card, are you?" Jonathan's eyes glistened with emotion.

"It doesn't mean I don't want to get a good punch in before they lock the door behind her, but I'm willing to let that go if you are. Forgive her. I will."

A stifled choke from Coco Churchill broke her gaze. Christiana kept her hand on Jonathan's chest, but turned her head to the Judge and his wife whose eyes stayed locked on Christiana.

"I'll need you to promise that you won't do anything about this," Christiana said to them. "No leaking rumors—"

"You mean the truth," the Judge said.

"Yes," Christiana knew the time for denying their relationship—all of it—had passed. "But I need to know I have your word, Judge."

"You're just a footnote in his long history of womanizing, little girl."

Peter stepped forward. "That's calling the kettle black."

The Judge's nostrils flared. "Bullshit. I've never done—"

"Sure you haven't, Judge. But remember. I have a feeling your word won't count for much after I start my series of profiles on federal judges in the nation's capital."

Coco dropped her arms from her husband and stepped forward. "Enough." She turned to Jonathan and Christiana. "I'll give you something better than his word. Mine."

"Marcella."

"No, Marcus. This is the way it's going to be." Coco smoothed down the front of her peach jacket. "No charges will be brought against our daughter. The D.A.'s a friend. Avery leaves tomorrow for St. Margaret's. You will never speak of the Brond and Snow families again, to anyone. Not ever. And we go on with our lives. All of us."

The Judge picked up her hand and caressed her knuckles. It was the single most intimate thing Christiana had ever seen the Judge do. He raised Coco's hand to his lips, and she gave him a slight smile.

At that moment, Christiana realized that she—all of them —had misjudged the real power in the room.

"You should've let me get one punch in," her father said to the back of Mark's head as he descended the two marble steps leading to the limestone drive.

Mark didn't respond, but Jonathan turned to face her father. "I know the feeling."

Christiana noticed Jonathan stood on the lower step, so her father looked down at him.

Jonathan took a deep breath. "Listen, I realize the Judge

said some things back there, things that you might be curious about."

"I don't want to know." Her father held up his hand. "I'm getting used to the fact my little girl here has a boyfriend. That's all I can handle right now. Besides, Christiana is far beyond her years." His eyes washed her in love, then turned to Jonathan. "But, know this, *Congressman—*"

"You have permission to kill me if I hurt her." Jonathan extended his hand.

Her father nodded his head and then reached for Jonathan's grip. "It must have been hard to give up your seat."

"It wasn't, actually." Jonathan turned his eyes to Christiana. "Giving you up would have been hard."

"Then don't," she said quietly.

"I have no intention of giving you up, lovely."

Christiana took his hand and studied his face. She'd spent so much time lost in his gaze, she'd memorized nearly every flicker of gold swimming in all that emerald. But she momentarily froze, seeing a new emotion flash across his beautiful eyes.

In her periphery, her father's attention descended on her, lightly, *protectively*. He bumped her shoulder, encouraging them to descend down the steps.

"Well, don't forget to get this little I'll-keep-my-mouth-shut deal in writing, Congressman," her father said. "I wouldn't put it past the Judge to find a loop hole."

"Paperwork is already being prepared, Peter." Jonathan squeezed Christiana's hand, as the two men descended side by side, silent and slow.

Christiana rubbed her neck. The tense scene should have catapulted her into a history-making migraine. Instead, she bounced down the final step and across the drive, her hand encased in Jonathan's larger one.

The gravel crunched under their footsteps as they walked

ELIZABETH SAFLEUR

toward Jonathan's SUV. Mark sat in the driver's seat, gazing over the hood.

Her lungs expanded, taking in the rose and lavender scents from the Churchill's front garden. She wondered if Avery had ever noticed how much beauty surrounded her. "What's St. Margaret's?" Christiana asked as they neared Jonathan's idling car.

"A mental institution," her father said slowly.

Jonathan pulled her closer. "An exclusive one. She'll be fine. In your words, she'll be *helped*." He tucked a strand of hair behind her ear. The touch, gentle and grounding, spoke more than his words.

Though he stood as tall and confident as ever, the last week's events etched his brow, and his left shoulder slumped forward in the sling. Her protective instincts flashed hard and fast at seeing him wounded.

"Jonathan, I have one last question. For you," she said.

He smiled. "Now that we've got you talking, you have a lot to say. Okay, go ahead."

"Congressman Jonathan Franklin Brond from Rhode Island, do you *like* being a member of Congress?"

"You know, no one's ever asked me that before."

"It's high time they did."

"Yes, it is, which is exactly why I'm not seeking re-election. That's why I came, to essentially fall on my sword and keep you out of it. I didn't care what the Judge wanted to do to my name from now until October."

Christiana clutched his arm, and he winced. She dropped her hand. "Oh, I'm sorry. I'm just so—"

"Happy?" His eyes danced with delight.

She could only nod.

"He may not drop it, you know," her Dad said. "The D.A."

"True. He wouldn't have had a choice if I had told them everything. The system would have taken over. But know

360

this. I will do anything, even refrain from disclosing information, to keep your daughter safe, Mr. Snow. That's why you're looking at the new head of public affairs for the American Mental Health Association."

Peter cocked his head. "The Judge would've still raked you over the coals, made you lose that position."

"That's why I came. To let him know he got at least a piece of what he wanted—a Brond out of office. I'll let him find out now from the story you'll write." His lips quirked up. "Of course, I'd planned to warn him if he tried anything, I could always file those charges. There's no statute of limitations on attempted murder. As a judge, you'd think he was aware of that."

Peter's eyes grew misty. "Yeah, well, fathers sometimes forget the most important details where their daughters are concerned."

Sarah touched Jonathan's arm. "Man, your father is going to be so pissed." Amusement colored her eyes. "Please promise me I can be there when you tell him."

"I wouldn't have it any other way."

Her father cleared his throat. "Well, Chris, I expect you'll want to go home with your *boyfriend* now. I'll get Sarah and Yvette home. Besides, I've got some stories to file. You know, just to make sure the Judge knows I'm serious."

"Dad . . . ."

"Don't worry, Chrissy. Nothing too bad. I'm going to cover some of his recent cases just so he knows I'm watching. And I'll conveniently forget . . . certain other things." He softly winked and headed to the car where Yvette stood as if waiting for him to open the door for her. He stopped halfway and turned to Christiana and Jonathan. "All's well that ends well. Thanks to Marcella . . . and Christiana."

It was the first time her father ever called her by her whole name. The dam she'd built to house her final tears burst. She jogged to her father and hugged him around the waist. He engulfed her in a bear hug. "You're very brave, my little girl," he said into her hair.

The familiar Old Spice scent broke into her sniffling. He pulled her back and held her face between both hands. Their eyes locked, and a thousand unasked questions with a thousand unspoken answers passed between them. Her eyes moistened.

But the tears dried in her eyes as the only words left to say tumbled from her mouth. "The bounty's been paid."

35

Christiana threw her cell phone onto her car's front seat as she took the exit for Afton Mountain off the interstate. Her father had sounded less shaky in this last conversation. Now out of detox, he was forced to face his real demons.

"Damn those therapy sessions," he had laughed. "They make me want to drink more." That progress alone was worth the uncomfortable confrontation she'd had with him after the Churchill standoff. After her impasse with the Judge, she had figured if Jonathan could defy his father over remaining in Congress, then she could confront her father about his love of liquor.

Of course, before Jonathan announced his congressional retirement the day after the Churchill meeting, he proved that being a member of Congress had perks. He got her father admitted into the most exclusive alcohol rehabilitation center in Maryland. Jonathan told her dad it was where all the congressional wives and agency heads went. Christiana was sure that tidbit helped quell the initial resentment he mustered when first approached about going away. When

Yvette agreed to drive him there, Christiana knew he might have an additional reason for getting sober.

She hadn't shed one tear during the talk with her father. She gave all credit to Jonathan. Normally tight-lipped about her thought and feelings, she could barely shut up now. Well, except for one topic.

Christiana braked as she took a curve a little too fast. Her impatience to see Jonathan was only fed by the decision she'd finally made just that morning.

Since that day at the Churchills three weeks ago, Jonathan hovered over Christiana like she'd drop off the face of the earth at any point. But while his attention never wavered, she'd find him studying her face, as if he wanted to pose a question but hadn't yet formed what he wanted to ask. She felt the unspoken truth lying between them, and neither one was yet brave enough to pick it up and present it to the other. So she'd have to. Someone had to say "I love you" first.

She had three days before school started. She wouldn't leave this weekend until she claimed his whole heart. He had hers, and she didn't care if no one approved.

Christiana pulled up to the smooth polished wood gate of *Covil Sereia* and punched in the code Jonathan had provided. The gravel crunched under her tires, and as she rounded the tree-lined bend, the house rose from the trees. Jonathan's broad smile beamed at her from his front stoop. His hair glinted gold in the dappled sunlight, and he wore her favorite jade-colored t-shirt. His emerald eyes shone with happiness. Nothing in nature could compete with that green.

"Come inside," he said. "I need you."

Jonathan sat up from the tangled mass of sheets and pulled her up to his chest.

Christiana drew her leg over his hard quad in a protective embrace. A spasm of desire shocked her inner thighs awake even though Jonathan had spent most of the night between them. He was more than her kryptonite. He lived inside her molecules.

"Is there anything you'll miss about being in Congress?" Christiana asked tentatively. She wasn't sure he wanted to remember.

"The marble smell when I first walk in."

Christiana laughed. "The smell of dust and cement?"

"The older buildings have marble steps with little dips from so many people stepping on them, like a million men—and now women—have jogged up and down them, going to meetings to make important decisions. People committed to making life better for people. Not enough people walking through those hallowed corridors realize the history they step on."

"Is that why you stayed? I mean, for the history?"

"Something like that. I was supposed to run for senator next."

"Did you want to be a senator?"

"No. Before you, I don't think I ever thought about who I was. I now know what power is, Christiana. It isn't about how many people you can get to do your bidding. It's about knowing who you are and being able to take care of the people who matter to you."

He kissed her forehead and then looked back up at the ceiling. "There's one thing I won't miss, however."

"What's that?"

"The trafficking of half-truths." He leaned up on his elbow. "I owe you an apology, Christiana." He released a stray hair stuck to her cheek. "When I first ran into you at the club—"

"The pink fundraiser."

He pulled her into a tighter embrace. "I knew you'd never be happy unless you were living your truth. It's why I haven't been the best for you. I showed you a side to yourself that lay dormant, but I required you to tell lies during that discovery. That wasn't fair."

Christiana watched his eyes glaze over a little bit more with each word. Was this what he'd been mulling over for the last few weeks?

A breeze from the open window moved the sheer curtains. A thin layer of air passed between her body and his. She shuddered at the thought the space could grow any wider, and she drew closer to his chest, trying to squeeze out the possibility of anything being between them.

Jonathan nuzzled the top of her head. "Washington is a small town that traffics in half-truths and never lets you forget your mistakes."

"It seems pretty big to me."

"You'll outgrow Washington in due time."

"I'll never want to leave." She tried to bury herself in his chest.

He tipped her chin up with two fingers. He cast his warm green eyes down on her. "Someday, Christiana. You will want something more than Washington." His fingers dusted along her hairline, over her scar and down her cheek.

Before she could speak, he reached over to the bed stand. "And on that note. I have something for you." Jonathan pulled an envelope from the nightstand drawer. "Here. A gift."

She sat up. "What's this?"

"You'll see."

Jonathan pulled out a letter from the envelope and handed it to her. His beautiful eyes danced over her face.

She read the print on the heavy watermarked stationery —twice. "How? I didn't even apply for this scholarship."

"It's more than fair. Coco *Jackson* Churchill is the founder

of the Jackson-Heard scholarship. It's the least she can do."
He sighed at the disbelieving look on her face. "She spends
more at Tiffany's buying Christmas gifts for her staff.
Besides, it's her money."

Christiana arched an eyebrow.

"You do know the Churchill fortune comes from her
family, right?" Jonathan asked.

Christiana drew a large breath. No wonder the Judge
stood down so quickly.

"It's unethical. My silence isn't for sale. Half-truths,
remember?" Christiana threw herself on to her back.

"That's not what this is about. This is a thank-you gift.
For the *help*. Besides, there are six other people who make
the decision. Coco submitted you at the last minute, and they
voted. You earned this fair and square."

"I'll think about it."

"It looks like it's a done deal. Now you can go discover
life without the burden of working yourself to death while
doing it."

Christiana wrestled with the thought of taking anything
from the Churchills—even through a scholarship fund—after
what Avery did to Jonathan. But it would be so much easier if
she didn't have to work two jobs next year to go back to
school.

Wait . . . discover life?

Christiana positioned herself astride Jonathan's lean torso
and pinned her eyes on his face. His face held shock, but he
didn't move to push her off. She let the moment hang in the
air. She didn't want to miss a single muscle twitch when she
finally let the words out. His eyes appraised her. He had to
know something was up.

All summer she'd prayed for this moment, a chance to be
with Jonathan without all the secrets and lies. Never good at
talking, she found the words threatening to lodge in her

throat.

"So serious, lovely."

God bless him for always wanting to make things easier for her.

"There *are* things I want to discover, Jonathan—with you. I have something to tell you. Something I didn't say before, but should have. I love you." She grasped her bottom lip between her teeth and forced herself to hold his gaze.

Jonathan's green eyes misted. The wind outside rustled tree leaves through the open window, the only sound breaking in to the silence that sat between them.

He swallowed. "Thank God."

"W-what?"

"I love you, Christiana. I *love* you," he said emphatically, as if he didn't quite trust his own words had landed. "You're the only woman I've ever said that to outside my mother. God knows, I didn't want to expose you to the kinds of things people will say. But if I learned anything this summer, it's that I'm a selfish man. The thought of you with someone else . . ." He shook his head. "I can't allow it. Marry me, Christiana. This weekend. Hell, *today*."

Jonathan sat up and grasped her arms. "I'll take you away to anywhere you want to go so long as we're together." Jonathan stole her breath away with one of his all-consuming kisses. She followed his tongue spreading his love inside her mouth. When he released her, his eyes still shone emotion.

He reached for her panties.

She pushed him back. "Wait. Please."

If *she'd* learned anything that summer, it was how quickly she could fall into Jonathan and never surface. She had to do this the right way. She jumped off him, needing distance from his body.

His eyes registered something she hadn't seen ever

before. *He's afraid of what I might say next.* Emboldened by the effect she had on him, she pressed forward.

"Would you do something for me?" she asked.

"Anything." He snatched her hand.

"Wait until after I graduate from school?"

His lips stretched into a grin. "I'll think about it."

"And I want to meet Blanca. I don't believe she's real."

"Oh, she's real."

"Well, I want to thank her. For taking such good care of you. You once told me I had a lot of need. Well, I see the same in you. It's different. But it's there."

He brushed hair from her face. "Truth becomes you."

"Only truth from now on."

"Deal. Okay then. June first, three years from now, and not a day later, you'll meet me at an altar, location to be decided."

"Deal." She straddled his lap and kissed him to seal her answer.

"Christiana, you're never going to stop speaking up now, are you?"

Her lips curled into a smile. "No, sir."

"Good girl." He ran his fingers over her forehead, and she didn't even mind.

∼

Thank you for reading Elite!

If you enjoyed this story, you'll love Carson Drake's story in **Untouchable**, the next Elite Doms of Washington novel.

Carson has a knack for assessing someone's true desires— and fulfilling them.

In particular, he relishes the verbal sparring that lifts a

certain female's chin to a defiant angle and lights her brown eyes afire. Too bad London is everything he can't trust in a woman. Spicy. Complicated.

But when she appears like a misplaced angel at his favorite club, his inner Dom demands he give her what she secretly wants. Though to do it right, he'll have to excavate her secrets…and come perilously close to falling in love.

For a sneak peek of Untouchable, turn the page!

UNTOUCHABLE

Chapter One

My future will be made in the next thirty minutes. Okay, perhaps she was being a tad theatrical. But the thought wasn't too far from the truth. London Chantelle took in a sobering, deep breath. Drama wouldn't help her. Carson Drake sat on the other side of that door. She had to focus on business today—and only business.

She smoothed her pencil skirt down for the twentieth time, pulled her shoulders back and marched her Kate Spade pumps into Whitestone International's boardroom.

The men around the table stood as she entered. Carson was conspicuously absent. *Good.* She'd dubbed the company's contentious head of legal and public affairs the "Gladiator." All too often she'd felt like the weaker opponent in the arena of his boardroom.

After the pleasantries of handshakes and good-to-see-yous were over, she launched into her pitch. It took under twenty minutes to explain why she believed Whitestone required a full-scale rebranding.

Isolated at the other end of the vast conference table, CEO Stan Whitestone and his CFO leafed through the thick packet she'd slaved over for two weeks. She sat still and silent in the enormous leather chair, taking the moment to assess his mood. You could tell a lot about someone by watching their face as they read. *So far, so good.*

Mr. Whitestone pushed his copy of her proposal forward on the table. He leaned back in his chair and smiled. *Oh, thank God. He doesn't hate it.*

Her promotion to vice president at Yost and Brennan Communications rode on his acceptance. She desperately wanted that VP title and all that went with it. As vice president, she'd slave over *her* ideas rather than other people's. And the money? For once in her life, she might live in a place with a separate bedroom instead of a studio apartment.

"So, Miss Chantelle, only $500,000?" Mr. Whitestone asked. His CFO stared at him as if gauging his tone. She'd learned over the years that clients didn't often tease, and certainly not the head of a multibillion dollar contracting firm.

She cleared her throat. "Spending less would be a waste of money. If we can't do it right, then we shouldn't do it at all." *Oh, no.* She led with the punch line. She meant to save that last line until she needed a clincher.

"Well said." A familiar voice filled the room, and the air seemed to shift, along with her luck. The Gladiator had arrived. On cue, her belly flipped at the sound of Carson Drake's confident tone.

"Carson, so glad you could join us," Mr. Whitestone said. "London was just talking about recasting our image."

"So I hear." He strode over to the credenza and poured himself a cup of coffee. The air crackled with the addition of his dominant energy. It was as if he, not Mr. Whitestone, were the CEO.

He took the seat across from her. He fit the oversized chair. Another subtle reminder she was a small player in this big man's world. His dark eyes raked over her body as if assessing her reaction to his presence. She'd fought so hard to hide the illicit, secret thoughts she'd had about him since they met months ago, but his gaze seemed to penetrate her mind. *Hearing my inappropriate thoughts.*

During their first meeting, she'd had trouble tearing her eyes from his face. She'd spent every meeting since avoiding his dark eyes, as if that would hide her scandalous daydreams. He, on the other hand, watched her every move.

Of course he'd kept a professional tone with her at all times. *Albeit combative.* It was just as well. Her life didn't allow for illusions that Carson elicited with a single, knowing smile. She'd seen how other the women in her office grew all swoon-y over men like him. Men who were accomplished, good looking and oh, so arrogant, and who would turn a woman's focus from herself to him with a wink.

"My apologies, Miss Chantelle. I didn't mean to interrupt." He looked at Mr. Whitestone. "Carter cancelled. I recommend to abort. Effective immediately."

"Agreed."

"Now where were you?" His brown eyes returned to settle on her. A shock of dark hair had fallen over his forehead like he'd finger-combed it all day.

When did the room grow so hot? She casually pulled her blouse a little from her skirt to ease the straining fabric from her clammy chest. *Focus, London.*

She had no time for flirtations. She had responsibilities and a brother who counted on her. Unlike her mother, she would not abandon those dependent on her at the first charming thing out of a man's mouth. Whomever she got involved with—*if* she ever got involved—would not be like any swarthy Casanova her mother had brought home. Good looks always came with a price.

She grasped her portfolio on the table, opened it and pretended to glance through her notes. *Carson isn't going to affect me. Not today.* She straightened in her chair and squared her shoulders.

"Go on, Miss Chantelle," Carson urged.

"Thank you, Mr. Drake." She pushed a copy of her proposal across the table to him, which he ignored as he casually sipped his coffee. His fingers wrapped around the entire coffee mug. She hadn't noticed how large his hands were before.

She addressed the person who really mattered, Mr. Whitestone. The man who *will* sign an acceptance agreement, she told herself.

"Mr. Whitestone, I understand that discussing your business dealings in the press has been . . . difficult."

"You could say that," Carson said.

Dammit, she wasn't talking to him.

"Refreshing your image will bring a desirable type of attention to your company. We will sidetrack sensitive information about what you do and how you do it. Instead we will focus on the expertise of your executive team."

"A new brand based on our executives will invite questions," he said. "Questions we might not want to answer."

"We can deal with them as they come."

"Is that so?" He arched his brow as if he didn't believe her. She noticed his intimidation technique. Well, she wouldn't let Carson frighten her. So what if he'd negotiated six multi-million-dollar acquisitions in the last three years, testified before Congress, and been on every "most successful list" in Washington for the last three years? *So what if I paid that much attention to your credentials.* She knew what she was doing when it came to counseling her clients.

"Mr. Whitestone, we have been working with your firm for over a year. Your competition is getting more ink and more play on social media than you. Media attention requires giving us some news. You need more transparency about your firm." She could feel his regard burn through her blouse, now damp from nerves. Or lust? "I recognize Mr. Drake may not appreciate the process, but—"

"I know all about news generation, Miss Chantelle." His words pierced the air. He was probably annoyed she'd dare challenge him. But she'd also learned over the last four months of handling his company's public relations, he enjoyed verbal jousting. She had hoped today wasn't one of those days.

"Tell me something I don't know." He leaned back in his chair.

"You have twice the business of any other firm in your field, yet a quarter of its visibility."

"Based on what calculation?"

"Page fifteen of my proposal. Charts and everything." A thin surge of victory filled her at the surprise on his face. But the pursed mouths around the table showed her the snippy tone wasn't appreciated. "We just want to bring Whitestone into the twenty-first century," she added. Okay, probably not the best comeback. But Whitestone International needed a full image makeover, *stat.*

Carson sat motionless. "I fail to see how changing the colors of our corporate logo will be *entering* the new century."

"Rebranding is more than a logo, Mr. Drake. What I meant to say—"

"We know what you meant, Miss Chantelle," Mr. Whitestone said.

"I'm not sure *I* understand." Carson said. "Continue. Enlighten us with your wisdom."

"I apologize if I offended. I meant we want your audiences to see you for who you really are. Your current branding does not do you justice." *There.* That was a vice presidential thing to say, right?

"I understand you've worked hard on this proposal." He tapped her packet. "But I have serious reservations about spending this money right now. I move we wait a few months."

"Agreed." Of course, the CFO agreed. She'd labeled him the "Miser." He'd rub two nickels together to see if they'd mate before spending either of them.

She gripped her notes tighter. "You have two acquisitions coming up, and launching the news under the new brand would be wise."

In her peripheral vision she caught the other two members of the executive team watching Carson. She'd been in many meetings with this group. As usual, all eyes turned to him when a decision was at hand.

He didn't seem to notice as his unsmiling face focused on hers. A muscle in his jaw twitched. No man should have such perfect cheekbones. Mustering as much fierceness as she could, she matched his gaze. She imagined few people could hold his alpha stare for very long. She wanted to drop her eyes to her lap. She saw him surrounded by a bevy of women dropping before him in supplication. This man had to have women parading through his bedroom every night. Anyone that looked like him would.

Mr. Whitestone's voice cut through her ridiculous musings. "Carson, I agree. But the idea has merit. Miss Chantelle. Tell Mr. Brennan we need more time. You may not get the full budget you've proposed. But we'll consider the effort."

"Thank you." *Thank God.* She really needed $300,000. If

she bagged at least that amount, she'd have scored a touch-down for her firm.

She closed her portfolio. "I'll give you a call on Monday to see if you've rethought your position over the weekend. We'd want to get started right away."

"We'll call you." Mr. Whitestone stood.

Carson glared at her. *He looks like he wants to spank me.* She flushed. *Stop it. You are Y&B's next rising star.*

As she gathered her things, she took a deep inhale of the warm scent of tobacco and expensive leather that Carson left in his wake. Her female parts clenched in a very un-executive way. She hoped he couldn't hear the thumping knocks of her heartbeat. Clearly her heart hadn't gotten the I-won't-be-affected memo.

"Mr. Drake," she said before her courage fled. "Did you even read my proposal?"

He turned to her in the doorway. "What do you think?"

She had no idea what to think. The searing smile he gave her held intense dislike. Only Carson Drake could put someone in their place with a grin.

He walked her to the lobby in silence. Her legs rubbed together, the friction heating her thighs. Those foolish, foolish suggestive thoughts returned.

"Miss Chantelle." He held the glass door open for her. His gentlemanly move surprised her. Someone important must be watching.

She skirted outside to join the taxi line before she said something she'd regret.

She checked her watch. It was almost five o'clock. She had two hours until she met Michael—a man who never should have been more than a coworker. He was the last loose end to tie up before approaching Mr. Brennan with the idea of her promotion. And finally advance her life.

As she eased herself into the cab, she noticed that Carson still stood behind the lobby's windows. She turned her back on his curious stare. Perhaps she'd gotten to him. *Nah.* She doubted he gave her a second thought out of the office. She wished she could say the same.

Well, today was a new day. Vice presidents weren't overcome by erotic daydreams. They kicked ass.

~

Carson stared out the window long after London's taxicab disappeared into traffic.

He couldn't tear his eyes away from her today. She kept crossing and recrossing those luscious, tanned legs underneath the glass conference table. Then when she leaned forward to pass him her proposal? The top button of her silk blouse threatened to release. He spent the rest of the meeting anticipating its pop. It didn't.

He wasn't sorry he'd given her such a hard time about her idea to rebrand Whitestone. He'd always had the ability to discern people's true desires and just how far he could push. London needed verbal sparring. Only then would the fatigue and worry in her eyes lift. Her décolletage would flush a beautiful peach color. Her eyes would fire defiantly, and she'd lift that chin in a haughty salute as if he was the biggest jerk on the planet. All her nervousness would vanish.

He stepped into the elevator bank and inhaled London's lingering perfume. The scent matched her personality. *Spicy. And complicated.*

Today, she'd fidgeted on that beautiful ass more than usual, which teased his desire to stroke her defiance even more. *You wanted to stroke more than that.*

She was smart, dynamic and a challenge. *With a great behind.*

While he had no interest in romantic complications, he often imagined the kind of man she would respond to outside the boardroom. It wouldn't be someone who'd break her like a wild horse. Or even relegate her to a corral. No, London Chantelle needed to be haltered, gentled and understood. *All that energy channeled.*

He punched his floor's button and told his cock to stand down. He scrolled through his e-mail on his phone as the elevator lurched upward. London had already sent a follow-up email, ostensibly from her cab. The woman who never quits? *Jesus, what a pistol.* His own pistol remained cocked and ready.

He really needed to get a handle on his reaction to this woman.

He'd learned his lesson long ago. Two years negotiating divorce settlements in his early days cured him of trusting any immediate attraction. He'd seen too many relationships dissolve under the harsh light of day. Men shattered by angry, disillusioned females. He'd encountered a few of those harpies himself, beginning with his first serious girlfriend in college. Now safe, short-term, uncomplicated liaisons suited him fine.

By the time he stepped out of the elevator into his office floor, London's scent had dissipated. But he couldn't shake the image of her slipping those legs into the taxicab. Given it was late on a Friday, he wondered where she was headed. *Not anywhere you are, man.* Jaded or not, he couldn't help thinking what a pity that was.

Untouchable can be found at all major online retailers or request the book from your local library or favorite book store.

Untouchable is also available in audio at most major audio book retailers.

ALSO BY ELIZABETH SAFLEUR

ABOUT THE AUTHOR

Elizabeth SaFleur writes luscious romance from 28 wildlife-filled acres, hikes in her spare time and is a certifiable tea snob.

Find out more about Elizabeth on her web site at www. ElizabethSaFleur or join her private Facebook group, Elizabeth's Playroom.

Follow her on Instagram (@ElizabethLoveStory) and TikTok (@ElizabethSaFleurAuthor), too!